I0730790

# WEST

## STACEY MARIE BROWN

Stacey Marie Brown

This is a work of fiction. Any references to historical events, real people, or real locales are used fictitiously. Other names, characters, places and incidents are the product of the author's imagination and her crazy friends. Any resemblance to actual events, locales or persons, living or dead, is entirely coincidental.

This book is licensed for your personal enjoyment only. It cannot be re-sold, reproduced, scanned or distributed in any manner whatsoever without written permission from the author.

Copyright © 2016 Stacey Marie Brown

All rights reserved.

Cover by Jay Aheer (www.simplydefinedart.com)

Developmental Editor Jordan Rosenfeld (http://jordanrosenfeld.net)

Edited by Hollie (www.hollietheeditor.com)

# ALSO BY STACEY MARIE BROWN

## <u>Contemporary Romance</u>

### *Buried Alive*

### Blinded Love Series
*Shattered Love (#1)*
*Pezzi di me (Shattered Love)—Italian*
*Broken Love (#2)*
*Twisted Love (#3)*

### *The Unlucky Ones*
*(Má Sorte—Portuguese)*

### Royal Watch Series
*Royal Watch (#1)*
*Royal Command (#2)*

### *Smug Bastard*

## <u>Paranormal Romance</u>

### Darkness Series
*Darkness of Light (#1)*
*(L'oscurita Della Luce—Italian)*
*Fire in the Darkness (#2)*
*(Il Fuoco Nell Oscurita—Italian)*
*Beast in the Darkness (An Elighan Dragen Novelette)*
*Dwellers of Darkness (#3)*

*Blood Beyond Darkness* (#4)
*West* (A Darkness Series Novel)

**Collector Series**
*City in Embers* (#1)
*The Barrier Between* (#2)
*Across the Divide* (#3)
*From Burning Ashes* (#4)

**Lightness Saga**
*The Crown of Light* (#1)
*Lightness Falling* (#2)
*The Fall of the King* (#3)
*Rise from the Embers* (#4)

**A Winterland Tale**
*Descending into Madness* (#1)
*Ascending from Madness* (#2)
*Beauty in Her Madness* (#3)
*Beast in His Madness* (#4)

**Savage Lands Series**
*Savage Lands* (#1)
*Wild Lands* (#2)
*Dead Lands* (#3)
*Bad Lands* (#4)

## **Dedicated To:**

Coffee, Starbucks, and the unknown hot guy from the Internet. Without you three, I would be impossibly cranky with no place to work and no hot guy to think about while writing. (Who, if he knew what I was picturing him doing, would have a restraining order against me).

Thank you, hot guy!

# **ONE**

I glanced over my shoulder. Six boar shape-shifters the size of small horses, with several sets of spearing tusks and tails with razors at the tips, charged out of the warehouse and headed for us. The bastards were as ugly as they were fast. They were gaining on us. Quickly.

*Cooper*, I yelled to my Second through our link, the dwellers' way of communicating. *Hurry up.*

*Then make this thing go faster*, Cooper shot back through the link.

I thumbed the throttle to accelerate. The bike puttered and jerked forward, finally hitting the speed of a golf cart.

"Goddamn piece of shit," I mumbled under my breath. I missed my Harley. Badly. But since the worlds crashed together and magic flooded Earth, the normal machines no longer worked. This piece of crap was an Otherworld version of a motorbike. Now with Earth and the Otherworld joined, I lamented how "humanized" I had become. I missed so many things: the vibrating of my sleek black bike between my legs, the roar of the engine, the speed it could reach twisting you around a curve. Fae had superior talents in many areas, but building motorcycles wasn't one of them.

Normally, a bunch of shape-shifters wouldn't be a challenge. No more than an annoying gnat. But with this piece of junk, they easily gained on us, their eyes glowing as they neared. I would have said *Screw it*, changed into my Dark Dweller form, and outrun them in a second, but... A lump of fear blocked my thoughts from continuing. Surely it was only temporary. My Dark Dweller would return.

I growled under my breath and pushed the accelerator again. Anger burst up my spine, and I stooped lower over my ride. We were in this shit because of me. It was my fault these guys even had a chance in hell to catch up. I was the weak link in the pack. The third-in-command of the feared Dark Dwellers was a kitten without claws.

Another growl climbed up my throat.

*Fuck this. Shift and stop these assholes. I'll take the merchandise back,* I grumbled to Cooper. Now that Eli had stepped down and left with Ember, Cooper was our new Second under Cole Donovan. We had lost quite a few of our family members in the big battle, and none of us were ready to deal with that now, if ever. Especially Jared. I quickly purged his image from my head. The loss of our youngest was too painful, rotting in my core.

Cooper turned to peer at me over his shoulder. *You sure, man?*

I shrugged lazily. *Yeah.* I hoped acting as if I didn't care would eventually make it so, but the pain was always there if I stopped to notice it. I did shift once during the war against Aneira, the previous Seelie Queen, but I didn't let on how much it hurt and how hard it was for me to stay in beast shape. Something was wrong. The Dark Dweller in me used to be dominant, but now I struggled to let it out. I hadn't told any of the pack, but I knew they could sense something was off about me. I no longer went on hunts, and I made excuses for why I didn't turn when we fought other fae. My temper was short, and I hardly stayed around the house anymore.

Cooper threw me the wrapped article, and I added it to the several items already in the front of my two-wheel, magic-operated bike. The SUV Lars loaned us to use for the last run was at the bottom of a ravine—on purpose. That thing was even worse than the go-carts we were using now.

Coop shifted as he jumped from the bike. The pathetic excuse for a motorcycle hit a tree and fell to the ground. His clothes shredded into pieces and long talons replaced his human nails. Spikes grew rigid along his back, his eyes turned red, and his skin became sleek black fur. His Dark Dweller form hit the pavement facing the fae trailing us. A deep roar from Cooper vibrated my skin as he leaped for the pursuers.

I kept my head forward. My irritation felt like a hot poker in my chest. I wasn't mad at Cooper, but that didn't stop my resentment.

I finally turned the bike onto Lars's property line, stopping at the twenty-foot gates. The protection spells were securely in place, searing the atmosphere in a dense bubble. Internally it created an unease, making you want to turn around and head the opposite way. Humans would without realizing why, but as a fae I could push past it. I leaned over and slammed the buzzer.

The Riders of Darkness were now partners with the Unseelie King. With the ROD's status and skills, we learned to live on Earth as a biker gang, which was a perfect fit for us. In the past we ran and traded a lot of illegal items as a source of income. Our current job wasn't much different.

Today Cooper and I had "reclaimed" several objects

Lars's lab and technical advisers needed. We inspired fear in Dark and Light fae alike, which created a perfect retrieval system for Lars. Because most of the items we sought people didn't give up willingly, we could get them easier than he could. We were efficient, fast, and direct. Our reputation compelled some people to bring items to us the moment they saw us riding up.

An enormous man stepped from the trees on the side driveway, his chocolate skin almost blending in with the shadows. "Hey, R-Man." I smiled slyly as he grimaced at my pet name for him. Blame Eli. He started it. "Another delivery." I motioned to the container holding the artifacts.

"Password." Rimmon's voice was more rumble than speech. The man, even to me, was a scary motherfucker—bald, arms the size of toddlers, a face so stern and ugly it caused most people to run away in fear. You'd think with his mass he would fight like a huge grizzly bear, but the man was like a freakin' cheetah.

"Seriously? Come on, man. I've already been here twice today."

"Password." Rimmon folded his arms over his huge, bare chest. His pants were a patchwork of a dozen khakis sewn together. There were no "regular" clothes that would fit him. He had to be part ogre.

"West is super sexy?" I grinned.

Rimmon's lids narrowed. I took joy in vexing the large man.

"No? Not that one?" I shrugged. "You're right, too obvious and easy to guess."

"Password, Dark Dweller, or I leave you standing here with your dick in your hands." The glint in his eyes led me to believe my dick would no longer be attached.

"You must be fun on game night."

Rimmon started to pivot on his heels.

"Fine." The instant I uttered the words, the spell released its hold, and Rimmon unlocked the gates, opening them for me. When I pushed the back tires across the line, the spell snapped back into place, sealing us into the safety of the Unseelie King's property.

The vast English-style manor came into view as I curved around the second bend in the road. The figure of a woman stood on the front stoop, her dark brown hair tied in a loose bun, showing off her high cheekbones and beautiful swanlike neck. Her slender arms were crossed, and her full bowed lips puckered up, looking way too inviting for their own good. The only "flaw" in her beauty was a frown furrowing her sculpted brows. Goddamn, she was stunning.

"I don't know why you provoke him. You know one of these times he's going to ignore Lars's instructions and kick the crap out of you," the woman said. Her voice was like the most beautiful song you'd ever heard. She could tell you to fuck off, and you would do it willingly in the hopes you could hear her speak again or get one more look at her beautiful face.

I'd spent quite a bit of time at this house when we were preparing for war with the former Seelie Queen. You'd think by now I'd be used to Rez, but her beauty was not something you ever got immune to.

She was a siren, the Unseelie King's mistress, and someone I needed to stay far, far away from. This was actually not a problem for me. Don't get me wrong; I enjoyed ladies. All kinds. But I kept them at a distance. It was easier that way. I was a good flirt, a great charmer. Better than all my brothers. But I never let women get close.

Dark Dwellers were secretive by nature, and our group was even more private since we had been banished to Earth. I slipped once and let someone in—completely. I would never make the mistake again.

"You know me." I grinned at her and stepped onto the stoop. She took a step back, peering up at me with her dark, penetrating eyes. "I am more afraid *you* will kick *my* ass, darlin'."

"Which is entirely possible." Her lips twitched with the need to smile, but she kept hold of them. "Come on; he's waiting for you." Rez looked behind me. "Where's Cooper?"

"Got held up." I gathered the items into my arms and followed her to Lars's office. He never left us Dark Dwellers unattended in the house. He was probably afraid one of us would pee on his thousand-dollar rug.

# TWO

I breathed a sigh of relief when I stepped out of Lars's office a little while later. He tolerated us since he needed us, and we were connected to him because of Ember, but the Unseelie King was still not the most comfortable person to be around. He remained a demon down under the king title. Cole and Eli seemed to get along with him all right, but I preferred being on the opposite side of the door, on my way to Mike's Bar, or somewhere I felt more relaxed.

"You already done?" Rez's voice slid silkily through the hallway. She stepped from the kitchen and leaned against the doorway.

"Yeah." I grinned and stopped in front of her. Her style was classic and simple, and she always looked put together. Even with bare feet, black yoga pants, an off-white long-sleeved top, and her hair in a bun, she looked amazing. This was the most casually dressed I'd seen her, and I liked it. Compared to her, I still felt dingy in my scruffy boots, jeans, and T-shirt.

"I was off to do yoga downstairs." She tugged at her top. I thought it cute she felt she had to explain her relaxed appearance. I guess a siren didn't let many people see her in exercise pants.

"You want something to eat before you go?" She pointed over her shoulder. "Once again, Marguerite made too much for dinner. She's used to making meals for more of us..." Rez's voice broke off, and she looked at her feet. A shadow of feeling flickered over her face.

I understood that look and knew immediately what it meant. I'd seen it too many times on my own family members. In war you understand people are going to die, but you are never ready when it takes your own. They lost two of theirs in the fighting, and we lost four. I would never get accustomed to the emptiness.

Rez's cream-colored top slipped slightly off her shoulder as she bent and dabbed at her eyes. My gaze trailed down the curve of her neck and over her shoulder. She sucked in air and adjusted her thin frame straighter, pushing away any signs of grief. I was accosted by an overwhelming urge to reach out and pull her into my arms, to shield her from pain in the hope it might take mine away. I took a step back and clenched my hands into fists.

*What the hell?* Charming and flirty was one thing, but I hadn't felt protective over a woman not part of my family in ages. Ember had been the first, but she had been safe from the beginning. Even before Eli realized it, all of us could feel him claiming her. As soon as he gave her his blood, she was one of us. When she became family, protecting her came with the territory. I told myself now my impulse to protect Rez had nothing to do with her personally. It was a reaction to the family we both lost.

"I've seen you eat." She reached for my arm. "Please, do us a favor so we don't have to eat venison stew for the next three nights."

I glanced down at her elegant fingers, then quickly looked at her face. A grin twitched at my mouth. "You know I can't turn down Marguerite's cookin'." Her food was unbelievable. Probably the best cook I'd ever come across since my time in the south. It wasn't shocking she'd be working for the Unseelie King. Though she was human, she was a seer and had known about the fae since she was little and had started working for Lars soon after. Everyone here treated her like family, and she returned the love in kind.

"Oh, Mr. West. *Venir y comer*." Marguerite came up behind Rez, her arms open to welcome me. The woman stood barely five feet, but her aura was so full of love and force you forgot how tiny she was. When she got angry or scolded us, we Dark Dwellers bowed our heads in guilt and shame. Ember told me one time she threw Marguerite over her shoulder by accident, and the woman popped up, tsked her, and continued on with the laundry. Strong and fierce. All the women here were.

"Hello, *mamacita*," I said as she pulled me down in a hug.

When she drew back, her gaze was critical. "*¿Su triste?*" She patted my cheek.

"Never sad when you're around." I winked.

"Oh." A blush crawled up her neck, coloring her cheeks. She swished her hand at me and turned back to the stove. She shoveled a mound of stew into a bowl, adding a slab of cornbread on a plate. "Come. Eat."

Rez stepped to the side, motioning me to the huge island.

"I'm all right if you want to continue on with what you were doin', sweetheart." I stepped past her, giving one of my typical side grins.

She studied me. Her brown eyes dug so deep into me my smile dropped. "What?"

She tilted her head. "Are you ever not on?"

"What are you talking about, darlin'?"

"That." She lifted her hand, motioning at me. "All the put-on charm and schmoozing. Don't you ever get tired of doing it? Pretending you're all right?"

It felt as if she had shoved me hard in the chest. I blinked. She crossed her arms, holding her chin up in a challenge. Damn! She was more like Ember than I thought, although Ember hadn't seen through me this quickly. I wouldn't allow Rez either. She was an itch that didn't need to be scratched.

"Has it ever not worked?" Her eyebrows went up.

I widened my stance and folded my arms over my chest, a smirk pulling up one side of my mouth. "No."

A flutter of annoyance wavered over her features. "Says a lot about the type of girls you go after."

"I don't go after them, darlin'. They come to me." I turned away from Rez and moved to the counter and sat where Marguerite set my food.

Rez's lips parted, ready to respond, but they drew back together. With a shake of her head and a mumble, she departed the room, leaving Marguerite and me alone. Marguerite leaned over the counter and patted my hand before she turned to finish cleaning the stove.

I stared at my bowl, holding my spoon midair. My shoulders drew in, suddenly tense. Who was Rez to talk about being real? Was her life here authentic? Wasn't she a glorified secretary to Lars, who treated her more like an employee than someone who slept in his bed every night? The sweet den mom at Camp Demon, who went out and dragged men to their deaths on the weekend? Yeah. Who's the one pretending to be all right?

I slammed the spoon on the counter, no longer hungry,

and stormed out. I could hear Marguerite calling after me, but I was in no mood to be cordial, and she didn't deserve this West—the angry, violent version.

Rez wants fuckin' real? I crashed through the front door, bypassing the stupid Otherworld bike slumped on the ground. I itched to change—to become what I was meant to be: a ruthless killer, something to be truly feared, no pretense or appeal.

My legs took me across Lars's property into the forest. I curled over, the beast tickling under my skin. Pain shot up my back and down my limbs. I crumpled to the ground with a gasp. Turning had never been especially comfortable, but it hadn't been this painful. It was part of my nature as a Dark Dweller.

Except now it had changed. My muscles twisted in agony. They wanted to stretch and grow into their familiar form, but stabs of anguish rippled through, keeping them from doing what they wanted to do. My body withered on the ground, tears seeping out the corners of my eyes. Since being held in the Seelie dungeons, I had only changed a handful of times, and each time was harder. At first I could ignore the pain, but now it crippled me.

"No!" I growled. I grabbed my wrist and put all my energy into changing my hands into claws. Torment shredded my arm, and I clamped my jaws together. I pushed harder. Sweat poured down my face. Nails sprang from the tips of my fingers; black sleek fur covered my deformed hand. A paw started to emerge. For one moment my human hand dissolved and became a beast's razor-sharp claw. Then it was gone. I couldn't even hold the shape for more than a few seconds.

My chest burned. Rez was right about one thing. I was a fraud. Nothing about me was true anymore. My entire identity was gone. I was no longer a Dark Dweller.

I had been locked in the dungeons for months, years to those on earth, with metal spikes digging into my throat, depleting my blood and magic. Dark fae can't be on the Light side for a long period of time without side effects. When I say side effects, I mean permanent ones, even death. Somehow I survived. Deep down I knew the reason had to do a lot with a certain girl—one with black-and-red-streaked hair.

Ember.

For a long time I thought she was merely in my head and I dreamed her next to me, touching my face. But the raven, Grimmel, would say something later and make me think she must have been there. She could put herself in a place in real life and actual time in a dreamwalk, but not physical form. I could not see or interact with her but the raven could.

I never told her she was a huge reason why I was still breathing. Why every time I closed my eyes wishing for death to take me, I would force them back open and hold on another day.

My thoughts would start out on Ember, but my mind would slowly shift to another. A woman with long, golden, wavy hair, soft brown eyes, and a southern accent and smile that could still bring me to my knees. A girl my heart reached for at night—whom I saw in my dreams so clearly I forgot she was no longer part of this world.

She was dead because of me—because I let her get too close.

A roar broke through the night, and the ground and trees shuddered with my grief.

***

Oxygen huffed in and out as I lay there. The physical pain was a thin shell compared to the agony inside. I couldn't even stay in my beast form at all now. The beast was slipping further and further away, tearing a hole into my soul.

I felt empty.

Worthless.

I stopped liking the man I was a long time ago. Now I couldn't even revel in hiding behind the dweller.

This made me want to run again like I had when we first came to Earth, leaving my group in the Northwest and traveling in the States. Anger and frustration had invoked the need to get away—to be by myself. Not a normal Dark Dweller trait. But my mother, Ciara, never set me up to be normal. She was the free spirit of the tribe. The one who would leave me when I was a baby in someone else's care and take off for days to be "free" with nature. This only got worse when I was two, after my father died. Like mother, like son, I guess.

My mom died when our clan was attacked by the Dae in the Otherworld. I had no brothers or sisters, which was also another abnormal trait for Dark Dwellers. Knowing my mother, there had been no plans for more. One child held her back enough.

# THREE

Now, staring at the night sky, my breath coiled in the air, and the cold dulled my body. I liked feeling numb.

A bolt of green light darted across the sky, like a shooting star. I sat up with a jolt. I knew it was no star. The green ball curved down, crashing into the force field Lars had spelled around his property, crackling along it like veins.

I heard a faraway battle cry, sinking my stomach. Then the sky ignited with luminous emerald light. As if it were raining, hundreds of small spheres the size of baseballs smashed against the protective barrier, sputtering and splintering the shield like it was glass. Contrasting magic drove against each other. The sizzling noise crackled against my skin.

*Holy shit. We're under attack.*

*Rez! Marguerite!*

I jumped to my feet and ran toward the house. Shouts came barreling at me from all around as Lars's men sped for the property line.

Who the hell would attack the Unseelie King's compound? Whose balls were that big? Individuals had challenged him but never bluntly attacked his complex.

No magic could ever counter what he had over his land. Right?

More waves of magic pummeled down on the shield. Loud pops and snaps sliced over the surface, but it held in place.

I gritted my teeth as the manor came into view between the trees. As I ran for the house, more and more men darted past me, rushing to defend their King's property. The beast only wanted to protect who was in it. I rushed down the drive, my eyes locked on the door. It swung open as Rez and Marguerite scuttled frantically out, their gazes locked on the glowing sky. The buzzing overhead grew louder, the raid battering more intense.

"What are you doing? Get back in the house," I yelled.

Rez's head snapped to me, relief filling her eyes.

"Oh, thank the gods. I thought you were out there. Maybe caught."

"I'm here…now get back in there," I responded. I pointed to the house and turned to follow the men to the border.

"Wouldn't that be their target?" Rez reached for me. "Wouldn't we be safer with you?"

"No." I shook my head. "Where is Lars?"

"He ran to see what was going on." She pointed into the night. "Goran is going to freak out he's out there."

"You ladies go back into the house. I'm going to go see what's happening." I turned to leave.

Rez's fingers dug into my skin. "I'm coming with you."

"No. You aren't."

"Yes. I. Am."

"Fuck, sweetheart. I don't have time to bicker with you."

"Then stop wasting our time," she exclaimed and squeezed Marguerite's hand. "Stay in the house and if anything happens..." She paused. "Go into the basement. You know the room. You'll be safe there."

Marguerite nodded, looking back and forth between us, and hustled for the house.

"What room?" I asked as we started moving toward the fighting.

"It's a room designed against nuclear blast, magic attacks, chemical warfare, or any other assault against the King."

*Damn.* "Stay close, darlin'." I headed toward the gates. Lars was not my favorite person in the world, but he was still our King and I respected him. I preferred the devil, a demon in Lars's case, I knew...and I would protect him if it came down to it.

We reached the gate, pushing past a few of the guards. Rimmon was gone from his post, probably already after the attackers.

My fingers wrapped around the metal; my gaze focused on the darkness past the border. The green glow illuminated the grounds in the distance. My mouth dropped open. Thousands of strighoul lined up, each carrying a sling containing magic orbs.

"Strighoul?" Rez exclaimed next to me. "They are not smart enough to pull off an attack like this."

"No, they aren't." My eyes weaved among them all. "They must have help." They were the bottom feeders in the fae world. Stupid and ugly as hell with teeth like thousands of tiny jagged blades. They were a kind of cross between ghouls and vampires. They ate fae to possess their powers, showing little interest in humans.

Since the fall of the walls between the worlds,

strighoul had been a prick up our butts. Their numbers were growing, and so was their confidence. They were now openly attacking groups of humans and fae. Taunting. But it was still a far cry from boldly striking at the King.

I pushed away from the gate and went deeper into Lars's land, edging the border to see how far the line of strighoul went. Rez strode quietly beside me, taking in the thousands of carnivores ringing the property. We passed strategically placed men holding their positions, probably awaiting word from a commander.

"Shit." I rubbed my forehead. There were so many more than I thought, but finally the end of the mass came, and I moved closer to the line.

"Hey." I spotted one of Lars's men at the edge of the property behind some trees. Travil, I think his name was. The King lost a lot of men in the war against the Seelie Queen and a few had gotten "bumped" in their positions because of the sudden gaps. Travil was promoted from night guard to private guard of the King in the last year. "What's going on?"

Travil jerked his head to look at me, his body tense, gripping his bow and arrow, if that's what you wanted to call it. It looked more like some modern torture device although it was high-tech and probably could slice a grape from a mile away. He was a large, dark-haired brute of a man, and had the kind of face so serious and stony you could never imagine him cracking a joke or laughing. Ever.

"*She* shouldn't be out here." His little eyes squinted so much they appeared closed. But I knew not to be fooled; his eyesight was like a hawk's, along with his hearing.

"Tell *her* that," I scoffed, approaching him.

"*I* can decide for myself where I should or shouldn't be." She cocked her head and stared at Travil. She held much more authority than he did and he knew it.

He flicked his head back to the open field with a snarl, aiming his bow and arrow out. I was about to ask what he could see when flames of strighoul energy plunged into the air and arched down on the compound like missiles.

The night sky lit up and the protection spell sputtered at the intrusion.

"What is the plan?" I kept my eyes locked on the outlines.

"We're getting in place now. Goran will give us the word, then we attack," he grumbled. "It won't take us long to cut through them."

More waves came crashing down on the barrier, setting the hair on my arms straight up.

"We're all in place, sir," a voice crackled over a walkie-talkie on Travil's shoulder. I recognized Goran's voice.

"All right. On my count."

"One."

"Two." Anticipation nipped at the air.

"Three!"

Energy sung like a choir, but Lars's men were soundless and deadly, rushing over the boundary like ninjas.

Everything in my body thumped with the need to follow. To become what I was good at: a silent killer. I couldn't stay behind. I was a fuckin' Dark Dweller. I was used to slicing throats and ripping apart bodies in seconds. I was not meant for the sidelines.

"West?" Rez called me just as I stepped forward. My shoulders hunched forward, and a growl vibrated my tongue.

"Stay here!" I commanded and slipped past the spell, magic pumping the blood in my veins faster.

*Kill. Kill. Kill,* the beast chanted, hearing the sounds of death already breaking through the night. The wails of slaughtered strighoul enhanced my need for blood, my craving the high of a kill.

The beast wanted to play. It rocketed to the surface like a charging bull. My legs crumpled underneath me, and I crashed to the ground with crippling aches.

No. This was not going to happen again. I *could* shift. I would make myself this time. It was no longer even about the fight. I was going to change simply to know I still could. The noises of metal slicing through flesh, the crunch of men colliding in rage, spiked my beast with a need to join.

*Shift! Now!*

My face slid into the dirt, my insides cramping. I gritted my teeth in pain. Only hair sprouted on my arms this time before retreating. I rolled onto my back. The beast wanted to come out no matter what. It slammed desperately against the blockade within. The more it was denied, the more it hit back, bruising my muscles from the inside.

My voice wedged in my throat, and spots corrupted my vision.

I stared at the stars, colors bursting in vivid shades, the clamors of battle and death echoing in my ears. And I lay there like a newborn. Vulnerable and useless.

Unbearable agony overtook me and forced me to hide under the comfort of oblivion, away from the pain.

---

When I woke, silence encompassed me. I heard no clashes

of combat or killing. I also sensed I was alone in the field. There may have been no sounds of death, but the smell of blood, guts, and flesh drenched the area.

It was clear Lars had won, not that I had any doubt. From what I could see by the outlines, more than half of the strighoul were now fertilizer. With a groan, I sat up, my muscles sore from constricting. I glanced around. The field was clear of living strighoul, but hundreds of lumps scattered the field in permanent sleep.

Don't fuck with the King.

Incense, embarrassment, and self-hatred quarreled inside me, pushing me back on my feet. The disgust at myself, the fact I didn't even help fight but passed out like a wasted frat boy, roused my fury. People danced and partied around me, having the best night, while I drooled and puked on myself.

"Dammit!" The word burst from me. I bent over my legs and hauled in deep breaths. It took me a while to calm down, and the only reason I shoved down my loathing was the thought of Rez and Marguerite. I needed to see if they were all right.

I turned toward the compound, or the direction I thought it was, but the more I thought about where they were or how to get there, the more confused I became. *Right*. Once you left the protective shell of Lars's property, you couldn't get back in unless you were linked in with a spell. There were probably just a few who were. I was definitely not one of them.

"Screw this." I spun the other way and proceeded into the forest. Rez and Marguerite had been inside the barriers and had a ton of people watching over them. Rez was the King's mistress. He could worry about her. I needed a fuckin' drink.

Mike's Bar reopened quickly after the war. In this new world where nymphs, trolls, and humans mixed, the demand for alcohol was even more crucial. Mike's had been a hangout for the seedy and outlaws and had mostly served humans. Now most of the customers consisted of the Dark fae underbelly and scum of the human world.

Strangely, I missed the old place. Early on, our clan had made it clear no one messed with Mike. He was a human under our protection who had helped us so many times it was second nature to take care of him. Since no one wanted a Dark Dweller on their ass, they treated Mike and any other human clientele who ventured in with respect. Rules were bending now, resulting in less respect and fear, and there were always punks pushing the envelope, seeing how far they could go.

Mike's Bar was stuffed full of all types of degenerates by the time I got there, the hour well past midnight. Mike took one look at me and poured me a triple whiskey. "Thanks, Mike. You're a good man."

I tossed it back in a gulp and nodded for another. Brown liquid pooled in my glass as Mike refilled it, then went to take care of other customers.

I glanced up at the multiple versions of myself in the mirror behind the bar. The glass was still splintered from when Eli had punched it years before when Ember had disappeared and he thought she was dead. After that, he had changed into his beast form for two years. It seemed as if he lost a piece of himself when she was gone.

I could relate.

Anger bristled along the ridge of my shoulders, needing release, needing to fight. My eyes caught a pair of blue eyes in the mirror, full of need. Or maybe fuck.

The woman could have been really pretty. She had long brown hair and a nice enough body, but a hard life and probably drugs and alcohol zapped the youth from her face and eyes. She was only about thirty, but her face looked like a map of leathered lines. I had done her a couple months back and ever since she had sought me out, purring in my lap every time she saw me.

I normally didn't go back to the same woman, but tonight I needed to take the edge off, and there would be no chase here. I set down my glass, stood, and walked for the back door, my gaze only landing on hers once.

She practically squealed and followed me out to the alley, where the sharp smell of garbage, stale alcohol, and rats doused the lane.

I didn't say a word as I grabbed her arms and turned her facing the dirty ally wall, pushed the leather skirt up to her hips. Bare beneath, no undies; she had come here for this.

I never learned her name, nor did I care to. She was using me too, and I was more than okay with that. The anger inside was like a razor, slicing, the darkness oozing out.

"Call me *darlin'*," she whimpered as I undid my pants, pulling myself out.

I didn't want to talk. I wanted nothing more than to be the beast I could not shift into. But one word whispered in her ear, and she was so wet for me it made my job much easier. No foreplay or lead-up needed. I thrust into her, and she groaned and arched her back. The more I plunged into her, the more the darkness swirled, sweeping away my thoughts.

Her screams and whimpers became background noise. I was not even in the vicinity of being gentle. My beast did not seem to care for my choice of victim, leading my release further from my grasp, driving me harder.

She held on to the wall, trying to keep upright, her cries loud and crude. She spoke, but I didn't hear a word she said. I felt her clamping around me. She was about to orgasm, and I was nowhere near relief. My annoyance flamed.

She bellowed, and I knew she'd gone over the edge. I didn't stop, only drove harder, jealous of not getting the same. *Dammit! Just let go,* I screamed at myself. It didn't help. I roared with ire, grabbing some of her hair and yanking it back.

Then an image flashed in my brain, gripping my chest. Someone else with long brown hair, her body bending over for me, taking the brunt of my abuse with moans. My dick tensed, heat and blood slamming into it, ready to burst.

"Holy shit." I ripped away from the woman, trying to get away from the vision, and backed up to the opposite wall.

"What?" The woman straightened, looking over her shoulder.

I couldn't speak.

"Don't stop, baby. I want you to come inside me."

Yeah, I'll bet she did. Hoping to get knocked up. Trap me and my bank account. The women here knew our group had money. It wasn't the first time one tried to become a baby mama to one of us. Wasn't going to happen. We were fertile as hell, but after Owen's woman got pregnant, then died giving birth to Jared, he had us all take precautions. Tree fairies have the strongest magic for birth control, and it stayed put till you took something to undo it.

I tucked myself back in, my cock angry at me for copping out so close to the finish line. But I felt sick, disturbed at my own thoughts.

"Go back inside, darlin'." I rubbed my head.

"But...you didn't get yours." She tugged her skirt down and sauntered over to me. "I could help you with that." Her knees bent, ready to go down in front of me.

"No." I grabbed her arm and tugged her toward the entrance of the alley. "We are done."

She blinked, hurt flashing over her features. I didn't mean to be so harsh, but right then I simply wanted her far away from me.

Right on cue her hurt turned to anger. "You RODs are all alike. Assholes. Take what you want and throw us away. You probably don't even know my name, do you?" she hissed.

My mouth opened and closed.

"That's what I thought," she snapped. "And when I say you are all alike, I mean the fucking's the same. At least Cooper and Cole got me off." She swung around, stomped to the bar door, and slammed it behind her.

I didn't care to remind her I got *her* off—multiple times. *I* was the one who hadn't gotten anywhere at all. She wanted to hurt me, but she couldn't even come close; I was too numb. It didn't faze me in the least. She would not be a mistake I would repeat. Her going after Coop and Cole only convinced me of my theory. She was hoping to trap one of us, and she didn't seem to care who.

I laid my head back against the wall. *Fuck.* What a bitch of a day. I needed to go home, crawl into bed, and end it. I pushed off the bricks and headed back for the bar.

Gravel crunched under my boot. I was only feet from the back door when it swung open. A man about six two, nearing two hundred and fifty pounds, pushed through the door, bouncing it against the brick wall as he stepped into the night.

*Crap.*

Bike gangs' battles for turf and dominance was not a new thing. And our tiff with this chapter of the Hells Angels went back almost two decades. With my assistance, Eli had killed two of theirs after they assaulted Ember and me in this exact bar years before. The thought of Puck's or McNamm's hands down Ember's pants sent Eli into a tailspin. They could never prove we did it, but they knew. They still were out for revenge.

"Moseley."

"Grouper." His moniker was perfect. That's exactly what he looked like—a large, dumb grouper fish. He was big, but not in shape, and liver spots from excess drinking patterned his face. To top it off he had an underbite, which gave him the resemblance to a gaping fish.

Two more of his buddies slipped out the door behind him. What was it with me? I attracted trouble like Velcro.

"So, pretty boy, I hear you're roughing up women." Grouper took a farther step out, crossing his arms. "We don't take kindly to that."

"What?" I jerked my head back. I had never hit a woman. Gabby didn't count. In training we kicked each other's asses all the time. But hurting women? My eye caught the brunette who had just been in the alley with me now standing at the bar past the men. A smirk covered her face, her hand on her cheek like she was covering a bruise.

*That bitch.* My not getting off really pissed her off.

"I only fucked her brains out. Made her scream and beg for more, so loud you all heard it inside. Is that what she considers being roughed up?" I lifted an eyebrow with a smug shrug. We all knew the entire bar had heard us. Hers had been cries of bliss, of being truly screwed. This was solely an excuse to fight me, a reason to take on a lone ROD the coward's way.

Grouper was my height, but we were opposites in every other way. He should have known better than to pick a fight with one of us. Grouper's gang had never won against the Dark Dwellers.

To the untrained eye some thought we were too young and good looking to fight like real men. Oh, I loved proving them wrong. Since I hadn't gotten off tonight, a fight might be the release I needed.

"And it's even more amusing coming from you." I motioned to him. "I heard four of your men have been jailed for abuse of their old ladies. If that's you not taking kindly to harming women, you might need to rethink your definition."

"Shut up." Grouper clenched his jaw, rage flaming behind his eyes.

"The only abuse women will get is through my dick…" I rolled my shoulders.

"This is going to be fun." Grouper smirked and glanced at the two men on either side of him, as though he liked his odds. "But like your dick, it might only take a few seconds before you blow your load and fall asleep on the ground."

That was just plain offensive. My brothers and I had extremely zealous reputations through the area among the women. Performance was not our problem in the slightest. Actually, a good number of the fights we got into were with men jealous because their women longed to be back with one of us. We were Dark Dwellers. Fucking and fighting were what we did best.

The three men took a step toward me, pulling out knives and chains. So much for fighting like real men. They had to bring in the toys.

I licked my bottom lip and bounced back on my toes. Right then a figure moved in behind them, framing the door. A smile engulfed my face, confusing the guys before me.

*Seriously. You're getting as bad as Eli. Can't leave you alone for a second,* Cooper linked into my head as he leaned against the frame.

*Don't tell me you don't want in on this,* I winked, and Grouper growled, slamming his fists together.

*Did I say I didn't? Hell yeah, I want in. Hate these fuckers,* Cooper replied. *Heard what happened tonight at Lars's. Haven't fought enough scum, huh?*

*Nope.*

"You ready for a beating of your life, pretty boy?" Grouper cracked his knuckles, moving toward me.

"Oh yeah." I grinned.

Cooper grinned back.

Let the party begin...

# FOUR

*A girl stood with her profile to me revealing her long, wavy blond hair, tall, lean body, and sweet face. I knew her so well, every curve, every freckle. My heart thumped in my chest at seeing her again. I dreamed of her all the time, but she still took my breath away and twisted my chest.*

*"Cammie," I uttered her name, basking in her beauty.*

*She glanced up. In one blink, terror entrenched her features, and she scuttled away from me.*

*"Cammie?" I reached for her, panic tapping against my skin.*

*"Stay away from me."*

*"Please, let me explain." I took a step toward her.*

*"You're a monster!" A blood-curdling scream tore through my mind, hammering chills up my back and ripping my heart open.*

---

"West! Wake up!" At the sound of a thump on my door, my eyes shot open. Sweat beaded my hairline, the dream slipping from my consciousness with every second. My dreams were becoming more frequent. They'd increased from once a month or so to every week. Cammie and Aneira both had starring roles in them. Most of the time, I couldn't remember more than a feeling, a wisp of an image, but that was starting to change too. This time Cammie's cries echoed in my head and tore through my soul.

"Hey, bastard, did you hear me?" Gabby yelled through my door. "Cole wants to see you right now."

I glanced over at my clock. Seven a.m. What the hell?

"Yeah. Yeah." I rubbed my eyes, and my cheek lit up with pain. I rolled out of bed, grabbed a pair of boxer briefs and jeans and tugged them on. My body was sore. I wanted to blame it on the fight last night, but I knew what really caused it. I grumbled and tossed on a T-shirt.

When I opened my door, Gabby still stood there, leaning against the wall and nibbling on a bagel with a cup of coffee in her hand.

"How sweet." I snatched both items from her, taking a gulp of the coffee.

"Hey, asshole!" She punched my shoulder. "My breakfast."

I chomped on the bagel, ripped more than half of it off, then gave it back to her. She stared down at the tiny piece left and then glared at me.

"Sharing is caring." I guzzled the coffee and handed her back the empty cup.

"You are such a dick."

I grinned, turning down the hall. "Think you'd be used to it by now."

"Some days I'm more tolerant of all you dickwads." She caught up with me. "Today is not one of those. Cole has been up since the crack of dawn. Woke me up."

"What's his problem? Why does he want to see me at this ridiculous hour?"

"Because you and Cooper got in a fight with those bastards last night. Nice shiner, by the way."

"Are you serious? Because we got into a scuffle? They asked for it, and they got what they deserved. He's really mad at me for that?"

Cooper and I had dropped those assholes and had been back to drinking faster than the time I spent in the alley with that girl. The girl quickly disappeared once she realized her plan backfired. Yet I knew she'd be back, trying to get with me again. That's what her type did. It was cliché, but sadly a lot of clichés were based on truth.

"No." Gabby's shoulder knocked into me. "I was totally messing with you. He couldn't care less about that."

I pinched the bridge of my nose and stopped in the family room. "Then why am I up? I feel like crap. I want to sleep."

"Don't yell at me." Gabby put a hand on one of her hips. "I'm merely the messenger. Cole's been talking to Lars the past hour. He's sending me out on a scouting mission with Alki to see if we can track down where the strighoul are holed up."

"You mean *you* requested." I smirked. Since the war she and Alki had become an enigma. We all knew they were together, but Gabby never talked about him. Never had him over to the ranch. They only met on missions, which they made sure took place more often than not.

"Whatever." She fluttered her hands, sticking her empty cup in my hand. "I merely had to get you up and to the office before taking off."

"Job well done."

She reached for a backpack on the ground, throwing it over her shoulder. "All right, loser. Tell Cole I'm out. See you later."

I reached out, messing her hair. The pixie cut had grown out to a long wavy bob past her shoulders, which she dyed violet-black.

"Hey!" She slapped my hand away.

I loved pissing her off.

"Like the helmet and wind aren't going to do worse." I chuckled and turned for the kitchen, her cup in my hands. "Be safe, Gabs."

"Always." She exited the ranch house as I went directly for the coffee maker. I heard the motorbike start up and her drive away. I filled the cup, grabbed another bagel, and headed to the office.

"I was summoned?" I plopped down in a chair, shoving the bagel in my mouth. I needed a soaker. Coop and I did way too many shots after the fight last night.

Cole held up his hand, his focus on the walkie-talkie phone. "All right, Lars, I'll get Cooper on that."

"Thank you. I will be in contact with you later." Lars's voice came through clear and deep before the line went fuzzy.

Cole turned it off and looked at me, raising one eyebrow. "Nice eye."

"I let him get in a hit so he wouldn't totally be emasculated." I slurped down more coffee.

"Least of our problems. Not that those guys don't deserve to be taken out completely." Cole sat back in his chair, scrubbed his face, and pushed back his reddish-brown, shoulder-length hair. He looked exhausted. "This whole strighoul attack on the King is crazy. It's bolder than I ever suspected from them, which is not good. Lars has Gabby out hunting them down and wants Cooper to do more runs for weapons."

"I can help Coop out."

"No." Cole shook his head, sitting back up. "Lars wants you for something else. He wouldn't tell me what, but he wants you over to the compound now."

"Now?"

"As in right now. He made the request quite clear."

*Shit.* The Unseelie King demanding your presence at the crack of dawn was never a good thing. Yes, seven a.m. was way too early for me. For night creatures like myself, day didn't usually start till late afternoon.

"Do you have a clue what he wants?" I shifted myself to the edge of the seat.

"No." Cole sighed. "And as we all know, whatever it is, it's not going to be good.

---

"Mr. West!" Marguerite greeted me at the door. By her smiling face you'd never know the place had been attacked the night before. She was her usual happy, loving self.

"*Mamacita*, always a pleasure." I winked. The swelling around my eye had gone down but still was sensitive.

"Oh, Mr. West. Such a tease." She batted my arm playfully. "Mr. Lars is in his office."

I nodded and entered the house. My senses picked up no activity downstairs except for in Lars's office.

"Come after. I cook breakfast." She quickly shuffled back into the kitchen, grabbing a pan.

"I'm good. Thank you, though."

"No." She shook her head fervidly. "*Debe comer.*" She picked up a spatula and pointed it at the cut under my eye.

*"Empaparse de alcohol."*

A smile hinted at my face. I was sure I looked awful. At least I'd taken two minutes to jump in the shower before coming. I wanted to wash the sex and alcohol off me.

"Thank you, *mamacita*." I kissed her cheek. She blushed from head to toe and shooed me out of the kitchen toward the office.

Life had changed a lot since the walls fell four months earlier. Humans no longer ran Earth. The Seelie Queen and Unseelie King were now in charge. Had you asked me even a few months ago if the Light and Dark would ever be able to work together, I would have said you were nuts. But Lars and Kennedy were doing exactly that—trying to restore the world to some functioning order and attempting to get humans and fae to form a truce.

Understandably, humans hadn't reacted well to the discovery of fae, and even worse when they learned fae had been living among them for centuries. Along with that knowledge, some human-designed structures didn't respond well to the force of magic crashing down on Earth. Buildings crumbled; bridges collapsed; electricity and Internet disappeared. We had to start over, and Lars, who was a demon as well as the Unseelie King, was leading the way in developing the new world.

My hand rose to knock on the office door when I heard his voice.

"Come in, Mr. Moseley."

A twinge of apprehension tweaked at my lungs. I sucked air in through my nose and pushed it out my mouth. I had no idea why he was calling me this early unless it he wanted to talk about the attack last night, which seemed strange. His own guards and men would know a lot more than I did.

I opened the door, stepped in, and shut it.

"Mr. Moseley, good to see you." Lars sat back in his chair, his watchful eyes studying me. Analyzing. Assessing. His gaze landed on the bruises and cuts on my face. He saw me the night before; he knew these were fresh. "Have a seat." Lars motioned to the set of chairs positioned before his desk.

"I'm good." I placed one hand over the other, letting my arms hang, but my shoulders were tense.

"Sit down, Mr. Moseley. That's an order," Lars said evenly.

A nerve in my neck twitched. I never liked to sit when I came in here. I had an urge to be on my feet, ready to pounce at any time. But when the Unseelie King demanded you sit, you sat. My feet moved around the chair, and I eased myself down, my gaze never leaving his.

He stared at me, steepling his fingers at his mouth. "You are curious why I summoned you this early?"

It really wasn't a question, but I never could seem to keep my mouth shut. "You missed me; it's no secret."

"Amusing, Mr. Moseley." Lars pressed his mouth together. "However, I am in no mood for your low-level humor this morning." He dropped his hands, straightening in his chair. "I will get straight to the point. The events of last night have succeeded in forcing me to act. Somehow the strighoul were able to find my private compound. We both are aware they are not smart enough to do this on their own. Someone is helping them.

"My enemies grow each day. Following Aneira's design, many want this new world to fall completely in the hands of the fae and to enslave humans. They do not have the intelligence to see the larger picture, to understand this system would fail, and fail miserably. It would be the end of our world, and the beginning of the decline for fae."

Lars may be a demon and the Dark King, but he was also a brilliant business man. He not only saw the bigger picture but designed it. With no rules, the fae would reduce the human population at an alarming rate, not thinking about a time when those numbers grew so low fae would die and create civil war among every fae clan. Humans and fae needed laws, limits.

"Now *my* home is being threatened." Lars stood and walked over to the glass doors, which opened onto the property he owned. The gray sky rumbled and lightning flashed as if it were reflecting the mood underneath his cool exterior. "I do not take those threats lightly. If they think they can intimidate me, they are sorely mistaken." Lars swung around to me, his eyes flashing black. "I will come back with everything I have. Show them exactly who is in charge and who should be feared."

My throat automatically swallowed, tamping down my need to go on the defense. As a Dark Dweller we were always ready to act, or be in a constant state of defense at the smallest hint of trouble. "And how do I play into this?" I shifted in my seat, wanting to stand.

Lars swiveled. "You, Mr. Moseley, are going to retrieve an object for me." He glided over closer to me.

"An object?" I leaned back, his proximity too close. His power syphoned off him, condensing around me, pressing down on my chest like air was seeping out of the room. I was not expecting him to ask me to fetch something. Fight, threaten, bully? Yes. But not be a gofer. "What does this have to do with last night or fighting back against your foes?"

"Everything." A small smile lit up Lars's lips, his eyes sparking with greed. "It is no ordinary object."

With Lars, nothing was simple or easy. He hadn't even told me what it was, and I could already feel his request was laced with danger and difficulty.

"What is this remarkable item?"

Lars moved to the edge of his desk, settled on the corner of it, and bent slightly toward me.

"You are one of the few aware of the existence of the Sword of Light." Lars's eyes seared into me. "The truth of its existence. The four treasures of Tuatha Dé Danann are not a myth."

"Yes." I gulped from fear. I didn't like the way this conversation had turned. Stripping entire bodies from bones was something I could do, or used to do. Speaking about the most powerful weapons in the world, created by fae and hidden because no one could handle their power? No.

I knew the four jewels were the Sword of Light, which Kennedy used to kill the last Seelie Queen, the Stone of Fál, the Spear of Lugh, and the Cauldron of Dagda. All had been considered mere legends and bedtime stories to scare fae children, but when a map appeared on Ember's back, leading them to the sword, we realized they were no myths.

Before the sword was found, there had been buzz about the Stone of Fál also being found, a fae and human possessing it, but then the gossip went silent and nothing had been heard about it in a while. Probably just a tall tale.

"I want you to find the Spear of Lugh for me."

"Wh-what?" I shot out of my seat. "You want me to find one of the most powerfully magical objects in the world for you to possess? Are you mad?"

"Quite the contrary, Mr. Moseley." Lars stayed

unruffled perched on his desk as I filled the room with my bewilderment. "I have carefully planned this."

I ran my hand through my long hair, which flapped back in my face. "No." I shook my head. "No fucking way."

I knew Lars's nonchalant attitude was only skin deep. He could turn on you in a blink, his demon always bristling right under his skin. But I couldn't seem to stop myself.

"I know you already have the sword. What do you need with the spear?" I exclaimed. "No one, including *you*, needs that kind of power. Plus, how would I even find it? It's been missing for thousands of years."

Lars stood, slipping back around his desk. "Why or what I need the spear for is my business." His words were clipped. "You only need to get it for me." His yellow-green eyes grew darker. "Which you will, Mr. Moseley. It is not up for debate."

"Oh really?" I folded my arms. "I am not your pet and will not fetch for you. The Dark Dwellers have a partnership; you need us. I won't be your errand boy."

Lars tilted his head, the demon stretching beneath his skin, sharpening his features. I stood my ground, holding his gaze. He could bend me to his will. He had the power to make anyone do anything, but I hoped the relationship he had created with Cole would prevent him from acting.

"You will." Lars's voice held no room for doubt. "However, I am willing to make this beneficial for you as well. A favor for a favor."

My gut squeezed. Favors owed and given by the Unseelie were never positive. "And how are you going to sweeten the pot exactly?"

Lars sat, and his chest puffed out, like a cat that caught

a bird. "I will help you with your little…inadequacies, I guess we'll put it."

Air locked in my chest. *No.* He couldn't know about my beast. No one did. But the way his eyes glinted with smugness, somehow I knew he did.

"You have been suffering since the day we brought you from the Light side, have you not? Every day the pain consumes you more?"

I huffed through my nose, trying to keep any emotion from reaching the surface.

"I can sense the beast in there wanting to come out, but the pain keeps it back. The difficulty in shifting is no longer in your control."

Anger pumped under my skin; he'd spoken my worst fear and weakness out loud.

"There is not much I do not know or sense." Lars clasped his hands together. "Now, sit down, Mr. Moseley, and we can discuss our mutually beneficial plan."

It took everything I had to walk back to the chair and sit. Stripped of the wall I built around my emotions, energy stirred through my veins.

"My power and reach are great. If you do this little favor for me, there will be no stone I won't turn to find a solution to your *problem.*"

"What? They don't have a pill for me take?" I quipped back. "So my beast won't go limp anymore?" With the beast confined inside, I did feel like a limp asshole. An amused smile hinted on his face. *Really?* That's what made the demon smile? My beast's erectile dysfunction.

"Do we have a deal?" Lars smirked, knowing there was no other answer I could give but yes. My teeth ground together and I nodded. "Please say it, Mr. Moseley."

My nostrils flared. "Yes. We have a deal."

Instantly I felt the weight of our bond like a lead jacket. Nothing was worse than an oath hanging on you, especially one put there by the Unseelie King. I couldn't get out of this. He pretty much had me by the balls.

"Now, back to the spear." Lars sat forward, laying his forearms on the desk, and waited till I filled the chair again. He began a moment after I sat. "Growing up, I am sure you heard the tales of Lugh. The Irish deity was a hero and high king of the fae long ago and was well known for his extraordinary talent in battle with a spear. He had been gifted the spear, which was said to be made from dark bronze and extremely powerful magic. Little is mentioned of the spear and what happened to it after his death." Lars took in a deep breath. "I have gone to great lengths to find any trail left to the whereabouts of this treasure."

"And let me guess...you found something." He wouldn't bring it up unless he discovered a solid enough lead.

"You are correct." He nodded. "What I found from several reliable sources was the spear had been stolen and traded many times after being taken from Lugh's deathbed. The last information I could find said it had been sold to an extremely wealthy man and was on a ship for Asia." Lars settled back again as he conveyed the story. "The ship did not sail far from the coast of Ireland. Said to be the work of sirens, who might have wanted it for themselves, the ship crashed into the rocks below a cliff and sank, killing everyone on board. The tale states anyone who tried to go after the sunken ship met the same fate as the others. After time, it became more lore than fact, and the treasure stayed buried below."

"But it could be folklore. You have no idea if it's really

down there or simply a story told to keep people from knowing where it really is."

"That's why I have you, Mr. Moseley," Lars replied. "You are going to find out the truth to these rumors."

"And get dragged under and killed like the others before me?" I waggled my head. "No, thank you."

"You will not be going alone."

"What do you mean? Who's coming with me?" My lids narrowed in on him.

"Someone who knows quite intimately how to deal with sirens."

"Oh, hell no!" My reaction snapped from me. "No fucking way."

Lars's eyebrows hitched up at my response.

"No. Rez cannot come with me. I can do this on my own."

"It is already done. I spoke to Rez earlier this morning."

I jumped to my feet, my hands on his desk, leaning over. "Well, tell her to unpack her bags."

"This is not going to be a simple exploring mission. Unfortunately, my queries have brought attention back to the spear's fable. You will not be the only one on this hunt. It will most likely get exceedingly perilous."

"Then that's even more reason for her not to go. She's too much of a risk. If this is going to be so dangerous, I'd rather not spend it worrying about her." Letting the Unseelie King's mistress get hurt or killed would make Christmas dinner especially awkward. Actually, I guess it wouldn't since I'd be *dead*.

"She is hardly defenseless."

"Below the water, but that is not where most of the attacks will come from."

"And above." Lars pulled at his cuffs. "She has trained with Alki. She is a decent enough fighter."

I huffed. She would only get in the way, nothing else. It was safer without her. I didn't need to bear the weight of her importance to the King on my back as well.

"She is going, Mr. Moseley. You will find her help crucial. She will be able to converse with the sirens, find out if they know anything, without drowning or succumbing to the siren song." He tipped his head around me. "Right, my dear?"

"Right," a sultry voice sounded behind me.

My back stiffened and I slowly stood, glancing over my shoulder. Rez stood in the doorway, leaning against the frame like she had been there for a while. Her long, silky hair hung in damp strips, showing she had recently emerged from the shower or pool. She wore stiletto-heeled black boots, black leather leggings, and a sexy lace-trimmed tank. As usual, her beauty sucked the air out of the room. But the glare she cast on me was brutal. No doubt she heard every word of my steadfast rejection of her tagging along. She pushed away from the wall, glided into the room, and reached my side, keeping her gaze locked on Lars.

"Though, if Mr. Moseley would like to do this without me, then let him." There was an edge to her words. "I would *love* to see how he would deal with sirens. I am *sure* they would instantly ignore their nature and tell him all their secrets."

"Hmmm… Am I sensing sarcasm here?"

She craned her neck to me, lifted her hand, and patted my arm. "Let me know how it goes for you."

"Definitely sarcasm. See, darlin', you can't get anything by me."

She glowered at me then snapped her head back to Lars.

"If the dweller thinks himself *so* unbelievably charming he can manipulate a bunch of sirens, then who am I to stop him?"

"There's not a fae or human I've found I couldn't charm."

"Seriously? Your ego is so big you'd rather get killed than admit you need my help?" Fury rattled the edges of her silky voice.

"I don't need anyone's help. I never have," I growled back. "Especially yours."

"You over-inflated, narcissistic—"

"Enough!" The King rose from his seat, shutting both our mouths with a scowl. "This is not up for discussion. Rez will be going with you. Case closed." Lars moved around the desk, buttoning his jacket. "You two will leave tonight. I suggest you go and do what you need to do to be ready and back here by six." He moved toward the door. "Now, if you excuse me, I have more important issues to attend to than refereeing the two of you bickering like children." He strode out of the door, leaving Rez and me alone in the room.

Rez clenched her small hands into fists. Her mouth dipped open to speak, then she shut it, shook her head, and briskly left the room.

*How the hell did my morning turn so bad so fast?*

All I wanted was to sleep in, nurse my hangover, and have a huge greasy breakfast. Now I would be packing to head to Ireland in search of some magical spear with a pain-in-the-ass siren. I rubbed my head, which still throbbed with last night's bourbon.

Marguerite's cooking smelled of huevos rancheros and chorizo and dragged me from the room toward the kitchen.

My chest twitched with a sudden feeling of doom. Something told me this was the stupidest, most dangerous adventure I had ever embarked on, likely to submerge me in ruin and disaster.

Let the good times roll.

# FIVE

With a folder of information on my lap, I sat back as I thumbed through it. There wasn't much to go on, basically the history of the spear and what little lore existed, a contact sheet of possible leads, the location, and the hotel Rez booked for us, but nothing really substantial. I wasn't surprised. We were chasing a myth, a fable told to children. I figured it would be similar to finding the Holy Grail to humans.

Yet eight hours later here I sat on the King's newly constructed private jet, designed specifically for our magically charged world. We were traveling to the motherland of Celtic fae lore, my parents' birthplace before fae had to go into hiding from humans.

I had been there only once, but never to the western side where we'd be searching from Dingle to the Cliffs of Moher. Not even legend could seem to decide on exactly where the ship carrying the spear sank.

I leaned back in the buttery leather seat, letting my tired eyes shut for a moment. At the sound of someone stirring across from me, I popped open an eye. Rez stared out the window, then back at her own packet, then shifted again. Her face never showed distress, but I could feel fear bounce off her like a paddle ball against the side of my head.

"Don't like to fly?" I lifted the other lid, staring at her.

"No." She shook her head. "We sirens don't like being far from water. I would have preferred to swim there."

"You might get your wish if this thing crashes."

Her dark eyes snapped to mine with a glare, and I grinned mischievously. She wrinkled her nose in annoyance and turned back to the window.

Humor was the only thing keeping me from freaking out. Dark Dwellers were earth-based animals. Up here, thousands of feet in the air, I felt trapped in a contraption which probably had a motor like that piece-of-shit scooter Lars had us riding, and further away from life as I knew it than ever before.

The plane shook, dropping a little. Rez's knuckles turned white, her chest fluttering. Magic in the air made for horrible turbulence. Actually, not only humor would keep me sane. I swiveled the chair and headed straight for the built-in bar. Lars was my kind of traveler. Never far from a drink.

"Want one?" I glanced over my shoulder at Rez, then to the opposite table to the other two passengers. "How about you Beefhead? Ginger-Nuts?" Normally Lars had "people" to serve him on the plane but clearly only for gold card members.

Besides Rez and myself, there were the two pilots and two of Lars's men, who frowned at their nicknames. They were here to see we got to the hotel safely, then they'd disappear. I'd overheard them discussing doing an "errand" for him after they dumped us at our location.

"No." The smaller, redheaded guard glowered at me, his thick Irish accent heavy.

"Really?" I started pouring whiskey into my glass. Top-shelf Irish whiskey. Nice. "Thought you Irish came out drinkin'?"

"We do. Believe me, dweller, I could drink you under the table without even hitting a buzz," Ginger-Nuts challenged.

"Then bring it. I would love to see you try, leprechaun."

The huge, beefy man next to him quickly grabbed his shoulder, holding him back. "Garrett, don't. The King is already mad at us for the last slip-up."

"That wasn't a slip-up, Cadoc. Fairies deserve to be put in their rightful place. It's about time those arrogant asses understand their status in the new world."

"So you're here as punishment?" I let out a sharp howl. "You piss off Daddy, so he sends you to babysit us. What do you have to do after, go clean up some kelpie's crap?"

Garrett's gaze boiled with fury, but he kept quiet.

"We are not here to babysit. We have our own mission. But I don't expect someone as simple as you to understand what I do. There's no point in explaining it. I'm not sure there are small enough words."

"Got it. Brains and brawn." I pointed to each of them. "He has to come along to tuck you into bed at night. I think that is adorable." Fury rose off them, swirling magic in the air.

"West, enough." Rez glanced back at us. "Tuck your testosterone back in your pants."

I smirked at the two lackeys and tipped my glass at them before strolling back to my seat across from Rez.

"Seriously, West. Do you enjoy pissing people off?"

she muttered, shaking her head, and flipped through the pages in front of her.

"It's part of my charm, sweetheart."

She huffed, flattening a page on the table, a map of Ireland. "Here's where we will be searching, and you need to understand sirens are fluffy bunnies compared to others hunting these lands."

"I'm a Dark Dweller, darlin'. I think I can handle it. Remember we were the most feared creatures in the Otherworld." I took a swig of whiskey.

"With your bloated ego, I'm surprised you haven't been killed yet."

"There's a reason my 'ego' is swollen." I winked. "I'm confident because I know how good I am. In fighting too."

"Please, I'm feeling nauseated enough." Her face scrunched. "Wish we could have used the doors to travel."

"And be lost in them for the next year?"

The thin gateways used to slip between worlds had gotten mixed up. After the walls between the worlds fell, the portals were no longer a safe way to travel. Ember was the only one I knew who had learned a pattern to them. Eli still wound up in Japan when he was trying to get to Italy. Some led you on an endless loop, trapping you for days or months. Many humans had gone missing since the crash, probably stumbling into a door and ending up on some remote island or Antarctica, never to be heard from again. Hence, the reason Lars wanted us to use the jet to get to our destination.

"We'll be landing in Cork in the evening and will rest and spend one night in the hotel. The next day we will head to the coast. Our next lodging is in Cahersiveen."

"You're a list girl, aren't you?"

She sat up in her seat. "Doesn't hurt to be organized and ready."

"Sure, darlin'." I winked and sat back in my seat. "Let me know when you need me to nod and say, *Yes, sounds great.*"

Her brow furrowed, but she kept talking, as though to reconfirm the plan more to herself than me. Her voice was like melting chocolate, so she could be reading the periodic chart and I would want to hear more. I finished my drink and let her voice lure my eyes shut. It was the most peaceful I'd felt in a long time. But I knew the moment I truly let myself go under the nightmares would come for me. I could feel them lingering at the edge, waiting for me to drift off.

The moment my strength gave in, they pounced.

---

*Spikes burrowed deeper into my neck with every tug of the chain, and blood slid down my back, splattering on the stone floor.*

*"Come, pet." The woman before me yanked on the heavy chain. "I will have you collar-broken by the end of the day...if it kills you." She smiled, her red lips parting in twisted humor, her flaming red hair braided and hanging over her shoulder. She pulled me through the halls, her ass wiggling proudly at her catch. Her dress was flowing and soft but sheer in areas that made you do a double take.*

*She was beautiful. But then the Seelie Queen would be. She was Ember's aunt, and I could see some family traits. But everything I adored about Ember, I despised about the Queen.*

*Aneira paraded me through the court, naked and bleeding with only a spiked collar wrapped around my neck that was slowly killing me. Soldiers, kitchen staff, and her circle of the fae high court all spit on me and yelled obscenities as I passed by. Their hatred for the Dark, the Unseelie, remained as strong as ours for them.*

*She had been coming daily for a week to humiliate me, but today something felt different. A giddiness showed in her step as she led me down a hallway. A guard opened the door for her the moment she approached.*

*"Come, pet. I have lots of fun in store for us today." She dragged me into a square stone room. My heart and lungs stopped. Chains hung from the ceiling with wrist, neck, and feet cuffs. A chair with metal restraints sat in the middle. Various leather whips and clubs with barbed wire laced between the strips lined the walls, along with a table full of sex-torture devices. There was more, but my brain couldn't absorb all I saw, sheer terror dotting my sight. "Think it's time you learned some obedience."*

*The door slammed so loudly behind me I jumped. The guard left me alone with the Queen. Acid built in my stomach, bile rising into my gorge, making me gag.*

*"Don't make that face. I promise rewards if you do well." She jerked me farther to her, showing another section of the room.*

*My lungs halted, and my gut fell through the floor. I was going to throw up—I had no doubt.*

*A bed sat in the corner with speared handcuffs dangling from the headboard. This was not a little S&M. This was designed to utterly break you, to brutalize and torment till you begged for death.*

*Darkness squeezed my vision as she dragged me forward, bellows reverberating off the wall full of anguish.*

*They were my own.*

My lids bolted open, and I wheezed in air. Rez stood over me, my fingers wrapped around her arm in a death grip. I jerked my head around, regaining my thoughts and whereabouts.

Plane. Rez. Right…

"Nightmare?" she asked quietly, her expression laced with sympathy, immediately setting my teeth on edge. Everyone knew generally what happened to me when I was held prisoner by Aneira, which I despised, but no one knew the full truth.

And they never would.

"No," I snapped.

"Really?" Her eyebrows lifted. "You normally scream out in your dreams?"

"No, usually she does," I quipped, trying to lighten the mood.

Rez's lips pressed together with a frown. Her gaze flashed to my hand then back to me. I then noticed I still clutched her small wrist like a vise. My hand dropped away from her, the imprint of my hand still marking her skin.

"We've landed." Rez stood fully, her appearance impeccable. She looked like she was going to New York for business in her knee-length heeled black boots, a gray pencil skirt with matching jacket, a deep red blouse underneath, and her hair pulled back in a sleek ponytail. She didn't appear like someone going on a hunting mission in remote parts of Ireland, where sheep outnumbered people.

"Garrett and Cadoc took our luggage to the car." She hooked her bag holding all the documents over her shoulder. The black antenna from the walkie-talkie phone stuck out of her satchel. Lars wanted us to check in and keep him updated with any news. "Shall we go, Mr. Moseley?"

Back to being formal with me. Her nervousness and teasing were gone. All professional.

I nodded as my eyes tracked her down the row to the exit. My gaze latched on to her ass as she walked away. *Jesus.* The woman's figure was amazing. *West,* I warned myself and swung back around in my seat, raking a hand over my face. *Stop. She's like a Gabby. Sister...or nun. Damn, there better be some Irish lasses I can utilize along the way.*

I stood, picked up the last of my whiskey, and slammed it back. Yeah, this was going to be so much fun.

# SIX

Ginger-Nuts and Beefhead dropped us off at the Hayfield Manor Hotel. My gaze locked on the thousand twinkle lights trimming the hotel, lighting our way through the cold winter evening, the building old and beautiful. Ireland had fared far better than cities in the States after the barrier fell between worlds. The older the architecture, the more resilient it seemed to be to magic.

Ireland had always been the most magic-saturated place, even with the walls in place. It was the first place after Seattle to get electricity and the new magical-based equipment to function. Besides some of the newer crumbled buildings, Ireland looked mostly untouched by the war's effect, and this hotel in particular.

"Are you freakin' kidding me?" I got out of the car, staring at the hotel. "This is your idea of being inconspicuous?"

It was like stepping into one of those chick movie sets from the 1800s. The three-story Georgian manor was built from old, red brick covered in ivy with white painted dormers. Topiary plants and a perfectly trimmed lawn lined the way up the cobblestone path to the door. A warm glow reflected across the drive.

"It's only for the night." Rez shut the door and came around to me. "There is no reason we can't hide in a luxury hotel as easily as a dump."

"You've never been on a mission have you, darlin'?" I smirked, glancing over at her. She pinned her lips together, not looking at me. "Believe me, seedy doesn't ask questions nor does it care to know your name or if you have a credit card. Easier to disappear or make someone else vanish."

She huffed lightly, then took off for the front door. "I am so sorry. You will just have to suffer the inconvenience of Egyptian cotton sheets, a Jacuzzi bathtub, an indoor pool, and a steam-powered shower for a night." She grabbed the door, twisting to me, her free hand going to her chest. "My deepest apologies." She dissolved into the buttery light of the hotel.

A grin hitched my mouth, and I shook my head. Feisty thing.

"Get your bloody bags out of the boot," Garrett yelled from the driver's seat. "I'm not your fuckin' butler."

My smile dropped and became a growl. I went around to the trunk, called a "boot" here, and retrieved the two bags. I actually was shocked when I saw Rez's suitcase. I expected a girl like her to bring five pieces, full of inappropriate clothes and shoes. But she packed light for the unknown journey ahead.

Slinging my duffle bag over my shoulder, I slammed the trunk. Garrett tore away, spitting dirt and pebbles into my face.

"Yeah, screw you too, Ginger-Nuts," I screamed after the car as I picked up Rez's bag and headed inside.

The interior was even more beautiful and elegant with dark mahogany furniture and paneling, delicate rich fabrics, chandeliers, and antiques. A grand staircase dominated the lobby, curving into two wings of the hotel on the next floor. I was so out of my element, the bull in a china shop. One look at me in my worn jeans, scuffed boots, faded T-shirt, and abused brown biker jacket, and you knew I didn't belong.

On the other hand, Rez fit so well, like the place was designed around her. This was her element, elegant and classy, and far from my world of bikers, coarse language, and even coarser women. This was where she belonged, while I should be at some low-class bar where I could relate.

She held her head high, confidently walking up to the check-in desk. Her gorgeous voice carried over to me, deep and fluid.

The old man behind the desk didn't even look my way when I reached her side, his undivided attention stuck on Rez with a dreamlike stare. The siren call, even when she wasn't "working," was hard to disregard. Simply walking in a room she demanded your attention, and when she spoke all eyes turned to her.

"Checking in to the two master suites, Patrick Murphy and Colleen Kelly."

I almost snorted. You couldn't get too much more common than Murphy and Kelly in Ireland, like Brown and Smith in the States. It was good for a cover. Names that didn't stand out were better and blended with the crowd.

"Yes." He nodded, his Irish accent thick. "Two master suites."

"Are they next to each other?" I queried, wanting to make sure she was somewhere I could reach quickly if needed.

"No, sir. They are down the hall from each other."

I shook my head. "No."

"Wes…Patrick, it's only for one night. It will be fine." Rez placed her hand on my arm.

Every instinct told me to fight, but being in this hotel already made me feel like a lowly commoner. Unsettled. I was overreacting, tired, and feeling out of place here. I relented with a grunt and grabbed the bags.

"We have someone to do that, sir." The man behind the desk nodded toward the bags. On cue a man dressed in a butler outfit came up behind me. He was of slight build and appeared to be in his late sixties.

"I think I got it." The man reached to take the bag, ignoring me. "I can carry my own bags," I snarled.

"Sir, I must insist I help," the butler replied, yanking on the handle.

"No."

Like two children playing tug of war, the old man and I tussled for the suitcases, bickering back and forth with an unspoken "mine, mine, mine."

"Harold, let the gentleman take his own suitcase," said the clerk behind the desk.

Harold let go, but his eyes narrowed on me as if I just insulted his entire family. *Shit.* I was saving his old ass from making another trip upstairs, and he looked like he wanted to short-sheet my bed later. He then grabbed Rez's suitcase, which lay out of my reach, and glowered at me with haughtiness. *Checkmate*, his smugness said.

Harold was about to get my boot up his ass when Rez clutched my arm, forcing me to follow her. Harold moved around us to the elevator, and we passed the gorgeous indoor pool and restaurant. The hotel was only three levels and I hated elevators, but I knew I had already embarrassed Rez enough. I got in, Rez standing next to me. Harold stood in front, his head only coming to my chest.

When we arrived at the top level, he proceeded to Rez's room. I followed. The moment he opened the door, I slipped past him and inspected the room. I'd learned over the years you could never let your guard down, no matter how safe you thought you were. My instinct was to get the lay of the land, study the room, entrances and exits.

"Sir, your room is down the hall." Harold placed Rez's bag in the closet.

"I know." I turned on the bathroom lights, peering in. Good. No windows.

"I am sorry, sir. Is the room not to your standards?" Harold folded his hands in front of him, staring at me evenly, but his shoulders were pinched.

*Oh…a bit snotty, Harold.*

"It is wonderful. Thank you, Harold." Rez placed a cash in his palm. He smiled at her, and after handing me my key, he withdrew from the room. The door snapped shut and laughter peeled out of Rez, her hand to her stomach as she bent forward.

My eyes widened in surprise.

"Wow, I thought I was going to have to put you both in a time-out." She sat on the edge of the bed, giggling. "Five minutes in Ireland and you've already pissed off people and made enemies."

Dark Dwellers were excellent at that. "I think I can take Harold." I grinned, stepping closer to her.

"Oh, I don't know. Harold looked pretty spirited."

"It would be like fighting a leprechaun."

"Have you ever fought one?" Rez wiped her eyes. It made me feel good she was back to teasing me.

"No. Even in the Otherworld, I only ran across a few in my time." Sadly they were becoming extinct. But a real leprechaun was nothing like the commercial image at St. Patrick's Day. They weren't red-bearded men hiding gold at the end of rainbows and were less mischievous and more like nasty, drunk assholes.

"Then you don't know. He could have head-butted you in the kneecaps." Her laughs trickled away, leaving the room silent. Suddenly I was highly aware of us being alone in the room together.

"I'll let you get some sleep." I rubbed my hands together, inclining my head toward the door.

"Breakfast at eight. The car will be dropped off at nine. We should be on the road no later than nine thirty. Arrive at Cahersiveen a little after noon, giving us time to settle in and have something to eat before we start our quest. All right?"

"Yes, ma'am." I saluted her. "Did you schedule in times when I can take a piss?" Her eyes flicked skyward. I grinned.

A few moments past. The awkward quiet rushed back into the room again, bristling the nape of my neck. *Why am I still here?*

"O-kay. I'm going." I turned for the door right when she stood up from the bed, our bodies colliding. My arms wrapped around her as she stumbled, pulling her back up. Her body pressed into mine, curving with heat against me. In her four-inch heeled boots, she could look straight into my eyes. Her mouth was only inches from mine.

Waaaayyy too fuckin' close.

"Sorry, darlin'." I forced a playful grin on my face with a wink. No big deal. I caught her from falling. A gentlemanly thing to do.

"Yeah. No problem." She brushed her hand over her smooth ponytail.

"See you in the morning. Sleep well." I grabbed my bag and retreated from the room, stalking down the hall. I shut the door and fell against it. What was wrong with me? Since the moment Lars mentioned her coming, I had been off. Okay, I had been off way before that because of *issues*. It was time to get back on my game. I wanted to forget my beast problems, the nightmares, the neurotic woman down the hall. The only important thing was finding the spear. That was all.

I ran my palm roughly over my face. I needed a drink.

Rich brown liquid swirled around my glass as I took another sip. It seemed like the only thing in this sophisticated place that felt familiar. Dark leather stools lined the mahogany bar. A black fireplace roared to my left with soft barreled armchairs clustered in groups for people to sit and unwind.

It wasn't making me relaxed. My shoulders were still taut, waiting for the whiskey to take the edge off.

"Another, sir?" the bartender, Sean, asked me. He was tall and lean with graying hair, and he prickled when I sat down. As a Dark Dweller, I was used to it. People couldn't put a finger on it, but they sensed danger. Something instinctual they feared.

"Yeah." I nodded, setting down my empty glass for him to refill. It was late and only a few of us remained in the bar area. Sean might have to turn out the lights and lock up the liquor to get me to leave.

I couldn't get rid of the edgy feeling. I shouldn't be surprised by it in the face of all that had happened, but usually I was the calm one. Or at least I pretended to be.

Since I came back from the Light side, I had to force my easygoing attitude more and more. The loss of the ability to shift might make me lose it completely as I was constantly tense and quick to snap. Rez and this classy joint only enflamed my already disgruntled mood.

Sean filled my glass again, and I slammed back another gulp. The rich, musky liquor glided down my throat. A notch between my shoulders loosened as the alcohol burned through my chest.

Better. But I still couldn't let go of my unease. The biggest thorn in my side was the vast difference between Rez's world and mine. She was chic. Even the way she moved and spoke screamed money and sophistication. I was seedy: bars, loose women, cheap booze, fast motorcycles, and fucking someone whose name I didn't know against a wall in a dark alley.

This seemed true even more now than since my time in a quaint beach town near Myrtle Beach. Cammie brought charm and sweetness into my life, but the bad boy was never far underneath no matter how much I tried to be a better man for her. Cammie had been far too good for me; Rez wasn't even in my universe.

*Jesus, West, why do you even care?* It didn't matter if we were on the same level, Rez was so far off limits it wasn't even funny. And I didn't want anyone for more than a good time anyway. I tried once and failed miserably. I'd never do it again. Anyway, Rez was someone you courted, wined and dined. Not my type, in other words.

I snorted into my glass at the thought of me trying to court a girl. I never had to. Cammie was the closest I got to pursuing one, which intrigued me, but even she didn't take much convincing. Our connection was there.

My fingers rolled around my glass, lost in thought,

when a tickle nipped at the back of my neck and traveled along my spine. My gaze darted around the room. Nothing seemed out of place. A man and woman sat by the fireplace. Two men sipped brandy, talking, in another group of chairs. The scene was no different from when I walked into the bar. But the vibe still pulsated lightly down my shoulders. I twisted in my chair, searching. Nothing.

I leaned back and scanned the lobby in the other room. I was just about to chalk it up to my overactive nerves and go back to drinking when I saw three men head for the stairs. They were dressed in jeans and work boots, more like me and less like the well-dressed occupants here. One was tall, bald, with a crooked nose, like he had been in so many fights it could no longer heal straight. The second one was short and stout with a reddish-brown beard. The last guy was tall and ripped. His scarred face also appeared to have been in many fights.

I sensed they were human, and humans didn't normally worry me. What could they really do to me? But now my instincts were ringing with alarm.

I tracked them walking away from the front desk and up the grand staircase. My feet hit the floor, and I tossed money at the bar as I raced after the men.

I took the steps two at a time, not even pausing at the second floor, my legs hauling me to the third. With every step, my nerves trembled and my legs moved faster. The itch grew stronger, like hundreds of tiny spiders crawled up and down my neck.

I reached our floor, scanning each direction of the hallway. At the far end, a shoulder of one of the men disappeared around the connecting corridor, heading to the section where Rez and I roomed.

The beast lunged against its cage, causing my heart to

beat faster. *Protect.* The beast growled, pulsing my muscles into motion. The pattern of the carpet blurred under my feet as I rushed down the hall.

I curved around the corner and came to a dead stop, my heart hammering in my chest. The three men were heading straight for Rez's room. My body coiled with rage. How did I let her talk me out of rooming near her? My hands curled into fists as I barreled toward the three men. I knew I could be a scary fucker without trying, and I wasn't holding back.

The bearded man suddenly shifted his direction, looking at the card key in his hands. He angled himself for the door next to Rez's and stopped.

I did too.

He unlatched and opened the door, letting the other two in. As he looked back at his buddies, he caught sight of me: the menacing figure in the hallway, poised to tear him in half. His eyes widened. Letting out a tiny yelp, he shuffled into the room and slammed the door shut.

The sound of the bolt sliding into place echoed down the quiet corridor, sending a rush of chagrin through me. *Holy shit, West. You are such a paranoid ass.* These human guys were probably innocently heading to their room, and I practically jumped them, wanting to beat the crap out of them in a five-star hotel.

Air huffed out of my lungs, and my shoulders drooped as I scrubbed at my face. With a turn, I moved in the opposite direction to my room, shaking my head. I really shouldn't be taken off my leash, should I? My quick temper, paranoia, and stress were a formula for catastrophe. When I snapped, I only hoped no one innocent was in my path.

I slammed into my room, pissed as hell, throwing myself back on the enormous Tempur-Pedic bed. The alcohol was supposed to ease my tension, but I was more restless and irritable than before.

I could think of only three ways to release this type of aggression. Shifting. *Can't.* Fight someone till you're bloody messes and can't lift your muscles anymore. *Probably frowned upon here.* Or fuck someone senseless. *Uhhh.* Options slightly limited, unless I departed the premises, which I'd never do, leaving Rez unprotected.

I rose from the bed and moved toward the shower, tearing off my clothes along the way. Under the spray of the steam shower, I tried to relieve some of the pressure, but every time I closed my eyes, Rez appeared. The curve of her neck, the roundness of her ass, the fullness of her tits. Her lips, eyes, voice...everything. Imagining her on her knees in front of me.

I lurched, anger rising. There were a million gorgeous girls I could be thinking of. Hell, most of the time I didn't even need a face. The memory of my many encounters with water fairies usually did the trick. Tonight nothing else turned me on. Typical. She was the one woman I couldn't have so I wanted her. Nothing more than my beast's instinct to conquer. My need would probably dissipate after I screwed her.

Still I wouldn't allow myself to picture her. And in the end I was left unsatisfied. Naked, I headed for the minibar. An awfully poor substitute. Each tiny bottle was a fortune, but I didn't give a shit. It was on Lars's bill. He forced me on this trip, and I would take advantage. I drank every bottle till I stumbled to my bed, landed face first and naked, and then passed out.

---

A hammering in my head rattled me out of a dead sleep. Pulsing, throbbing pain drove nails into my brain. My lids struggled to lift. The insistent pounding wouldn't stop, and it took me a moment to realize it wasn't only in my head. The door to my room thudded with harsh knocks.

I groaned and lifted my head. Heavy curtains kept my room dark. Only a sliver of light around the edge of the window squeezed through. I winced as another round of drumming hit the door, sending shockwaves into my skull.

"Yeah. Yeah…I'm coming." I slowly put my feet on the ground, though the room kept spinning. I used the nightstand to gain my balance. "Stop the fuckin' knocking already."

My feet shuffled across the carpet, and I slapped at my cheeks, trying to wake up. At last I made it to the door and unlocked it. My eyes flinched at the onslaught of light, and I put my hand up to shade them.

"Yeah, what the hell do you want?" My bleary gaze cleared the moment I saw the person on the other side.

"Oh." Rez's gaze traveled down my body then she quickly snapped her face to the side, a deep red blushing her cheeks.

*What?* Oh right. I was naked.

Rez's head jerked around trying to look at something else other than my body, and let's be honest, my dick, which stood greeting her this morning, too. So polite of it.

"What can I do for you, darlin'?" A mischievous grin engulfed my face. Was I in the presence of the one fae embarrassed by nakedness?

"Get dressed, for one." The flush in her cheeks creeped down her neck.

"Nothing you haven't seen before."

"Yes…but…well…not exactly…" She rolled her lips together, stopping whatever she was going to say. Her eyes briefly darted to my crotch then down the hall.

"You're the one who woke me up. I always sleep naked."

I tried to grip the door and missed, stumbling to the side.

"Are you drunk?"

"That's an extremely good possibility." I grinned, regaining my hold.

"It is already past nine, and the car is here. We need to get going." She huffed then shifted her weight. Watching her squirm helped my hangover. My playful smile only seemed to grow the more flustered she got.

"No, we really don't. Cahersiveen won't be going anywhere. I promise it will still be there an hour after you dictated." She leaned back to glower at me.

Today her silky, dark brown hair hung to the middle of her back. She had on a cream-colored, fuzzy-looking sweater, cashmere I think, and heeled black boots. Dark designer jeans were tailored to fit every curve of her body but looked more chic than any jeans needed to be. She looked like she should be shopping on streets in Paris, not going to humble fishing villages on the coast of Ireland.

"Is that what you are wearing?"

She folded her arms, her eyes tapering. "Yes. Is that what you're wearing?"

"If you want it to be."

Rez actually rolled her eyes, her frustration with me mounting. Damn, she made this easy.

"Meet me downstairs in ten, Mr. Moseley." She swung around and marched down the hallway. I loved how I turned to "Mr. Moseley" when she was pissed with me, which was more often than not.

I splashed cold water on my face and quickly grabbed my clothes, my hangover already easing. In an hour it would be gone totally. Perk of being fae.

Once dressed, with my duffle bag slung over my shoulder, I proceeded downstairs. Rez was sitting on the edge of her seat in the lobby sipping from a delicate flowery china cup, her knee bouncing. I was going to have to work on this control issue of hers. She really didn't like her time schedule being off, but to me schedules were meant to be thrown into disarray.

My stomach growled. I was ready for an enormous breakfast with several cups of coffee.

"You hungry?" I pointed at the dining room, the scent of eggs, sausage, and coffee making my mouth water.

"I already ate." She stood, her long legs drawing her up to my eye level. "I was down here at eight like we planned. I had the most *delicious* spinach-and-cheese omelet. They had these hot scones with homemade cream and jam, which melted on my tongue, fresh-squeezed orange juice. And the coffee…oh, don't get me started. Dark and rich." She emphasized each description, her voice low and sexy, her eyes rolling back like she was about to have an orgasm.

Now I was extra hungry and even hornier. "Evil, darlin'." I shook my head.

She grinned impishly, then grabbed her rolling suitcase and headed out the front door.

Yeah. She was trouble. If I were a smart man, I'd back away and stop playing this game.

Too bad I wasn't a smart man.

# SEVEN

A silver Range Rover Sport waited for us in the parking lot. Rez had done all the booking for our trip, but she didn't comprehend the concept of blending in. Or maybe this was her version of it. Still it made me feel like a yuppie ass. I shoved her suitcase in the back. "Don't tell me the few things you brought are similar to this." I motioned to her outfit. "And those definitely have to go." I pointed at her boots.

She glanced at her feet. "Are you telling me how to dress?"

"No. I'm saving your ankles from breaking. You can't hike or run in those," I exclaimed. "I'm also saving my back from having to carry you because your feet are aching."

"I'm not an idiot. I have a pair of flats in there."

I raised an eyebrow.

"Fine, they're ballet flats, but I can run if needed."

"Oh, sweetheart." I clicked my tongue, shutting the hatchback. "Think we're gonna have to do a little shopping on our way out. You haven't quite grasped how to be one of us mere mortals."

"*You're* not mortal."

"A technicality."

"I'm in jeans and a sweater." I burst out laughing at how plain she made her outfit sound.

Hurt flickered over her face, and she looked down.

"Hey." I instinctively reached out for her face, pulling it up. "Darlin', you don't understand. You already stand out. You are the most stunning woman there is, without the fancy clothes. We need any help we can to go unnoticed. At least as much as a siren and a dweller can."

Rez's breath faltered, and I felt a catch in my chest. The intimate moment stifled the cold morning air. What was I doing touching her? Especially like this? I backed away, pushing my hands in my jeans pockets.

"We should get on the road. Keys?" I held out one hand.

She blinked, then jerked open her bag, which held all the paperwork, took out a set of keys, and placed them in my open palm.

"Okay. Let's get this shit show on the road." I forced myself to smile cheekily, trying to break the strange energy, and went for the driver's side.

Flirting with women, taken or single, came so naturally to me it was like breathing. Safe. Fun. But with Rez I was all too aware I was doing it. The moment she called me out in the kitchen the night before we left, I had become conscious of it. All I should see when I looked at her was the face of the man she crawled into bed with each night looming over me, threatening death. Even flirting harmlessly with her could get me killed.

"Are you planning to drive?"

"Uh. Yeah." I grabbed the door handle.

"Good luck with that."

I swung the door open. *Shit.* "Right." I smirked. "Wrong side."

She chuckled, grabbed the door from me, and hopped into the passenger side.

Walking to the driver's side, a gust of unease blew over me, as though we were being watched. I halted, my eyes drifting around. Only one other couple was outside, but they weren't looking at us. I gazed at the windows of the manor. Not a whisper of fabric moved or a person stood looking out, so I sought out the room where the three men had slipped unwittingly out of my dangerous path last night, but no sign of life showed behind the heavy drapes covering the window.

I shook my head and climbed into the car. Even if it were only my paranoia, I wanted to put some major distance between us and this hotel.

---

"Here, try this on too." I handed Rez a fake-fur-lined puffy coat. Ireland in winter was freezing at best, but along the water, with the wind, rain, and thick mist, it could be downright arctic.

Rez stared at the items in her hands, a crease lining her forehead.

"Sorry, darlin'. No designer clothes here." I grinned. We found a sports-and-camping shop where she could at least get the basics: boots, cargo-style pants, couple of wool sweaters, and a jacket. "You will thank me later, I swear." I winked at her.

"Never did I think you'd be picking out clothes for me." Bemusement twisted her mouth. She turned to one of the dressing rooms with several outfits draped over her arm. The shop appeared small with only two changing stalls. I trailed behind, sipping the coffee I'd picked up next door. I'd already demolished the bacon-and-egg sandwich.

Sitting in a chair across from her tiny curtained room, I took another swallow of coffee and almost choked. The coffee burned up my nose as I struggled to keep it from spraying all over the floor. An inch of curtain was not pulled all the way to the wall. The mirror on the other side reflected Rez inside, tugging her sweater over her head. Her long hair pulled through the fabric and tumbled down her bare waist. My gaze latched on her, unable to part from the sight of her smooth olive skin and her black lace bra cupping her exquisite breasts. My shoulders were peppered with sweat. My breath faltered at the tousled mop of her hair, which looked uncannily like she'd been fucked. Really good.

I couldn't stop the image that popped into my head, even though I should have. I wanted to be in the dressing room with her groaning and gasping, legs wrapped around my waist, hair getting more ruffled every time she slid up and down the wall as I thrust deep into her. *West. Stop!*

It was too late. The beast flared to the surface with a crash, and my muscles reflexively tried to change. I shot out of my chair, falling to the ground on all fours, the coffee splashing over the floor as it hit. A grunt gouged my throat under the sudden onslaught of pain.

"West?" The curtain whipped open. She stood there holding a sweater to cover up. Her eyes grew large, and she dropped the sweater to rush to my side. "West? What's wrong?"

Her half-naked body rubbed against mine, only slamming the beast more into primal mode. *Dammit, woman. Not helping.* My hands curled into the rug, digging into the fibers damp with my coffee. My spine curved up, elongating, my body ready for the change.

Except nothing happened. Torture ripped through my veins and guttural noises climbed up my throat. My muscles contracted and locked and my whole body cramped, firing razors through my nerves. The longer I went without changing, the more intense the pain grew.

"Miss, what's going on?" The plump, blond storekeeper walked over. "Is he all right?"

A growl of warning vibrated in my throat. Rez grabbed my face, forcing me not to turn to the lady.

"Yes. Please, stay back. He has these fits occasionally."

"Do I need to call the paramedics?"

"No!" Rez yelped. "Needs some space. He'll be fine soon."

The woman nodded and retreated to the front of the store.

"West, listen to my voice. Just breathe in and out." Rez rubbed her fingers over my temples and hair, easing the needles of fire weaving down my body. Her boobs were right in my face so I closed my eyes and focused on her voice. "I need you to calm down. Your irises are bright red and your pupils are horizontal. Seeing you like this might give the clerk a heart attack."

She kept talking, a soothing hum to her voice. The siren's gift began to center me, calming the beast, and the pain eased with it. I took in labored breaths and eased back on my heels. Slowly I opened my lids. Rez sat in front of me, her face lined with worry.

"Jesus, woman, put a top on," I grumbled through my teeth.

"Thought people being naked didn't bother you," she quipped back, but hurriedly pulled on the sweater lying on the floor next to her.

"Normally it doesn't," I whispered and glanced away. Naked women turned me on like it did any other man, but she was far more than merely any woman.

The beast had never responded like that, but right now everything was new territory for me. It seemed a good possibility the longer I wasn't able to turn, the more "fits" might happen. Danger had always turned the beast loose, but never desire. No woman had ever meant enough. Well, except one. And the beast had calmed around her; it hadn't gone ballistic.

"What happened?"

I shook my head, feeling anger warm my ears. My weakness was showing itself. And I hated it.

"West, talk to me. You were in a lot of pain."

"Nothing," I snapped and rose abruptly. Rez didn't need to know about my bestial dysfunction. "You ready to go?"

She stood, her lips pressed into a thin line. Her critical gaze roamed over me, lids narrowing.

"Come on. We're already off your schedule by two hours." I turned for the front, walking to the counter, and threw down my credit card. "Whatever she wants."

Bursting out the door, I walked into the chilly morning air, heading for the car.

This was starting off to be a *wonderful* day.

---

The first part of the car ride was tense, but when I turned up the music and started singing at the top of my lungs, I finally got a smile out of Rez.

"You know you don't have one lyric correct?" Rez shook her head, turning to look at me.

"Mine are better." I leaned my head her way and grinned. "Come on, sing with me."

"No." Her head swung back and forth. "No way."

"Why?" I kept my head straight but flicked my eyes to her. "I doubt sirens have to worry about having a bad voice."

"It's not that."

"Then what?"

She folded her hands on her lap, twisting her fingers.

"Please don't tell me it's because it's not what respectful ladies do?"

Her lips curved down.

"Get the giant stick out of your ass and sing with me, darlin'." I turned the knob again, and the music boomed through the car. I wailed out words, sounding somewhat close to what the guy was singing, my thumbs drumming the steering wheel, my shoulders bouncing.

Rez laughed and peered at me like I was crazy.

"Come on!" I nudged her with my arm. Finally I saw her lips moving, copying the words. "Louder!"

Her voice rose, and after a few beats, it went even louder. Of course she had a beautiful voice, sultry and deep, but I enjoyed it more when she sang a wrong word and turned to me, beaming.

Rez's body wiggled in her seat, her head swaying side to side. When we came to the last chorus, she lifted her arms and closed her eyes, and screamed out the words at the top of her lungs with utter abandonment. As the crescendo reached its end, Rez dropped her arms and twisted to look at me.

My heart almost stopped. The most dazzling, beautiful smile I'd ever seen stretched across her mouth. Her eyes sparkled with life. And then she started to chuckle. It was the most incredible sound because she didn't hold back. My face spread into the biggest grin as my head jerked from the road to her and then back.

"That's better."

She wiped her eyes, still fighting her giggles.

"Don't tell me you've never done karaoke?" I turned the music down.

Her whole face beamed. "I can't remember the last time I sang for fun."

I raised my eyebrows. "Seriously?"

"Yeah." She shrugged, her smile fading. "I sing when I work." She glanced out the window. "I guess there hasn't been a lot of opportunities or reasons to sing otherwise."

"Well, we'll have to change that." I nudged her with my arm. I meant find a karaoke bar or something like that, but the moment her gaze snapped to mine, my statement felt a whole lot heavier. Doused with meaning and sinking below the appropriate line.

"Do you enjoy it?" I locked my eyes on the road.

"What?"

"Being a siren?"

"Does it matter? It's who I am. It's not about liking it or not. I can't change it." Her head twisted to the window. Her body language screamed there was a story, one that told she did not enjoy what she was.

"True. It doesn't mean you can't love it." I tried to examine her through my peripheral vision. "I love being a Dark Dweller. Sometimes more than being a man."

Her head turned back, critically observing me, her forehead lined. She jerked her gaze back out the window, and the silence grew in the car, the music playing softly in the background. Rez's finger tapped on the door handle, growing steadily more intense.

"What?" I asked.

She licked her lips, running her hands through her hair. "Tell me, darlin'."

"I know you can't change anymore," she said softly.

"What?" A block of ice sat against my neck.

She cleared her throat and faced me. "You can't shift. That's what happened today, wasn't it?"

The ice slid down my spine. My mouth fell open, but I swiftly shut it, keeping my stare locked on the road. How did she know? Was it so obvious? Was my weakness stained on me like my tattoos? Marked on me like the scars around my neck?

"You don't have to keep it from me."

"How...?" I gritted.

"Lars."

My nose flared.

"Don't be upset. He told me because he wanted me to know you wouldn't be able to turn even if you wanted to."

There was more to her sentence, the words she didn't say: I couldn't truly protect her. The feared Dark Dweller was no more than a caged lion at the zoo. Something enemies would poke with a stick and taunt, if they found out.

"I can fight better than any fae." My knuckles turned white on the steering wheel. "I can still protect you."

"I know."

"So why did you act like you didn't know back in the store?"

"Because..." She twisted her fingers together. "I wanted you to tell me. But then I realized you never would. You would make up every excuse and lie to keep me from knowing the truth."

She was right. I would have.

"It does not make you weak, West."

My foot slammed on the brake, and I pulled the Range Rover to the side of the road. The car came to a shuttering jolt, a cloud of dust engulfing the car. Anger coiled up my neck. "How would you know?" I roared. "No one knows how this feels."

"Then tell me." Rez didn't pull away from my anger. "I want to understand."

I twisted in my seat, facing her.

"I am a beast without the beast," I yelled, wanting my declaration to stop there, but my mouth kept moving, the words flowing out. "You don't think every adversary would use it against me the moment they knew?" I slammed my fist into the steering wheel, the metal groaning under the force. Rez didn't even flinch. "I can't change. I can't protect myself or you like I should be able to. So don't tell me it doesn't make me weak. It does. It's like being ripped in half. My very essence is gone. Everything that makes me whole causes me excruciating pain. It dangles in front of me like a carrot, but the moment I reach out, it tears my soul into pieces. Losing the man would not be as painful as this is. The beast is who I am. My being." My breath came out in harsh drags. "And it's the precise thing I can't be."

*Why did I tell her all that? I had never told anyone. Especially about my feelings.*

I swiveled in the seat, setting the car back into drive, signaling an end to the conversation.

Telling Rez was a mistake. One that would never happen again.

---

The rest of the drive into Cahersiveen was silent. When

we reached the small village, we found our B&B in the middle of town: a quaint two-story with a converted attic and restaurant on the lower level.

We needed to mingle among the locals and start getting people to talk. Lars had one contact in this town, but we didn't know how to get hold of him. I figured we'd go to the one place where everyone knows everyone else's business: the local pub.

We settled into our rooms, and this time I demanded hers be next to mine. They gave us the two rooms with connecting doors.

We spent most of the day apart. She set her room up like the FBI center, going through all the useless information we had, trying to make sense of the information, while I walked around and got a feel of the place. There were a couple of tourist trap pubs nearby, but I wanted to find where more of the locals went.

It was already dark by the time we made it to the restaurant for dinner. Rez was dressed in the clothes I had bought her earlier but kept tugging at them. She looked amazing, more appropriate than she did in a flouncy blouse, and she fit in a little better.

We grabbed stools at the bar that was already full of fishermen and workers. Rosy cheeks were everywhere I looked, whether from drink or the cold wind outside, I couldn't tell. But I hoped for the former. The drunker they were, the looser their tongues.

"How's it going there?" The bartender came over and threw down coasters. He was average height but stocky with graying brown hair and green eyes. His eyebrows were so thick it looked as if two tabby cats were wiggling on his jovial face.

"We need some food and some drinks." I grabbed the menu off the bar. "A Guinness, please."

"Pint of gat for you. What about you, lass?"

"Uh." Her gaze flew to the back of the bar. "Grey Goose and soda, please. With two limes."

The bartender's mouth curved up in an amused smile as he shook his head and went to grab our drinks.

"Wow." I snorted. "You are even snooty about your alcohol. Hope he doesn't give you three limes...might have to commit you."

"Nothing wrong with knowing what you like." Rez shot me a glare.

"No." I shed my coat, securing it on the hook by my knees. "But you leave no room for something you might like even better."

She pursed her lips, took off her jacket, and picked at a leg pocket of her cargo pants, wiggling on the barstool.

"Relax, darlin'." Without thinking, I placed my hand on hers, pressing it onto her leg.

Creases threaded her forehead, but she stilled at my touch and her eyes moved to mine. Heat from her hand lit my arm on fire. The desire to curl my fingers around hers flicked at my muscles, but I tugged my hand back to stop the impulse.

"Sorry. I feel uncomfortable in this." She plucked at her sweater.

"Uncomfortable? It's the most relaxed attire I've ever seen you wear."

"Exactly." She lifted her head with a tilt, staring at me. "Casual is not something I'm used to being; haven't for a long time..." Her words drifted off, and I couldn't help but feel there was more behind them.

"I've seen you in yoga pants." She looked gorgeous in them. I actually preferred her in laid-back clothing. She felt more real.

"Only because I was working out." She sat straighter. "I like being put together. Looking nice."

My eyes wandered over her. Her long dark hair flowed down her back, displaying her high cheek bones, blushed by the heat in the bar. Her lips were full and inviting, her almond-shaped brown eyes luring me in. My hand wanted to curve around her long neck, bring her into me. She had sensuality that couldn't be hidden, even in the worst outfit. But gorgeous people, especially in the fae world, were a dime a dozen. Don't get me wrong. I was a man, a Dark Dweller, who enjoyed a pretty girl, but extremely few captured me past a moment together in some bar bathroom or parking lot. Something about Rez, a guarded depth and sadness she hid behind her ordered world, called to me. And for the first time since a girl in South Carolina, I wanted to know more about the woman across from me.

The bartender came back with our drinks.

"Irish stew with soda bread," I ordered, breaking my stare from the siren, facing him.

"Same." Rez set down her menu and smiled at the bartender.

"Sure thing, luv." He grinned at her. "I'm Seamus. Need anything, *you* just let me know."

"Thank you, Seamus." She smiled back.

I tried not to laugh. "Think you might be my lucky charm here." I took a sip of beer. "You need to be the one asking Seamus if he knows of our lead. Look around, sweetheart. This bar is mostly men...and they are all staring at you."

It was no joke. Old to young, the men kept peering over at Rez with admiration. Their gazes weren't dirty or degrading, as far as I could tell. She wasn't even wearing makeup. Her hair was windblown, her cheeks and nose were red with cold, but this only made her even more stunning.

"Look at the women here." She turned to me, jerking her head back. "They are about to rip your clothes off, public indecency be dammed."

I couldn't disagree with her assessment. A handful of women, old and young as well, were staring at me like I was dinner. *West, here's your chance. You could have any one of these lasses in minutes. Get Rez out of your system.*

My shoulders sagged. The thought of getting off the stool and leaving Rez to try and fuck some chick I didn't even want sounded exhausting. Boring. Unfulfilling.

*Shit.* What was wrong with me?

"If you..." Rez looked down at her drink, her fingers twirling the glass. "If you need a night *off*, I totally understand. I figured someone like you would need to."

"Whoa..." I rocked back. "Wait... Did you just tell me to go fuck someone?"

Rez's cheeks deepened with crimson. "You are a Dark Dweller. I know you guys are...are..."

"Horny as hell? Sex crazed? Beasts?" I laughed when I saw the scarlet run down her neck. She squirmed in her seat, not meeting my gaze. Even the mere mention of sex caused her to fidget.

"Yeah." She nodded. "I am quite aware of *your* reputation, Mr. Moseley. Of the needs of Dark Dwellers. It isn't a big secret, too many rumors about you. All of you. I lived in a house with Ember and Eli for a while, after all."

"Yeah, those two would give you an idea." I chuckled, then leaned into her ear, whispering, "But that is only a small taste of what we are capable of. What we can do..."

She inhaled sharply and tensed.

I don't know why I did it. Why did I keep taunting her about sex…sex with me? It was dangerous. Stupid.

Thankfully Seamus came with our food, and I scooted away from her. I finished off my beer in a gulp and nodded at Seamus for another. Day two with Rez and I was already struggling to keep it together.

As we ate, we listened to the voices around us.

Several women brushed or touched me on the way to the bathroom, giving me a wink or a smile, inviting me to follow.

Rez rolled her eyes and finished her drink. Then something in her demeanor changed. She leaned on the bar and flipped her hair to the side, a dazzling smile traveling over her lips. She curled her finger, summoning Seamus.

He practically ran over.

"Ya, lass?" He grinned from ear to ear at her.

The moment she opened her mouth, I felt the magic, working her abilities.

"Seamus, you said if I needed *anything*, you were the man I should ask?" Her voice was like the richest syrup, sliding over and bathing you in its power.

"Anything, luv." He was entranced.

As was I. And I was somewhat immune to other fae charms. But damn, with every word I felt my body lean toward her, wanting to be close.

"I was wondering if you had heard anything or knew of a man they call Lil' Mack?"

Seamus's head lurched back, but his body stayed bowed over the bar toward her. His lids narrowed, and his lips pushed together, but his gaze did not leave Rez. His head shook slightly. "No. Never heard the name before."

He was lying. I could hear his heartbeat peak alongside his breath.

"Seamus," Rez purred. "I know you aren't telling me the truth."

To see this side of her, the seductress, I almost slid off my barstool. She wasn't even close to the level a water fairy or succubus would go, but there was something even hotter about sirens. Subtle. She sucked you in and dragged you down without you even realizing it.

People mixed up the three a lot, but water fairies were blunt and forward, whispering what they'd do to you without shame. They were simply horny off the rush of life around them and used sex to defuse all their energy. A succubus *had* to have sex. It is where they got their energy to live. Sirens didn't have sex with their prey. They lived off the sacrifice, the life force leaving the drowning victim.

"No. No...I'm not." He shook his head, trying to fight her.

Rez reached into her bag and pulled out an envelope. "That could be for you, Seamus. And if this Lil' Mack decides to come forward, there is even more for him."

Seamus picked up the packet filled with paper money. He gulped.

Lars hadn't told me about the bribe money, but I wasn't surprised. This was chump change to him, and he would do anything to find this spear. And money talked.

Seamus's eyes darted around the room, then moved closer to us, stacking our dishes.

"Lil' Mack is dead," he mumbled.

"Dead?" Damn. I stared at Seamus, hoping to see he was lying about this too.

"Some old folklore has been swirling around anew about some treasure. People looking for dangerous things again. Ruthless folks." He swallowed, picking up our bowls. "People have disappeared. Those who know anything about..." He stopped speaking. "I will not be one of them. I can't help you any more than that. Sorry." He flipped around and moved toward the kitchen.

With my dweller senses I caught the scent of fear a man has for his life. People were disappearing? Those who knew about the spear?

Lars had stirred up interest again, and it looked like we weren't the only ones out searching for it.

# EIGHT

We headed back to the hotel after that. Rez went to her room with a hasty good night, and I couldn't have been more grateful, though the thin walls did nothing to keep me from hearing her in the next room.

I undressed and fell back on my bed. Tonight had been little more than a dead end. I knew this wasn't going to be easy, but the news our lead was dead and others were disappearing left me dispirited.

With a sigh, I rolled onto my stomach and dropped the pillow over my head, needing to block my thoughts. Sleep. We'd start fresh tomorrow.

---

*She stood in front of me. The beautiful creature I ruined. The dimming magenta glow of the sun reflected off her pale skin. The dozen freckles I knew well that sprinkled across her nose and cheeks were adrift in shadows.*

*We stood on the beach, the sand dunes where we had made love on the first night together. The image so sharp in my memory I could taste the salt from the air, see the yellow sundress she wore. Her tan skin glowed under the moonlight, her smile lit her face with beauty, and her golden hair blew in the light breeze.*

*"Will." She held out her hand to me. This time she showed no fear. This was the Cammie who loved me, wanted to grow old with me, have children together. "Come with me."*

*I took a step, reaching out for her hand.*

*"Let me take you away from all this. No more pain. You deserve nothing but happiness."*

*"No, I don't." My feet shuddered to a stop. "I don't deserve anything good. Not after you."*

*She kept her hand out. "I've missed you so much. I want us to be together. Forever."*

*My gut screamed out in agony, wanting nothing more than to follow her. To let all my pain go. "Cammie, I love you. But you know I can't come with you."*

*Hurt flicked over her features before she looked away from me. "You don't love me," she whispered. "You never really did."*

*"Yes, I—"*

*"No, you didn't...not enough." Her eyes filled with liquid, crushing my heart. She dropped her face into her hands, her body rocking with sobs.*

*My feet took me close to her, and I gripped her wrists. "Cammie," I uttered softly. "Look at me."*

*She shook her head.*

*"Please." I gripped her arm firmer. "Look. At. Me."*

*Her head snapped up.*

*"Holy—" I gasped, stumbling back on my ass as terror clipped at my veins, cutting off my oxygen. The beach morphed into Aneira's chambers. The many hours she had tortured me inside these same walls came flooding back.*

*"What, my pet? Not happy to see me?" Aneira's violet eyes tore through my flesh into my soul.*

*"Not you," I choked out.*

*"I've missed you." Her beautiful but cruel features pinned me in place. The chains and torture devices hung behind her, curling bile up my throat. "We had such good times together, didn't we? That's why it would have never worked with that little naïve child. She could have never fulfilled you. Only I can."*

*"No."*

*"Oh, I think we both know it's true." She cackled, grabbed a collar with spikes, and walked toward me. "I think you grew fond of this."*

*Oh gods. "No!" I bellowed, trying to scramble away, but my body wouldn't obey. "Nooooo!"*

*Everything started to spin, going dark. Only Aneira's mocking laugh echoed in my ears.*

---

"West, wake up!" The voice belonged to neither Aneira nor Cammie, and it dragged me to the surface.

My eyes surged opened, confusion clogging my mind as my gaze rolled over the person above me. Dark hair and eyes gleamed down on me, the moonlight etching a beautiful face. I was in the dark room with paintings of the sea hanging on the walls.

*Rez. Cahersiveen.* My brain latched on to the familiar things, understanding this was real. I was no longer in Aneira's chamber. My body still didn't realize it and shook with the memories, while sweat trailed down the side of my face. It had felt so real I couldn't quite let go of the torture. The humiliation. The disturbing way Cammie morphed into Aneira.

"Hey." Rez's finger brushed the hair off my forehead, quieting my pounding heart. "You're all right. You're safe."

I licked my lips, my throat struggling to make words.

My attention moved over the room, making sure this was all real. Something lumpy and scratchy dug into my back, anchoring me to earth. I was no longer in my bed, but lying on the floor, as if I were moving toward the door.

"West?" Rez's voice drew me back to her, and it was like a cord, finally breaking me from my nightmares.

Then it seemed like entering another tortuous dream, but this one was the good kind. Rez kneeled over me, her silky pajama tank top hung low and displayed the top curve of her bare breasts. My body couldn't help but respond.

And I slept naked… *Shit.*

The impulse to reach up and drive my hand through her hair, grabbing her neck and pulling her to me, felt overwhelming. I imagined kissing her lips then slowly moving down her neck till I reached those lovely creatures. I sat up so fast she fell back on her heels. I clambered onto my feet, turning away from her. I grabbed the boxer briefs from the chair and pulled them on. I kept my back to her, scrubbing my face.

I could feel her wanting to say something. It hung in the air like a clothesline. My soul was so soiled it could never be clean, no matter how many times you washed it.

"I appreciate you coming in here, but you can go back to bed now," I muttered.

Rez rose from the floor, but she didn't retreat to her room.

Dammit. This was not something I wanted to talk about. She was supposed to stay on the other side, the flirty but safe side. She already breached that wall this morning, and I wanted to keep her from crossing it again. Discussing what tormented me, what could make me shake like one of those small dogs, was deep into territory I hadn't gone with anyone in a long time.

I glanced over my shoulder at her. She stood with a look of determination set on her face. A rumble curled up my chest.

"Bark. Snap. Yell. Even hit me…I don't care. I'm not leaving till you talk to me."

I swung around, shock jerking my shoulders back.

"You think I would ever hit you?"

"You wouldn't be the first." She folded her arms.

I blinked several times, a roar of anger flaring up my spine. "Has *he* ever hit you?" My feet moved to her without my consent. "Has Lars *ever* struck you?"

"No. No, he would never." She shook her head. "Lars has been nothing but kind to me."

"Then who?" The raging fury sparked through me at the thought of anyone hurting her. My lungs clenched and my muscles constricted with need to find the fucker. "Tell me!"

Her neck inched back, looking at me, her gaze challenging. "Tell me about who is terrorizing *you*."

"What is this?" I huffed. "I show you mine, you show me yours?"

"You scream out her name." She bit down on her lip. She didn't have to say who. Aneira had forced me to cry out her name, taking a piece of my soul every time. "You did it on the plane too. You look like you are being tortured, fighting against ghosts."

I took a huge step back, gulping for air. Oh no, this was not something I was going to talk about. Not to anyone and certainly not to her.

"Good night, Rez," my voice sounded void of emotion.

"What did she do to you?" she asked quietly, her hands rubbing her arms.

She wasn't simply asking about the prison. The forever marks on my neck told the story. She meant beyond that.

I gritted my jaw. "I said good night."

She stood there, her gaze unwavering.

"Damn," I growled, spinning around, needing to get away from her intrusive stare. "Just go! I'm not discussing this, especially with you."

"Why especially me?"

Rotating around, incense latched on to my shoulders. My defenses boiled up. My conflicting feelings of wanting to throw her out of my room or throw her on my bed and fuck her till all my pain and anger was gone scared the shit out of me.

"Because I don't need to rehash what happened and to relive it over and over. I want to *forget*." My words fired from my lips like cannonballs. My pain only wanted to afflict someone else. "You are not my therapist, my family, or *even* my friend…" Rez took a sharp breath at my words. "You're simply the King's tart I have to deal with on this mission because he said so. That's it. Nothing more. Got it?"

She didn't pull back or even get teary. She stared at me, the life in her eyes dying away till all I saw was a cold, empty night in her dark irises.

"Good night, Mr. Moseley." Her voice sounded void of emotion. She turned her back to me and walked through our joint door. I was ready for it to slam, at least then I'd feel the anger I deserved. But it closed with a soft click and felt like an arrow straight to my chest.

My legs collapsed, and I fell into the chair, my face in my palms. The agony I felt earlier only intensified. I hadn't meant to lash out at her, to be such an asshole. But what did she think? I would tell her my deepest, darkest secrets? We needed to keep this relationship clear cut and squarely in the lines of working together for a common goal. Nothing more.

I still couldn't stop my gaze from returning to the closed door between us. I felt a need to pound on the door and beg for her to forgive me. To wrap her in my arms and feel her heart against mine. My fingers raked over my face. The last time I held someone merely to feel their heartbeat was the day my world crumbled around me.

I bolted up. What the hell was wrong with me? Only a few days earlier it seemed easy to stuff the siren in her box and tape the lid. *West, get the fuck a hold of yourself. Get that shit locked up.* I grabbed a pair of pants and a T-shirt out of my duffle bag, dressed quickly, and I took off out the door.

The freezing night's air stung my lungs the moment I breached the doors. The smell of salt water lay on my tongue, and goosebumps streamed up my arms. It helped clear my mind. My feet started to move. The need for the beast to come out and dive into the night cranked my legs faster. I ran, trying to escape the devils nipping at my heels.

---

When I returned, physically drained, I felt only slightly calmer. The sun was crowning the sleepy village. My eyes were aching with the need to close, but the things waiting for me behind my lids kept them open. I jumped into the shower, leaving it on the chillier side to help me wake up, then headed to a bakery. The lady barely turned the open sign over before I was in, pointing at pastries.

I still felt right about keeping Rez and my relationship purely on the appropriate side, but I had gone way too far. I acted like a complete bastard, and she hadn't deserved it.

I hoped a peace offering of coffee and croissants would help ease the awkwardness a little.

Balancing the coffees and paper bag between my hands, I was almost at the hotel when the sensation of fingers glided up the back of my neck. I twisted and peeked around me. The streets of Cahersiveen were quiet. Only a few local fishermen passed, heading out to catch dinner for the restaurants.

The tingling grew, but I didn't stop moving. If someone watched me, I wanted to appear unaware. Sucking in air, I tasted all the smells near me: last night's dinners in the alley, salt, seaweed, musty smells of the constant fog and rain. And humans.

I rubbed my nose with my arm, using it to look around again. That's when I saw him. A tiny gray-haired man, probably only a little over five foot tall and small boned. He wore a newsboy cap, gray pants, a green sweater vest, and a gray sports coat with leather patches on the elbows. He was human, but he was aware of me. Unafraid but cautious. He leaned out of a passageway, his eyes boring into me. His hand lifted, and he motioned me over.

I casually walked over to him, on guard but curious. As I neared him, he fled deeper into the alley, hiding behind a dumpster smelling of spoiled food. At least the cold and the constant barrage of wind eased the smell.

"I heard you were asking about me." The man's voice was nasally, his Irish accent forcing me to be more attentive.

"I'm sorry? Who are you?"

"Seamus said you were looking for me." He nervously bobbed on his feet, peering out to the street.

Seamus, the bartender from last night. "He told me the guy I'm looking for was dead." This guy's nervousness was rubbing off on me, making me jittery.

"I am. If they catch me. To the world I am dead. Seamus is the only one who knows."

"If who catches you?"

"I don't know who they are. They come in like the fog and disappear before anyone notices. Anyone who knows anything about the spear has turned up dead. I didn't want to be next so I killed myself off first. Went into hiding."

"How do you know I'm not one of them?"

He snorted. "Didn't you hear me, sonny? They are invisible. Silent. You came clopping in with your shiny car and gorgeous lady friend, practically screaming my name in the streets."

I think I was slightly offended. Dark Dwellers were known for their stealth. But in human form, we didn't go unnoticed as well as we hoped. My clan drew a lot of attention, especially from the women. Not that I hadn't been hit on by men more times than I cared to count, but women were a lot less subtle about it. Being fae, our looks were part of our hunting equipment. Rez and I might as well have come in on a float.

"What do you know about the spear?" Now I glanced over my shoulder neurotically, the taste of excitement at this first break swirling in my body.

"Not much, but it doesn't seem to matter how little. They are out to silence us," he jabbered. "I shouldn't even be here—"

I cut him off. "Then get to it, Grandpa."

He pressed his lips together. "I'm only telling you because I'm afraid they will find me. Then what I know will die with me. Plus, I need the money to stay hidden."

So this was all about money. I didn't care since it all belonged to Lars. I growled impatiently for him to continue.

"Okay, okay." He held up his hands. "The story is my great-great-great-*athair crionna* was a crew member of the ship supposedly holding the treasure." I knew enough Gaelic to remember the term translated to old father or grandfather. "There were only rumors and hushed whispers, but one night Da got drunk and told me the story of the spear and how my *athair crionna* was on board. The whole crew was killed for trying to take it away from its home."

"Story?" Great. Some passed-down, elaborated tale with dubious origins.

"It's the truth." His ears and nose turned red, showing his Irish ancestry.

"Sure." I shifted the cups in my hands. "So did dear ol' Da happen to tell you where this ship left?"

"No." He shook his head. "The ship documents are long since lost, and I know little about my ancestor."

"How is this helping me?"

"Because my family origins put me at risk."

"They'd really kill you because of your family's history?" I snorted.

"Yes." He nodded fervently. "Because my family was the famous O'Brien Clan, who dominated the coast around Lahinch. There were only a few ports back then around that area." He took a shaky breath. "You are looking in the wrong place."

# NINE

With this new information, I moved quickly back to the hotel. I didn't even think as I ran through my room, setting down the coffee, and burst through the door Rez and I shared.

I should have knocked.

My feet went still, my brain emptying of anything but the view in front of me. Rez, with her back to me, staring out the window, toweling off her wet hair...naked. My gaze followed every curve of her body, from her feet to her ass, hips, back, to the one breast I could see from here as she lifted her arms to her hair.

"West!" she yelped, jarring me from my trance. She draped the towel in her hand around her torso and swung around to face me. "What are you doing?"

"Uh." What the hell was I here for again?

Her lids constricted the longer my mouth came out with nothing. "Mr. Moseley, as the King*'s tart* I feel barging into my room without notice is highly inappropriate." She fastened the towel tighter around her. "I didn't think you would need to be reminded of this."

I cringed, breaking my gaze to look at the floor. Clearly she was still *really* pissed.

"Please leave so I can change."

"Look, I'm sorry for what I said last night." I stepped farther into the room, ignoring her request. "But it doesn't matter right now."

Her eyebrows lifted, and her hand stayed locked on her towel.

"You know the guy on the list? The one the bartender told us was dead?"

"Yeah?"

"The dead man was alive enough to pull me into an alleyway this morning."

"This morning? It's six thirty."

"Yeah, well, I didn't sleep. So I went to the bakery right when it opened." I waved my arm. "It turns out this guy faked his death and went into hiding because anyone who knows anything about the spear turns up dead."

"What?" All anger dissolved from her face.

"He heard about the money we're offering and thought it worth the risk to come out of hiding."

"What did he say? Does he know where it is?" She took the last few steps to me, her barely covered body forgotten by her. It wasn't something I could get past. It took a lot of focus for me to stay on point.

"His lineage is from the Clan O'Brien, and they owned most of the coast along the town of Lahinch. His great-grandfather, times like ten, is thought to have been a member of the crew on the ship which carried the spear."

"So…we're looking in the wrong spot." Rez reached the conclusion a lot faster than I did.

I nodded. "It's all fables and folklores told down generations, but it's all we got."

A smile inched across Rez's face as she stared at me. "Guess we are heading to Lahinch then."

"Guess so." I grinned back, both of us elated by this sudden break.

The moment took a sharp swing, from us talking about the mission to us standing there staring at each other. The insignificant towel barely hit the top of her thighs or covered the top of her chest. My hands twitched, wanting to move to the top of her towel. One tug and it would be gone.

I balled my hands so tight into fists my bones cracked. The zing of adrenaline from the news mushroomed under my skin, metamorphosing into desire. Her nearness caressed my senses, provoking deep desires. My gaze drifted from her eyes to her lips. Drops of water from her hair trailed over her collarbone and slipped between her breasts.

There was a slight hitch in her breath. Her body jolted back, putting a huge gap between us, clearing her throat. "This is great news. Give me a few moments to get ready, Mr. Moseley, and we can get on the road." Rez held up her head, her tone lacking any reaction. Both her hands held tight to her towel.

"Oh. Yeah. Of course." I nodded, swiveled, and headed out of the room. I shut the door and walked to my bed, falling back on it. My hand covered my face.

"Fuck. Fuck. Fuck." I growled under my breath. I was the one who made such a big deal of us not crossing the line, and the next morning I was the one who wanted to rip the towel right off her.

If I were really smart, I'd send her back to Lars with some excuse why she couldn't continue with me. I was tempted. Very tempted. Why didn't I? I wasn't sure. I didn't want to think about it.

It was starting to look like retrieving this spear was going to be the easy part of this task. But if it took everything I had, Rez would stay firmly on her side. And if I had to find several cute Irish lasses to rid her from of my system, then bring them on. I'd be grateful to get back to easy sex with no strings, because the woman with me on this mission right now, in my dreams and next door, was torturing me every way possible.

Even with this exciting break, Rez stayed icy toward me on the drive, not veering from one- or two-word answers. And she seemed perpetually stuck on calling me Mr. Moseley.

Tension and formality drove me bonkers, like trying to sit down while wearing armor: uncomfortable, awkward, silly, and unnecessary. We could keep the lines between us and still be relaxed. Right? But everything I tried to get her to laugh fell in my lap with a flop.

"Rez, come on. I'm sorry about what I said last night." I sighed. We'd been on the road for almost two hours, and I was about to lose it if she uttered another one-syllable response. She kept her head down, going over the paperwork spread out on her lap, circling and writing notes in the column.

"I know. You've told me several times now." Her marker circled another spot on the map.

"But you haven't forgiven me yet." I smiled and glanced over at her. "Please forgive my beastly behavior. I don't know where it comes from."

She cocked her head, and her lids tapered with a deep scowl, not wavering under my charm.

The smile dripped from my lips. "Really. I'm sorry," I said sincerely.

"Yes. I understand you are. And I'm not mad at you, Mr. Moseley."

She tucked her hair behind her ears and went back to the map.

"Not mad, huh?" I snorted and gazed out at the deep green grass rolling by the car like waves. Dots of sheep and stone fences dominated the land between the small, sleepy villages. The gray sky greeted the turbulent ocean in an almost seamless line. "Because you always call me Mr. Moseley when you're happy with me."

Rez dropped her hand, crackling the paper, and turned to me. "What do you want from me?"

Taken aback, my mouth opened but nothing came out.

"I am doing as you asked. Keeping this professional." Her voice rose with indignation.

*Damn. Even yelling at me, I could close my eyes and drown in her voice.*

"You were right. We are not friends or anything else. We are coworkers. So let's keep on the task at hand. Do our job. And get home to our loved ones." Rez set her jaw, then went back to the files on her lap, letting her hair fall, covering her face from view.

I had said pretty much the same thing to her, but hearing her say we weren't friends stabbed painfully at my chest. And the *back home to our loved ones* line twisted my gut into a knot.

What did I want? The thought of not even being considered a friend prickled my spine. I had only said it to push her away. I didn't really believe it. We had all gone through a lot together during the war. If anything had bonded us, it was the loss of family and friends. How many nights and days had I sat in Lars's kitchen, talking and joking with her?

The problem was having her as my friend meant letting other lines slip. I didn't care. If being friends meant I had to take even more freezing showers or slip out to find a water fairy around here, I would do it. She meant more to me than some "coworker."

The words sat on my tongue about to cascade out, when my attention was caught by a dark gray Saab in the rearview mirror. It looked like almost every other car on the road we passed, but this one had been behind us since we left Cahersiveen. I thought it turned off, so I let it go. But now it was back. It could be a coincidence. Travelers journeyed the same path as we were, but since my encounter with Lil' Mack, I felt on edge.

Being out in the middle of the country with few cars on this unmarked two-lane road with us, I could do nothing but keep going. We were nearing Limerick, where we'd curve west toward another finger of the Irish coast.

I spent the rest of the trip watching the car in back, relaxing when we passed Ennis and it turned north. Jesus, I really was paranoid. It wasn't a bad thing in our case, being on guard. But paranoia was a thin line before you were sure everyone was out to get you.

Rez picked the Clare Coast Hotel to stay in, which was more sensible than the place we stayed in Cork. Nice, simple rooms next to each other, right in town. I hated they weren't connected, but at the same time I was relieved. Something about having a door privately linking our rooms felt strangely intimate. Almost taunting.

Rez's coolness hadn't ebbed any when we separated to our rooms. I was back to doubting if friendship was a smart idea, deciding to let her dictate the formality of our partnership.

After throwing my duffle bag on top the dresser, I flopped on the bed, the springs squeaking under my weight. I stared at the ceiling, my stomach rumbling with hunger.

I wanted to eat. I needed to sleep. But the thing I required the most was sex. The lack of it was starting to make me crazy. I was so freakin' tense and coiled up I could barely breathe. The beast scratched at my insides, needing to be let out. The nightmares were ready to pounce the moment I shut my eyes, and the tension with Rez was causing anger to simmer under the surface. I had been angry for a long time. At myself, at Eli, at Lorcan. I learned to live with it, hide it under the humor. Now it seeped out my skin, and I was trying as hard as hell to patch the holes. But with everyone I covered, two more burst open in another spot.

I rubbed my forehead and growled.

My hearing wasn't as strong as it when in dweller form, but I could still hear Rez move around on the other side of the wall, the squeak of her bedsprings bouncing.

I crushed my lids together. It wasn't even noon, and I already needed a drink. And about ten water fairies. I was close to the water, so they were probably around, except I couldn't find the appeal in locating them. The thought of dealing with them only exhausted me. *What the hell is wrong with me?* The image of ten naked, curvy, horny women should have me running toward the ocean…dick first.

The bed in the next room whined again with a slight groan, like she had lain back on it. The idea of her pleasing herself slammed into my brain and my cock pulsed, pressing painfully against my jeans. Oh no. This really wasn't good.

I was about to get up and go for a run, anything to separate myself from the picture of Rez in my head, when I heard a soft moan. Oh, holy shit. Was she…? My throat went dry, the fabric of my jeans straining. My breath went shallow. *Leave, West. Get out of here.*

But I neither wanted to nor could. The soft panting I heard through the wall tied me to the bed. She was probably thinking of Lars, missing him, but I didn't linger on that. Desire consumed me. We were both stressed and fae. Two things relieved by sex.

I stirred, the buttons of my pants rubbing against me sent pleasure through my body. *No. No. No. No.* The last bit of logic pleaded with me. *Don't do this.* But merely breathing set my dick throbbing.

Another soft moan came through the wall.

"Screw it." I tore at the top, popping my jeans open desperately, grabbing myself out of my boxer briefs. Palming myself, I began to stroke. I let out a heavy sigh. The thought of Rez doing the same on the other side of the thin wall had me so turned on I couldn't even see straight. I closed my eyes, letting myself have this moment. My hand worked faster, picturing her on her bed doing the same. The way her body would first constrict with pleasure and then go limp. Without thinking, my free hand went to the wall, wanting to feel her.

Energy slammed into my hand, flowed into my fingers, pumped down my body, tingled every nerve, and exploded through me. "Holy shit," I whispered hoarsely. This was something I had never experienced. The energy coursing through my veins heightened every sensation to almost painful levels, and created sharper waves of pleasure.

A harsh gasp and moan came from next door. Had she felt the same thing?

I was completely undone, no longer in my head or even in my body. I didn't care who heard or if she knew I was getting off with her. It was past that, as if I were possessed. My fingers curled, digging into the wallpaper. I was semi-aware I was swearing. Loudly. My hips rocking frantically, leading myself to the ledge. Jacking off was nothing new to me. It was natural. Normal.

But never in my centuries of life had it felt like this. It was something you did in the shower or quickly when you couldn't actually get sex or some girl to do it for you. This was a hundred times more intense than ten water fairies going down on you. It felt like her energy was going straight into me, wanting nothing more than to give me the most intense bliss. My head began to spin, feeling myself ready to peak.

A cry so sharp and full of ecstasy vibrated through my hand and into my body, shoving me off the cliff. My mouth parted and a roar tore through my lips, so loud the hanging light shook. My release pumped out as the world blurred around me. My hand slid down from the wall, my lungs trying to catch up with what just happened.

*Holy shit.* What *did* happen?

I was not someone who got embarrassed for something like this. Ever. I was quite open about sex. Fae were the most sexually charged creatures around. Dark Dwellers were near the top of the sex-driven list. But this…

I had no doubt Rez heard me as well. The entire hotel did. I had wailed and cursed louder than a banshee.

Did she get off hearing me, knowing what I was doing? Did she get turned on as much as I did at the thought of the person in the next room doing the same? Did she feel the power pulsating between us? Almost like she had been in the room with me…

*West. Stop.*

Before I let any thought settle, I shot out of the bed, tearing off my soiled shirt, and went straight for the shower.

I couldn't deny I felt a hell of a lot better, every muscle relaxed, but it was something that would *never* happen again. Ever.

And if we didn't acknowledge it, then it never happened.

# TEN

My stomach was about to eat itself, and it was what propelled me to finally go to her room. My knuckles rapped on Rez's door. She had to be starving as well. She barely ate the croissant I got her, which was hours ago.

*Play it cool. Act like it never happened.*

The door unlocked and swung open, her scent drifting out to me. My grip on the doorframe crunched, my body immediately reacting. The beast pawed under my shell, constricting every muscle that had finally relaxed.

Her hair was swept into a ponytail, a few loose strands hanging around her face. A line etched between her eyes, and I wanted nothing more than to run my thumb over it softly till it disappeared.

"Hey." I cleared my throat. "Thought you might be hungry?"

"Oh. Yeah. I am." Her gaze wouldn't meet mine, splotches of red dotting her neck and cheeks. If I held any doubt she was aware of what happened earlier, it vanished.

My instinct was to call it out. Laugh about it. Make a joke…like I always did. With anyone else in the world I would have. But Rez could see through my bullshit, and I didn't like feeling transparent right now.

"Was cross-referencing ports in this area with the notes Lars gave us." She stepped back into her room, nodding to the table.

Lars. The elephant constantly paraded between us. Probably it had been him she was thinking of while I was picturing her mouth on me. I ran my hand through my damp hair and stepped into the room, afraid to get too close to her.

The desk was peppered with files and maps, markers, and notes strung across the surface. "Find anything?" I touched the map, scanning her circled indicators.

"No. The leads we have are so vague it's hard to count on them for anything." She came to my side, her arm brushing mine, and she almost jumped away. "The one thing I found was a claim the ship actually got far out to sea before they brought it back in, and it crashed on the rocks. This, unfortunately, means the port could be miles away from its resting place. Finding the port where it departed still won't help us."

"No, but at least it gives us a jumping-off point." I tapped on the chart. On a map a dozen miles each way looked like nothing, but underwater, you could be feet from ruins and still miss them. "At least I feel we are in the right area now. That deserves a celebratory dinner, right?" Actually, I needed a frickin' drink.

"It's three in the afternoon."

"There you go with those rules again, darlin'." I smirked, looking down at her.

She waggled her head but let a grin inch over her mouth. "Fine. Only because I can hear your stomach rumbling from here."

"It's about to devour itself." I groaned, rubbing my stomach, and my T-shirt hitched up. Rez's gaze darted down to my exposed V-line.

She blinked, the red on her cheeks flushing deeper as she bit on her bottom lip. I don't think she even realized she was doing it, but holy shit, if it didn't turn me on again. Heat crawled up my back. The images in my brain were far too vivid: me tossing her on the table, her body arching back, crinkling the maps.

Both of us reacted at the same time, turning opposite ways.

"Let me grab my coat."

"I'll go get my jacket."

We both bumbled out, running from each other.

Damn! This had to stop. We couldn't even be in the same room longer than two minutes before I was peeling off her clothes in my head. I didn't want to test how long it would be until I actually tried. Because I couldn't. I shouldn't even be fantasizing about it.

We needed to find this damn treasure now so I could send her off back to Lars and get my head screwed on straight. Get back to kinky girls in alleys. No baggage, no commitment, no names. That was what I deserved. The seedy trenches with people like me. Those were the people I belonged with...I only ruined good people, dragged them down to the dark, and destroyed them.

***

The more Rez called me Mr. Moseley, the easier it felt like what happened earlier was only a dream. I actually wanted to believe I fell asleep and it had all happened in my mind. At least then I was the lone asshole, and Rez was unaware of my dirty thoughts of her. But walking to the local pub, I had a horrifying thought... I was faintly aware I might have called out her name. I kept my head locked forward, not once glancing over at her.

In Europe it doesn't matter what day of the week it is, the local pub is full. People use it as their extended living room, socializing and hanging with their buddies after work. Today, in the dreary, late afternoon, gatherings of mostly locals milled around the cozy pub.

Rez and I sidled up to the last two barstools available. We knew bartenders were always the best to befriend and talk to. They knew more than anyone.

"What's your poison, darlin'?" I nudged her shoulder. "Don't think they'll do Grey Goose martinis in this place."

"Wow. You really think you have my number, don't you?" She flipped her long hair over her shoulder.

I leaned into her. "Am I wrong?"

She glowered at me, only proving my point.

The bartender made his way to us. "What would you like?"

"I'll take a stout on tap." I nodded to the beers.

The bartender nodded and looked over at Rez. "And for you, lass?"

"Uhhh." Her gaze wandered over the taps. "Same."

My eyebrows lifted. "Same? You don't strike me as the beer type."

"I'm not." She shrugged. "But when in Ireland… You were right. I should try the local stuff."

"This is the not the kind of beer you ease into for the first time. It's strong, dark, and thick."

"Just the way I like them." She grinned.

My lungs constricted, partly from her sexual innuendo, and partly because she might as well have been describing me. Or most likely Lars, which reminded me of who she usually slept with every night and that I better stop this line of thinking quick.

I grabbed for the beer set in front of me, trying to banish the image of her on top of Lars, head thrown back, screaming his name.

The awkward silence came zinging between us. She reached for her beer, taking a sip. Her face scrunched up, and she shook her head, like it would help dislodge the taste from her tongue.

"Told you, darlin'." I snickered, taking a deep gulp of mine. "Yum."

She shot me a look but picked up the beer again, taking another sip. She shuddered again.

"Okay." I grabbed for the beer. "You don't have to drink it. Get something else."

"No." She snatched it back possessively. "I want it."

I chuckled at her grabby hands and determined expression. "If you say so."

"I ordered it. I will finish it." She sat straight in her chair, like she was setting herself up for a challenge.

"Is that a Rez rule?"

"Rez rule?"

"Yeah, one of the thousands keeping you on the straight and narrow and your very controlled life."

One eye narrowed on me. "Structure isn't a bad thing."

"I didn't say it was bad." I leaned an elbow on the bar, twisting to look at her. "But it keeps you from experiencing the really good things."

"And the really awful," she retorted.

"Yeah…" I nodded. "But you can't have one without the other. You can't fully appreciate ecstasy if you've never experienced misery."

Her gaze darted away. "Who says I haven't?"

My eyes moved slowly up and down her. "Because one look at you, darlin', and you can see you've had a cushy life."

Her eyebrows furrowed, a spray of anger blooming under her face. She reached for the beer and took a huge gulp, which caused her features to sour more. She shook it off and took another drink.

Getting under her skin only spread a satisfied wickedness through me. "What's wrong, darlin'?" A mischievous grin inched across the side of my mouth.

"Nothing," she said, but I could see it was all a front. It made me want to push her more, crack a wall and actually see her get flustered. Get beyond her comfort and protected façade.

"Let me ask you a question." I licked my lips. Her eyes darted to them then back up. "Are you this uptight in bed? Do you like to be in control there too?"

Her mouth parted, a blush hinting at her olive skin. "That is none of your business."

"Have you ever been so thoroughly fucked you've completely lost yourself?"

Her jaw tightened as she tried to swallow, her head turning forward.

I was probably going too far, but that's what I did. I enjoyed making people squirm. And now that I saw I was affecting her, I couldn't seem to stop.

"I'm talking an orgasm so fierce they hear you two towns over. Fucked so good, it's all you can think about, until you crave it like a drug."

Rez jerked in her seat, her head snapping to mine. Anger and what looked like terror blistered in her irises. I was waiting for her to yell at me. Shit, I wanted her to.

Every time she got rattled and mad at me, it turned me on. And for some reason I was determined to finally break the perfect persona. I wanted to see the flaws, the true emotions.

Her lashes lowered, and she took in a deep breath, regaining the restraint she was about to lose. Her lids opened, void of the emotion I saw earlier.

"Wouldn't you like to know?" Her voice was cool.

Uh, actually I did. That was the problem.

"And my screams were heard *four* towns away. At least." She took a sip of her beer.

*Damn.* Now my brain was full of tantalizing images of her. My cock strained against my pants so bad I had to shift to ease it. She smirked, noticing me adjust.

"Well played," I mumbled and gulped down the rest of my beer. She smiled, a mix of smugness and irritation, then motioned to the bartender for another round.

"Martinis to stout beer." I nodded, impressed.

"I'm not as prissy as you make me out to be, Mr. Moseley."

She was still mad.

"Prissy? Did I ever call you that?"

"Probably many times behind my back."

I laughed. I couldn't fight her on that one. "I don't even want to know the names you called me behind my back."

"Some were signed." She wiggled her fingers, causing me to laugh more. For the life of me I couldn't picture Rez flipping anyone off. It didn't fit her classy image, but at the same time I would love to see her do it. Make her more real.

"Show me." I nodded to her hand.

"What?"

I wrapped my fingers around her hand.

"Show me," I demanded.

"You want me to flip you off? Seriously?"

"Yes."

"Why?" Her cheeks reddened, and she squirmed like she was uncomfortable.

I had no real answer. I simply wanted to see her do something out of character. "I'll bet you've never flipped off anyone in your life." My thumb rubbed at her middle finger.

"My mother was extremely strict. I was raised to be a proper young lady. It was not something I would have ever thought of doing. Now it feels crude and inappropriate."

That made me only want to fuck the lady right out of her, till all she desired was crude and inappropriate. *Keep it in your pants. Seriously, man. Get a grip.*

I let her hand drop. She immediately brushed them over her cargo pants, like she could wipe the unexecuted vulgar gesture off her hand. For some reason her reaction pissed me off. *Get off your high horse and roll in the pigpen with me.*

We went back to drinking, going for another couple rounds. We should have been working, getting more information. Splitting up and flirting our way into more local lore, but for the life of me, I couldn't get myself to want to. I wanted to stay here. Sitting next to her, drinking, laughing. This woman was seriously messing with my head. Or heads. Both of them.

I switched to whiskey, my brain fuzzing. The fish and chips I ate did nothing to soak up the alcohol going down. The more I drank, the more I recalled the earlier incident. Had she gotten off to me, too? The possibility was hard to ignore. I wanted to repeat it…this time in person.

My eyes tracked her mouth, sipping at her beer.

"I have a theory about you, darlin'." My brain and tongue were no longer attached.

"Oh really? Another one?" Her eyebrows curved up as she crossed her legs, looking superior. "Please, do tell."

"I think like your rules, your clothes keep you safe. They're your armor."

Her smile dropped.

"I think you hide behind your designer garments and heels as a defense. No one can reach you way up on that pedestal. Untouchable…therefore no one can hurt you in return." I leaned in closer, watching her jaw twitch, her eyes going back and forth between mine nervously the closer I got.

Again, I felt every word I said hit a target. "I call bullshit on anyone ever making you scream loud enough to even be heard in the next room. You are too uptight to ever fully let go." *Shut up, stupid*, I muttered to myself. But of course I didn't. When did I ever listen to anything I should? "All your lists and plans are to *control*…" The air thickened around us. Our mouths were only a few inches apart, my voice low and taunting. "When deep down all you want is to roll in the dirt, have someone completely unhinge you."

Fury flashed over her features, and she lurched back, her lids tapering, jaw clenched.

"That's the second time tonight you have presumed to know me. Let me tell you: You. Know. Nothing." She slid off the stool, grabbing her coat. "Don't assume you understand me when you can't even see the truth in yourself. We all hide. You do behind a wall of bullshit. You use jokes and taunts to make sure no one is really looking at you." She swung around and rushed for the door.

"Shit." I sighed, rubbing my hand over my face. *Nice job.* Jumping up from the stool, I threw down money and ran after Rez. The chill of the night nipped at my skin the moment I exited the door. My eyes scanned the low-lit street, and a figure moved quickly away from the pub.

"Rez?" I called out, jogging after her. "Hey. Stop."

She ignored me.

My fingers latched on to her elbow. "Rez, please."

She stopped, whirling around on me. Her fingers flew up, all of them folded over accept her middle one. Rez was flipping me off. Pigs should be flying. Worse, I found it so hot. This was so twisted.

"There. Are you happy?" Her arms fell back to her side.

"Actually, yeah." I nodded. "But everyone knows I'm a sick jerk."

She tried to fight it, but a bubble of laughter emerged from her throat. She wrapped her arms around her waist and moved to a wall of the bakery shop a few doors down from the bar and leaned against it.

I moved squarely in front of her. "I am a dick." I shoved my hands in my pockets. "Sorry."

"Yeah, you are." She raised her chin up to me. "But it doesn't mean you aren't right."

"Wow, that's a first."

A grin wobbled on her mouth. Then she took a deep breath, the humor fading.

"My past…" She licked her lips. "Yes, there are reasons why I have the need to control everything. Present an image to the world so they don't know the mess inside or the person I used to be."

A desire to keep her talking, telling me the things she hid from everyone else, locked my tongue in my mouth. If I spoke, I'd probably ruin it.

She looked at her boots, her arms clenching her body harder. She struggled for a few more moments, appearing to debate telling me her story or not.

"Before Lars brought me to the compound, my life was quite different." Her hand went to her necklace, twirling it between her fingers. "I ran away from home at a young age with nothing. I was naïve, immature, beautiful, and easily manipulated and desperate for money right after I arrived in Seattle. I met a fae who ran a club. He was charismatic and charming and promised me luxuries beyond my imagination." Rez looked to the side, her lids blinking back emotion. "Let's say it became anything but…"

My stomach squeezed, a sickness washing over me. Part of me didn't want her to go on, the fury building as I thought of anyone hurting her. But I was already too far in now and needed to know it all.

"What did he do to you?" My voice rumbled.

She pushed herself off the wall and walked a little away, her back to me. "Nothing and everything."

"What does that mean?" I shoved my hands deeper into my pockets, trying to control the desire to touch her. I wanted to grab her, swing her around to face me, demand she tell me. Then kill whoever this fucker was.

"*He* never physically touched me; that's not what he wanted me for." She slowly pivoted around, her attention on her boots.

"Please explain," I said through gritted teeth. This was her story, her painful past. So why did I feel like tearing the world apart? The beast wanted to run, shredding the night like toilet paper.

"He ran a club upstairs and a seedy opium sex den downstairs." She tugged on her necklace harder. "Most of my years there I don't remember. He had us girls so drugged all the time I could barely recall my name. I was an addict. Nothing mattered more to me than being high. Reality was an abstract concept. Sex with whoever and how many didn't matter. It became all a hazy dream. And the moment I felt myself coming down, I begged for more, offering whatever they wanted in return."

Bile burned up my throat. I didn't dare speak, didn't dare move.

"That was how Lars found me." Her voice cracked, and she wiped one eye. "Skin and bones, curled in a corner, in filthy rags, coming down from a high."

*Holy shit.* Never in a million years would I have ever guessed this was Rez's past. This meticulous, confident, beautiful woman was once a sex slave in an opium den?

"I don't know what made Lars save me, what he possibly saw in me, but he picked me up and carried me out of there, bringing me home. He and Marguerite spent weeks breaking me of my addiction. It was the worst time in my life. The pain, both physical and mental, was overwhelming. But the things I did and said to get them to give me a hit were despicable. I would do whatever I could to get what I wanted. Sex, violence, pity…anything." Rez shook her head. "I went a little crazy. Did things I can never forget." She wagged her head, as if trying to dislodge the recollections.

"Finally, when I started to come out the other side, I could barely live with the memories of what I did in the den. It took me a long time to feel safe and to understand Lars's interest in me wasn't simply another man wanting sexual favors for payment. He went out of his way to make sure I felt worthy, valued as a person, desired, but not only for sex. He put me to work, slowly giving me more and more responsibility, building me back up.

"He kept it professional. Never even hinted at crossing the line…to the point it made me crazy." She scoffed, her face reflecting the memories trailing through her mind.

"Marguerite quickly became the mother I never had. She fed and loved me without anything in return." Rez swallowed. "That was something new to me. Unconditional love. It was years later before Lars and I started anything, and I initiated it. This man gave me everything…eventually I wanted his heart too. How do you ever repay someone for saving your life? Giving you a whole new one. An amazing one."

Now I understood her relationship with Lars even more. What he did for her. No wonder she was completely devoted to him. Gratitude and adoration were strong emotions. A deep loyalty and respect *could be* confused with love. Not that she didn't love Lars.

"What happened to the guy who ran the club?"

"I don't know. Lars never talked about it with me. All he told me was he shut the place down, and the guy would never be running another 'club' again." She curled her fingers in quotes.

I pinched my lips together. "What was his name?" Knowing Lars, he probably had this guy taken care of. But I needed a name just in case, so if I ever ran across him I could give him the slow, painful death he deserved.

She rubbed her boot into the sidewalk. "Vadik."

"Vadik?" I repeated in shock.

"Yes. Why?" Rez stiffened.

I had heard of him. He was mid-level demon who tried to rise up and take Seattle from Lars in the brief time when Lars was distracted dealing with his newly acquired

Dae niece, Ember. Then suddenly Vadik disappeared.

"I know him in name only." I folded my arms, glancing away. "There were rumors of him being spotted on the Seelie side before the war, but no proof. Most likely he's dead."

I couldn't imagine a Dark demon surviving long on the Light side. I knew all too well how it tore you in half. A demon wouldn't last, but right then I wanted to bring him back to life simply to kill him again. Especially because at the mere mention of his name Rez's eyes filled with terror. Another emotion exploded behind my ribs, not unlike a punch. A mix of feeling honored, grateful, and strangely joyous because she picked me to confide in. She trusted *me* with her secret.

"Knowing Lars, I'm sure Vadik is long gone."

She bit her lip and nodded; a humorless laugh came from her. "Now you know why I'm a control freak. I promised myself I would never be that girl again. I'd forget my past and would move on with my new life." She seemed to stand straighter then glanced at me. "Besides Lars and Marguerite, you are the only other person who knows."

"Thank you for telling me." I took a tentative step to her and placed my hands on her upper arms. She flinched but didn't move away as she looked down. "What you've done and gone through, darlin'…" One hand went to her chin, lifting her face. "It makes you even more amazing to me."

She inhaled, her gaze locking on mine.

My eyes danced with her rich brown irises. And then it happened again: the need to kiss her deeply and wrap my arms around her, protect her from the world. It consumed my body, itching and twitching every muscle to act. I wanted nothing more than to taste her lips, to fiercely take them with my own. Heat arced between our bodies and drew me closer to her. Oxygen dissipated, leaving my lungs scrambling to pump more in. A voice in my head told me to stop touching her. The rest of my body ignored me.

Something flashed in Rez's expression, her lashes dipped to my mouth. Desire flamed as the other beast in my pants strained against my jeans. My body leaned forward, wanting to give in to the craving.

*West, what the shit are you doing?* A voice bellowed in my head. It bore an uncanny similarity to Lars. I yanked my head back and stepped away. Shit. What the hell had I been about to do? Was I a complete bastard? Not only hitting on another man's woman, but right after she told me the horrendous story of her past?

I rubbed my hand through my hair. "We should get back to the hotel. We have a lot of ground to cover tomorrow."

Rez nodded, staring again at her feet. "Yes. We should."

I pivoted toward the hotel down the street, while my dick pointed like a compass to the woman behind me. *Get a hold of yourself,* I chastised myself. She's no different from the thousands of women you've encountered in the past. Maybe it was because she was completely off limits.

*That's it. My desire exists only because I can't have her. She's safe to want because nothing can ever come from it.*

It was the only theory I had, and I clung to it.

---

The moment we walked up to the hotel, I saw what looked like the gray Saab that had been following us. My already jangled nerves twisted tighter, intuition rolling through me. I sniffed the air. Someone was watching us. I grabbed Rez's arm.

"What?" She started searching around, reacting to my firm grip, the way I was smelling the air. Magic was so thick all the time now it made it hard to pick out a particular odor as if there were fae near.

"We're being watched." I didn't see anyone but could sense someone. "Let's get inside."

She nodded, hurrying. With every step, each of my senses raised a new alarm. The lobby was empty this late at night, but it didn't calm me. With sudden desperation to get upstairs, I took the stairs two steps at a time, and Rez padded quickly behind me.

Dark Dwellers were programmed to detect threats, even when no one else did. An insight, like a weight scale. If everything was fine it stayed level, but the moment it changed, the scales dipped, letting us know something was off. Pinpointing exactly where the threat was coming from was harder, but I could sense it, and I wanted to tuck Rez safely in her room.

The silence in the hallway was unnervingly alive, brimming with the tension of something just about to happen.

We turned down the hallway to our rooms, and I halted. The door to her room was cracked open, the smell of magic heavy in the air. I thrust my arm in the air to bar Rez from going in. She grabbed my arm.

"Stay here," I whispered in her ear and inched toward the door. Funny, until now I had never thought about carrying a weapon. My body had been enough. Now it was like bringing a knife to a gun fight.

I nudged the door open, scanning every inch of the dark room. My heartbeat sped up the moment I took in the scene before me: chairs knocked over, mattress shifted off the frame, clothes flung around, and shredded paper covered the floor. The contents of Rez's suitcase were strewn everywhere. All the documents we'd left on the table—the maps, the research from Lars—were gone.

*Shit!* I stepped farther into the room, my head jerking to every dark corner. Was this the group Lil' Mack mentioned? Others looking for the spear, using us to get all the information and sneak in and take it?

The sound of squeaking door hinges jolted me. Air locked in my lungs as two massive men stepped out of the bathroom, their mouths stretched open with daggered teeth, and claws growing out of their mitts.

Shape-shifters. Bears. "Huh. And here I thought Irish brown bears went extinct thousands of years ago."

Neither one of them spoke, their eyes vacant, as if they were robots. The shorter man, whose mouth was misshapen by a twisted scar, was the first to leap for me. The larger one curved around and blocked my escape to the door.

The animal in me prickled, heating my insides with stabs of pain. I had fought plenty of times in human form, but when my beast sensed magic, knew its own, it wanted to frolic. Biting back the pain, I stood my ground, ready for the bears. The larger one, who had a scar from his eyebrow to his cheek, lunged for me. At the last moment, I snaked to the side, letting him bypass me as I swung for the smaller one with a missing pinkie claw.

My fist landed in Pinkie's face, shoving him back to the wall with barely enough time to feel Scar come back for me. I dropped to the ground, kicking my legs in a sweeping motion. He fell back on the table, breaking it with a loud crack.

I had no time to think. Both came for me with determination. Punching and kicking, I fought back, knocking them as hard as they gave it to me. My fists crunched into the nose of Pinkie. He stumbled into the doorway.

Claws slashed across my torso. I roared, whirling around to the bigger guy, whose face looked like an animal's in its contortions. His jaw snapped, his long teeth dripping with saliva. I jumped back, ready to swing when a scream vibrated the room.

"West! Behind you!"

My head twisted over my shoulder, and I saw Rez by the doorway, the smaller bear between us, ready to pounce on me. He snarled, whipping around to her.

"No!" I bellowed, but it was too late.

Claws slashed across Rez's body. Screams tore through the room, digging holes into my chest as he tossed her to the ground. The beast screeched inside me, and pain shredded down my body. I couldn't shift to protect the woman I…

"Rez!" I bellowed. Pushing through my pain, I barreled into the shape-shifter standing over her, our bodies crashing into the ground. I pummeled the back of his head and bounced it off the floor like a basketball. Fury ignited me into flames. Red was all I saw and heard as blood rushed into my ears. Then I was in the air, flying across the room. My bones crunched as I slammed into the wall and slid to the floor.

The bigger guy snarled, his elbow pulled back, and a clawed fist crushed deep into my temple, sending me into darkness.

---

I had no idea how long I was out when my lids finally lifted open, the ceiling blurry and spinning. My fingers reached up and touched my throbbing head.

*Damn.* Was I just taken out by Smokey the Bear? That's bad for the ego. Fair enough, there had been two of them, both able to shift, but still. Fuckin' embarrassing.

*Rez…* Nails tearing through her skin, her body falling. I jumped up, already searching the area where the bastard tossed her. In the dark, I saw her crumpled body, blood pooling around her, soaking the carpet.

"Shit. Rez." I scrambled over, dread leaking into my lungs. *Please be okay.* Relief at seeing her chest rise and fall eased me slightly. I rolled her over, trying to see the damage across her stomach.

Her tattered top exposed deep, jagged cuts peeking out through the gaps. The drying blood stuck the fabric to her skin. My finger curled around the neck of her sweater, carefully splitting it open, the tattered fabric peeling away, sticky with blood. Her lacy bra had ripped away along with her sweater. Earlier today I would have given anything to see her almost naked. But all I saw now was blood and gaping flesh, her lungs fluttering to catch air.

I was up and in the bathroom before I could register anything. On autopilot, I wet a towel and rushed back to the room.

I halted when I peered at her sprawled form on the floor. Her head lolled to the side, her hair haloed around her, top ripped, and chest to hip gouged with claw marks. Blood everywhere. All my organs felt like someone put them in a blender, and they threatened to rise back up my throat.

Sinking back on my knees, I carefully cleaned away the blood. I knew she would be all right. She would heal, but knowing it wasn't the same as feeling it.

"That's it. You're done," I whispered hoarsely to her. "I won't allow you to get hurt again. I can't protect you like I should." The agony of my failure was my own private hell. The dweller could have fought them without even trying. And I had no doubt I would have eventually won against them in human form. But the sight of her, bloody and nearly lifeless, had crippled me.

I was searching for a reason to send her home. I had it. But now that I did, my chest clenched at the idea of her going. Leaving me.

I finished washing her other cuts and grabbed the easiest thing to dress her in. My hoodie engulfed her, making her appear smaller and more fragile, but she wasn't. I knew she was tough as nails, but I still wanted to shield her from any more abuse and pain.

Packing what was left of her stuff, I zipped the suitcase. With one arm, I shuffled it underneath her, picking her up. A soft moan escaped her lips as I hitched her higher.

Somehow I got my duffle bag over my shoulder, leaving both rooms wide open and vacated as I headed for the car. I would dump it the moment I got us somewhere safe. We couldn't have anything leading back to us. We needed to get far from here. Off the grid.

I stepped out into the parking lot, my gaze quickly going to the space I sensed would be empty. Yep. The gray Saab was gone. We had been followed from the moment we got off the plane. I didn't know how those humans at the first hotel worked into this, but I had no doubt they were sent to watch us. I had ignored my instincts and look what happened.

It wasn't going to stop me. I had to keep going, deal with Lars. But Rez? No. I didn't want her caught up in all this. No matter how much she fought me, I was sending her home.

No argument.

# ELEVEN

I drove into the night, zigzagging and looping around the small country roads, making sure we weren't being followed. I took us north to the town of Doolin, near the Cliffs of Moher, and parked the car behind an old, run-down building off the main road.

Dawn was still hours away, and we had nowhere to go till it was light enough to figure out what the next step was. Finding an untraceable place to stay in the middle of winter was actually trickier than it would seem. Some places were closed down, and others were vacant enough so we couldn't hide behind the hordes of tourists who ran around this area in the summer.

The gusting wind blew over the cliffs and rocked the car. I wanted to keep the heat going for Rez but was low on gas, and I didn't want to dump the car till we found a place to stay. Then I needed to take it far enough away to get people off our trail.

Twisting around to check on her stretched out on the backseat, I was startled to see her dark eyes on me. "Shit, darlin'." I shook my head. "I didn't think you were awake."

Rez continued to watch me.

"How are you feeling? You okay? Need anything?" I unbuckled my seatbelt. "You cold?" I didn't even let her answer before I was out the door, popping open the back, scrounging my bag for my other hoodie and a sweater. The bitter wind cut through my jacket.

"Damn, it's cold out here." I padded the extra clothes on top of her. "Gonna stay put here tonight. When it gets light, I'll find us a place to hide." I was babbling, but something about the way Rez was silently tracking me made me chatter nervously. "Get some sleep. Your body needs to recover." I tucked the clothing around her and backed away to shut the door. Fingers shot out, curling around my hand, stopping me.

My chest locked when her eyes met mine. *Don't go,* they pleaded with me.

Being close to her always led me down the wrong path. I couldn't. It was the one rule I needed to stick to.

"Please," she uttered so softly the breeze almost stole it from me.

I dipped my head in response. The need in her voice curled around my lungs, strangling the capability to talk. Tonight I couldn't deny her solace. *Who the hell are you fooling? Tonight or any other night.*

She flinched as she sat making room for me to get into the backseat, her hand clutching her stomach. I loved the way she looked in my sweatshirt. Warmth buzzed through my rib cage. When I settled in, she scooted closer, lowering herself, and laid her head on my lap.

*Oh. Hell.*

It was hard to turn off my body's initial response to her being so close to my cock, but I shoved it back, focusing on her. *Dude, stop being a fucking dick.* If she needed my body as her pillow, I would do that. The idea to put down the seats and make a bed out of the back crossed my mind, but sitting here with her head on my leg was already driving me crazy. Lying with her would be far too tempting… the more uncomfortable I was, the better. Anyway, I needed to keep watch.

A small contented sigh emerged from her, and I looked down to see my fingers absently threading through her hair and over her temple. I hadn't even been aware I was doing it. Not good. I knew I should stop, but the blissful expression on her face impelled my fingers to keep moving. I would do anything to keep that look on her face.

I let go of the rights and wrongs of my actions and let myself believe I was a friend providing comfort after a frightening night. After having your guts almost fall out of your body, you deserved to be consoled. Nothing more. *Keep telling yourself that, asshole.*

Another gust of wind knocked against the car and chilled the last of the warm air left. I tucked the sweaters tighter around her when I felt a violent shiver run through her.

When fae healed, we were at our weakest. Our bodies working hard to repair and recover, we shut down and went into a deep sleep. Her body was also trying to keep itself warm, working even harder. She needed to heal and if my body heat kept her warm, then my dick was going to have to shut the hell up. I twisted, popping the seat handles, and slipped out the door.

"West?" She lifted her head when my arms went around her.

"Shush, darlin'." I scooped her up in my arms, lifting her off the seat like a baby, and went around the back, opening the hatch. I placed her down, pushing down the seats, and lay her back.

The biting air numbed my hands and face quickly as I

opened our bags, grabbing every piece of clothing we had to drape over her. I quickly climbed in next to her and slammed the back shut.

Rez curled in a ball, trembling like a paint mixer.

"Come here, darlin'." I moved in behind her, pulled her frame into mine, and wrapped my arms around her.

Her head knocked into my chin and her muscles jerked, forcing me to curl farther around her like a strait jacket. I hitched a leg over hers and folded completely over, pulling her so tight against me it felt like I'd consumed her. It took several minutes for the shuddering to ease, her muscles melting into my warmth.

Being a sexual beast wasn't always a great thing. Okay, I had never even remotely thought that before, but with Rez's body pressed firmly against mine…yeah, I was an asshole. But my dweller didn't seem to give a crap who she was. All it understood was the curve of her ass pressing into my dick and the incredible way she smelled and felt.

If human boys thought puberty was rough, it was nothing compared to Dark Dwellers. I went through mine in the Otherworld before we were banned to Earth. There we were given a lot of freedom to act out and do anything. When we came to Earth, I watched Cole try to raise Eli, Cooper, and Gabby through that time and did not envy him. Earth provided far more temptations and far more trouble. Nothing horrible, but Cole was going to the police station every few days.

I'd experienced blue balls only once in my life, and only for a few days, until Cammie realized she wanted me as much as I wanted her. And in the week of courting her, it never felt like this. This was painful. The beast clawed and knocked at my willpower so fiercely I moaned when Rez shifted into me.

By forcing my brain to think of our next steps like a checklist, my body began to ease, and I drifted off to sleep.

*I lifted my head and recognized the room. Even though it appeared bare of its normal torture devices, I knew every crevice of this place. Acid sizzled in my stomach, and I would have retched, except I couldn't move. I wasn't even able to open my mouth to scream.*

*I stood naked, invisible chains bearing down on me. This was how she liked me best.*

*"I've missed you," a beautiful voice said behind me, but it caused my spine to shudder, fighting against the unseen hold. "It isn't the same without you. I'm so bored now."*

*Red hair danced in my peripheral, the curve of a woman's body in a tight, revealing dress moved around me. Damn. She looked so real. Nothing blurry or hazy about her. I was right back in my real-life nightmare.*

Wake up, West! Wake up.

*"Oh, love, you think you will wake up if I don't want you to?" She let out a peal of laughter. "You know I have always been in control. Your soul is mine, dweller. You gave it over to me." She purred, trailing her hands over my torso. "Who knew the moment I broke you you'd become such a magnificent, uninhibited beast?"*

*My jaw tightened, and my lids blinked rapidly, trying to fight the onslaught of emotion. Being back here... I didn't know if she was real and I was truly in hell, or my subconscious wanted to annihilate the last part of me trying to survive. It didn't matter. My body shook with hatred of both her and me. "Fuck off, Aneira," I forced the words out of my throat.*

*"Oh, we did that, love, countless times," she whispered and continued to run her hands over me. "But I am more than willing to revisit our time together. How about you?"*

*"No." My teeth barely let the word slip past my lips, anger pumping through my veins.*

*"You can deny it all you want." Aneira raised an eyebrow as she looked down at my naked body. "But you liked it. Still do, clearly. That's what you hate the most. It's like the ultimate dirty secret. It makes you hate yourself." Her red lips curved in a cruel smile. "Because you feel you deserve no better. The more perverse, the more you revel in it. Punish yourself."*

*"Shut up," I growled, fury breaking through.*

*"Anything good you destroy. The poor, sweet, naïve girl." Aneira clicked her tongue. "You ruined her."*

*Bile coated my throat and burned holes in my gut. My lungs fought the truth in shallow pulls.*

*"So you can lie to yourself." Aneira circled me, her hand running over my bare ass. "But I'm inside you." She stood on tiptoes and nipped my ear. "I am the worst part of you. You can't lie to me, but I am you now. You put yourself in chains a long time ago. The way I made you fuck me...scream my name... torture you...that was the first time you felt alive in a long time. Free. And once you were...wild, ravage, primal... Don't tell me that wasn't the truest you've ever felt."*

*I stared ahead, immobile against her claims, vomit rolling up from my stomach. I wanted to disappear, to no longer exist. Because I couldn't live with this...*

*The truth.*

*I had felt free. For once, I had let Cammie go. All emotion or sentiment sank in the tar, leaving me vacant.*

*"Look at what you did to Cammie. You think you deserve someone like Rez? You'd destroy that beautiful creature and you know it. How long before you'd shatter her? Ruin and obliterate her with your demons, like the others?" Aneira leaned into me, her fingers tickling my chest. "Come join me. You belong with me...we are alike, you and I. You may cover your secrets with charm, but you are twisted like me. Let the cruel, bitter, perverted beast out." Her hand wrapped around me, stroking me.*

*Tears pricked up at the vile disgust I felt toward myself. What I'd done. I kept pretending I could escape it, that I had hope. I didn't. Some things even a Dark fae cannot recover from.*

*The same person who banned us from Earth, who tortured me on a daily basis, ripped my soul away with degrading humiliation, killed and tormented others for the fun of it, stood in front of me. The woman I hated with every fiber of my being...I fucked her.*

*It started out with her dragging me to her chambers and forcing me. She batted me around like a toy. Every day she shredded me down to nothing, convincing me my true nature was vile, warped, cruel, and soulless. I let myself drown in it, welcomed it...even enjoyed it. My anger and self-loathing mounted with every encounter.*

*Then I would go back to my cell with my spiked dog collar, draining me even more of myself...of life, of my will. I was close to letting her have me; my life meant nothing anymore. I wanted to be taken fully underneath and hoped to never come up again.*

*Until Ember saved me.*

*When she appeared at my cell with Lily, she told me not to give up, that she would get me out. The purity of her strength and belief, her forgiveness and love, gave me hope. The dweller bond we shared provided a rope for me to grab on to. I clung to the vision of her face, her words, the image of my brothers.*

*I fought Aneira, even when my disobedience inflicted more wrath and humiliation. I no longer let her break me. But in doing so I became a shell of myself.*

*When I returned home, I did everything I could to forget, to push it away. I acted normal on the outside when depravity haunted me on the inside, that truth no one would understand. Hell greeted me most nights, but now hell had come back to claim me. And I wasn't sure I could fight it again.*

*Aneira smiled, caressing the fear and doubt rolling off me.*

*"West?" My name came softly over the air, spreading over me like a blanket.*

*Aneira stiffened, moving in front of me, filling my line of sight.*

*"Are you ready, dark one?" She held out her hand. "You know you will only be truly free with me."*

*"West?" My name stirred around me, spinning my head to search for the owner. A smudge of light appeared in the corners, the walls thinned and grew transparent.*

*"Dweller," Aneira beckoned me, but I heard another call my name, circling me like a lifeline. "Come with me. Now," Aneira demanded, her expression growing more frantic.*

*"West." My name anchored me, giving me strength.*

*"No..." I snarled at Aneira. Her lids narrowed, and her violet eyes glimmered with hate. "I will never go with you."*

***

With a snap and a jolt, my lids blinked open. Aneira was

gone, and I was standing in a field, fully dressed, surrounded by sheep, the ocean smashing into the coastline a quarter of a mile away.

What the hell?

"West?"

I swung around to the familiar voice. The cloudy dawn revealed her in shades of gray. Rez walked to me. Her body stiff, still healing itself together. "I woke and you were gone. It scared me." She huddled in her jacket, the wind blowing her hair around.

"Yeah. Sorry." I stared around, my brain fuzzy and confused. My hands shook; I curled them over. *Aneira felt so real...*

"Hey." Rez tipped on her toes, putting her hand to my cheek. "Are you all right? You're trembling."

The concern in her face and the worry in her voice almost made me break down and tell her. Ignoring the secret I kept only caused it to grow, flourish, and coil its way around me.

"What's wrong, West? Talk to me." Rez's sweet brown eyes compelled me to look away.

I couldn't put this on her. It was my burden, my horror to live with. We needed to keep our distance, and telling her the one thing I had never told anyone went against that.

"I'm okay." I took her hand away from my face, squeezing it with mine. "How are you feeling?"

Rez tilted her head, eyes watching me critically. "Could be worse."

"You hungry?"

A frown dug between her eyebrows, but she let my bullshit play out. And I was grateful for that. I couldn't have handled her digging at this wound.

"You must be starving. Healing consumes a lot of calories. The day after I healed from a deep injury, I inhaled the kitchen, then went to our local diner and ordered everything on the menu. Just for breakfast."

"Yeah. Food would be good." She took a step back, staring at the ground, gloom weighing her down.

"Hey." I grabbed her chin. "Are *you* okay?" Being gutted by Yogi Bear probably messed you up for a bit.

She let out a shaky exhale. "I didn't like waking and finding you gone." She looked straight into my eyes, her voice unwavering.

Not what I was expecting. I dropped my hand from her face and shoved them in my pockets.

"Sorry, darlin'. Won't happen again." For many reasons. The main one was she wouldn't be staying here long enough for me to do *anything* to her. I wasn't looking forward to bringing up that topic. Feeding her first was the best plan before I told her I was sending her back to the States. "Let's go get some breakfast." I put my hand on her lower back, turning her toward town. We trudged over the mucky hill, dodging the sheep droppings, to the road.

Before we hit the path, I glanced over my shoulder to the spot where I had been standing.

*"You think you deserve someone like Rez? You'd destroy that beautiful creature and you know it. You know you will only be truly free with me."*

Even from the grave, Aneira could still reach me, tearing the only bit of happiness I had, driving her claws deep.

The truth always finds you.

# TWELVE

We found a café in the tiny village of Doolin, the smells of frying ham and eggs ran around my empty stomach like a dozen chickens at feeding time. Rez and I both ordered two meals.

"Hungry this morning?" Our waitress was short and plump, her face angelic. Her eyes lit up, and she winked at both of us.

"You have no idea, sweetheart." I gave her a full flirty smile and red splotches appeared in her creamy white skin. "And if you could grab us a basket of muffins to tide us over, I would be most obliged."

"Uh. Uh…of course," she stammered. Her name tag read Noreen.

Rez rolled her lips together, looking at the table. I received a sharp boot kick to the shin under the table.

"Oh, and if you have clotted cream and jam…" I licked my lips, staring straight into Noreen's eyes. "I think I would just die of happiness." I laid my southern accent on even thicker.

"Of course…anything." She nodded, patting her forehead before she took off for the kitchen.

"You are awful." Rez snorted. "I swear even if they

didn't have cream, she would be out churning it for you right now."

I sat back in my chair with a laugh. I knew how women responded to me, especially with the accent. I can't say I hadn't used it over the years to get my way. But the one person who seemed completely immune sat across from me.

"Do you always get what you want?" She slipped off her coat, laying it back over the chair, still wearing my hoodie underneath. I looked anywhere but at her, knowing she had no bra on beneath. Dammit. I shifted in my seat at the thought. "Smile, toss in the accent, and have them wrapped around your finger?"

"Or my dick." *Speaking of...*

She rolled her eyes, sitting back in her chair, a scowl fluttering over her face.

"How are your wounds?" I wanted to unzip the hoodie at the table to see if they were healed. "I want to look at your cuts after we eat."

"They're healing. I looked at them when I woke up." She touched her side. "Only sore now."

I exhaled and sat back, running a hand over my hair. I wanted to wait till after we ate, but now seemed a perfect time to bring up her leaving. I grabbed my coffee and took a chug, burning my tongue. I could feel her eyes on me. Did she sense what I was about to say?

"Rez..." I started. Noreen stopped me, bringing a basket of muffins and bread and six ramekins full of cream and jam to the table. I gave her a big smile, but it dropped the moment she walked away. "Rez—"

"Don't." She cut me off, waggling her head.

"Don't what? You don't even know what I'm going to say."

"You want me to leave." Well, so much for her not knowing. "And I'm telling you right now, I am not going anywhere, so you can forget it."

"After what happened last night…" I rolled my fists into a ball. "I can't protect you. Not like I should."

"I don't need your protection." She leaned over the table, darts of anger pinching around her eyes.

"You don't need my protection?" I let out a derided laugh. "Really? Your guts pouring out on the floor last night says differently."

"That was *with* your protection."

I inhaled, the sting of her statements cutting deep.

She grabbed her necklace, running the charm along the chain. "I didn't mean that," she fumbled. "I knew what I was getting into. I wasn't disillusioned. I knew this would be dangerous. I may not be a fighter like you, or Ember, but I can defend myself. You don't need to protect me or bubble wrap me. I'm stronger than you know."

"Jesus, Rez, everything you've been through, you are one of the strongest women I know, but you are not a fighter. It's not anything to be ashamed about. Sirens aren't designed for battle. It's not in your nature, but fighting is mine. I can't help wanting to protect you; it's who I am. Plus, I want to keep my head…and if anything happened to you, under *my* care, Lars would *kill* me."

"No, he wouldn't." She folded her arms over her chest. "Death is part of battle."

"What?" I scoffed. "Are you serious? You are the Unseelie King's mistress. I think he'd be a little more than put out. Believe me, losing the woman you love…you want to take the whole world out."

"I am *not* the woman Lars would destroy the world for." Every muscle in Rez's neck and face strained, fury rolling off her. She spoke cool and steady. "*She's* already dead." The chair scraped the floor as she scooted back, standing. "And I am certainly not the one he loves. So you can stop worrying over what happens to me. I am on this mission with you as an equal partner, and you will not dictate if or when I leave. It is *my* choice. *Not* yours." She grabbed her jacket so furiously she knocked over the chair in her rush out the door.

*What the hell happened?* My mouth hung open in shock as I tried to ignore the stares from the tables around me. I felt like an even bigger ass. In my fear, I had committed the ultimate caveman move: treated her like she was less than me, that my rule was dominant.

Dark Dwellers were protective, territorial, and possessive, but we weren't sexist. Women in our clan were treated exactly like the men, even in battle. They were actually far stealthier and faster than the males. I would never have treated Gabby like this or Samantha. In my defense, I worried more because she wasn't like Gabby. Sirens could kill without even touching their victim, but only underwater. Rez was vulnerable on land, but I had no right to tell her to leave. I groaned, raking my hands over my face.

"Uh..." A voice popped my head up. Noreen stood over me with four dishes stacked along her arms.

"Noreen, would you do me the biggest favor and wrap those up?" I forced myself to smile sweetly at her.

"Certainly." She nodded, her gaze trailing from Rez's overturned chair to the door.

"Thank you, sweetheart." I chuckled lightly. "Looks like I might be in the doghouse."

"She'll forgive you." Noreen smiled sweetly, her green eyes bright. "Only a moment with you two and it's not hard to see you're both completely in love."

She turned and walked away.

I opened my mouth to object to her observation, but she was already halfway to the kitchen. In love? *Oh. Hell. No.* Lust maybe…I liked her. A lot. But nothing more. I had loved only once. I would never let myself again.

———

Containers in hand, I ventured out onto the street, searching for Rez. I spotted her a block away sitting on a stone wall and staring at the gurgling Aille River. Her hair cascaded around her while she huddled deeper into her jacket against the cold air.

I jogged toward her, my apology already on my lips.

She beat me to it. "I'm sorry." Her shoulders drooped, and she stared at the darkening clouds. "I shouldn't have run out like that."

I pitched one leg over the wall, straddling it so I could face her. "You are not the one who should be apologizing." I set the cartons between us. "I had no right to tell you to leave."

She jerked her head to me, her brown eyes sweeping over my face.

"We're partners," I said, feeling myself being drawn closer to her. "I'm not sorry for worrying about you, but I will try not become a sexist dick."

She let out a laugh, which sounded like music. "Don't make promises you can't keep."

"Did I promise?" I widened my eyes in mock horror. "No, I said *I'll try*…big difference, darlin'."

She grinned and our eyes connected. An electrical current zapped between us. Her smile faded, and her gaze became more intense. It felt like a brick dropped on my lungs, smashing out all the air. Every inch of my skin was alive, aware of the slightest breath of air or brush of skin.

I leaned forward with the impulse to kiss her, to run my hands through her hair, cup the back of her neck.

Then I saw her lips part.

The explosion of desire set off an alarm in my head. *Code red. Code red.* The warning bells went off. *Need distraction pronto.*

"Um…" I looked down, my fingers tapping on the takeout boxes. "Figured you're still starving."

"Yes." She cleared her throat. "Remind me to stomp out *after* I eat."

"It's still warm." I handed her the top box.

"We don't have utensils." She took the container, lifting the lid.

"You do. They're called fingers." I wiggled mine and dug into my food, popping a piece of omelet into my mouth. "Come on, let etiquette go. I swear it tastes as good without a plate and fork."

She swung her leg over the wall, matching my position and delicately pinched at her omelet, barely picking up a morsel, and placed it on her tongue.

"You can do better than that." I shook my head, challenging her.

Looking at me through her lashes, she grinned mischievously, and my heart slammed into my ribs. She picked up half the omelet, shoveled it into her mouth, then clasped her hand over her mouth, fighting between laughing, choking, and chewing.

"That's my girl." I guffawed, enjoying watching her relax and be silly. *Wait. What did I just say?*

Her eyes darted to mine then back at her breakfast, still trying to finish her bite.

"Oh, those look good." I grabbed for the small potatoes drenched in butter and salt.

"Hey." Her hand slapped mine. "Back off my breakfast, or I'm going after yours."

"All's fair in love and war, including breakfast, sweetheart." A twinkle glinted her eyes. I already sensed her next move.

Her hand jetted out for my food, but my fingers caught her wrist, stopping her. "I didn't say mine. Technically, I bought them. Gives me rights to all."

"Oh really?" An eyebrow curved up an instant before her other hand grabbed for the huge slab of ham in my container. I tried to snatch it, but she shoved half of it in her mouth, the other half sticking out between her lips. She squealed, twisting her head as my fingers pinched the end, ripping off what was left and chucking it into my mouth.

"Now it's war." I grinned, broke open her second container, and seized an egg. Getting a poached egg into your mouth without breaking it is a lot harder than it looks. She retaliated by stealing my bacon. But I nicked a pancake in return.

The prim-and-proper Rez disappeared. Giggling and snorting, she stuffed food into her mouth until she had chipmunk cheeks. All I could think was she looked frickin' adorable. Then the siren did something I wasn't expecting. Picking up the last poached egg, she leaned in, like she was going to feed it to me, and smashed it into my face.

"Oh…" I laughed, yolk and bits of egg sliding down my chin. "Now, you're asking for it, darlin'." I scooped up the last bits of food in my tray, grease, butter, and sauce oozing over my fingers.

"Oh no." Rez scrambled off the wall, her laugh tainted with alarm.

"Oh yes." I leaped for her.

Rez darted to the side, trying to get away from my reach. My long legs took only two strides before catching the hood of her jacket with one hand. Her body reeled back into mine, and I looped my free arm around her, holding her tight to my chest.

"Like I said. All's fair," I whispered into her ear. She squealed, withering against me as my hand smeared food all over her face.

She yelped and continued to try and fight me. I grabbed the front of her jacket, swinging her around to face me. Rez's lips were slick and shiny from the butter, cream sauce coating one cheek, pieces of bacon and potatoes plastered to the other. The sight of her sullied face, her hair messy, and happiness brightening her eyes overpowered me, desire buckling my legs.

"Fair? You got an egg. I'm like a buffet here." A huge grin engulfed her face, her fingers wiping away the bits of food.

*A buffet I want to devour.* I wanted to reach up, grab her chin, and slowly lick every morsel from her face, like an appetizer. Then move on to the main course. Every inch of her body. *West...* I turned away, grabbed napkins from the bag, and walked back to her, my boots hitting hers. Slowly I raised my arm, giving her a chance to stop me. She didn't. My fingers held her chin as I wiped away the smeared breakfast off her face.

"Would you believe that was my first food fight? Seen them in tons of movies, but always seemed like a waste of food. And messy." Her gaze met mine.

"You *are* a mess." My throat felt tight, causing my voice to be low and gravelly. I could see her swallow, her gaze tracking mine. *Damn.* I wanted to kiss her. Badly.

Her eyes glided to the side, like she sensed what I wanted to do. "So? What is our plan now? Those guys last night took most of the paperwork and maps."

Her face was clean, but I didn't stop. The need to be close to her overruled my logic. "I saw a little bookshop down the street. We'll see if they have any old books or maps of this area. Then we find a place to stay. Far off the grid." I paused. "We're close. They wouldn't have attacked us if we weren't on the right track." I dropped away from her. "There. Breakfast free."

She touched her cheek, a slight frown on her lips. "I still feel like I rubbed my face in a butter dish."

"It's good for the complexion."

"I don't think grease and butter are good for the complexion."

"No, darlin'." I bumped past her, heading toward the bookshop. "I meant laughing."

# THIRTEEN

The bell chimed as we entered the bookstore. It looked old and creaky and smelled of dust, paper, and cat. The husky black feline looked about as old as the store and slept on the counter atop a pile of dated magazines. It didn't stir until it took a whiff of the beast within me, then its head popped up and it hissed at me.

Yeah. Shape-shifters, especially Dark Dwellers, and domestic pets sometimes had a problem getting along. The more alpha the animals, the more we didn't. I had to establish dominance. "Hey, fat bastard." I scratched his head, staring him down. "You want to take me on?"

Rez scoffed. "Be careful, it might be one feline even you can't conquer."

"*All* pussies love me." I held back my chuckle when she rolled her eyes. "Haven't run into one yet that didn't."

"Seriously, your ego is massive."

"So am I...that's why." I grinned.

Rez rubbed her temples, groaning, and moved deeper into the small shop.

I enjoyed taunting her and driving her out of her comfort zone way too much.

Bookshelves stuffed the cramped space, holding books with leather or fiber covers. Maps and music posters dominated the walls. An entire section was dedicated to only Irish music. Doolin was known to be the center of their traditional music, where musicians played live in the pubs every night.

"Hello?" Rez called out. Only the murmurings of Gaelic tunes played in the background.

"Probably went out for a coffee or something. Not like tourists are pounding down the door this time of year." I shrugged, looking around the racks.

"And you two certainly aren't tourists." A musical Irish brogue rang from the back of the store. Rez and I jumped, jerking toward the woman. Definitely human, she looked to be in her fifties, short and round, and each of her voluptuous curves blended in with the other. Long, gray, frizzy hair stuck out of a colorful scarf tied around her head. She wore all black but had a multicolored shawl hanging over her shoulders. An earth mother type. Her energy was bright and warm. She was the kind of person you wanted to hug, taking consolation in her softness.

The woman took a step closer, scanning over us. "You are not what I was expecting."

"Huh?" I jerked back, my defenses rising. "What do you mean *expecting*?"

She tilted her head, clasping her hands. "I've been awaiting you two for a while now."

Rez was the first to fill the stunned silence. "I'm sorry?" She shook her head. "Waiting for us?"

"Who are you? How do you know us?" I belted out after Rez, keeping my body in front of hers.

The older woman smiled at us. "Not exactly you, but I knew someone was coming." She swished her hand. "I wish the visions came to me with more detailed descriptions and a time frame. It would save me a lot of energy."

Visions? "You're a seer?"

"Psychic, actually." The woman walked between us to the counter, rubbing the cat's head as she walked around. "People always confuse us as the same thing."

Like it mattered right now. "But you saw us arriving?"

"Well, 'saw' is not really how to describe it. I was doing a reading and the cards told me you would be here."

"Cards? Seriously?"

"You should be the last person to be skeptical. I have the gift, no matter what tool I use to understand the message." Her lids narrowed with irritation.

"You're right." Rez stepped to the counter, taking over before I insulted the lady even more. "What message did you receive? How do you know it's about us?"

"It told me a couple would be coming to the store, searching for an item."

"Wow, you just described pretty much every person walking in here." I threw my arms up. This lady was probably a complete fraud.

"An ancient, coveted, precious item lost to the sea?"

Rez shot me a look over her shoulder, then turned back to the woman. "Was that all you saw?"

The woman assessed us for a moment, silent, and then said, "A woman with the voice of an angel and a man who lived in darkness. I'd say that's you two."

Now she had my undivided attention.

"The cards said you would come to my store after the winter solstice, seeking knowledge and refuge."

Rez inhaled sharply at the woman's words.

"Do you have information for us?" I barged up to the counter, skimming Rez's shoulder. "Where this lost item is?"

"I don't even know *what* it is. I have no idea what you seek or where it is. It doesn't work like that. I didn't even know who I was expecting. Do you know how long 'after the winter solstice' is? Months. Every day I came in wondering if today was going to be the day. Or if in the time I went to get a tea, I missed you." She fluttered her hands dramatically, becoming agitated. "Believe me, my ability has been more of a burden than a gift. It varies on how much information I get. But there's always enough to make me crazy."

"We appreciate you've been waiting for us. For what you *do* know." Rez reached out, placing her hand on the woman's, her voice low and soothing. The woman immediately inhaled through her nose, centering herself as she let go of her breath, calming down.

She nodded appreciatively at Rez. "You really do have the voice of an angel."

"Angel of death," I mumbled. Rez's elbow hit my ribs, and she glared at me. I lifted my eyebrows innocently.

"I am Cara." The woman held out her hand to Rez.

"I'm R—"

"I think it's better if you don't know our names." I spoke over Rez. Anonymity was the only way to survive.

Cara pursed her lips but then slowly nodded, her gaze analyzing me. "You are probably right."

"Now, about that information. Do you have any books on ancient shipwrecks, the family O'Brien, or treasures?" I rubbed my hands together.

"No," she replied, deflating my hope. Then her body stilled, her eyes widening. "But I have a map of all three."

"I'm sorry, what?" I couldn't have heard her right.

"It's a family heirloom given to me by a friend when his uncle died. He thought I'd like it because I love old maps." Cara patted her hand to her chest. "Every time I touched it I kept getting flashes of a weapon…like a spear or dagger?"

My head spun, my hands clutching the table to keep me upright. Holy shit, did we just find the key to the location of the spear? "Where is this map?" I gritted my teeth, trying to keep from leaping closer to her and demanding she show me.

"I'm sorry, but it's not for sale." Cara face lined with remorse. "It means too much to me."

I moved, ready to jump over the counter and scare her shitless till she handed it to us.

Rez's hand grabbed my arm, keeping me in place. "That's okay," she interjected. *What? It is not okay.* "We don't want to take it from you." *Yes, we fucking do!* "We only need to see it. Please, Cara, this is extremely important."

Cara nipped her bottom lip, glanced at the cat sleeping, then at the door. She huffed and went for the entrance.

What the hell? Was she leaving? Kicking us out?

Cara reached the door, flipped the open sign to closed, and swiveled to us. "Come with me."

Was it wrong to roll naked on an old piece of parchment paper like it was the treasure itself? If it was, then so be it, because that was exactly what I wanted to do when Cara pulled the framed map from her office wall.

"This map shows several places where treasure is 'supposed' to be, from various shipwrecks." She curled her fingers in quotes. "They are just legends and folklore. Tall tales of those wanting to find pirate treasure."

"What if it's not? What if these are real? Or at least some of them?" Rez glided her fingers over the glass connecting all the X-marks showing locations. "You said the O'Brien name was connected to this map?"

"Yes." Cara nodded. "On the back of the map are names associated to the different wrecks. You know, tales that claim a particular captain was at the helm when the ship went down."

"Which one's linked to O'Brien?" The muscles around my lungs spasmed, anxiety and anticipation lighting them on fire.

Cara looked at me, and her eyes glinted with excitement, as though she knew she was a part of something extremely significant.

"This one." She tapped at the glass.

Adrenaline pounded in my temples. "Holy. Shit."

"You said we were close." Rez's eyes met mine with shock and excitement.

I didn't think we were *this* close.

Cara's finger sat on the X symbol right on the coastline. The script next to it read: *The Cliffs of Moher*.

We weren't simply near. We were sitting fuckin' on it.

# FOURTEEN

The bells of the entrance chimed, declaring someone's arrival into the shop.

Cara's head jerked up. "They must have not seen the closed sign. I'll go see what they want."

She had taken two steps when my sense of smell picked up on the intruders. Bears. "No!" I hissed, grabbing her arm. Cara gasped. Rez's gaze snapped to mine, her expression made of stone, but her eyes moved with questions.

My nod was subtle, but Rez understood and immediately reached for the knife strapped to her leg.

"What is going on?" Cara yanked against my hold. "Let me go!"

"Shhh." I covered her mouth, feeling the dark beast rise, sensing the threat on the other side of the door. My eyes must have shifted red, my pupils elongating, because she yelped under my hand, pulling harder against me.

"Stop. Now," I growled. "These men are here to kill us. And you too, if they find us."

Cara went quiet, her face full of fear, but she pulled her hand away.

"There's a back door."

Bangs resonated from the front of the store. The bears knocking into shelves. I instantly wanted to fight them. To spread Smokey apart for what he did to Rez, but her safety meant more. Both these women were in harm's way and would be used against me if caught.

"Where?" Anxiety bounced my feet.

"It's right on the other side of here, but you have to go out this door and around the corner. You will be seen."

*Damn!* I glanced at Rez to see how she was handling the thought of another fight. She may claim to be all right, but that shit last night had to affect her more than she admitted.

She looked back at me with a slight shrug. *We have no other choice.*

Seeing her strength, her courage, knowing she couldn't really beat them in a fight, but still wanting to stand next to me…did things to me I didn't want to think about.

"I'll distract them." Cara turned for the door.

"What? Wait!" I grabbed her arm again. "These guys are evil assholes. Shape-shifting bears. They will tear you apart." It still felt strange to be open about fae to humans in this new world.

"No, they won't."

"How do you know that?"

"Because I trust the cards." She patted my hand. "And I don't die today."

"Cara. No." Rez stepped in front of the door.

"Oh, I almost forgot. Take these." She pulled keys from her pocket and a slip of paper. "It's my little cottage. No one will find you there. Here's the address."

My mouth gaped.

"You are seeking refuge, right?"

I nodded, taking the keys.

"See? Trust the cards." She nudged Rez out of the way and clutched the handle. "Now. Run."

Cara turned off the lights and stepped out of the room, walking with false ease toward the men. If I could hear her heart slamming in my ears, they could too, but going forward was our only plan.

Rez kept close as I eased toward the door.

"Gentlemen, can I help you?" Cara curved herself toward the front so the men would look that way. Smart lady. "If you need help finding something, I can assist, but please don't throw my books on the floor."

The bigger one rumbled under his breath but turned to face her.

I grabbed Rez's hand and tugged her through the door and around the corner, keeping low. I could hear her heartbeat pumping strongly behind me, serenading the store. Bears also had a great sense of smell.

We scarcely got to the door when I heard one of them grunt loudly. It was creepy how they didn't talk. Almost like they couldn't. I glanced over my shoulder, and both bears were tearing after us.

"Shit!" I yanked Rez, shoving her through the exit to the alleyway. "Go!"

She didn't hesitate and bolted down the alley. I slammed the door, reaching for the garbage bin closest to me. It wouldn't hold them long, but I would take any time we got. I wheeled it over, blocking the exit, and locked the brakes. They shoved the door roughly against the metal bin but it didn't open all the way, buying us time. Swiveling, I darted down the backstreet and ran across the road.

"West!" Rez called me from a lane up the street. I swerved toward her, pumping my legs faster at the sound of metal scraping across cement behind me. Crap. They were out.

We darted through another alley. This town was small so it was really hard to get lost. I cut through a parking lot, heading behind a strip of stores and pubs. I ran faster than Rez but glanced behind me to make sure she was there. Movement caught my eye and suddenly an object leaped at her from behind a dumpster.

"Rez!" Her name tore from my throat. It was too late. Her scream pealed through the morning air, gutting me. I wheeled around, my chest hammering in my throat, going back for her.

A man's arm wrapped around her body, holding a knife to her throat. He was tall and lean, but muscles corded his arms, his green eyes shaped like diamonds. His arms strained through his shirt, and his hand shook as he dipped the blade into her neck. Red liquid trickled past the blade.

My beast roared, fury curling my shoulders forward. "Get the fuck away from her," I growled, my back hunching over more, pain flashing down my legs. I pushed against the instinct to change, and the beast screamed in agony inside me.

The man's eyes met mine. They looked dead, vacant, similar to the bear brothers. He didn't say anything, but his forked tongue darted out, tasting and smelling the air around him.

*Fuck!* Snake-shifter. If he weren't threatening Rez, I would have found him funny. The irony of a snake being in Ireland was almost too much. Like the bears, snakes had also allegedly been purged from this island a long time ago. A silly legend. According to the historians there never actually were snakes here.

"What do you want?" I inched forward.

He stared as if he didn't even realize I was talking.

A screeching of wheels ripped my attention to the van backing down the alley.

The bear brothers jumped out from behind the snake-shifter and opened the back doors of the vehicle. Snake Man hauled Rez back toward the van.

They are taking her. *Away from me*. The beast inside went berserk, shutting logic down, and rage poured through my veins. I flung forward with a roar. Stabbing pains wrenched my body, and all I saw was red, but I couldn't stop.

The bears came after me, shifting their hands and mouths into weapons.

"West!" Rez's voice gutted me, driving the dweller inside to scrape at the surface. My legs collapsed underneath me, agony pitching me forward on all fours.

*Noooooo!* I bellowed in my head.

There was always a point when the beast went too far. It didn't care if you wanted him out or not, he was ready to kill. I was past the point of no return, even though no monster emerged to the surface.

My hearing was centered on Rez, hearing her screams and struggles against the snake. The bears watched me, not sure why I had crumpled to the ground. The bigger one tried to get near me. My mouth opened, letting out a thunderous roar, rattling the garbage cans next to me.

The smaller one grabbed him and pulled him back, shaking his head. They both stared at me as my body tried to attack them. Blinding pain shredded my insides, and bile leaked from my mouth. I couldn't move. Every muscle locked up, suspended in this painful limbo where I could not change.

"West!" Rez's voice was lost as the doors shut on her and the men hopped into the van.

Wrath exploded inside, demanding to release my beast. Black dots consumed my vision, and I felt my shoulder slam into the cement. A guttural howl came straight from my soul. The vibration of the van driving away thumped against my temple.

*Rez...* She was gone. I had failed her. Again.

Aneira had done more than twist my mind. She had taken away my essence—the one thing that made me who I was. I was simply a shell filled with bullshit pretending everything was fine. When in reality my walls were crumbling down, leaving me nothing but a husk.

Gradually my bones and muscles relaxed and air flowed through my lungs. I pushed myself to sit, spitting acid burning my throat. I wiped away saliva. My body ached like I'd been beaten, but anger propelled me to my feet.

Rez. Finding her was my only thought.

Who were they? Why would they kidnap her? It seemed clear they were after the spear as well. Lars warned us his interest might have alerted other groups who would be trying to beat him to the finish line. Stealing our information, our leads...they wanted to get to it first. Surely that's why they took Rez, hoping she would give them its location.

Shit. Lars. What would I tell him? *Hey, sorry, your woman was hijacked by Yogi, Boo-Boo, and Hiss while I curled on the ground like a pussy.*

"Fuck!"

I yelled, running a hand through my hair. I didn't care about Lars or the damn spear. I needed to find her. *If those assholes hurt her in any way...* The thought drifted off.

*What? What would you do? Roar at them, you toothless asshole?*

I shoved my fists into my pockets, my shoulders tight and hunched. I had to do something. Find her somehow... My boots clipped the pavement, moving before I even finished the thought.

"Cara?" I screamed, ripping the back door open. "Cara!"

"What?" She bustled toward the back, her hands going to her mouth. "Oh my goodness! What happened? Are you all right? I thought you got away."

"No." I clenched my teeth. "They took Rez." I was past caring if she knew our names. It was a moot point anyway. They had her.

"Oh no." Panic and fear widened her eyes.

"I need you to find her."

"What? How do you think I can find her?"

"Do a reading on your cards. A séance! Get out a fuckin' Ouija board. I. Don't. Care. Just find her," I yelled, my patience out into wisps.

Cara's hands shook, tears glassing over her eyes. Yeah, I was being a dick. I didn't care. Getting Rez back by any means possible was my only drive.

"That's not really how it works." She fluttered nervously under my gaze. "I don't pick and choose what the powers want me to know."

"*Try.*" I slammed my teeth together, growling.

She licked her lip and patted her chest rhythmically, like it helped her keep from freaking out. She didn't even know how scary I could get. Cara ran back to the counter where the cat still sat stretched out. He lifted his head and glared at me.

*Right back at you.*

She pushed him off, producing a strained cry from his throat. At least now I wasn't the only one the brat scowled at. "Sorry, Othello," she uttered remorsefully, but tossed her tarot cards on the table, shuffling them frantically. "Pick one." She held them out.

I'd asked her to do this, but I felt irritated, like she was wasting my time. A clock ticked in my head, every second putting more distance between Rez and me. I pinched a card and tossed it on the table. What was I thinking? Did I really think this would help locate her? The problem was I didn't know what else to do.

Cara frowned at the card. It showed a man hanging upside down.

"What does that mean?"

"Reversed hanged man shows martyrdom, indecision, and delay," she said. "You can't let go of something because it's keeping you from moving forward. Being happy."

Like a punch, the accuracy of this card jabbed at me, only angering me more.

"How the hell is this helping me find Rez?"

"I told you. That's not how my abilities work." Lines dug in her forehead. "Try another."

I yanked at a card, tossing it down.

"Hermit card," she noted. "Upright, which means soul-searching, introspection, inner guidance."

"This is bullshit." I shoved all the cards off the table, scattering them across the room. "This is not helping me find Rez."

"I'm sorry, but this is what the cards want to tell you." Her jaw grew tight.

I bent over, trying to control the rush of irritation pumping in my body. "What do I do?" I muttered to myself. "I *can't* lose her too." The words slipped out before my brain understood what I had just said.

"Hermit...guidance." Her hand went to her mouth like she figured something out. "Of course."

"What are you going on about?"

"I think I might know who could help you."

I froze. "What?"

"Olwyn. She lives close by. You might call her a hermit of sorts, but she has a young apprentice living with her. I see the girl come into town for supplies sometimes. Olwyn's been around since I was a baby. She has to be in her nineties at least, but everyone knows who she is. The rumors about her being some kind of witch have been going around since I was a child. Kids and adults stayed away from her but, having abilities myself, I was intrigued by her."

"A witch?" Witches were on the low rung of magic, but I was desperate. "Where?"

"She lives over the hill from the cottage." Cara nodded to where I put the keys in my pocket. "If you head north from the house, follow the stone fence on the right, it will lead you there."

Hope bloomed in my chest, and I grabbed Cara's hands. "Thank you."

"Hopefully she can help you. Give you guidance."

"Seriously, thank you for all you've done and giving us a place to stay. You don't even know us, and I can be a jerk. So Rez would want me to thank you for her too. Dealing with me."

"You are a handful. It's a good thing you're so handsome." A tiny smile hinted on her mouth. "Now go rescue your girl."

"Uh. Not really *my* girl. She's someone else's."

"Really?" She lifted her eyebrows. "That's strange because I pulled the lover card for you two."

"Must have been a mistake."

Cara slanted her head with a knowing grin. "I always trust the cards."

# FIFTEEN

The address to the cottage was on the key ring, but Cara gave me directions, warning me it was challenging to find being so remote and there were no real roads to it.

When I finally pulled up to the single-story stone house, I realized it couldn't have been a more ideal hideout. Even without trees, there was something about this rolling countryside you could get lost in, disappear.

I quickly grabbed our belongings from the back, unlocked the door, and walked in. The phone/walkie-talkie rang in my bag, but I ignored it. I knew who was checking in, and he was the last person I wanted to talk to at the moment. Lars could wait till I had Rez back safe.

The place was freezing, dusty, the air stale from being vacant since the summer, but other than that it appeared perfect. It was a large one-room house with two queen beds decked out in flowery comforters. A round table with four chairs sat next to the kitchenette facing a window with a couple of window seats. On the opposite wall was a fireplace, a bathroom at the far end, and a closet. Simple, but everything you needed.

I tossed the stuff on the bed, zipped my jacket, grabbed a beanie, and took off out the door. Following Cara's directions, I trailed the wall and traveled north. The wind snapped at my face, turning it numb after a while. The already dreary sky darkened the afternoon.

Billows of air puffed from my mouth, and the marshy terrain sucked at the bottom of my boots. "Over the hill" in Ireland clearly didn't have the same meaning as it did back home. I traipsed over many hills for more than a mile before I saw the smoke from a chimney rolling into the sky.

"Finally," I grumbled. With a flash of fear for what might be happening to Rez, I jogged the last bit to the house. I crossed the gate and felt the slam of magic, heavy and dense. Complex. Not something I'd imagine a witch to be capable of. The curtains were shut, but I could see a soft glow illuminating from the slight gap. Thank the gods for hermits. I didn't have to worry no one would be home.

The thuds of my knocks almost drowned in the howling wind. I perked my ears, hearing a sudden whisking of movement along with dishes clanking. A full minute passed before I heard the door creak, then saw a sliver of a face, one brown eye peering out.

"May I help you?" a quiet but firm woman's voice asked. She sounded young. The apprentice?

"Yes. I really hope so." I stuffed my hands in my pockets, trying to look as unthreatening as possible. "Cara from the bookshop sent me. Told me an Olwyn might be able to assist me?"

"I can't imagine we could do anything for you. I'm sorry." The girl went to shut the door, but I shoved my boot in before it closed.

"I'm sorry, I don't have time to be polite. I know you guys are witches. My friend was kidnapped by some real assholes, and I need your help to find her." I put my hand on the door, pushing against her weight. I knew it would take only a little shove on my part. From what I could see she was a tiny thing. "Please. I don't say that word very often, but I'm desperate here. I need to get her back. Now."

Her eyes scrutinized me. The girl glanced to her side, then nodded, letting the door open.

"Thank you." I stepped in, shutting it behind me. The house was bigger than Cara's, but not by much. It included a loft, which was probably where they slept, and a full kitchen. The beams along the roof were lined with hanging dried herbs and flowers. A tall working table was covered in cuttings, liquid jars, and several mortars and pestles. The room was divided into the kitchen area and the living space by the fireplace. A huge black pot hung in there, boiling something which smelled sharp and herby. The lights were low, which seemed to set the mood for a witch's lair.

The girl turned to face me. She appeared to be in her early to mid-twenties. Five-three and barely a hundred pounds, with long, glossy brown hair pulled back in a low ponytail, brown eyes, and a dash of freckles sprinkled over her nose. She was really cute, almost beautiful but hid behind the boxy brown pants, brown tunic, and long, knitted grandma sweater. Something seemed familiar about her. Knowing me I probably "dated" someone who looked like her.

"Do you have anything of your friend's?" the girl asked, folding her arms. "It helps with the locator spell."

"Shit." I shook my head. "Not on me."

"Olwyn has worked without before." She sighed and turned toward the chair by the fireplace.

I almost yelped when I realized an old woman was sitting in the rocker.

"Olwyn?" The girl's voice sounded soft and sweet as

she touched the woman's arm. "This gentleman…?" She looked at me.

"West," I replied.

"Fionna." She motioned to herself, then turned back to the old lady. She sat so stationary it was hard to believe she was breathing as she stared at the fire hypnotically. "He needs to locate his friend. Can you help him?"

The woman glanced up at her, coming to life. Her face was weathered, her white hair cut close to her head. She seemed even shorter than Fionna but much rounder than her young protégé. The magic was so thick around her I was beginning to think I had long underestimated witches' magic potential.

Some witches became Druids when they won the favor of the gods and they were given magic, extending their lives and powers. What we considered witches now were completely human and usually did little more than make herbal poultices and perform solstice rituals, rarely true magic. Most weren't capable of doing any more than a charm or two, but based on the palpable energy of Olwyn's magic here, she was capable of a hell of a lot.

Olwyn nodded. Fionna kissed her hand and put it back on the chair.

"I always have to get her permission first. Her power takes a lot from her." Fionna went to a shelf in the corner, grabbing a map and crystal hanging from a chain then went back to Olwyn, settling in front of the old woman.

"Since you don't have an object of your friend's, I will need you to come here." Fionna motioned me over, and I moved to them, squatting down next to Fionna.

Fionna's delicate fingers laced the chain around Olwyn's fingers, lifting her hand, and scooted the map on the woman's lap. "She's gotten shaky over the years, so I have to hold her arm." Fionna reached over and grabbed mine. "You need to hold on to her hand and mine. Close your eyes and think of your friend. Especially the last moment you saw them. It's easier for Olwyn to follow her journey from there. Understand?"

I nodded and settled my knees into the carpet, clutching both Fionna and Olwyn's hands, shutting my lids.

"Ready, Olwyn?"

"Yes, dear. I know," the old woman spoke, her voice heavy with age, but there was something innocent and naïve in her tone as if she were proud she did. Hell, if I remembered anything at that age, if I lived that many more centuries, I'd be glad to remember when I peed last.

They both started chanting, and energy trickled down my arms. I focused on Rez being dragged back into the van. It felt like torture. I was ashamed I let it happen, but I locked on the image, replaying it in my head and straining to see where the van took her.

Their incantations grew louder, pushing behind the words and into me. Energy filled the room, shoving down on my shoulders, forcing me onto the ground.

Fionna's tiny hand gripped mine tighter, as if she were telling me to concentrate harder. I drove further into my mind, hearing Rez scream and struggle, seeing the fear on her face, the way she called my name. Needing me.

Sweat dribbled down my back, coating my forehead. The pressure was growing so tense; I squeezed my lids together with a grunt. Olwyn let out a chilling wail, stabbing the air like it was made of glass. It shattered, pushing me back, and I lost hold of the women.

I opened my eyes to see Fionna still clutching Olwyn's hand, the crystal touching the map, the chain pulled taut.

"It worked." Fionna glanced over at me, smiling. "We have the location of your friend."

"Where?" Anxiety and relief orbited my lungs.

"She's outside of Lisdoonvarna, a small village to the east of here." Fionna set Olwyn's hand down, patting it before taking the charm and map from her. "Thank you, Olwyn. Now rest," she whispered to the woman. Olwyn immediately let her lids drop, slumping in the chair, going straight to sleep.

"Outside? Is it any more specific than that? That's still pretty vague." I climbed to my feet.

Fionna walked over to the table, brushing a few items away before placing the map down. "When I say it's small, I mean it. Where the crystal landed there is only one place she could be." Fionna stabbed her finger at the spot. "An old abandoned granary."

Hope sprang in my chest like the freakin' Easter bunny, bopping around with exultation. I was already moving for the door. "Thank. You." It was the truest my words had ever sounded to me.

"Wait." Fionna reached out for me, her grip firmer than I'd have imagined for a girl her size. "Do you even know where you're going?"

"There." I pointed back at the map. It wasn't detailed, but I was in too much of a rush to think straight. I'd find it. I had to.

"Let me go with you. I can show you where."

"No." I waggled my head firmly. "No way. It's too dangerous. These guys aren't playing around, and I can't watch out for you too."

"I won't go in, just get you there. Besides, if it's locked up or has a spell over it, you might need a witch by your side. I may be an apprentice, but I know a few things."

Her smile was so sweet as she boldly offered her witchy services to me.

I hadn't even thought about the granary being enchanted. But there was a good chance it would be. Depending on the strength, it could block me out.

"You can spend the whole night driving around, trying to find it, or I could lead you straight there. Your choice." Her eyes slyly inched over my body but quickly looked away. Ah, little witch liked what she saw. Her shyness was adorable. Probably not too many guys had knocked on this door in the middle of nowhere.

The thought of touching her did nothing for me. At all. Only one woman was on my mind. And I needed to get her away from those bastards. Now.

"Fine." I ran my fingers through my hair. "But only as far as the building. I go in alone, and if you hear or see anything, you run. Got it?"

Fionna nodded, blushing deeper at my authoritative tone.

Looking back over at Olwyn sound asleep, I realized this was probably the most excitement Fionna had experienced in a long time, if ever. It couldn't have been terribly thrilling for a young girl here, all alone to tuck in an old woman by seven every night.

# SIXTEEN

"There." Fionna pointed to an enormous old barn in the distance. The headlights bobbing over the road were our only light. Evening had encroached fast and neither moon nor streetlights lit the inky darkness. I begrudgingly admitted to myself I was glad Fionna was with me, showing me the way. Without her, I wouldn't have found this place with all these turns and curves over the hills along one-lane roads and dirt paths.

I drove the car behind a vacant outbuilding, far enough away, turned off the lights, and killed the engine. "Take these. Just in case." I handed her the keys. "Like I said, after I'm in, come back here. If you sense any danger, if the worst happens, take the car and go. Okay?"

Fionna met my gaze and nodded. "If that happens, you walk straight through those trees to the east, and you'll eventually come to a main road. Follow it back to town." She pointed out the window to the forest.

"All right. Let's do this, sweetheart." I slid out of the car, my boots squishing into damp earth.

Not far down the road I felt the pulse of magic. It didn't seem as strong as that around Lars's compound but more solid than I thought it would be. I could get in, but it would probably set off alarms.

"Wow." Fionna held up her hands, sensing the barrier. "This is tightly woven."

Again, I was surprised at her awareness and that she could sense the threads of magic twisting the protection spell together. Witch or not, most humans didn't have the perception to detect fae magic. But Olwyn was more powerful than any witch I'd ever met, so she probably taught Fionna well.

"Can you break it?" My legs jittered. Rez was somewhere in the building, possibly being beaten or worse.

"I think so." She nibbled on her lip and held her palms close to the magic field. She closed her eyes and started chanting under her breath.

I looked back at the structure in front of me. The granary building was the main one, with a few smaller structures off to the side, probably offices at one time, but my gut told me Rez was being held inside the barn.

Fionna's chants grew more strained, wind blowing her ponytail around, and her lids squeezed firmly together. Watching her there, I saw a power and strength behind her shyness. She no longer looked sweet and fragile but confident and strong. Beads of sweat spread along her hairline, words shooting off her tongue. The barrier wobbled, weakened.

*Shit.* She was doing it.

Fionna grunted and fell to her knees, the invocation coming out choppier. The protection spell dimmed a little more. Fionna cried out, then the barrier blinked out.

"Now," she screamed.

I didn't hesitate, I leaped over the line and waited.

Nothing. No bells or magic. I turned around to nod at Fionna, to tell her to get back to the car, when magic slammed down on me with a high-pitched noise reverberating in my ears.

*Shit!* There must have been a trip wire or something. Too late. I was here and I wasn't leaving without Rez.

I swung back to Fionna. "Run!" I screamed and took off for the entrance to the barn. Determination drilled my legs into the ground as I ran, my eyes fixed on the barn door. The alarms ceased, and the air hung in unsettled silence.

*Rez. Rez. Rez…* My head chanted along with my steps.

I ignored the sinking feeling in my gut, the eerie sensation rippling over my skin. I wrenched at the door, flung it open, and plowed into the old massive barn full of rusting granary equipment. The musty smells of grain, metal, and oil from the machines lingered heavy in the space, almost covering the slight odors of fae and human.

The weird feeling tripled, wiggling over me like worms. I dug in deep, searching for Rez's smell covered by a fresh ocean breeze traced with something sweet. My nose finally picked up her scent, which was faint and hard to distinguish. Wanting to scream out for her, I bit my lip. Why was it so quiet? Were they even here?

Thick shadows draped the barn in almost pitch darkness, my eyes adjusting slowly to make out shapes. I slinked around a large hopper tank, my boots squeaking over the cement floor as I came to a sudden stop.

*Dammit.*

A line of eight men stood before me, waiting. Their eyes were vacant. A sinking sensation told me this was too fast for them to already be ready for me. The alarms had just gone off, so how would they know I was coming? Three of them were human, the ones from the hotel. *I knew it.* The others were fae, but I only recognized Smokey Bear, his mini-me, and the reptile.

"Sorry I'm late. Traffic here was a bitch." I casually searched over their heads, taking in the eroding hopper tanks and equipment left in the barn, trying to form a plan. Behind the men sat a tiny go-cart, keys dangling from the engine. "Sheep-jam on the R478 again."

None of them so much as flinched or acknowledged me. Their faces remained blank.

"You guys are a blast to hang out with. Seriously, you wouldn't want to head to Vegas with me? Think it'd be fun; plus, you guys have killer poker faces."

Hiss lifted his lips, his forked tongue sliding out.

"Is that a yes? No? Sorry, hard to tell." A plan was finally forming in my head. "I appreciate you watching my girl for the day, but I think I should take her home now. It's bath night."

Yogi Bear rumbled at last, stepping forward.

"Yeah, enough of the chitchat," I replied, stepping to him. He swung out for me. I ducked, darting under his arm, moving faster than the others could respond. I ran to the cart, turning it on, but the engine died.

*Of course.*

A hand grabbed my shoulder and twisted me around, his fist cracking the side of my jaw. I kicked out, slamming my boot into his crotch. Yogi fell to the ground, and I whirled around, turning the key again. This time it started.

Another arm slipped around my neck, pressing on my jugular. Choking, I leaned forward, fighting his hold, my fingers barely managing to slip the gear into drive. I threw back my head and the sound of cracking cartilage snapped through the air. I bent down and tossed his body onto the floor of the cart, shoving him down on the gas pedal. The vehicle jumped forward, heading for the leg of one of the tanks.

Boo-Boo grabbed me by the back of my jacket, dragging me into him. My elbow drove into his gut, and I kicked back into his knee. He went down.

The sound of bending steel filled the room with squeals. The cart had driven straight into the eroding leg, cracking it. My eyes widened as the tank wobbled forward. The men were so set on coming after me they didn't even look up. With a shrill peal of twisting metal, the tank gave way, crashing to the earth.

*Run, asshole!* I screamed at myself.

It was only seconds between the force of the drum hitting the ground and the deafening boom in my ears. The force tossed me in the air. I sailed over and hit a conveyer belt, rolling across it with a grunt before hitting the ground.

*Ouch.* I winced, looking over my shoulder at the damage behind me. Not one body to be seen. The rusty container filled up more than half the room, all the men caught underneath. Old grain left in the tank spilled out, heaping over the bodies underneath.

"Not bad." I nodded in pride. "Didn't think that was going to work." I pushed myself up, feeling aches already across my torso and face.

"Rez?" I called out.

Nothing.

"Rez!" No voice, but I thought I heard a sound like someone stomping their feet above me.

I looked up to see a catwalk above my head. I ran for the stairs. With every step I could sense she was close, and I sprinted for the catwalk. At its end was a single room. It had no door and was filled with more equipment and pulleys. In the dark it took me a moment to find her far against the wall. Her arms were tied over her head, and she was muzzled.

"Rez!" Joy sprang up like bubbles inside me.

Her head jerked to me, and excited grunts muffled through the rag in her mouth. Four huge strides and I crossed the room, squatting down to her level. I ripped the gag down.

"How are you? Did they hurt you?" My words spilled over her like a tidal wave. My hands ran over her face, needing to touch and check for wounds. She had a black eye and split lip but otherwise appeared all right.

"I'm fine." Relief washed over her face, her voice a whisper. "You found me."

"Did you doubt it?" I grabbed at the ropes tying her. It was cord rope, not thick, but so dense and firmly bound it made it difficult to break through.

"No. Not really. I knew you would track me down." She rolled her jaw, loosening it. "What the hell happened down there? Sounded like a bomb going off."

"Decided they needed close-up, hands-on experience with the equipment here. Only way they'd learn." Adrenaline pumped through my arms, and I tore at the rope tied in the infinity loop around her wrists. I hissed through my teeth, tugging at the knot. It felt like the tie was bound by a spell.

"Shit." I searched the room frantically, time was ticking by, my heart slamming into my ribs.

"There's the knife in my boot. I hid it there." Rez nodded to her leg. "I tried to reach it but couldn't."

"So lovin' you right now," I mumbled, my fingers ripping off her shoe, the knife clanking onto the floor. I grabbed it and sawed at the rope. A burning sensation fizzed up my veins. Magic. It was fighting me from breaking her free. The more I hacked, the more it grew, till I was grunting in pain. With one last cut, the rope fell away. Fire pierced my gut but quickly dissipated.

"Not nice," I grumbled. Rez was already on her feet, shoving her foot back in her boot. "Come on, darlin'. These guys really seem determined to have you as their house guest."

I grabbed her arm and ran out of the room, searching below at the overturned granary tank. A few men had scrambled back up. The fae, naturally. I had a feeling the humans would stay under. Permanently.

Eyes turned to us. Hiss and some other fae were instantly moving toward the stairs—the only way up, the only way down.

*Fuck... Think, West.*

"There!" Rez yanked on my jacket, taking off down the catwalk, her boots pinging over the metal. It took me a moment to understand her plan, but when I saw the hopper tank near the wall, its flue leading outside, I was right behind her.

Great plan, except the catwalk ended fifteen feet from the tank platform. There was no other choice but to jump. Rez got to the end and crawled up on the railing.

"You got this, darlin'." She wouldn't die from the fall, but it could break her legs. Always hard to run with broken legs.

"Hope so." A clanging sound revealed itself to be men hitting the catwalk behind us.

"Push off with everything you have. Imagine yourself soaring through the water." I rubbed her back, feeling the men gaining ground. "Now. Go, sweetheart."

She closed her eyes, gnawing on her lip and jumped. Terror wedged between each rib as I watched her body fly through the air. There was nothing I could do. I was surprised and completely impressed at how little hesitation she had. She leaped, not thinking or overanalyzing. She just acted.

As Rez began to descend, my voice was pinned in my throat, my gaze locked on her. She still had a few feet to go when she yelped, stretching out farther. Her fingers grasped the rail and pulled herself in, her body crashing into the railing with a harsh bang. Shit, that was close.

I climbed on the top of the barrier, ready to jump, and glanced over my shoulder one last time. The men had stopped and turned around to head to the tank ladder. Boo-Boo and Yogi were already on their way.

I leaped, the beast qualities easily eating up the space, helping me make the platform in a crouch. When I sprang up, I saw the bears now at the ladder.

"Go!" I shoved Rez into the funnel. We could feel the vibrations from them climbing up, the rungs of the ladder pinging from their boots.

Rez let out a tiny yelp as she let go, her clothes generating a whistling sound as her body sailed down the flue.

My fingers gripped the ridge, about to fling myself after her, when pain tore into the back of my calf. Claws dug into my flesh. A bellow overflowed my lips. The nails burrowed in farther, scraping close to bone. I tipped to the side, nausea swirling in my head, coating my tongue, my fingers losing their hold.

With a cry, I crashed onto the small platform, pulling free of his claws, which shredded my muscles and tendons. I clutched the edge of the platform, watching the ground spin below me.

Yogi climbed the rest of the way up. There was only room for two, but it still felt too crowded. I had enough of this fucker.

Ignoring my injury, I hopped up on one leg, facing him. Pain pissed me off. I channeled my wrath through my fist, crunching his throat with force. Yogi stumbled back; his hand cupped around his throat.

His gaze lifted to mine, and I saw rage behind his eyes. He had partially shifted, his head and arms already full bear, while his legs stayed human. The space was too small for him to be full animal, and it would only hinder him. His mouth snapped out for me, teeth grazing my jacket. His claws sliced down on me. I had nowhere to go. There was only one move I could make before I was gutted. I hugged him.

Okay, it was less of a hug and more of a tackle. It's difficult to use your arms when someone is "bear" hugging you. I bowled into him, running his body back to the railing. We rammed into the pole, which bent him so far back he started to fall.

He wrapped his arms around my back and drilled in his nails, taking me with him. I howled. My feet came off the ground, my breath catching as I felt myself start to go over. The railing zipped past my vision as we plunged. I reached out and grabbed for anything I could. My fingers wrapped around the metal, my head going over. I bit down and held on tight.

Agony screamed through my ligaments when gravity caught up with me, jolting me to a stop, ripping Yogi's claws from my back. The embedded nails scraped along my body as he continued to fall.

He hit the concrete with a crunch. I hung on, swinging for a moment, my joints pulled out of place, blood dripping to the floor with resounding taps.

No one spoke, but I saw Boo-Boo rush to his partner, his face contorted with concern and fear. His hand gingerly cupped the other's cheek.

I was so tired and hurt like hell, but there was no time to take a break. More clangs from the ladder hummed in my head. Hiss was on his way up.

I kicked my legs, gritting my teeth, blood and sweat dampening my forehead. Grunting, I hooked my leg to the ledge and climbed back up. Hiss was almost at the top. His face peered over the side, and I locked my jaw, kicking my bad leg back. With as much effort as I could muster in my weakened state, I slammed my foot into his face. He cried out and fell, hitting the other two guys behind him, all three crashing to the ground in a pile.

With my energy dwindling, I fell back into the tube and let myself go. Gravity sucked me to the bottom. Air pushed from my lungs and my head spun when I was chucked out of the shoot eight feet from the ground. Otherwise I didn't feel anything.

"West!" Rez rushed over to me. "Oh gods. I was so worried."

"Sorry, darlin'. Was held up." I tried to smile. "Boys' night."

"Next time have the decency to call and let me know you're gonna be late." She curved her arms around my back, helping me sit up.

"Think I'm getting a taste of what it would be like to be married to you." I moaned. My back felt like it was on fire.

"Believe me, if you were married to me, you wouldn't want to leave." She pulled me to my feet, her voice teasing. How with so much pain could I still get this hard? Her being flirty only mushed my brain more.

"I don't doubt that, darlin'." I sucked in a deep breath and looked back at the granary. "Let's get out of here while we still can."

---

Rez was my crutch for most of the way home, but my body healed quickly, giving her a break. I didn't even look to see if the car was gone. I hoped Fionna used it to get away. We needed to ditch it anyway. Parking it in front of the cottage was dangerous.

Getting over the dark rolling hills and bypassing main roads was tedious and long. But not once did I feel we were being pursued, which was a relief. I didn't think I could take another fight.

Eventually, we passed close enough to Olwyn's place where I saw the silver Range Rover parked behind the house. Fionna was safe, which was all I needed to know. I'd go over and check in later, thank her again, but right now I wanted to get Rez and myself inside the cottage, safe.

Once we were, I checked every lock and put a chair to the door, keeping the lights off.

"Let me look at those wounds." Her fingers brushed the hem of my shirt.

Now that we were back in the snug cabin, her proximity felt dangerous. Her honest but flirty tone still had my pants tenting. "No, I'm good. Merely need a shower. I'll heal by tomorrow." I grabbed her hands and pushed them away.

Rez nodded and sat on the farthest bed, where I'd tossed her suitcase, rubbing her hands together. "Thank you, by the way."

I jerked to look at her. "You're thanking me for coming to rescue you?"

"Yes…?" She leaned her head to the side. "Did I not say it right or something?"

"You don't have to thank me, darlin'. Nothing would have kept me from tracking you down."

She looked down at her lap, a soft smile teasing her mouth. "Well, thank you anyway."

"You can get me back next time, sweetheart. I can play the damsel."

Her brows hitched, her eyes glinting.

Hell. I didn't need to see that look from her right now. I was already riled enough.

"Uh…let's see if they have anything to drink in this place." I went to the mini-fridge stuffed under the counter. Awkward tension jumped around me like a dozen screaming children. I opened the fridge and peered at the contents. "Beer, mustard, and baking soda…sounds like my typical dinner."

Rez chuckled, rising from the bed. "Actually, I think I'm going to crawl into bed. Put an end to this day."

"Are you sure you're all right?" I stood, shutting the door, and leaned against the counter.

"West, if you ask me again, I'm going to go beg those guys to take me back."

I folded my arms. "Not funny."

"Oh, look who's lost his sense of humor in the last eight hours." She crossed her arms, mimicking me.

"And look who still doesn't have one," I grumbled.

"West, I'm fine. They only roughed me up when I tried to escape while they were tying me up. Otherwise they didn't do anything to me. They didn't ask me anything or even talk to each other. That was creepier than anything else."

"Strange. Why kidnap you and do nothing? They didn't even ask you about the spear or what you know? It doesn't make sense." I tilted back farther against the counter. Nothing about these fae or humans felt right. They had yet to utter a word. To tell us why they were after us.

"No, it doesn't." She rubbed her head. "But maybe they were waiting for the person in charge and you showed up first...I don't know. I'm simply glad to be away from them. They acted like zombies."

That was exactly what I had thought.

"Tonight I want to forget about it. Take a shower, crawl into bed, and deal with everything tomorrow." She grabbed toiletries from her bag and headed for the bathroom but quickly snapped back to me. "Because we *are* going forward with the mission tomorrow. No buts. We know where it is now and have men after us for it. We need to get it before they do."

She watched my reaction, seeing if I would contradict her. I only nodded, which caused her to frown with skepticism. "That means no secret calls to Lars and getting me sent home or sidelined somehow."

"Wouldn't dream of it. We're partners. In this to the end. Together." I crossed my ankles, the tabletop creaking under my weight.

"O-kay then..." Rez's lids tapered in mistrust, taken back by my declaration. She was ready for me to fight, to demand she go home because it was too dangerous.

And I wanted to. Gods, how I wanted to. But I learned my lesson earlier. She was equal in this with me, and I had no right to demand her to go. If anything, tonight had showed me she could handle herself and was far stronger than I gave her credit for.

Plus, I couldn't deny, as much as I wanted her to go

and free myself of temptation, as much of me wanted her to stay. To keep torturing me.

Rez gave me one last suspicious glance then went into the bathroom. Only a few seconds passed after I heard the water turn on. The sound of cascading water was relaxing. I wanted to take a shower too, but merely getting over to the bed was an exhausting task.

I stripped off the layers and slipped under the covers in my briefs. I really wanted to be naked but thought it might be a little too much with the King's mistress sharing my room.

I was drifting off when I heard the bed next to me squeak as Rez climbed in. Her presence was like a fresh breeze with sweet and salty undertones. Her smell sparked something deep in my core. I felt myself sigh deeply before sleep took me under.

*"I've missed you so much, Will." The soft southern drawl was so familiar, like honey, soothing the unhealed wounds in my heart. I looked to her face and wanted to cry.*

*"Cammie." Her name caught on my tongue, aching in my chest. No words seemed to be good enough, no apology or declarations fitting for what I felt.*

*"Don't you miss me too?" She sloped her neck to the side.*

*"Oh gods, yes," I choked. "Every day."*

*"I feel like I'm losing you." She held out her hand for me. "I don't want you to leave me. I love you so much."*

*Every step I took felt like I was slopping through mud, not bringing me any closer to her.*

*"You left me, Will." Sadness lowered her lashes. "How could you do that?"*

*"No…no, I didn't." She had left me. And it was all my fault. "I loved you."*

*"Did you?" Doubt coated her accent. "If you really loved me, you wouldn't be leaving me. I can feel it…you don't love me anymore."*

*"That's not true." I kept moving toward her, wanting nothing more than to touch her, to feel her skin on mine. "I will never stop loving you, Cam."*

*"Not in the same way." Tears glazed her hazel eyes. "You're forgetting, letting what we had die. Don't you think I deserve more than that? After what you did?"*

*She deserved everything.*

*"You can so easily forget me."*

*"Forget you? I think about you all the time."*

*"Not lately. Your thoughts are being taken away from me. I'm being replaced by another."*

*"You could never be replaced."*

*"Prove it." She beckoned me again. "Come with me, join me. Say you want us to be together again."*

*A sharp noise broke through the air, pulling my focus away from Cammie.*

*"No," Cammie shouted, her hand reaching out for me. "Come with me. We belong together. You and I. We deserve this…forever."*

*The sound came again, piercing my subconscious. I glanced behind me, searching. I didn't know for what, but a nagging feeling tugged at me.*

*"West!" Cammie yelled my name, desperation in her voice, bringing me back to her. "Take my hand. Come with me." A tickle of reservation shot through me. My feet scuffled to a stop. That was not the name she knew me as. It sounded strange coming from her.*

*"West, stop!" I heard the voice again, a deeper call,*

*singing to every nerve ending in my body with a strange desire. I was about to turn around, when Cammie cried out.*

*"No...don't leave me. You promised me forever." She reached for me, her face growing anxious. "Please, I need you. Just a few more steps, my love."*

*I hesitated, but those hazel eyes full of longing and sadness were always my undoing. I lifted my arms, taking the step to Cammie. Our fingertips almost touched.*

*Then something hit me, taking me down. My head slammed against the ground. I blinked my eyes. A form sat on top of me, the glow of the moon sparkled off her long hair, her face completely hidden in the shadows of the dark night. All I could see was long blond hair, a girl riding me fiercely. It reminded me of the night we devoured each other under the night sky on the sand dunes. The air hot and sticky. The soft waves rolling onto shore.*

*"You're here." Her skin was soft upon mine, the weight of her body solid, corporeal. My brain didn't want to know if this was a dream. It wanted to feel peace for once. My hands went to her face, pulling her to me.*

*"West. I'm—"*

*"I'm so sorry. Forgive me," I whispered, anxious to feel her lips on mine again. My lids closed, my fingers laced through her hair to the back of her head and drew her to me. My mouth took hers with rough, unrestrained need. I heard my name again, but I answered by gripping her head tighter, my mouth devouring hers. Any resistance I felt at first quickly dissolved as I crushed her tighter into me, breathing her in with every demanding kiss. My tongue prodded her mouth to open more for me. She responded in kind, deepening our already hungry mouths.*

*Oh Jesus. It was better than I remembered. The beast rousing inside wanted her. Badly.*

*One hand stayed in her hair, the other slid down to her hip, to her pants line, dipping below and curving around her ass. Strange. Hadn't she been wearing a sundress? A slight moan broke from her. Hands glided through my hair, sending sensual chills throughout my body as she raked them over my scalp. Our lips were desperate, only wanting more.*

*This was a dream. One I didn't want to wake from. Nothing felt so real, so unbelievably good. The beast was going crazy. It wanted to claim. To take her. To thrust into her until we exploded and broke, like the waves against the shore.*

*I took a deep breath. Another alarm curled around my mind. Cammie had smelled like lilac and jasmine. But in this dream she smelled more like a perfect evening at the beach, with a dash of sweetness, like someone making cookies in the distance. Sweet and salty. This smell twisted my beast into a fury. I enjoyed Cammie's flowery smell, but this triggered something deep in my core. Something I wanted to fall into and never come out of again.*

*I growled and flipped her on her back, crawling between her legs. My hands tore at the tie at the front of her soft pants, my mouth on her neck. Nipping.*

*"Oh gods, West, we need to stop," she whispered, but her tone was full of need, urging me to keep going.*

*This was my dream. And I wanted to feel myself sink into her, even if it wasn't real. I had been waiting much too long to feel this way again. No matter how many girls I had bedded, nothing felt like this. Electricity sizzled through my body at her touch. Her smell.*

*My mouth moved down her chest, pawing at her jacket. My jacket. The symbolism only rallied the beast, which liked the small token of me on her. I unzipped the jacket, my brain sending me more reservations: a silky camisole. No bra. Cammie had not been curvy up top. She was lean and thin, and had legs for days. I didn't mind. I loved all shapes and sizes. Women were gorgeous whatever way they came. Period.*

*"I want to be inside you," I huffed harshly, my body straining with yearning, cupping the fuller breasts.*

*"West," she breathed heavily into my ear, pulling my ass into her.*

*"Cammie…" My teeth grazed up her neck.*

*The moment I muttered the name, her body went tense beneath mine. "Stop." Her hands pushed at my chest. "West, stop. Wake up." My cheek stung and I jerked back. Shit. That felt far too painful to be a dream.*

---

"I'm not Cammie!"

I blinked several times. Wavy blond hair changed into long, silky chocolate tresses, hazel eyes into brown. Rez's face came into focus. She was propped on her elbows, half her body still beneath mine. Her pajama pants were untied showing a slip of silky underwear, her lips swollen.

Holy. Shit. Rez.

I scrambled to safety faster than you'd leap out of an alligator-infested river. "Oh gods." I ran my hand over my face and turned away, taking a few steps to gain distance between me and the King's girlfriend.

"West. It's okay." Rez got to her feet. Out of the corner of my eye I saw her retying her pajama bottoms, and I cringed.

I swung around. "Okay? It's not *anywhere* near that. I kissed you…"

"You thought I was someone else." Her gaze slid to the side, and she folded her arms against the chronic breeze blowing over the cliff.

I did. Mostly...

"Why didn't you stop me?" I demanded. The heat of her still clung to me.

"I tried. You really didn't give me much of a choice." She shifted her weight, her hand touching her swollen bottom lip. Puffy because I kissed the shit out of her.

I bent over, pressed my hands to my knees. *Breathe, West, breathe.* Whatever the premise, innocent or not, I had just stuck my tongue down the throat of the woman bedding our King. And I would have stuck other things into her, too, if she hadn't slapped me out of my trance.

The beast hit against the cage, wanting more. A warning rumbled in my chest, telling it to shut the hell up and sit in the corner. It basically flipped me off.

*It's only because I thought she was Cammie*, I told myself. *It was simply a mistake. Nothing more.*

"Don't worry. It's no big deal." She shifted her legs again and brushed her tangled hair behind her ear. Her cheeks were flushed. She was probably lying, but I wasn't about to push for the truth. Hiding behind a lie sounded excellent to me.

"Already forgotten." Another lie.

The severe chill in the air helped clear my mind, moving me on from making out with Rez to the fact I was standing on the cliff in the middle of the night and wearing only my briefs, my cock displaying its eagerness to continue.

"What...the...hell?" I circled around, holding my arms out. "How did I get here?"

"You were walking in your sleep again," Rez answered. "I woke and you were gone. *Again*. It was lucky I found you in time." Her gaze trailed to the edge of the cliff.

"What? I was about to walk off it?" A chill iced the back of my neck.

"Yes. I had to tackle you. You didn't hear me...and you were about to go over." She shook her head as if trying to toss out the vision.

The image of Cammie motioning me forward, to *join* her, flooded back. Were my dreams trying to kill me? They started out as occasional nightmares, then grew to frequent night terrors with me waking up on the floor in cold sweats. Now my guilt was taking me over cliffs?

I gaped for a moment at the ledge, keenly aware of the jagged rocks below. Fae were hard to kill but not impossible. Actually, we were more vulnerable since the worlds merged. Those rocks would have probably ripped me into tiny pieces.

"Thank you." I nodded at Rez.

"You're welcome." She nodded back. "Now let's go back. I'm freezing." She was shaking, even beneath my jacket.

"You are?" I waved down at my mostly naked body. "You wouldn't be a *gentleman* and let me have my jacket back?" I gave her a half smile.

"Hell no. Your jacket is the only thing keeping me from hypothermia."

"You didn't bring it out here for me? I'm only wearing boxers."

"You're mostly beast. I think you can handle it. I'm wearing a thin camisole." She smirked, turning for the cabin, wrapping it tighter. Devil woman. "It was the first thing I could find. You should be thankful I didn't take the time to find mine."

"You mean the one hanging right by the door?" I teased, remembering her hanging it there earlier.

"Shut up," she muttered and picked up her pace.

I chuckled and followed her back to the house. Truth was, I liked her wearing my clothes more than I would ever have admitted. But I had already made things really awkward for us.

Nothing about this night should ever be talked about again.

Especially the kiss.

Damn...that kiss...

When would I stop destroying everyone around me with one impulsive act?

# SEVENTEEN

Not long after we walked in, I built a fire in the stone hearth and insisted Rez sit right next to it on the rug. I tugged off the bed comforter and wrapped it around her.

She was right, I could handle cold. My beast burned hot underneath, although even I found the wind whipping off the water and shooting over the Cliffs of Moher bone chilling. I had pulled on a pair of sweats, keeping my chest bare. We seemed past the "appropriate" clothing rule.

"Thank you." Her teeth chattered when I handed her a warm cup of tea.

"The least I can do after saving my life." I snorted. "Guess we're even. Didn't think I'd be playing the damsel this soon."

"Not quite even." She cupped the mug close to her.

My jaw snapped together, and I turned back to the sink, looking outside.

"Talk to me, West. I want to know about these nightmares."

"They're none of your business." I wrapped my fingers

around the lip of the sink and leaned over, defensive anger coiling up my spine.

"Don't you think you walking off a cliff in the middle of the night is my business? The last time was across a field leading to a bluff." She kept her voice soft but strong. "We're in this together, remember? We have to depend on each other. I need to know why my partner is wanting to fling himself into the ocean." She shook her head, her hair covering her face. "And *I am* your friend, West. I care about you."

"You don't know me at all."

"Enough," she snapped, whipping me around to face her. "I'm not going to pretend tonight didn't happen. You thought I was this Cammie. You cry her name a lot in your sleep. Along with Aneira's."

"Not the only names I've ever screamed out in the night, darlin'." My lips lifted in a smirk.

"West! For once," she glanced at the ceiling, "can't you be real with me?"

"This is real."

"No. It's not." She glared. "Don't think for a moment I don't see past the façade. The cheeky, flirty thing is a part of you. But not all of you. You have so much darkness in you, but you hide it behind the jokes."

"I'm a Dark Dweller." Anger bristled under my skin, but I wasn't angry at her.

"You know what I mean." She set down her mug. "Who is Cammie? What did she mean to you?"

"No, we're not doing this."

"Yes. We. Are. Sit down and talk to me. Now," she yelled, motioning to the spot next to her. Even screaming at me, the woman's voice was like butter. More the kind you pulled out of a really cold refrigerator, but still creamy, rich, and soothing. I knew I wouldn't deny her.

"Shit," I mumbled and grabbed a beer from the small fridge. I sat, slamming my back against the bed frame next to her, my jaw cracking with tension. Cammie was the last person I wanted to talk about. She and Aneira haunted me, consumed my dreams, but for two completely different reasons. One because she destroyed my soul, and one because I destroyed hers.

I carried the memory for so long. What I did. The true monster I was. What Aneira subjected me to was nothing compared to what I did to a sweet, innocent girl.

Aneira's humiliation and torture wasn't surprising. She did what was in her nature, and I was the enemy. We both knew it. There really were no surprises. She went beyond the normal torture, but still I went in somewhat prepared. A prisoner understands it's not going to be a good time.

But Cammie was unaware. Naïve. She thought she knew the guy she went to bed with at night. Every lie I crafted, every time I kissed her added to her doom. My own selfishness couldn't leave her be. The need to find happiness, peace, a home, a life...took away hers. Cammie's memory had become so vivid. Guilt and sadness engulfed me, bringing her back to life to torment me. I could feel her pushing against the lock where I had her contained, wanting her story to be heard.

I leaned forward, grabbed the fire poker, and stuffed it deeper into the ashes, stirring the flame and my memory.

"I was a man in love. Stupid and impulsive."

Rez didn't move, her lids lowered on the fire, but I felt her undivided attention on every word.

"Her name was Cammie. Cammelia Delilah Montgomery. Couldn't get any more southern than that," I said with a chuckle. I took a sip of my beer, setting down the poker. "From the instant I met her, the thought of being without her felt like a death sentence." I shook my head at my naiveté. "It was the first time I had experienced love like that. The kind which completely engulfs you." I glanced over and our eyes caught and held contact. I squinted back at the fire, rolling the bottle between my fingers. "The other members of my clan always had a sense of home, a sense of each other. I didn't." I swallowed, the declaration hard for me to say out loud. "Growing up the way I did, I always felt separated from them. Restless. Searching."

The fire crackled and popped, sparks drifting up the chimney like lightning bugs.

"I thought I found it with her, whatever hole I was searching to fill. I ignored everything and pushed away the truth." My chest clenched, more memories streaming in, cutting off my words.

"What truth?" Rez gently encouraged me to keep talking. What she didn't realize was I couldn't have stopped now if I wanted to, the memories crashed against me, needing to get out of their prison I kept them in for so long.

The bed frame creaked as I rested back into it.

"That we could never be."

"Why?"

My tongue slipped over my bottom lip and I exhaled. "Because she was human. And back then the rule was…"

"No human could find out about us," Rez filled in for me. Before the wall between worlds came down, fae were a guarded secret. No gray area existed.

"My clan has killed many. That's what we did. We were hired assassins. When we lost most of our tribe and were banished to Earth, Cole became leader. Our life here was different. He and Owen were the eldest and ran the clan, but some of us realized we were more than executioners. We kept to ourselves, stopped killing... unless they came after us or hurt one of our own. We could never totally change our nature; we only curbed it. Some of us took the adjustment better than others. I was one who struggled. Not with killing, but finding my place. No one knew. Keeping to myself was usual for me.

"Watching everyone else adapt to Earth only made me feel like more of an outsider. I took off, leaving the only family I had ever known and traveled around, seeking a place to fit in." I finished off my beer, setting the bottle down with a clink.

"Dark Dwellers are like pack animals and live in clans. But unlike Cole, Eli, or Cooper, who would do anything for their family and sacrifice anything to protect them, I was different. I loved my family and would do anything for them, but I didn't feel the same undeniable devotion to stay.

"I traveled for months, going wherever my bike took me. Feeling as lost and even more alone. But then I was passing through a small town near Myrtle Beach. She was a waitress, and the moment she walked up to the table, with her southern accent and wholesomeness, I was hooked. Growing up in the Otherworld, naiveté is a death sentence. She was a breath of fresh air, and I needed her sweetness in my life then. Not that she hadn't gone through shit. Her mother and most of her past relationships were a horror show, but she came out okay somehow."

I smiled, recalling her walking to my table with a pink diner uniform on, her long wavy blond hair pulled back in a ponytail, her hazel eyes guarded but full of sass. She had legs that went on forever.

"She resisted my advances at first, but I knew it was

only a front. It wasn't long before we were completely consumed. She invited me over for dinner on our third date, and I never left. We barely came up for air. We both fell fast and hard. For eight months we lived in happy bliss." I rubbed my chin, choking back another wave of emotion. "I thought she was it, the one. I had found home. The beast had finally calmed for the first time ever. It had never claimed a mate before, so I thought the serene mood meant it was going to. I wanted to believe more than anything."

"What happened to her?

I blinked, the picture of Cammie's face forming behind my lids brought waves of grief.

"The only rule Cole was clear about, the only one we could not break," I said hoarsely, "was to never let a human find out about us. If only I'd listened. Deep down I still was a Dark Dweller. No matter how far I'd run, I could never escape that or my brothers. They found me in South Carolina."

My jaw clenched as a memory flickered through my mind. It always came back to *her*—the woman who gave her heart to me completely—her soft skin, long blond hair, soft hazel eyes staring at me with adoration. Then came the memory of those same eyes looking at me with utter fright and betrayal. I shook my head, trying to dislodge her face from my mind. It was pointless. She was burned into my memory. The sounds of her terrified screams were etched into my soul forever.

"After almost four years of being on the run, they suddenly showed up. Strange how one impulsive choice can change everything. End everything..." The day flooded back like a movie in my head. One I wished I could rewind and do over.

*Blond tresses curled over the pillow, and I buried my nose deeper into her locks, smelling the honey-and-flower shampoo she used. Her golden skin, tanned from the summer on the beach, curved temptingly into my body, making me desperate for her again. I bit down on my lip. I had to take it easy with her. Humans didn't have the sex drive fae did, nor could I completely let myself go. Humans, I was beginning to learn, were tough on the inside, but their bodies and lives were fragile. Fleeting.*

*I had pushed it enough with her. I had almost gone too far last night.*

*My hand brushed the hair away from her face, a smile hinting at her lips at my touch. Even asleep she was the most beautiful thing I'd ever seen. Fae or human. Dark Dwellers had been on Earth for seven years, but this was the first time I truly felt happy.*

*But the future loomed over my head like a heavy shadow. She told me last night she was in love with me. Saw her future with me. Marriage. Kids.*

*I wanted those things too. The entire dream. Blond rug rats running around on the beach with my gorgeous wife by my side. I'd work in the motorcycle shop down the street, while she opened a café of her own near the water. A perfect, simple life. Deep inside I understood it was a dream, but as I stared at her right then, all I wanted was to make it true for her. For me.*

*I didn't want to think I was either condemning her to a life with no kids or one where she could die if she had mine. When Owen lost Jared's mother in childbirth, it practically killed him. Could I do that to Cammie?*

*Every day I lived a lie. Human, William Miller from Georgia, with accent and all. No family, no home, no direction until I found her. I told her the truth—I lost my parents young, but I hid the truth of my clan, my brothers and sisters living on the other side of the US. I had not told her who I was. What I was.*

*I kissed her temple and slipped from the bed, settling to fulfill my need for her in the shower. Then I got dressed and walked out of our three-bedroom beach cottage to work. The bike shop was only four blocks from our place. Bill finally hired me after two months of hounding him. I took pride in my first legitimate job. Back in Washington, my family had been involved in procuring and selling illegal items. But a bunch of terrifying bikers, who scared even the toughest fae, didn't fit easily into society. We quickly joined the dark human underbelly, gaining a name and prestige in the biker community as dudes not to mess with.*

*I clocked in, clocked out, and got a check every other week, which was pitiful from what I used to make. For Cammie, it was worth it.*

*"About time, Miller," Bill grumbled, stepping out of his office, wiping his greasy hands on an even greasier cloth. "Was about to clean out your locker."*

*"Sure, Bill." I rolled my eyes, heading to the employee room. He'd never fire me. Once he realized how good I was with bikes and how many people, especially woman riders, requested I do custom upgrades on their hogs, he doubled my schedule and upped my pay to keep me happy.*

*I slipped on my work coveralls over my clothes, grabbed coffee, and set out for the bike I was working on, greeting the other employees as I passed.*

Jesus, you're so mundane…normal, *I thought, shaking my head. If anyone knew the truth, knew the slaughtering beast lurking only feet away from them…*

*My morning slipped by quickly, my mind absorbed on*

*the job. I was surprised when I heard Cammie's voice talking to Bill.*

*"I brought you guys jerk chicken, coleslaw, buttermilk biscuits, and brownies for dessert."*

*"Sweetheart, if you ever get tired of him, you can cook for me any time you want," Bill said. Cammie was the only person Bill softened around. She had all the guys here around her finger. She was an incredible cook and enjoyed bringing us all lunch before she went to work at the café.*

*I heard her laugh. "Not sure I could ever get tired of Will, but I'll keep it in mind."*

*I strolled around the corner, my smile spreading across my face at the sight of my girl. Her hair was loose around her shoulders, and she wore a cornflower blue sundress and brown sandals. She was breathtaking.*

*"Thought I heard my girl." I swept her up in my arms, kissing her deeply.*

*"I brought food," she muttered when I let her breathe.*

*"Think I'd rather have you, darlin'." I nipped her lip, the beast stirring.*

*Bill cleared his throat behind me, and I set her down.*

*"Thank you, Cammie. I'll take this back to the breakroom. The guys have never been fed so well." Bill picked up the basket and walked to the back. "Don't lose that one, Miller. She's the only reason you have a job here. Can't lose food this good."*

*"Yeah, yeah." I brushed off his comment, keeping my eyes on Cammie. "Don't worry, I won't let this one go. Ever."*

*A smile spread over her face, and her hazel eyes glinted with love. She rose on her toes, her mouth finding mine, and we quickly got lost in each other.*

*"West," a deep voice called from the garage doorway.*

*One word. One moment.*

*Everything changed.*

*Ice spread over my lungs, my head jerked to the door, where three men stood at the entry. My careful, comfortable world shredded into thin slices. Panic tore into my veins, making me feel cold and guarded. I pulled away from Cammie, stepping in front of her, my brain still struggling at the sight of my pack standing before me.*

*"How did you find me?"*

*"You always knew we would," Eli replied.*

*I had been gone for more than four years, and he had grown into a man in my absence. He was huge, at least six four. Taller than me, and built like a swimmer or soccer player. Broad shoulders, muscles bulging down his arms. His brown hair long and scruff lined his jaw. But it was the same piercing green eyes which used to see through me as a kid that stared at me now. Lorcan, his older brother, stood next to him. He was around my age and hadn't changed much. Same green eyes as Eli's, but shorter and took more after their mother, with the round face, but still there was a striking resemblance to their father, our old leader, Dragen. Cooper was on Eli's right. He had developed as well and was built like he spent time between a gym, a bike, and a surfboard.*

*As Dark Dwellers, violence and sex pulsed beneath their skin, like they could go either way at any time.*

*"You're family. We will always come for you." Eli took a step forward. My hands automatically shot back onto Cammie, pushing her back protectively.*

*"Will, what's going on?" She tried to look around my shoulder, her eyes widening at the three men. I could hear her heart beat extra fast.*

*"Will?" Cooper lifted one brow.*

*"Nothing. They were just leaving, right?" I nodded to the door.*

*Cooper folded his arms. "Cole wants you home. With your family."*

*"Home?" Cammie repeated. "What does he mean home? You told me you didn't have any family."*

*One of many lies.*

*"Ouch, West." Lorcan palmed his chest in false hurt. "Trying not to take it personal."*

*I glowered at him before turning back to Cammie. "Get out of here, darlin'."*

*"What?" She shook her head. "No. Not till I know what is going on."*

*"Go. Home. Cammie," I seethed through my teeth, my temper surging with my anxiety.*

*"Do as he says." Eli took another step closer, his voice commanding. I could feel his power. His magic throbbing in the space.*

*Holy shit. The alpha in him condensed the air, ready to punish me for my insolence. My beast bent his head to his leader. When the fuck did that happen? Eli was the second? Not Lorcan? This made me even more nervous. All Lorcan ever wanted was to eventually be alpha. Take his father's place, but his little brother got the second spot instead? That couldn't have gone over well.*

*"Please." I clutched her wrists, shaking them.*

*Her hazel eyes looked into mine, fright consuming them. For me.*

*"Don't worry. They won't hurt me, darlin'."*

*Lorcan snorted. "I could still kick your ass. Especially now." Lorcan's ego always got the better of him. Ever since we were kids, he had something to prove. He once had been a cool guy, the one who snuck me food when my mom ran out, but something happened, he changed. Grew bitter and angry.*

*"Go. I'll be home later," I whispered softly.*

*"Promise?"*

*I nodded, cupping her cheek, and pulled her in for a quick kiss.*

*Cammie slowly stepped away from me, her gaze darting nervously from me to the guys. She squeezed my arm, then headed for the door.*

*The moment it shut, I swung around, anger blazing off me. "What the hell are you guys doing here?"*

*"Good to see you too." Cooper frowned.*

*"Don't you think we should ask you that? Picked up more than the girl. Love the southern accent there, lover boy. Part of your cover, Will?" Lorcan smirked.*

*It had been at first. Now it was part of me.*

*"Don't tell me you work here?" Lorcan held up his hands, motioning around the space in horror.*

*"Yeah, I do." I folded my arms. "I have a job, a girl, a life."*

*"A lie." Eli lifted an eyebrow, cutting straight to the bone. "What are you doing, West? She's human. You know this can't last."*

*My nostrils flared.*

*Lorcan walked to me with his arrogant strut. "She's a hot piece of ass, I'll give you that, but I know you better than anyone. I can tell she's different. She's more than a place to stick your dick."*

*"I think she'll notice when she ages and you don't." Eli's green eyes burrowed down on me, and I looked away.*

*"When the fuck did you become alpha?" I mumbled.*

*"When you were gone," Eli replied coolly. "You've missed a lot. Jared is growing up, gonna be five soon. He doesn't even know you." Eli's comment nipped at my soul.*

*Jared.*

*The day he was born should have been a happy day, but Owen lost his love, the mother of his child, the same moment. Still, we gained this brilliant light. The moment Jared came to us was really the day we fully changed. He steered us away from our old life. The half-Dark Dweller, half-human baby, fragile and innocent, peered at us with those hazel eyes and Donovan family features. He had us completely in his tiny hands. Any one of us would have turned the world upside down for him. Missing his first years drove a nail into my heart, but for so long I had pushed all of them far in the background so I could forget. I forgot his giggle and chubby cheeks.*

*Now it was exploding in my face. How could I have left him? So many nights I had stayed by his crib, making sure he was fed and protected. Then one day I just got up and left. Left him.*

*But I had found peace, and I would not let it go. "You wasted your time. I'm not going with you. I'm happy here."*

*"You can keep lying to yourself, but if you really care for this girl, you will let her go now. We need you home."*

*"No."*

*Eli was on me in a split second. He seized my collar and slammed me against the wall. His eyes flashed red. "I don't think you understand the severity of what's going on."*

*Adrenaline surged through me.*

*"We're here because your family needs you, not because we had nothing better to do," Eli growled.*

*I swallowed, glancing around at the other two. They stood rigidly, not smiling. Eli wasn't playing with me.*

*"A group of Dark fae have found out we're on Earth. They killed Dex."*

*"What?" I jerked my head to Lorcan. Dexter and his twin brother, Daxtan, were notorious troublemakers in our pack and best friends with Lorcan. The three were inseparable. Dex treated life like he was invisible and no one else mattered. I never liked him much, but he was one of our own.*

*Eli loosened his grip, and I stepped away. "Sorry, man." I nodded to Lorcan. He pursed his lips, sliding his hands in his pockets. "But this doesn't change my mind. I don't want to be part of that life anymore."*

*"Please. We all know that's a lie. I can sense your beast from here, ready to let go. When was the last time you let him out?" Lorcan cut to the truth. I barely let it out anymore.*

*"This isn't up for discussion. They know about Jared. They say they are coming for him. Cole demands your presence back home." Eli shifted, rolling his shoulders back. "We will give you an hour to say your goodbyes, then we will come for you. Sorry, West, but family comes first. You owe Jared that."*

*I gritted my teeth, my chest lowering and rising in my chest. "Is that an order?"*

*Eli tilted his head, a hint of disappointment in his face. "Yes."*

*The alpha had spoken, and I could feel the order curl around my muscles. For so long I believed I was on my own, starting my new life.*

*With one word that life was over.*

---

*I burst through the front door of the tiny house Cammie and I shared. I didn't even give pause to tell Bill I was leaving. The job no longer mattered. The life I had been building here had been wiped away in seconds. I would never set foot in there again. The only thing that mattered was Cammie. Panic clogged my head, shutting down logic. My beast felt like it was being backed into a corner.*

*"Will?" Cammie jumped as the door banged open and I stomped in. She stood in the kitchen, worry contorting her features. She rushed to me. "You're home. Are you okay?"*

*"Get your stuff."*

*"What?" Confusion knotted her eyebrows.*

*"Pack. We're leaving." I stormed to the bedroom closet, grabbed her suitcase, and threw it on the bed. "Take only what you need."*

*"Will, stop!" She clutched my bicep. "Tell me what's going on. Are you in trouble?"*

*I grumbled, heading to her dresser, my hands swooping a handful of her undergarments and tossing them in the suitcase.*

*"Will, please. Talk to me. Who were those men?" She flung her arms around.*

*"They're the closest I have to family." I reached for another bag, stuffing more tops in it.*

*"Then why are you running from them? I don't understand."*

*"Let's say my family is kind of like the mafia. You're born into them and you can never leave."*

*"Are they going to hurt you? What do they want?"*

*My family would never hurt me, physically, but Cole's demand I come home would kill my heart. I couldn't take Cammie back with me. Humans were a strict no-no. It was the only stringent rule we had. And I was stupid enough to let myself fall for one.*

*She danced around me as I continued to tornado through the room, grabbing anything I could grab.*

*"Will. Enough!" She seized my hand, stopping me. "I'm not leaving. This is my home. My job is here. Your job. I just put a down payment on the café on the water."*

*I whirled around, gripping her arms. "We can start over somewhere else. You don't understand..."*

*"You're right, I don't." She reached up, touching my face. "I love you. I want to have your children in this house, grow old with you here. I want to create a life in this home."*

*I squeezed my lids together as her fingertips trailed my face. How could I take that away from her? This was her grandmother's house, and she spent every summer here growing up. Every inch of space held a memory of hers. When her grandma passed, she left it to Cammie. She would never leave. And I couldn't ask her to.*

*I rubbed at my face anxiously. The idea of forcing her to leave and never giving her a clear reason why broke me as much as walking away from her.*

*Could I look at myself in the mirror if something happened to Jared and I turned my back on them? If one of us was threatened, the whole family showed up. I was one of the best fighters. When it came to a pack, we each had our role, like wolves. When one left, a part was missing.*

*"You told me you had no family. Why did you lie to me?" She twisted me back around to face her.*

*"There is a lot you don't know about me."*

*"What? Are you a fugitive or something?" She laughed.*

*I hesitated. Technically in the Otherworld we were.*

*Humor slid from her features, her hand covering her mouth. "Oh my God."*

*"No." I reached for her, but she jerked away. "It's not what you think."*

*"You don't know what I think." She stepped back.*

*"Cam..." My hand went for her wrist. She batted it away.*

*"Why did they call you West?"*

*Again another lie wrapped around my tongue ready to fall on her like the rest. Lying had gotten too easy for me, but remembering the lies was getting harder.*

*"Is William even your name?" Her huge eyes widened farther.*

*I pressed my lips together.*

*"Oh God." Her hand went to her stomach.*

*"Darlin', listen."*

*"Don't darlin' me." Her eyes filled with tears. "What is your real name?"*

*"That's not important."*

*"Yes, it is! Tell me!"*

*I rocked back on my heels, bowing my head.*

*"West. West Moseley."*

*"Oh my," she muttered, turning away. Her hand went to her mouth again, a tear rolling down her cheek.*

*How could I not see this coming? The pain I would cause her.*

*"Is there anything you didn't lie to me about?"*

*"Yes." I grabbed her arms again. "I was totally honest about how I feel about you. I am in love with you, Cammie."*

*A crazed laugh came from her. "Love? You have no*

*idea what love is. Love means being truthful, completely honest and open."*

*I couldn't respond, which only sent her off more.*

*"I told you! I told you how I felt about being lied to. I have been betrayed so many times in my life. It was the only thing I asked of you. Just to be honest with me. Why? Why was that so hard to do?"*

*"Because I can't."*

*"Why? What have you done? Who are you running from? I mean, have you killed someone or something?"*

*I'd killed a lot of people, so I kept quiet.*

*She swore and turned from me, running out of the room.*

*"Cammie." I bolted out of the door after her.*

*"Stay away from me!"*

*I ignored her pleas and circled my arms around her, bringing her into me. "I'd never hurt you. You know that, right? I love you."*

*"That's usually when people do." Agony and confusion rippled over her face, tears raining down.*

*"I don't want to lose you, darlin'," I whispered against her ear.*

*"I need to know the truth." She was rigid in my arms but stopped trying to pull away. "All of it."*

*"I'm not sure you're ready for that. It's more than just my name. I'm only trying to keep you safe." The words fell from my mouth before I could stop them.*

*Cammie ripped out of my hold, her wavy blond hair tangling in my fingers as she shoved me away.*

*"Don't act like you're shielding me. You're only looking out for yourself."*

*"No. Believe me. This is for you," I yelled back. Energy blasted into me, and I knew a few seconds before they knocked my brothers were there. Fuck. They were already here. Panic steamrolled through my veins.*

*"West, it's time," Eli broke into my head, talking through our link. It jolted me to hear him so strong through the connection. I hadn't heard any of them for years.*

*Cammie flinched when a fist pounded on the door.*

*"Cammie, listen to me. We don't have a lot of time."*

*Her attention was still on the door when I grabbed her chin to bring it back to me.*

*"You want to know the truth? The real me?" I could feel where I was going, desperation making me act, turning off every warning bell and logical thought.*

*"Yes. I want to know everything about you. Whatever trouble you're in, we can figure it out together."*

*"West?" Eli spoke through the door, a slight warning in his tone. He could hear every word I said. His presence only seemed to induce me to act faster.*

*"I'm not in trouble. It's not like that. It's not who I am but more of what I am."*

*"West! What the fuck are you doing, brother?" Eli beat on the door again. Anxiety tightened his voice. They would break through that flimsy door in a moment trying to stop me.*

*"What are you talking about?" Her head kept snapping to the door then back to me. Her southern politeness struggled with not opening the door and greeting the visitor, but I held her in place.*

*"I need you to be really open to what I'm about to tell you."*

*"West. Don't." The door shook as someone slammed into it.*

*Cammie yelped, her body trembling. The beast could taste her fear on its tongue, waking it from the slumber I put it in.*

*"I'm not...I'm not what you think. I'm not human." I ignored the shuddering of the door, the creaking of wood. Cammie's unease rose with every breath and boiled under the surface. I should have stopped, should have known her human brain was not calm enough to accept what I was about to show her, but I couldn't. I thought this was the only way I could save us. If she really saw me, the beast would claim her. He wanted to, I could feel it, but hadn't yet. Once she was my mate, they couldn't part us, or hurt her.*

*I dropped one hand from her, raising it between us. I would start out small. Let her first see I was more than human.*

*Out of the corner of my eye I saw Cooper come around the glass doors in the back, his fist breaking through, going for the lock.*

*"Don't do this, man. You know the rules." He swung open the door. The front door burst open at the same time, Eli and Lorcan charging into the house.*

*It was too late. My arm shifted into the beast's claw. Silky, deep black fur grew up my arm. Claws like scythes protruded from the tips of my fingers, displaying the killing machine I was.*

*Everything froze for a moment. Then Cammie's eyes widened as she took in my hand, a gurgled cry humming in her chest.*

*I had to speak. Calm her down. "Don't be scared." I ignored the guys, keeping my gaze on her. But my words had little effect on her.*

*Her body went from shaking to convulsing and a shrill scream came out of her lungs, flushing chills down my back. And the shrieks didn't stop.*

*"Cammie, it's okay. It's still me." I let go of the beast, my hand shifting back to normal. "I'm what you call a Dark Dweller. I'm a fae from the Otherworld." I could hear my desperation for her to understand, the pleading growing more frantic.*

*She backpedaled away from me, her terrorized eyes glancing around the room at the huge figures looming around her. I could sense she knew we were all the same. Something she didn't understand. Threats.*

*I'd considered telling her before, but every time I played it out in my mind, I eased her into it. Slowly let her see my true nature. Reality gave me no luxury. I threw her in headfirst. I wanted to believe her love would overcome her fright. Noting the hysterical fear pumping off her, this would not be the case. "Cammie. Please." I reached for her. She screamed louder, painful, frenetic wails.*

*She thought she wanted to know the truth.*

*"You are a fucking idiot, West." Lorcan came closer. "You know the rules. Why would you do this? Killing her was not on my agenda today."*

*Fuck... Lorcan. The moment Lorcan's words emerged, the air transformed into a wild river.*

*"You won't touch her!" I whirled on Lorcan. "My beast has claimed her."*

*"No, it hasn't." Eli curled his hands into tight fists. Shit. As the alpha, he would know most of all.*

*"It will. Once she accepts it."*

*"That's not how it works," Eli snarled, stepping farther into the room, away from the door.*

*Cammie's cries turned into words. "Help!" she screamed, and bolted for the back door.*

*"Sorry, girl. We can't let you go." Cooper stepped in front of her. His eyes were soft, but his large taut arms threatened to capture her.*

*"Help! Help me!" High-pitched shrieks echoed off the walls. The neighbors were close. Someone would hear her soon.*

*"Cammie, please calm down. No one is going to hurt you." I tried to get near her, my voice soothing.*

*Her gaze turned on me, and I felt as though my guts were being ripped out through my throat. She no longer saw me. William Miller, the man she fell in love with, was gone. All she saw was the freak, the monster underneath. She twisted on her heels and dashed for the broken front door.*

*"Cammie!" I leaped for her. But as I sprang for her, Eli did as well. In a scared daze, Cammie jerked forward and slipped on the tile. Eli stretched to catch her, grabbing her by the neck. Cammie's body went one way, her neck the other. With a crack, her spine twisted and snapped. Her body collapsed to the ground.*

*Lifeless.*

*My love.*

*My life.*

*Gone.*

# EIGHTEEN

"All it took was one moment. One moment that changed everything. It was my fault." I struggled to swallow over the knot in my throat. Time had eased the consuming pain and guilt I felt for so long, but it would never go away completely. And clearly my subconscious was being haunted again. "I was so naïve and stupid. And I killed her."

"You didn't kill her. It was an accident." Rez touched my arm.

I pulled away. "You and I aren't that innocent. I may not have killed her right then, but her life was over the instant I walked into her café. It had only been a matter of time. I should have walked away and left her alone. She could be alive right now. Living the life she always wanted with kids, a husband who adored her, in the house she loved, and working in her café.

"Lorcan was the most honest. We would have had to kill her. She was human. I should have left with my brothers, made the sacrifice for her. But I was greedy. I wanted it all. I kept hoping I could force the beast to claim her, but even then it knew more than me. And I took everything from her because I was selfish. I didn't care about the consequences. I only saw my happiness.

"The first few months after Cammie's death, I had let myself go into the darkness. I killed without conscience. I fucked without care. I drank without limit. My brothers stuck by me, got me out of jail many times, but Cole had to curb me from doing deals or going out in public. After a while I settled down, hid behind the humor and appeared the easygoing guy. The charmer. But the darkness was always there. The guilt. The regret."

I scratched my stubble and stared at the flames.

"I told Eli I didn't blame him. But years later when he met Ember and started acting like a fool in love, I couldn't deny the bitterness I felt. The anger I kept down resurfaced, and even though I really liked Em, all I could see was Cammie…what I had been denied. The love and connection between Ember and Eli was so off the charts I resented him.

"Those two were meant for each other. No matter how often I felt Ember was someone I could have fallen for, she was Eli's, and Eli was hers. Seeing them together stirred pain in me I wanted to keep buried. I vowed I'd never let myself love like that ever again."

"Is it why you chose Lorcan's side?" Rez tilted her head as if she finally understood something. "Ember told me the story about how Lorcan thought Eli lost his way because of her and separated with a few of you."

"Uh. Part." I grunted a harsh laugh.

"There was more to why I followed Lorcan, the loyalty I deemed for what he had done for me in the past, but Cammie had been a big part. Another thoughtless decision." I picked up my head, turning to Rez. "Seems I am full of them, darlin'."

"You act with your heart. You jump. Think after." Her shoulder brushed mine as she curved more toward me.

"Not foolish at all. I'm kind of envious."

"Envious?" I snorted.

"Yeah. I overanalyze and overthink everything. No emotion. Sometimes I feel dead inside. Always thinking but never feeling."

My gaze met hers. The flames flickered over her irises. Suddenly the fire felt blistering, sucking all the oxygen from the room.

"How about you take some of my impulsive actions, and I'll take some of your overthinking."

"Sounds like a plan." She smiled.

"I guess we'll have to have joint custody of them."

"You can have them every other weekend."

"Okay, but I'm the one who gets alimony."

"What? Why?"

"Because your job is much better than mine, darlin'." I lifted an eyebrow and winked. "Better perks."

Her eyes met mine. An emotion flickered through them too fast for me to capture it. She turned away from me, like she was hurt or angry. I had meant to tease her, like I did every day with every girl. This felt odd, uncomfortable. I swallowed hard.

We were silent for a few minutes. Unlike my brothers, I tended to talk, fill empty space with meaningless chitchat. For the life of me, I couldn't think of one thing to say. It had never been a problem for me. I enjoyed twisting an awkward moment into the unbearable.

Rez's voice was soft. "Just so you know…the perks, as you call them…aren't." She kept her head forward. "They haven't been for a long time."

I could feel my eyebrows knit together. What was she saying? She and Lars weren't sleeping together? The idea seemed highly unlikely. The Dark Unseelie King merely slept beside a stunning siren? No way, no way in hell. I would find it impossible to resist Rez if she were lying next to me. No man had that kind of restraint.

"What do you mean?"

She wrapped her arms around her legs, pulling them tighter to her chest, then leaned her chin on her knees, staring at me. "You're not the only one haunted by ghosts."

My frown deepened as my confusion increased.

"The moment Ember came into our lives, she brought with her the ghosts of his past. That's what lies between Lars and me in bed now."

"Aisling," I filled in the name.

"The love of his life." Rez turned her chin to face the fire. "How can you fight a memory? The only one he ever loved. He still mourns her...I've caught him a few times, staring off, a sadness in his eyes. She will always win."

"Do you love him?"

She took a long inhale. "I love him the way I love anyone close to me. But not the way I should. I am not in love with him."

"What do you mean *like you should*?"

"You know." Her voice went quiet again. "Passionate, consuming love. The kind that gives you butterflies." She tucked strands behind her ear, showing off the slopes of her high cheekbones. "Lars and I work well together. We are exceptionally compatible, and I have a great life, help run the house and a lot of the King's business. We could have contently kept living harmoniously together." She stopped, her lids blinking.

I sensed the "but" not vocalized and waited for her to continue. My mouth was dry, the heat in the room seeming to go from freezing to boiling in minutes. Time ticked by. Finally I heard the word fall from my mouth like it couldn't help itself. "But?"

Her lids closed briefly before they lifted, and she pushed her legs out straight.

"I'm starting to feel like I want more, that being content isn't enough anymore."

My mind buzzed with wanting to ask her why. What made her decide that? Why now? But I didn't. I had no right to know. Even this much of the King's personal life was more than I felt I should know. I had no idea how the Unseelie King felt about her, but she was his. It was about power.

Roles in the Seelie court were opposite because their Queen was in control. Kennedy wouldn't take advantage of it, but the last Queen did. I knew all too well. I had been *her* prisoner to do with as she pleased.

My lungs were suddenly full of tar, and I had to close my eyes to get control of my breathing, pushing away the awful memories.

I felt a hand brush softly through my hair, and I opened my eyes. Rez quickly dropped her hand, but her eyes were crimped with concern. Instead of getting angry or defensive, I stared back at her, desire spreading heat through my body.

She sensed it. The worry dropped from her features, turning unreadable, but she didn't look away.

*All it takes is one moment. One moment can change everything.*

Kissing Rez earlier was not something I would ever forget. The feel of her lips, her mouth as desperate as mine, and the feel of her moving against me would be forever ingrained in my memory.

What really pissed me off, the icing on the truth cake,

was looking back, I think I knew… I knew it had been Rez from the moment her lips touched mine. Rez tasted, smelled, and felt different from Cammie. My beast reacted differently. But I wanted to believe so badly it was Cammie so I could touch her again and tell her I was sorry. For one moment I let myself pretend it was a dream. But what dream did I want to stay in? The one where I had Cammie back, or the one in which I had Rez?

The ghost of Cammie now vanished from the room. From me. All I saw was Rez. Her beauty was almost painful, but during the week I had seen passed that, to the real woman underneath the gorgeous face. I loved the times when she was relaxed, laughing, and joking, or stressed and pissed off at me. I'd grown to appreciate the woman who hated chaos but found amusement in the anarchy I delivered daily to her life. I liked them all.

Suddenly, all I wanted was to kiss her again. To take off her clothes. Nibble her skin. Taste her everywhere. To know what places I could touch her to make her lose her mind. To know how it felt to be inside her. My chest squeezed, and I looked away. No way. No how. I had already made enough stupid decisions in my life.

Rez was off limits. That was the only certainty here.

# NINETEEN

The next morning, after a rare, peaceful slumber, I left Rez to sleep in and walked to town to grab groceries and diving stuff. My chest felt lighter, like unsealing Cammie had finally set her free. Set me free. I had loved her. I always would in some way, but it was time to let her go, along with the guilt and anger. I would always regret what I did and the choices I made, but I couldn't change them, and the girl I knew would want me to be happy.

I wished I had been stronger for her, loving her enough to walk away. Even my beast knew deep down she wasn't the one. It never actually claimed her, no matter how much I wanted it to.

Keeping my hood up, I slipped in and out of the stores, getting some things we needed. The less we were out in public, the better. The shifter gang would be out in force searching for us.

Carrying a diving suit, tank, and groceries more than three miles in sheep-shit ridden fields and squelching in the muck was a pain in the ass, but the items were essential. Rez was about to be in her element...I was not. Water in general I liked: showers, drinking it, pools, and even skinny-dipping in *calm* waters was cool. A vast, deep, wild sea? Nope. No, thank you.

I liked my feet on the ground. But there was no way I was going to let Rez do this on her own. This was where I really understood the partnership part of our work together, our strengths and weaknesses, and why she wanted to fight next to me. She was up to bat now, and I wasn't going to be left sitting on the bench.

"I swear, West Moseley." Her yells clobbered me the moment I stepped into the door. "If I wake up *one more time* and you're gone…with no note, no idea if you actually tossed yourself over a cliff this time…" Rez flayed her arms around in anger. "I will toss you over myself."

"Sorry, darlin'." I set the diving equipment down, taking the groceries to the kitchenette. "Guess I'm not really used to having to tell someone where I am."

"Get used to it." She put her hands on her hips, looking so frickin' cute in her PJs, hair in a messy bun, pissed as hell at me. "Because if you make me panic like that again…" Her eyes were narrowed in crinkled slits.

I moved to her without thinking, sliding my hand beneath her jaw and pulling up her head till our gazes met. "I'm truly sorry. It won't happen again."

Her eyes searched mine, the fright still etched in them. I wanted to take it away, to fill them with joy. Yet her concern for me twisted something deep in me I didn't fully understand.

Wanting to kiss her was a continual struggle, but now that I knew how her lips felt on mine, how she tasted, it became a full-blown battle. I wanted to explore her mouth, nip on those full lips, and this time be fully aware it was her.

When she cleared her throat, I realized I had been

staring at her the whole time. *Shit*. I pulled back, hitting the air tank.

Rez looked at the object and a smile bloomed on her face. "You got a diving tank?"

"Got to keep up with you, don't I?"

"Oh, I highly doubt, Mr. Moseley, you could *ever* keep up with me." She flashed me a mischievous grin and turned for the bathroom, grabbing a pile of clothes on her bed.

I stood there, my mouth on the floor, my dick pointing to the ceiling.

Forget the dreams, this woman had to be here to cruelly torment me. *She* might be the reason I'd fling myself off the cliff.

---

I spent most of the day playing with my diving gear while talking over a generic plan with Rez. She sat at the table making a checklist. Of what I had no idea, but I knew it made her feel better.

The walkie-talkie buzzed when Rez was in the bathroom. I knew I should have answered it, told Lars what we were up to, but my fingers wouldn't click on the button. The memory of my mouth hungrily on Rez's scrambled my mind like a snare. A tangle of guilt...and need.

*I'll call him after we go down. Might have something more substantial to tell him.* I convinced myself this made sense, letting the call go unanswered, and shoved it under some papers on the table. Out of sight, out of mind.

If only this were true.

We didn't want to head down to the area until after sunset. There weren't a lot of tourists this time of year, but a few milled around the bluffs. We needed to sneak unseen to the strip of rocky beach below the cliffs, which was far off the trails and not permitted, especially at night in the dead of winter.

Rez's legs were bouncing by the time we headed over.

"You are so ready to go, aren't you?" I laughed, watching her fidget behind me.

"Yeah." She pulled on her coat. "It's been a while since I've been in the water. I miss it. I don't feel right when I've been away too long."

I nodded and glanced away, grief flaming the loss of my beast I experienced on a daily basis.

"I'm sorry. That was extremely insensitive." She touched my arm. "You'd know more than anyone."

"Don't worry about it, sweetheart." I shrugged and stepped into the bitterly cold night, the tank on my back.

Rez huddled close to me, using me as a shield against the robust winter wind as we hiked the trail and descended the steep cliff to the beach. There was only one trail with access to get down; the other side was a mile of sheer rock cliff poking out into the wild sea.

My body prickled with goosebumps, the wind spraying water so cold it burned on my exposed skin. The water crashed against the rocks like a child having a tantrum. Everything in me wanted to retreat from the brutal water, while Rez gobbled up the distance to the sea like she was ravenous for it.

Here was another reason to stay away from her. She was water; I was earth. We were never meant to become friends, let alone lovers. Back in the old days of the Otherworld we wouldn't have associated at all. Maybe times had changed, but how much?

Rez ripped off her boots and socks the instant we hit the bottom. Her toes were eager to caress the water. She tossed the articles at the rock face and began to undo her pants.

*Uh...* My brain went dead as she bent over, pulling her legs out from the fabric. My eyes bugged out at the sight of her *tiny* white silk panties, her legs lean and toned. And her ass… I gripped a boulder to keep myself standing.

"Darlin'?" I choked.

She looked over her shoulder, ripping off her jacket. "Can't go in with my clothes, can I?" She smiled coyly, her eyes gleaming under the moonlight.

Damn. She was even more breathtaking while stripping and full of life. Buzzing, glowing, and vibrant. She was home. When her sweater came off, I was thankful it was so freakin' cold. Although it didn't help all that much. She could overshadow below-freezing temperatures.

In the dark I could still make out each curve and her hair skating over the middle of her back. My hands were desperate to follow every arch of her body.

She turned around, tossing her clothes to me. "Put them over by my boots," she ordered, then moved toward the water.

No one ordered Dark Dwellers around. No. One. But damn if I didn't waggle like an obedient puppy. No doubt she could demand anything from me and I would comply, which scared the hell out of me. But seeing Rez in only her bra and underwear…yeah, I was so screwed.

"Let me go down, see if I can find anything first."

My eyes finally tore from her figure and went to her eyes. "Rez…"

"I'll come back and get you, I swear."

Her feet touched the foamy water cresting the shore. It looked like someone turned the light on inside. A hazy glow illuminated from her, pulsing with energy. It slammed into me with the force of a club to the head.

My feet moved to her. The need to follow her wasn't even a question anymore. My heart thumped in my chest, understanding the magnetic draw, but it didn't stop me from inching to her. I was more than an obedient puppy. I was her slave.

"We're in my world now." She glanced over her shoulder at me. "This sea is *extremely* powerful. Whatever you do, keep your distance. Stay put until I come right back to this spot and get you. All right?" It was not a question but a mandate. She waded farther out and then dived into the sea, the waves devouring her underneath their hungry currents.

The desire to trail her ebbed when she disappeared, letting me breathe. *Hell.* Never having a run-in with sirens before, I didn't know what kind of power they had. *Shit.* This was the first time I had really experienced her power. No wonder thousands of human sailors, swimmers, or surfers would willingly go to their deaths.

I climbed over the rocks to where her shoes were and set down her clothes and the air tank, tucking them in a crevice to keep them dry.

Time ticked by as I waited for Rez to return. I paced the beach, anticipating her return and about to lose my mind when the most beautiful song carried over the wind, jerking my head to a cluster of boulders sticking out of the sea.

Only a sliver of moonlight broke through the clouds, but I spotted a female figure coming up from the water, climbing on one of the protruding rocks. The water hit the rocks around her and sprayed in the air like a fountain. The white cloth she wore absorbed light, displaying how it clung to every curve of her body like a second skin. It was a Grecian one-sleeve dress and transparent in tantalizing areas. Dark hair hung to her waist, curtaining her figure. Deep brown eyes caught the moonlight, glinting with a beckoning entreaty.

I knew those eyes.

Rez.

I knew she didn't go under wearing the white cloth, but my thoughts didn't care to analyze it. The image before me was so breathtaking, so exquisite, my chest clenched. My mind only longed to follow her. My body wanted to drop to my knees in reverence. But *all* of me wanted to worship her—in every way possible.

As a fae, I was *mostly* immune to another fae's glamour but not entirely. Compared to a human, it was like receiving only a half dose of strong medicine. If this was only a little dose of what Rez's kind was capable of, I had severely underestimated her capacity as a siren. I should have known better. I struggled to keep away from Rez in her everyday clothes, with no glamour.

"Come, dweller, I have something to show you." Her voice floated seductively over to me. The call twisted so beautifully with the sound of the crashing water it was almost as if she spoke through the waves. Every break against the rocks was a song in itself. "Follow me, dark *beast*."

*Dark beast? Hmmm…can't deny it kind of turned me on even more.*

As my feet moved to the water, a tiny bell tugged at my gut. The warning went through my brain but landed on marshy land and sank. I hopped on a large, slimy boulder, my boots slipping over the moss, and my gaze locked on every curve in the distance.

*Rez…*

Why was my heart thumping at the thought of her naked body fitting against mine? *Stop. Now. You can't touch her. She is not yours, nor can she ever be.* Instinct had already taken hold, though. My beast moved and thought for me, locking on its target.

She turned, glancing over her shoulder. "Come, dark one. Let me show what you covet." Then she dived into the water.

I clambered after her, poised to jump into the roiling sea. *West, man, you're a Dark Dweller, so you don't swim especially well, nor can you breathe underwater.* I ignored these thoughts, took a deep breath, and submerged beneath the dark water. The salt of the sea stung for a moment when I opened my eyes but was gone as soon as I saw her underwater. My lids locked open.

A glow of light emanated off her skin, casting an even more ethereal beauty around her. *"Follow me below, to a world you have never known,"* she sang, wrapping around me like the softest warmth I'd ever felt. Her voice brought tears to my eyes.

*Oh gods, don't ever stop talking to me.* The pleasure of her voice was so complete I craved nothing else. She was far enough in the distance I couldn't make out her features exactly, but I needed to be with her, the girl who shocked me so many times, made me laugh and strive to fight my demons and still want to come out the other side. I would trail this woman to the depths and beyond.

Her legs kicked together like a fish's tail as she swam lower to the seabed. My lungs already constricted, seeking air, but I ignored them, pushing my arms faster through the water to get to her. She stayed just out of reach so I couldn't touch her, her song luring me farther.

*"Let me rid you of the pain, come out of the rain, where you will find freedom from the chains."* She turned

around to face me, still slipping lower to where rocks and sea life were entrenched into the ground.

*Strange thing for Rez to say,* I thought, but still it was only a fleeting thought. Black dots impeded my vision, but I followed her song like a nomad spotting an oasis in the desert.

*It's an illusion. Wake up!* A desperate call screamed into my head. Blackness began to seep around the edges of my vision, my lungs clawing for oxygen. I blinked a few times and saw the woman before me was still stunningly beautiful, but there were little things I noticed now. Her nose was slightly longer, her face rounder, her eyes a different shape.

It wasn't Rez.

Certainty slammed into me, and I automatically sucked in. Water flooded my lungs, driving more air out of my lungs. Panic took over like a kitten thrown in a bucket of water. My legs and arms flayed around as I choked. My hands went to my neck, knowing there was no point. I was going to drown, the surface of the ocean too far up to reach in time.

*"Let go, dark beast, stay with me beneath the sea,"* the siren sang. My lids drifted closed to the lure of her voice and the lack of oxygen. *"Here is your grave, under the wave. Forever mine."*

My body went limp, giving up the struggle, my mind a murky mess. I could have sworn I heard my name being screamed, piercing my head in pain before I let go.

The ocean digested another victim in its belly.

# TWENTY

A swell burned up my lungs and spilled out, tearing at my throat as I purged the ocean, drawing me out of the depths of death. My ears rang with a strange noise, but I couldn't decipher any particular sound. Syrup clogged my brain, swirling it with confusion and exhaustion. I wanted to keep sleeping, but as each noise became clearer, I was tugged from the darkness. The voice crystalized till I wanted nothing more than to follow it wherever it wanted me to go.

"Dammit. Wake up, West."

*Rez.* I tried to say her name, but no sound ventured out.

"I swear to the gods, if you hurt him in any way, I will kill you," I heard Rez almost growl. Before I could wonder who she was talking to, another voice spoke.

"We both know you will never do that." I recognized the woman's voice. It came from the one who lured me under. Now hearing them together, I wondered how I let myself believe the other siren had been Rez. Their voices were similar, both deep and sultry, but the other siren had an older, more confident tone. She spoke slower, less emotionally. Also, Rez teased me, but she would never have called me *dark one* or *dark beast*.

"Don't underestimate me." Rez's words were full of hate.

"Wow, you really care for this one. Sirens don't let ourselves love. You know that."

"Who said anything about love?"

"Please, you can't fool me. You never have. Look what happened last time," the other woman responded. "You have the ideal situation with the Unseelie King. Oh yes, I know all about your life now. You are provided everything, without the nuisance and hassle of love. Don't be a fool. Do not give it up for something you know will only end in tragedy."

"I'm not giving up anything." Rez's voice tightened at the end.

"You better not."

There was a moment before I felt breath tickling my face. "West, please. Wake up." Rez's fingers lightly touched either side of my face, her contact giving my eyes the burst of energy they needed to open.

I blinked a few times, and her features came into focus above me. "Rez," I forced the word out and instantly regretted it. Fire burned my esophagus like someone poured acid down my pipes, and it sent me into a fit of gagging coughs.

Rez helped me sit and twist so I could evacuate more water from my lungs. When the spasms lessened, I rotated back, curling my arms loosely around my knees. I leaned between my legs, grappling for more breath without stirring my lungs so I wouldn't start hacking again.

Rez's hand slid up the back of my neck, softly rubbing. "Are you all right?"

I looked at her, hair still soaked and clinging to her bare arms, still nearly naked. The freezing air dimpled her flesh. She had told me her body adjusted to whatever temperature the water was but couldn't adapt as fast to the element of air. The impulse to put my arms around her and protect her from the unforgiving environment was hard to ignore, but I could not cross that line. Not that my own saturated clothing would help warm her.

"Yeah. I'm okay." I nodded. Her shoulders relaxed, and a small smile hinted on her mouth. That damn mouth. My gaze couldn't seem to pull away, her lips only a few inches from mine. The beast stirred in my chest and rubbed against my ribs. She didn't move, her gaze dropping to mine, her chest rising and lowering. I don't think she realized she did it, but her nails dug lightly into the back of my neck. My dick and the beast both came alive, growling with need as they seemed to do at awkward times.

Life-and-death situations always excited the beast, coiling extra energy and demanding release. *It would happen with any beautiful woman. Right?*

"See, he's perfectly fine. All the fuss was for nothing." A voice broke my trance on Rez, the beast switching quickly to defense, and I jumped to my feet. My muscles lit with pain. My beast wanted out, to be let free, but agony compressed it in a corner.

Rez held on to my arm as I wobbled a little, but I quickly found my equilibrium and curled my shoulders forward, a rumble of warning directed at the other siren.

"Easy, dark one. I am not here to hurt you." The other woman held up her hands, her tone lulling me into a calmer state. I fought against it and snarled at the woman. She was as beautiful as I remembered. So similar to Rez in stature and features it felt a little disturbing. Her white dress was still sheer and wet and clung to her hourglass body, taunting any red-blooded man. Her long hair was pulled to one side, hanging over a shoulder to her waist. She watched me with her dark eyes.

"You didn't feel the same earlier," I snapped.

"I was only doing what was in my nature. You should understand that, Dark Dweller," she replied, tugging at her flimsy covering, like she was trying to straighten it, which only drew my attention to the curve of her hips. It was subtle, but I knew what she was doing.

Sirens understood seduction better than anyone. It wasn't about sex with them. They seduced with their song or their sensual movements, touching their hair or licking their lips. It was crafty and cunning.

But now I was aware of it. I was a man, so of course I noticed, but she did nothing for the beast inside.

"I won't deny you would have been one of my greatest kills. The energy off you is unfathomable. There's two of you in there, fighting, and so full of power I would have been satisfied for months." She sighed softly, her lashes fluttering at the thought. "Oh, it would have been exceptional to be so thoroughly gratified. But Mareza seems ardent on keeping you alive."

Mareza? My head snapped to Rez. Okay, they clearly had a past.

"Don't call me that." Rez folded her arms, her chin rising.

"Why? It is your given name."

"It is not who I am anymore, Morweena."

"Morweena? When did—"

"I stopped being that girl the moment I walked away from you." The muscles along Rez's neck tightened as anger smoldered her words. "What are you even doing here?"

"You know why I'm here. Why I had to leave. You

broke a contract. I was ostracized, and I came here soon after you *left*."

Morweena's brown eyes narrowed on Rez as she scoffed. "You take so much after *him*."

Rez inhaled sharply, her arms coiling with tension.

"What I did was for your own good. I wanted you to have the best in life." Morweena took a step closer. "You were so naïve and childish in your dreams. You needed to see the truth. What your nature truly was. I saved that boy from a worse fate."

"Saved him? You killed him!" Rez screamed, rage and sadness cutting at the beauty of her voice.

"I saved him from eventually being killed by you. You don't think being betrayed by his love would have destroyed him even more? I also protected you from being the one who took his life. You would have never forgiven yourself," Morweena rallied back. "You can't fight your nature, who you are. The moment you met him, the boy's life was doomed. You held on to those young whimsical ideals far too long."

"You can pretend you murdered my love as a teaching session, but I know the truth. Killing him made the path clear to the ruler of the selkies, who happened to be looking for a new wife."

"He was a king. Rich, powerful, and would have given you a great life."

"No. He would have given *you* a great life," Rez hissed. "Did you not care he hit women for fun? He was a cruel, evil man...but none of that mattered. You only wanted the money and power my marriage would have brought you."

*Jesus.*

I marveled at the depths of Rez's past and the loss and

cruelty she had experienced. Instead of folding under it, she rose higher. The incredible, strong woman next to me blew me away with every new discovery.

"You are even more disgusting than he was. You killed the boy I loved for your own greed and need for power."

"Love?" Morweena laughed. "You are still living in a fantasy. Sirens don't love. We can't."

"You can't," Rez volleyed back. "After my father broke your heart, you never let love touch you again. Even for me. You get off finding men who are in love and killing them. It's your revenge for what he did to you."

*Whoa. Father?*

Everything suddenly clicked. It probably would have sooner if my brain wasn't half drowned.

"Deep down, you killed Philip because he loved me. You wanted to destroy that. Make me feel the same pain."

"You can believe what you want, Mareza, but I only wanted to protect you."

"I think I am better without your protection, *Mother*."

And there it was. My gaze darted between the two women with new awareness. The similarities were so strong I realized why I thought Morweena had been Rez from a distance.

"I don't think you are, my girl." Morweena tilted her head, her gaze flashing to me, her eyes drilling in so deep I felt turned inside out. "I know you are in even more trouble."

Morweena's words hurt even more than the icy wind whipping off the rocks and slapping our faces.

Rez rubbed at her arms, glancing at her toes, the unforgiving rocky beach not appearing to hurt her feet.

"You two need to walk away from each other now."

"You know nothing about what is going on," I finally

spoke up. She was with Lars. It wasn't even a consideration.

Morweena let out a silky laugh. "Sirens can see to the deepest, most hidden parts of your soul. It is how we lure you."

"What?" I peeked at Rez.

"Only in our truest form," she responded. "When we are taking someone to their death. Otherwise we can't."

That really didn't make me feel better.

Morweena stepped to me, her head leaning back to take me in. "I saw you, Dark Dweller. I know what you are hiding from your family, and I know what you are concealing from yourself."

My body stiffened and muscles clenched with the need to fight. I wanted to tear something apart when I felt vulnerable in any way.

Rez reacted quickly, grabbed my arms, and hauled me back. I let her. If I didn't want to be, she wouldn't have been able to use a bulldozer to budge me.

"Mother, stop. It's not wise to piss off a Dark Dweller."

"He's struggling with even calling himself that anymore. If the beast is lost, then so is he."

My growl vibrated the loose stones underfoot.

Morweena only smiled. "Is this why you are coming for the treasure? To release the beast from his prison?"

I froze. "Wh-what?"

"The Spear of Lugh. Surely it is why you are here." Morweena tucked her arms beneath her breasts and circled us. "Rumors travel fast in these parts. And when talk of the spear connected to the Unseelie King occurs, you take notice. Even more when his mistress and henchman land on the island."

"I am *not* his henchman." My gaze tracked her moving around us.

"Really? What do you call someone who does the bidding and serves the King?"

"Trapped."

Humor pinched at her mouth. "I see."

"Mother, what do you know about the spear?" Rez pulled her drying hair over to one side to keep it from blowing around.

"After you left, I came here and started a new home. It wasn't long before I became the leader of the group of sirens here. That was when I was told about the treasure, where it was hidden and what lengths we go to protect it."

"It's really here?" I needed her to confirm it.

"Yes. My clan guards the treasure. Anyone searching for it would either never find it or be killed if they got too close." She came nearer to us, her arms still crossed in front of her. "We have taken extreme measures to protect it. It is guarded by things even a Dark Dweller would fear."

"I doubt that, sweetheart," I snapped back.

"I already sense you will disregard my warnings." A smug expression formed. "If you proceed, you will sincerely wish I had taken your life."

She didn't strike me as an empty-threat kind of lady.

"But you will allow us to go down and search?" Rez asked, her tone full of skepticism.

Morweena lifted her hand toward the ocean. "Be my guest."

"What do you want in return?" Rez stiffened.

"Nothing, daughter."

Rez folded her arms tight around her body.

"I miss you, but I think you are perfectly placed with the demon king. I am happy you found true happiness. Don't mess it up."

Rez shifted her weight.

"We can search in your sea for the treasure and you want nothing?" I asked. It had to be a setup. No doubt about it. She wouldn't so willingly let us go after a treasure they had guarded for centuries. Not unless she was completely convinced we would never reach it. But I still couldn't walk away from the chance. "You and your people will let us be. We can go after it freely?"

"I swear none of my clan will touch you."

"Or sing, talk, whistle, or hum?" Always cover your bases with fae. Tricky bunch. "You won't come anywhere near us?"

"Correct."

Damn. I hated knowing I was heading straight into a trap and still understood it was a better option than showing up on Lars's doorstep empty handed.

I looked at Rez. Her furrowed brows mirrored my worry, but she shrugged and nodded. No other option remained for either of us.

"Then I guess this is goodbye," Rez said to her mother, not making a move toward her.

"I hope not for good, Mareza." Morweena's voice was beautiful, but I realized it held little if any love. "You have grown into a stunning woman. I am pleased."

"Thank you, Mother." From a glance, the women looked like sisters, perhaps five years apart. But the loss of heart, of emotion, aged Morweena. Life laid heavy on her shoulders and deep in her eyes.

"My advice, Mareza. Let him go." Those ancient eyes flashed at me before returning to Rez. "You will only find pain in that future. Leave him in the depths…it will save him from what is ahead. You are doing him a favor."

With those words, she turned, walked back into the sea, slipped in the darkness of the water, and disappeared.

Rez set her lips in a grim line, staring at the place where Morweena vanished.

Awkward tension filled the air between us. What did she mean Rez should let me go? Pain in that future? A future with me? My brain quickly shut down the thoughts, pushing them away. No. That was completely impossible. The only way I dealt with uncomfortable silences was with humor.

"So…that was mommy dearest?"

"Yeah." Rez sighed, still keeping her eyes from me. "Never thought I would see her again, especially here."

"Didn't sound like you guys had a warm, fuzzy relationship."

Rez chuckled. "That is an understatement. Instead of nurturing and loving her daughter, I became competition and a commodity to trade. She constantly compared our beauty, or the number of men she could lure to mine. The older I got and the more my looks evolved, the more difficult she became. She struggled between being jealous to wanting to use my beauty to snag eligible men. So her lessons for me were relentless and cruel. I found escape on land…away from her."

"Where you met this Philip?"

"Yes. He was my first love. My first everything." Rez blushed, a slight smile on her mouth at the memory.

It came like lightning. Jealousy. Why the hell did I feel envious of some twat human kid? The twat who first got to love her, touch her body, know her taste, the sounds she makes.

"After she killed Philip, I couldn't take it anymore. Any of it. The arranged marriage, the mental abuse from her. I left. Never looked back." Rez moved closer to the waterline. "My desperation to never have to return was what made me easy prey for someone like Vadik. I was willing to do anything to make it on my own. Deny what I was and hide behind the haze of the opium. Until *it* became the nightmare I was trying to escape." She dipped her toes into the cold water and her shoulders relaxed.

"Is she why you don't seem to like what you are?"

Rez clung to herself harder, her feet wiggling in the water. A flash of pain crossed her features.

"She was the reason at first, the grief of losing Philip tore me apart. Especially when I knew she was right. I was young and couldn't control my powers. I probably would've killed him eventually." Rez took in a deep breath and looked up at the moon. "You know why I'm barely ever away from the compound? Why I need to live so structured?"

I tilted my head to stare at her, feeling the sorrow bleeding off her.

"Most addicts replace their addictions with another. Gum-chewing, smoking, sex." She rubbed her arms. "Mine was death. When Lars got me clean, I went back to accepting what I was. Finding a release in being a siren again. I got addicted. Had no off switch..." She swallowed, her lids blinking. "I killed every night. One was not enough, I started taking down groups at a time, getting such a high off them...I couldn't stop.

"It got so bad it made the national news. Lars had to step in. He realized I needed rules. Boundaries to keep myself in control." Rez turned to me. "It's why I'm so fanatical. Why I freak out if things go off plan."

"You think you will lose control." I nodded, more puzzle pieces clicking in. Rez's depth unraveling another layer for me.

She nodded. "Just like being a siren, I've recognized the extreme side, the addict will always be part of me. I will continuously have to keep it in check."

"And seeing your mother…influences that?"

"Normally, I would say yes." Her gaze clicked on mine. "But having you here helped."

I tried not to react, to take it more than face value.

"What's sad is I know everything my mother does comes from her pain. She fell in love with a captivating pirate who stopped in port. A double no-no to our kind. We don't fall in love, and we especially don't fall for someone not fae. She thought he felt the same so she broke the rules." Rez exhaled. "He didn't."

"Did she kill him?"

"No. He simply pulled up anchor one night and left without a word. It was the night she was coming to tell him she was with child. It destroyed her. I think when she saw my naiveté and wistful ideals…"

"She saw herself." I nodded.

"And all the pain resurfaced. It also didn't help I have some of his features." Rez tapped at her face. "I used to see so much anguish when she looked at me. Then she tucked her emotions away and became cold. Cruel."

"Do you know who he is?"

"No. Mother wouldn't talk about him. My grandmother told me he was a fae pirate stopping in Greece on his way to the Orient. She said he comes from both Asian and Spanish ancestry. With his almond-shaped eyes, tanned skin, and high cheekbones, no one—not even a siren—could fight his charms." Rez snorted. "Even my grandmother blushed telling me about him. But that's all she would tell me."

"Fae? Your father could still be out there."

"He's not my father. Merely someone who impregnated my mother and left without a word."

"He didn't know about you."

"You think it would have changed anything?"

"Maybe." I clutched her arms, turning her to look at me. "Listen. I lost my parents, and there isn't a day that passes I wouldn't love the chance to see them again, especially my father. You might have the chance."

"No. I have lived quite happily without him. I'm not going to dredge things up that are better left buried." She yanked out of my grasp. "Now, let's focus on why we are here. So I can return to where I belong. To my *real* family. To Lars."

She twisted back for the water and dived in. The sting of her words broke over my chest like waves, crushing my lungs. But I shoved it away and followed her toward the sea, where a trap was set, ready to annihilate me.

Hell. I might be okay with that.

---

"Rez?" I hollered when my toes hit the waterline. "We need a plan." In the dark it was hard to make her out in the obscurity of the waves.

"I'm going to check it out. See if I can find the shipwreck and I'll come back. Be ready with your oxygen tank."

I was about to put it on before Morweena showed up and tempted me into the water. Even if I had it on, she probably would have convinced my brain I didn't need it. I would never underestimate a siren's power again.

Strapping the tank on my back, I waited for Rez to return. I hated being the one to wait, dependent on someone else. I danced on my feet, fidgeting with agitation. This was her strength, and I had to give it to her, but it didn't calm me.

Even with my clan, I preferred not to rely on anyone. I couldn't have done this mission without her help, and my stubborn nature took a hit when I realized that.

Time ticked by, my legs pacing back and forth across the rocky beach.

"Screw this."

I popped in the mouthpiece, switched on the tank, and waded into the water. The ocean was so dark my little torch didn't penetrate the murkiness past a few feet, but I dived deeper.

Swimming farther and farther down, in what felt like a vast alien world, I was uncomfortable, claustrophobic, restricted. My beast hated the suffocating feeling of water on all sides and ached for earth between my toes.

I was about to call it quits, when a hazy glow rose from the bottom of the sea, fifty yards out in front of me. The luminosity moved and glided through the water like a fish.

*Please be Rez. I can't take another siren.*

My arms and legs cut the water as I swam to her. The closer I got, the more her light reflected off objects, like metal and glass. Human-made items. Deep in the ocean valley against a ragged rock, pieces of an old wooden pirate ship lay half buried under the seabed. There were a lot of shipwrecks along the coast, but I sensed exactly where Rez was heading. Magic was thick here, seeping through despite the spell cast to hide it.

She almost reached the object of her focus when something crossed in front of her, her light bright enough for me to see. I squinted to see what the object was that moved. It didn't make sense...it looked like toes. Boulder-sized toes.

Rez's body jerked to a stop as a blistering roar broke through the water like a shockwave. Water pushed me back, rolling and twisting me with its power. I finally slowed. Rez's light let me lock on to a focal point to decipher up from down. When I steadied my vision, I saw her swimming toward me, like a speeding train. Then movement behind her took my gaze away from her. My mouth fell open, the mouthpiece slipping out. *Holy shit!*

I had been right. Those had been toes—attached to what looked like a five-story monster. My mind took in his muscular legs as it stepped over the shipwreck, its heavy steps hitting the seabed, billowing sediment and debris creating murkiness. I wasn't sure if I wanted to see it anyway.

*"West, take my hand, we must head to land,"* her siren voice sang to me as she raced up. My mind suddenly forgot why I had been scared, all I could focus on was the woman before me. Her voice was so exquisite, her face so ethereal and stunning I wanted to cry.

*"West! Snap out of it before we become a mishap."* Her eyes were wide and huge with fright, but all I saw was their beauty. A sharp sting to my cheek jolted me back in surprise, clearing me from Rez's siren trance. I shook my head, waking myself up.

*"No time."* She shoved the mouthpiece between my lips, grabbed my hand, and swam toward the surface. The water thundered as the beast headed for us.

Now I was awake.

I didn't even try to swim on my own; her speed and agility in the water were supreme. I kicked as hard as I could to help her, but it probably did little.

I glanced over my shoulder, seeing only arms swinging through the loose silt. He did not seem to be giving up the chase.

He bellowed again, pushing us farther to the top as the sound broke through the water. The glimmer of the moon gave the top of the water a patchwork effect, glittering and simmering. If I weren't being chased by a giant sea monster, I would have found it serene, especially holding Rez's hand. But I was nowhere near relaxed. Everyone pees in the ocean. Don't judge.

Rez and I broke through the surface and scrambled for the shore.

"What the hell was that?" I tore the air tank from my back, getting the weight off me, letting it fall next to my feet.

"Not what but who." She turned her body to face the water, her body trembling. This time it was not from the cold.

"Then *who* the fuck was that?"

"That was Balor." Rez panted, dripping with seawater.

"What?" I swung toward her. The snapping of the wind and roar of the water cascaded up from below. "Are you sure?"

"Positive."

My jaw slackened in disbelief. "Balor? As in Balor, the dead demon king?" All fae grew up hearing the legends of Balor. In the Celtic-Irish mythology, Balor was the god of death and the king of a race of giants. He had a third eye, which he kept closed because anything he looked at would die instantly.

"Not so dead." She nibbled on her bottom lip. "We fae can't seem to stay dead."

"Clearly," I exclaimed. "All right, so what you're telling me is the Celtic high demon king, who can kill and destroy everything in its path by simply opening its third eye," I stabbed at the space between my eyebrows, "is guarding the spear?"

"That's the one." She nodded. "I heard rumors a Druid brought him back."

Only a Druid could. "And you forgot to mention this?" I bellowed as the head of the giant poked out of the water. *Fuuuuuck.*

"They were simply mumblings underwater. Old stories no one took seriously. I mean, it is impossible magic…bringing someone back from the dead. It shouldn't be feasible."

"It looks pretty possible to me." I waved toward the beast, whose shoulders had now breached the waves. "And I don't think it's a coincidence Balor, Lugh's grandfather, whom Lugh *killed*, happens to be guarding his grandson's weapon. One of the most powerful objects ever created."

I heard the legend as a child: Balor tried to kill all his grandsons because of a prophecy saying one of them would slay him in battle, destroying Balor's kingdom by using his own eye to kill his people, the Fomorian. Balor tossed all his grandsons in the sea to drown, but one survived—Lugh, who grew up and killed Balor and became the next high king of the Tuatha Dé Danann.

"Bringing Balor back to defend the spear is kind of poetic genius. His hatred and need for revenge is probably the best defense. He'd want no one to obtain it and let Lugh's power back out in the world and possibly Lugh himself." I looked out to see where Balor was. "So, grandpappy is back and really pissed off, holding a grudge on his long-deceased grandson."

"Seems so." She leaned over and grabbed the knife wrapped on her leg. I wanted to laugh. The six-inch knife wouldn't be so much as a splinter in his massive body. "Uh, there's also something else."

"We need to move now." I gulped, watching the monster ascend.

"There's another rumor Lugh used a piece of Balor's eye after he killed him, lacing the spear with the magic stored in his eye. It's said that's why the holder of the spear will never lose a battle and will be the ultimate killing machine."

I groaned. "You've got to be kidding me." This was even worse than I thought. The missing part of his eye was now a piece of the spear. No wonder Balor wanted it back, or at least near him at all times. Hell! Now I understood why Morweena had no problem letting us go after the spear.

Balor rose higher out of the water, like a skyscraper emerging from the earth, water gushing down and around him like a tsunami.

"Do you have a plan, sweetheart?"

"I was kind of hoping you had one."

My brain looped in unhelpful circles as the demon rose to his full height, my mouth gaping. He was an ugly son of a bitch, but I had to give him props for his physique, which was mostly on display except for the tiny loincloth. His body, unlike a giant or ogre, was ripped with muscle, like a true warrior and king. His skin had a grayish tint, and long white hair dripped down his back in braids and dreads, but he was completely bald on top. His hair circled around his pointed ears and down his face, giving his cheeks tuffs of white.

So many people portrayed him as having only one eye, like a cyclops, but he actually had three. The two normal ones were used to see, the third, the one in the middle of his forehead, was used to kill and destroy. Legend said he mostly kept it closed until he was ready to kill. Supposedly this beam of light would blow up anything it pointed at.

I gulped. The moment he decided to open it, we were dead. "Rez, it's time we leave. Think we've overstayed our welcome."

"I couldn't agree more." Rez backed into me. "Come up with anything yet?"

"Yes."

"What?"

"Run."

I grabbed her hand and tore down the beach. A cry boomed from Balor, and the earth thundered behind us in little earthquakes with his every step. There was only one way in and out of this little cove: a steep trail difficult enough to climb on a day when you didn't have a giant demon king after you.

I glanced over at him. He wrinkled his forehead and scrunched his eyes in fury. His eyes wandered over the rocky beach like he was still searching for us. In his hand was a large javelin. He let out another growl and his eyes flashed with a green color, then the lid of his third eye lifted. A beam like a laser hit the side of the cliff in front of us, halting us in our tracks. The light tore into the mountain, ripping large chunks away from it.

"Oh. Shit." I barely got my words out before an avalanche of rock tore from the surface, gravity tugging it down with speed. Rubble tumbled down the cliffs, breaking into car-sized pieces as they shattered and rolled with force straight for us. We would be crushed and buried in a matter of seconds.

Twisting, I dived for Rez, ripping her roughly off her feet. My body slammed on top, taking us to the ground. Using a large boulder as a shield, I pressed us tight against it. Dust and rock rained down in a heavy barrage, pounding and slicing at our skin. The large chunks rolled over the boulder, flying like missiles into the sea. All I could do was curl tightly around, shielding her from some of the impact. The rumbling stone cascaded around us like thunder.

Warmth soaked into my waterlogged shirt, and I knew blood slipped down my sides as the debris tore our clothes into shreds. The screech of the tumbling rocks quieted enough I became aware of Balor's grunts snapping crisply in my ear. The earth vibrated with each step.

I craned to the side and saw the giant coming for us. We couldn't defeat him. Our only chance was to flee, which was not my natural mode. We had blindly jumped into this and now understood the consequences of our impulses too late. If we had any hope, we needed a plan. Even with that, I felt our odds were almost nil.

"Darlin', when I say the word, I need you to run…as fast as you can." I cupped her face, forcing her to see the desperation in my face.

"You're running too?"

My teeth slid over my bottom lip.

"Right, West?" Her voice rose sharply, her eyes widening. "I'm not leaving you."

"I'm not willing to chance going separate ways, and then he decides to go for you. If we both ran, he could reach us easily. One step and we'd be in his hands."

The earth pounded under us, his heavy steps getting near us, shooting up my anxiety.

"West—"

"No time for debate." I shook my head, my heart thumping. "On three you run. Don't look back...whatever you hear. All right?"

"No, West."

"This. Is. Not. A. Choice!" I almost screamed, my face turning to ice. "You are not dying here tonight. I will *not* allow that."

Balor roared. At any moment he could open his third eye and charbroil us right here.

"No." She shook her head.

"One..." I climbed off her, pulling her to sit up with me.

"West, I can't..."

"Two..."

Her eyes glossed over with liquid. A small whimper emerged from her throat.

With her arms still in my hands, I looked briefly into her eyes, her face full of fear, sadness, and something I couldn't place. A strange agony engulfed my chest. *Would I ever look into these eyes again? Would I ever have the chance to kiss those lips again?*

I reached up and, without realizing it, I grabbed her face and crushed my lips against hers for a brief kiss. I pulled back, my forehead still touching hers.

"Three," I whispered against her mouth, then stood, turned, and ran straight for the demon, waving my arms. "Hey, you ugly bastard!"

Balor's head jerked to me, a snarl forming on his face. He pulled his arm back and aimed his javelin at me, but he stared around as though searching for Rez. I couldn't chance looking behind and only hoped Rez followed my order, but if she were there, I had to keep him occupied.

"Come on, Balor, show me what your wrinkled,

ancient ass is capable of," I screamed at him. His normal eyes focused on me, his grip tightening on his spike. His enormous size gave me a second to see his moves coming, but he was still a hell of a lot faster than I thought. My body leaped to the side as his lance penetrated the ground, crackling the earth right where I had stood. I fell on jagged rocks, which sliced a deep gash across my stomach and hip. He tugged out his javelin, twisting to find me again. It took him a few moments to locate me, so maybe his eyesight wasn't good. I might have that going for me. Then I caught sight of a black shadow darting toward the water.

Shit, Rez. What was she doing? I told her to run, but I didn't have time to dwell on it. Balor grunted and raised his weapon to strike again. Scrambling up, I barely got to my feet when the blade sparked against the rock where I stood, sending me flying. I curled into a ball, scraping the side of my body as it grazed the razor edges of stone before tumbling into the damp sand. I pushed up quickly, my toes digging in and helping me stand.

Balor drew out his spike, and at not seeing my dead body speared to it, he howled with aggravation. He reminded me of a zombie. At one time he was the high demon king, worthy of legend, someone respected and feared. Now he grunted and moved like an ogre. Rez had said bringing someone back from the dead was a myth in its own right. Dark, twisted magic like that didn't come without a cost. I wondered how much was left of him inside the husk.

I ran, moving across the beach. Where was Rez? Had she gone into the water? Actually, it probably was the wisest move. She could swim faster than she could run. She was much safer there. I hoped she was way down the coast by now, far from danger.

I glanced over my shoulder and saw Balor's eyes land on me. I caught the green glint as his third eye began to rise. Shit.

My feet zigzagged across the beach, taking a sharp turn at the exact moment a beam of light shot down where I had been, exploding the ground like a bomb. Once again I went sailing into the air, the power of his magic shooting me to the far end of the beach. Rolling, skidding, and banging, my already bruised and bleeding form grated like cheese over the rocks.

Finally I came to a stop when I dropped between two boulders, wedging so tightly a rib cracked. My ears rang, and it took me a moment for my head to stop spinning, bile coating my tongue.

The ground shook, and I knew Balor was coming to investigate. I tried to move, my teeth grinding together in agony, and I sucked in a sharp breath to steady myself. Ignoring the slashing pain, I yanked my head enough to see over the top. And I froze.

Balor was making his way to me, but that was not what my focus caught on. Rez was climbing up the back of one of Balor's legs.

*Holy shit! What is she doing?*

Balor took three steps and loomed over me. I had nowhere to go. Besides being stuck, sheer cliffs surrounded me and boxed me in like a cornered animal. The beast inside was impossible to ignore, stinging my muscles with its urge to change to beast. I roared. It wanted out. It wanted to survive. But all I felt was unbearable pain.

Green flashed in his eyes again, and I closed mine. This was it. No more running. This was how my story would end: in charred beast bits.

The moment I expected his eye to burst me into

flames, I heard him bellow with pain instead. I snapped my lids open.

His attention was focused over his shoulder on one of his legs. That was when I saw Rez twist a knife deep across his Achilles heel, where the skin was thinnest. Blood squirted out like a tiny fountain.

Balor swung his hand at Rez, trying to rid himself of the nuisance. His hand missed her. She took the opportunity to stab the knife into another part of his heel, causing another spray of blood. Balor boomed, his fingers knocking Rez off his leg and into the ocean.

Balor stumbled back and crashed exactly where Rez had fallen, the ocean sucking him back below. I tried to scream her name, but he created a tidal wave of water around him, which pummeled down the beach on me. The water jiggled me out from the rocks, shoving me roughly through them like I was a sock in a washing machine. My head cracked against a rock and plunged me into the dark depths of nothing.

***

I had drifted into pure darkness when a sharp sting sliced my face. "West!" A beautiful voice sang my name, pulling me back to conscious. "Wake up, please."

I groaned, coughing up at least a gallon of seawater. Rez stood over me for the second time tonight. Her shoulders sagged with relief when I winked at her.

"We have to stop meeting like this, sweetheart," I said hoarsely, hacking up the rest of the water in my lungs. "If you want me wet, I know easier ways to go about that."

"Shut up. You've been out for ten minutes. I was scared to death." She smacked my chest, and I clutched my torso with a moan.

"Ow."

She lifted what was left of my shirt, and a small intake of air filtered through her lungs. My stomach resembled a plate of burnt lasagna. Blood, skin, muscles, and veins protruded from the wounds over my body.

A deep depression coiled inside me because I couldn't become the beast and heal my soul. It felt so dark there; all I could do was use humor. If I gave over to this kind of darkness, I would be lost forever.

"What happened to Balor?" I lifted my head and looked past her.

"He didn't come back up." She helped me sit up. "All I can think is we weren't worth the effort up here after I sliced his heel."

I sucked in, grinding my teeth together. "What the hell where you thinking? I told you to run."

"Don't be grumpy because I saved you again. Just accept being the damsel," she quipped.

I huffed with aggravation.

"We can talk when we get home. We need to get you stitched up." She got to her feet, still only in her underwear, which were ripped and streaked with dirt and sand.

She quickly tucked my diving stuff in a small crevice since I wouldn't be able to carry it back. It was restrictive and too dangerous.

I nodded, wrapped my arm around my waist, and rose to my feet. Rez slipped an arm around me and helped me walk. My strained leg muscles and fractured rib were healing, but slowly. My head spun from being cracked like an egg against the rocks. There weren't many places my body didn't hurt.

Rez helped me slip on my boots, got into her clothes, and walked carefully with me as I limped toward the trail to the top of the cliffs. I gave the beach a last look over my shoulder.

On top of the opposite ridge stood a hooded figure, a cloak billowing in the wind. I blinked and the form was gone, leaving me unsure I'd seen it in the first place, even though my entire body prickled with a warning.

# TWENTY-ONE

We didn't talk much the entire way back to the cottage. It took all my strength to keep walking, my body wanting to shut down and heal. When we entered, Rez sat me on the edge of the bed.

"I'm going to start a bath with some healing salts. They'll help close some of these superficial wounds faster. Then I will stitch the others." She proceeded to the bathroom. The sound of water filling the tub lulled me and I began to doze.

"Hey." A hand touched my face and I jerked awake. Rez dropped her fingers, but her face was inches from mine. "The bath's ready."

I nodded and met Rez's gaze. She quickly looked away and hastily moved from me. The kiss. I had kissed her. Again. It was now the only thought in my mind. The small cottage created an intimacy that slinked over my skin, rousing me. Again. *Aw, shit!*

"Thank you." I gripped the metal footboard and stood, then hobbled to the bathroom. The smell of salt mixed with the sweet odor of magic. These weren't your normal bath salts.

"Didn't I get enough salt earlier?" I stared at the milky water.

"And sand, dirt, rocks." Rez came in behind me. "The magic in this will help you mend faster…" We both knew she left off "because you can't." We were quiet for a moment.

Rez shifted on her feet, waving her hand at the tub. "Will you be okay?"

"Think I can handle it." I gave her a half grin. Turning away, I reached for the back of my shirt to pull it over my head, tearing some of the wounds open. I hesitated. Air heaved in my lungs, and I grabbed the side of the tub. Warm blood oozed along my torso and back, seeping into my damp, stiff shirt.

Rez tilted her head. "You sure you're all right there?"

My nose scrunched up in a snarl. She smiled smugly.

"Let me help you." She took a step to me, grabbing the hem of my shirt and turned me toward her. No man, especially a Dark Dweller, wanted to appear weak, but this was different. A woman wanting to undress me, especially Rez, made it so I couldn't deny the nurse thing got my heart pounding.

Her hands felt warm against my skin as she skimmed my sides and she carefully drew my shirt up. Her body pressed against mine, her eyes on her hands, though her breath fluttered against my skin. She was gentle with the pieces of my sliced shirt sticking to the wounds. Her fingers hit my chest and her lashes fluttered, lifting to my face. It felt like I was in a trance and could not look away. Her breath faltered when I lifted my arms as far as I could. It hurt like hell, but I could withstand pain in her presence. She tugged the fabric over my head and threw the shirt on the floor.

She didn't move away, her gaze still on me. The whole

room seemed to disappear. All I knew was I wanted her. Wanted to be deep inside her. The urge overwhelmed me. Consumed me.

*Lars. Remember fuckin' Lars.* My brain shouted at me. I clenched my jaw and shot backward away from her.

"I think I can handle the rest." I ran my hand through my hair.

"Yes. Of course." Rez moved away, thumbing toward the door. "If you need anything, I'll be out here."

*If I need anything? Yeah, to be in between your legs.* I shoved the thought away as soon as it crossed my mind. I waited for her to shut the door before I finished undressing. My body was so aroused it hurt.

I eased into the tub, trying to clear my head of shooting pain. I struggled to relax, but the thought of her right outside the door was too hard to forget. Images of her wearing only her underwear flashed in my head. We'd only been on this mission over a week, and I never had to relieve myself so much in my life. It scared me she was the only one I thought of when I did. She was the cause and the cure. I tried to force myself to think of women in general, a bunch of them together, but no matter what, my mind returned to her. Just her.

*"Fuuuuccckk,"* I growled. Doing it myself now wasn't good enough. It only made me more tense and aggravated. There was a reason people didn't see my bad mood much. It was something no one should experience.

A light knock tapped at the door. "Want to make sure you didn't fall asleep."

"Nah. Getting out now," I called back. It took me a bit of effort to get out of the tub, but I already felt the surface wounds closing. Overall, my body felt a lot less sore and tired. The magic in the salts was amazing. I wrapped a towel around my waist and moved into the other room.

Rez stood by my bed, placing alcohol and a sewing kit on the nightstand.

"Okay, nurse, your patient is ready."

She glanced over at me. I wore only a towel. Her cheeks slightly pinked but she motioned to the bed. "Get in."

Without warning, I dropped my towel and went to climb in. She swiftly stepped to the side and dropped her eyes. Fae were not ashamed of naked bodies, but it felt different to have *her* looking at me. Oh yeah, it was different.

I settled against the headboard and pulled the sheet to my waist.

She sat on the edge of the bed, her back straight. She looked so elegant even though she still wore the damp, sand-ridden clothes from earlier.

"Go shower."

"I'll sew you first, some of the cuts are still bleeding."

"I know you are uncomfortable." I tapped my fingers on her dirty cargo pants. "I'll be all right for another ten minutes."

She sucked in her lip, leaning her neck to the side, a strange smile echoing on her mouth. "You know me so well, huh?"

"Yeah." I nodded. "I know you don't mind getting dirty but hate having to stay that way. You'll be twitchy and uneasy the whole time, craving a shower." I grinned. "I'd rather have your full attention on me."

She returned my smile and stood. "Be just a few minutes."

She grabbed some clothes and disappeared into the bathroom. My eyes closed and I drifted off to sleep to the movie of her naked in the shower. But quickly my dreams shifted, and my mind returned to the mysterious figure on the cliff.

---

*I squinted, staring harder at the spot. Suddenly the sky lit up with a flash of lightning, igniting the outline of a small hooded figure. A woman. I felt her power. It crackled the air, feeling vaguely familiar.*

*Her cloak fluttered in the wind as she raised her arms. Then magic rushed into me, crashing me back onto the rocky beach. The moment her magic hit me, the beast broke free. My body shifted with elation, and my paws hit the ground, feeling the freedom and peace it had been wanting for so long.*

*A roar tore from my throat as I took off down the beach.*

*"West!" I heard Rez scream from behind. I looked behind to see Rez and the hooded figure standing on the rim of the cliffs, the cloaked woman holding a knife to Rez's throat.*

*"She will merely be another one you doom to death." Without hesitation the figure sliced Rez's neck and pushed her body off the ledge into the sea.*

*Nooooooo! Agony howled through the beast.*

---

I bolted awake, ready to attack.

"West." Rez grabbed my rising arm. "It's me."

My gaze danced around the room, reassuring myself we were safe. She was alive. Oxygen left my lungs, and I sagged back against the headboard.

"Nightmare?" Rez perched herself on the chair, smelling amazing, fresh from the shower. She was in her silky cream camisole and soft cotton cream pajama bottoms, her wet hair draped over one shoulder.

"Yeah, but featuring a different woman."

Rez's eyebrow shot up.

"When we were leaving tonight, I looked back and could swear I saw someone standing on the opposite ledge," I explained. "But I blinked, and they were gone…so it could have been my imagination."

"But…" She grabbed for a hand towel and the bottle of rubbing alcohol.

"In my dream it looked like the same hooded figure. A woman. Her magic was so strong it blasted through me, bringing the beast to life. That's when I woke up." I left out the part where Rez was killed. "What if it was the Druid? The one who awakened Balor?"

"I was thinking whoever revived him might have to stay close," Rez responded, leaning me forward to look at my back. "This type of magic might need to be refueled. Bringing someone like Balor back from the dead has to take constant magic to keep him animated."

Aneira had killed most of the Druid line, afraid of the power they had. Druid magic was more powerful than fae magic, and fae could not control them. The Queen did not like being less powerful than anyone. She created a fear campaign and had them slaughtered by the thousands. Until Eli became aware of Kennedy, Ember's best friend, we thought all Druids had been annihilated. Since Kennedy, the first Druid Queen, had been installed on the throne, Druids had come out of the woodwork. And some felt the right to avenge the fairies, the fay who were the elite group of fae, who had wronged them.

"Balor is not naturally magic. Druids are capable of doing dark magic, but usually don't. It's dangerous, evil, and corrupting. Everything they stand against." Rez touched the cloth lightly to my skin.

I grunted as alcohol sizzled in the cuts on my back. "Usually. We might have found one quite all right with their dark side."

"Are you thinking if we find this Druid, we might be able to break the magic over Balor?" She plastered bandages to my back, most of the sores healing from the bath, before laying me back again.

"My exact thought," I said through clamped teeth, the movement stretching my stomach wounds. "I might know a few witches who possibly know of a Druid around here. Or at least a rumor. Either way, we go forward." I had told Rez about visiting Olwyn and Fionna on the way back from the granary.

"So, we're going to face Balor again?" She paused, glancing up at me.

"We have no choice. You know that. But first we see a witch about a demon." I hoped Olwyn could help us if there were a Druid connected to Balor. Breaking the magic between them was our best bet.

She nodded. We didn't have an option. The King had spoken. You got what he wanted or died trying.

"Balor doesn't look like he has too much awareness rolling around in that empty head, but whoever is retaining him will be expecting us this time." I sucked through my teeth as she pressed another alcohol-laden pad to my wounds. "The only thing we had going for us tonight was the surprise element, and we still lost. Badly."

"I don't think it would have made a difference." Rez doused the cloth with more disinfectant.

"Sure I can't drink that?" I wanted whiskey more than I wanted food. And my stomach was grinding like an ungreased crank.

"You could, but it would probably make you sick, besides tasting like troll piss."

My eyebrows reeled up in surprise. "Okay, darlin', you saying *troll piss* is either disturbing or extremely hot."

"Which one?"

"Can't decide. Probably both." I eyed her suspiciously. Every day her guard was falling away. "Do you actually know what troll piss tastes like?"

Her eyes lifted coyly to mine with a hint of a mischievous smile.

"Wow. Now I really want to know."

The impish expression stayed on her face as she shrugged. "Women are allowed their secrets."

Damn. And here I thought I knew most of them by now. My jaw loosened to ask her, when she spoke instead. "I am sorry. I reacted too hastily tonight out of anger and frustration." She kept her tone even. "My mother does that to me."

"Like only mothers can." I watched her lace some fishing line through a needle. "Believe me, my mother was a piece of work as well."

"What was she like?"

"A complete and utter hippie. Didn't want me, but Father was adamant about having kids. She hated limitations. Kids, clothes, rules. She resented staying home with me. After my father's death she grew steadily worse at pretending to even give a shit, running away whenever she felt like it. She'd leave me for weeks on end, putting dry grain in bowls on the floor like I was a pet. She'd be gone longer than we had food or supplies. I was just a kid and I'd get so hungry. A few times I ate the neighbor's trash.

"Lorcan realized what was going on. He snuck me food and milk or brought me home for dinner. He kept it secret. Never exposing my mother's horrible parenting. It meant a lot to me. Even when she abandoned me, I still loved her. Wanted to protect her."

"Ah. Another reason why you felt obligated to follow Lorcan."

"I knew I made the wrong choice the moment I followed him, but loyalty is a funny thing. It can overpower your better instincts."

An odd expression filtered swiftly over her face and was gone. "Yeah, it can."

Was she thinking about Lars? I wanted to know badly but kept quiet.

"But you changed your mind. Is that why Lorcan turned you over to the Queen? Because you turned against him?" Rez knew I ended up in the Queen's dungeons but not how. She flicked open a lighter, burning any germs off the needle. "Em said she didn't really know what happened. You wouldn't talk about it." She squeezed my wound together. "Take a breath and let it out." I did as she said. On the exhale she pinched my skin together and stuck in the needle.

"Lorcan didn't turn me over to her. He's a dick, but we're still family. I know he would never have done that to me." I looked at the ceiling. Suddenly the story was tumbling from my lips.

"The moment Lorcan kidnapped Ember and locked her up, I knew I'd fucked up. Eli wasn't the one who lost his way, but Lorcan. When I found out he was working with Aneira no matter if he believed he was doing the right thing for his family, it felt like a knife to the gut. That was one of the worst betrayals to us, especially after she had banished us from the Otherworld." The needle weaved through my skin with a sharp tug as she drew the skin together.

"I was on my way to tell Eli and Cole what was going on, where Ember was being held, before the Queen could get to her. I didn't get far before I ran directly into Aneira and her men. She didn't let me shift or contact my clan through our link." I swallowed, remembering the tremendous magic she held, the soul-crushing humiliation she put me through. "Realizing I was about to betray Lorcan and mess up her plans, she knocked me out and had a soldier take me through the doors to the Otherworld. I woke in her prison, chained with a spiked choker. The rest you know." My hand automatically came up to my throat. The scars from the collar still circled my neck, a constant reminder.

"I can't imagine what you went through down there."

My gaze darted away, mortification twisting to anger.

"Think you've experienced enough of my nightmares to get it." There was so much more Aneira did I wanted no one to know. I buried the memories so deep I hoped they would cease to exist.

"Yes." She pressed her lips into a grim line, looking down. "But those are memories, shadows, not what you actually experienced."

"Sometimes I think the nightmares are worse. Even after it's over, they're torture...never letting it go away."

"I am sorry, West," Rez murmured, tying off the wound. "For all you've gone through."

Rage bristled under the surface. "I don't need pity."

"It's not pity. If anything it's understanding. As you know, my past holds a lot of pain and loss, but it has made me who I am."

"I don't want to talk about it anymore."

She nodded, setting down the needle and thread, and picked up the cloth to clear the blood off the stitched lesion.

*Shit.* The topic had gotten too serious, stirring my ghosts, and allowing in all the dark memories I wanted to forget. I leaned my head back against the headboard and watched Rez from under my lashes. I could tell she sensed my gaze on her, but she wouldn't look up.

I needed to say something. Take away the tension in our silence. "So…Mareza, huh?" I licked my dry lips, quirking them into a cheeky grin.

Rez tensed; her forehead lined as she continued to clean the abrasion.

"What does it mean?"

She finally sighed. "It means 'of the sea.' Not especially original for a siren."

"It's pretty."

"I hate it. My mother is the only one who uses it." Her eyebrow curved up, a hint of a smile on her mouth. I jerked as she pushed on one of my cuts. "So if you know what's good for you, you will never say it again."

"That's the problem, darlin'." I chuckled. "I never seem to know what's good for me."

Her gaze lifted slowly and met mine. Her irises glinted in the dim moonlight. I hadn't meant anything when I said it, but staring at her now, my statement held a chasm of truths. I'd spent decades going after all the wrong things to keep myself safe from the right ones. To save myself the suffering again. My gut told me I had the right one in front of me, but my brain told me I was all wrong for her.

She glanced back at my chest, focusing on cleaning an already sanitized gash. She had cleaned them all, but she didn't stop, nor did I interrupt her. An intimate tension sparked the air, and my body responded to her feathered touch. I wasn't one to ever be embarrassed over an erection since it was a natural part of being a Dark Dweller. "Permanently aroused" should be our motto.

She lay the wet towel on the table, once again purposefully keeping her gaze from mine. She was done, but she did not rise and walk away to the safety of her side of the room. Part of me wanted to command her to leave, go as far from me as she could. The other was begging for her to stay.

Neither happened. I stayed motionless and waited for her to choose.

Rez's eyes moved over my body. She lifted her hand and touched my skin. She had been doing it all night, but something changed. Before her hands had felt almost as distant as a nurse's. Now as she glided slowly down my torso, curling around the Celtic tattoo on my side, lowering past my hip, I sucked in a breath, blinking, every nerve responding.

Merely a touch from her and I was harder than cement. She saw it. The blanket was pitched like a frickin' tent, but she didn't say anything.

"What do the markings mean?" she whispered, her voice like magic. Even if I were more immune than a human to her ability, she had the capability to ask anything from me and I would give it to her. It probably had little to do with her gift and more that *she* had the power to undo me.

"It's our clan's symbol. We all have one." I lifted my head, glancing at the symbol. "As soon as you hit a certain age and are trained to fight by a leader, you go through an initiation ceremony. You get a tattoo and head out on assignments with the elders." My thoughts went back to my time. I was already centuries old, but in human years I was about eleven. "That was before we came to Earth. "Our clan doesn't do it anymore. The only one who would have gotten one was Jared…"

I trailed off, the hurt of his death still excruciating. I could barely say his name without losing my shit. I rubbed my face, laying my head back again.

"Sorry." Rez placed her full palm on my markings. "I know how much it hurts to lose those you love."

"He was a kid. He had so much more life to experience. I loved Maya and Koke and miss them all the time. But losing a family member so young…"

She shook her head, her long, silky hair tumbling down her arms.

"As a Dark Dweller, death is part of us. We are trained killers. Losing one of our own is rare, but it happens. We mourn, we move on. Losing Samantha and Owen was difficult, but it's not the same. Jared…fuck…I miss that kid so much I can't breathe sometimes. It makes me so angry at life."

"Ah." She nodded.

"What?"

"It's another reason to guard yourself from letting anyone in." Her stare locked on, holding me prisoner. "If you don't sit still, then no one and nothing can catch up. Keep it cheeky and fun. None see the pain consuming you underneath."

My head knocked into the headboard, and oxygen filled my nostrils. The beast wanted to close down and shove her words back. Growl. Bite. Anything but hear the truth in them. Twice tonight she had reached in and pulled out my soul and shoved it back in my face.

"What the hell do you know?" I snapped. "You think spending a few days with me makes you an expert?"

"Hardly." She didn't react to my harsh tone. "You, West Moseley, are one of the most complex, straightforward, layered men I've ever known. I could spend the next thousand years and not understand you."

A rush of heat went through my body at the thought of her permanently by my side. The rumble in my chest, the beast reacting to her words, shocked me. It didn't fear. It wanted.

"Too bad, darlin', I would have enjoyed your hands-on assessment for the next thousand years." I half grinned.

"Who said it would be hands on?"

"Believe me, that's the only way you'd want to evaluate me." I winked playfully, trying to keep it light, but it failed miserably. I felt the heat rush off her body and slam into me. My hands curled into the sheets, fighting the primal reaction. Being naked only cranked every nerve ending to aching levels.

She licked her bottom lip and dropped her gaze. I was afraid to move, wanting nothing more than to take her. Her fingers rested on my torso and glided down to the edge of blanket, right to my V-line.

"You are gonna have to stop doing that, darlin'." I struggled to swallow.

"West." Her voice was deep and raspy. The sound of my name licked at my skin, igniting my nerve endings. The air grew thick, and I gripped the bedsheets, my knuckles turning white.

"Please." I stared up at the beams, taking measured breaths, trying to ignore the way her hand kept moving farther down my hip. "If you know what's good for you...you will stop. Move far away."

"That's the problem, *darlin'*." A sly grin curved her gorgeous mouth as she mimicked my earlier words. "I never seem to know what's good for me either."

My chest stopped pumping air. My muscles paralyzed with desire.

"When you kissed me tonight..." She gulped in air, her hand touched the place between her breasts, like she was trying to breathe. "It's all I can think about. All I want."

Whatever flimsy wall I had been trying to keep up splintered into a million pieces. I reached out, clutching my fingers along her jaw, and drew her in. Our mouths crashed against each other's with ferocity. Hungry. Feverish. My tongue parted her mouth, and she welcomed it with hers. Nipping at her lip, I growled, igniting my blood. She climbed on the bed and straddled me, the thin sheet barely covering me. The reserved façade melted as her kisses became more passionate and wild. She dug her hands through my hair roughly and ground against me.

*Oh. Holy. Shit.*

She leaned back as she stripped off her camisole. "I think your breasts are flirting with me," I said.

She smiled coyly. "Then teach them a lesson. Punish them." I don't think I could have been more surprised by her words or more turned on.

Her bra hadn't even hit the floor when my lips moved over her breasts, making sure I appreciated each one. Rez's breathing grew more labored as she arched into me. I could feel the heat building, especially between her legs, and it only twisted my thoughts, ignoring the alarms going off in my head.

*Warning. Warning. Unseelie King's mistress. Step away now. Keep penis and hands to yourself at all times.*

"Rez..." I forced myself to pull back, trying to ignore her bare chest, toned stomach, and curves.

She took my pause to start untying her pants.

"Stop." I grabbed her hands. "I am going against every instinct and desire in my body, but we have to stop. We can't do this."

"You're telling me no?"

"Barely." I looked away. "I like my life and my dick attached."

A glint sparked in her eyes as she took my hand, sliding it into her pants. "Feel that?"

I gulped, nodding, scalding heat pulsing off her. She pushed my hand farther down, encouraging me to feel her. Without my consent, my fingers dipped between her skin and her underwear, finding her. Her lashes fluttered and she moaned.

"That day in the hotel…" She swallowed, licking her lip. "The thought of you getting off to me. I know you felt it, too. That intense power was like nothing I have ever experienced. You were all I could think of. I wanted so bad to actually feel you inside me. And I have every day since." She leaned back so my fingers could slide deeper inside her, her voice husky and sexy. "This is more than merely enjoying the act of sex. *You* do this to me. I can't breathe or think when you are around me. And right now I want nothing more than you to *fuck* me. Over and over."

The more brazen and vocal she became, the more I lost my mind. I was getting the slight impression the little siren who kept reserved and controlled in her daily life let it all go behind closed doors.

I laid her back on the bed, tugged off her pajama bottoms, and tossed them across the room. I wasn't surprised I found the match to her bra…lace-trimmed black panties. She was the type who would always be put together. But here and now, I was going to do everything in my power to unglue her. Shatter her in the most unbelievable way.

Slipping the underwear over her hips, my mouth worked from her stomach to her thighs. My tongue and lips replaced my fingers. She let loose a sharp hitching cry, then a string of dirty words. She clutched my head, opening herself more for me.

I knew I was good at this. Many, many women had told me I ruined them for others. I got off on it, but more as a competitive thing. I didn't do it really for the girl, but for the guy after. Satisfied in knowing the women would compare everyone to me. With Rez, no thought filled my head except wanting to please this woman beneath me. I listened for cues, for what she wanted and liked. I was about to lose my shit at her noises and cries.

"West...please," she begged, tugging at my hair. "I want you. Now."

"But I'm not done, darlin'." I grinned at her.

"No. You aren't." She dug her nails into my scalp, riling me. "So get going and fuck me till I can't breathe."

Seeing the fierceness in her eyes, the wild need in her expression, I was a lost man.

"And don't hold anything back." Her mouth pressed to mine as I moved up. Our kiss was deep and aggressive, her legs tightening around my waist. Common sense was gone. Reality stepped outside. I positioned myself, teasing at her entrance.

"West...please," she begged.

I slid inside her. *Oh. Jesus.*

She gasped. We both paused as I moved farther into her. The magic we had felt before was nothing like this. It engulfed us, rubbed against my body with intense strokes, heightening every nerve till I couldn't breathe. My head spun.

Sex always felt good, but this was beyond pleasure. I had never felt anything even remotely close to her. She shook underneath me, vibrating with need, her hands pulling my ass toward her and me deeper into her as I started to roll my hips. Her soft moans became louder the harder and faster I moved.

I put one foot on the floor, gripping the metal frame, her body curved up for me, wanting more. I pulled back and then plunged in deeper, rocking her. A cry came from her throat, her nails digging into my back. I drew back and thrust in again.

She felt so incredible; I could barely keep standing. My leg shook, but it gave me more leverage as I drove deeper and faster into her. A small voice in my head was screaming at me to stop. I was sticking my dick in the Unseelie King's woman. The biggest no-no ever. You could slaughter a whole neighborhood under his protection, try to kill him, or break a bond, but nothing was as bad as taking something he felt he owned. Rez was his. He would not let anybody touch her. And no one would be stupid enough to try.

Except me.

Sweat trickled down my back, and I pumped harder, Rez bucking wildly against me. All I knew was the King could have walked in and I wouldn't have stopped. Nothing felt so right or so good.

"Oh gods, West..." She put her arms over her head, pushing back against the footboard, keeping herself in place.

The classy, elegant woman was gone. Her eyes sparked with heat, her mouth screaming out obscenities, telling me what she wanted, and her body violently moved with mine.

"You like it dirty, don't you, darlin'?"

"Yes," she growled, her gaze fierce. "But only with you. *You* do this to me. I want to completely lose myself. Shatter me. Break me free so they hear me in the next country." Her words undid me. The beast inside roared to life with vigor, taking her...demanding her with everything it had.

We both made noises I had never heard before. The bed rattled the room like an earthquake. The metal frame bent under my fingers, curving with the force I thrust into her.

"Holy shit," I bellowed, the beast taking over my cry as I felt her climax clenching around me. Mine followed in a heavy intensity causing me to feel I was nowhere near earth. Her body still pulsed and clamped as I gasped for breath with a moan. My body went limp, dipping over her. The twisted metal was hot in my hands as I loosened my death grip. I shut my eyes, riding the last bit of the wave, not ready to leave her body. *She's mine.*

Fingers skated over my ass to my back, opening my eyes. My gaze caught her deep brown eyes, which sparkled in the light. Neither of us could talk as we stared at each other, catching our breaths.

Her hand came to my face, she leaned up, and kissed me deeply. In that moment I knew—no question this time. The feeling consumed my body, so clear, so firm, there was no doubt. I was a goner. The beast had claimed her. Claiming someone was not in a dweller's control. The beast saw past rules and offenses. It was primal and comprehended only what it wanted.

It was also rare. I had been with a mind-boggling number of women, human and fae, since I turned fifteen. I couldn't give a ballpark figure, but they would fill several ballpark stadiums. And only once before had the beast gotten close to declaring its claim.

I stared at the beautiful woman below me. The one it had no right to possess. *Shit. What were you thinking?* I pulled away, moving off her.

"What?" She sat up, her cheeks flushed from excitement and physical activity. Damn, she was insanely beautiful.

*Get away. Get away,* logic screamed at me. I rose from the bed with a jolt, rubbing my temple, I sauntered over to the window. Anger at myself for letting it happen slipped down my arms, crunching my hands into fists.

"West?" Rez's voice softly said my name, uncertainty ringing through it. The sound of her bare feet padded over to me, but I didn't need to hear her. I could feel her now. Her magic, her energy hummed along my skin and in my body like an alarm. *Mine.*

*No! Not yours.* I bit down on my lower lip, keeping my gaze out the window. She came behind me, timidly touching my waist. Only a moment ago there was nothing reserved or sweet about her as she tore into my skin. Her uninhabited side only caused me to like her more. Rez didn't fit into a box. She was sassy, sweet, strong, timid, funny, serious, passionate, timid, shy, dirty, sophisticated. And insightful.

"Hey." She kissed my shoulder blade. "Not now. Not in this room."

I snorted. "Then when, Rez? The walls don't make it a safe area where you are suddenly available."

She sucked in through her teeth and moved to my side, staring out the window. I tried not to notice how the moonlight spread over her naked, sweaty body and reflected off her long, dark hair.

"Do you want me available?"

"Doesn't matter. You're not."

"Yes, it does." She turned to me. "Tell me honestly, do you only want me because you know I'm safe? If I were single, would it be more than sex to you?"

"It's not you're merely dating another man, darlin'. You are the *Unseelie King's* mistress." I clenched my jaw and fought the natural instinct to take what the beast declared as his. My nature was far more primal than a demon's, but Lars's status and power gave him full right to his possessions. Rez was not someone you controlled or owned, but the basic need of my beast didn't understand "sharing."

"Yes, I am. But as I told you, that has been in title only for a long time." She folded her arms and glanced away. "The moment Ember came into Lars's life, he was reminded of his true love. I tried to fight Aisling's ghost for a long time. But it was pointless. Even in death, she will always win."

"Doesn't matter." I swung to face her. "You think he will let me take you from him?"

"Let you take me?" Her eyebrows curved up, her lips pressing together. "Do I have a say in what I want?"

I dipped my head. "Of course."

"Well." She brought her hands to either side of my face, lifting my head. "What I want is for one night to forget everything. No pain, nightmares, memories, past lovers, or right or wrong. Because the only thing I know is when I am with you everything feels right in a way I haven't known in a very long time. If ever."

The Dark Dweller stirred in my chest…along with other parts of my body.

She pressed her body into mine, tugging my face closer to hers, her voice sultry. "Who knows what we'll have to face tomorrow? Tonight I want to be with you."

A growl logged in my throat, and I wrapped my arms around her, drawing her in. "I'm at your command, darlin'."

"Then I order you to screw me senseless," she whispered against my mouth. "All night long."

I blinked a few times, a grin hitching my lips. "I am loving that dirty mouth of yours."

"And I am loving everything…" Her hands ran over my torso, slithering lower. Her fingers wrapped around my dick as she kissed me deeply. "Now, let me show you how dirty my mouth can get." She shoved me against the window, my butt cheeks squeaking around the glass as she went on her knees.

The rest of the night we gave over to our relentless passion, our mouths and hands never losing contact. We paused once to get water, but all it took was watching water trickle down her chin and breasts and I was ready to go again. Dark Dwellers were insatiable by nature when it came to sex, never feeling quite satisfied. Even with Cammie, the beast was always restless for more.

Rez was as voracious as me. My endless need to be inside her was not only about pleasure but also because this was the first time in ages I'd felt stillness in my soul. It was hard to explain. The peacefulness I had with Cammie had been wonderful, but this was on an entirely different level. I never felt more alive—buzzing with intensity and at the same time calmer.

The beast was happy, finding peace in the worst place possible. But it didn't care. Whenever I was in her it made itself at home.

# TWENTY-TWO

The morning brought reality back with a blinding light. My lids squeezed against the rays of rare sunshine in Ireland for this time of year. I couldn't help feeling mocked. I just condemned my life, but the sun shone, the birds sang.

Bastards.

I dug my face into the pillow, stretching out like a lion, my injuries stinging slightly, but mostly I felt fine. Better than fine. The beast was calm…humming. It was so freakin' content and happy I didn't even know how to respond. Never in my life had I not felt it treading on the edges, restless and ready to act. This new sensation was bizarre.

With Rez, my beast was completely content and relaxed. I mean, so calm the supposed killing machine was fuckin' purring like a kitten. What the hell was that? Damn. This was not good.

It didn't stop me from reaching out, to feel her skin, the arch of her hip beneath my fingers, her taste. But my hands hit empty space, and I popped my eyes open. I was alone in the bed.

Her name was on my lips ready to call, when my eyes caught her over by the window. She was folded up in the chair, a coffee cup in her hand, wearing socks and one of my hoodies, which hit her mid-thigh. The steam rolled and danced in the sunrays as it rose from her cup.

The sight of her in my clothes aroused me all over again. Her long, glossy hair draped around her to her waist, glinting in the sun as she stared out the window. I couldn't help but notice the imprints of my butt cheeks on the glass, rousing memories of the night before. We had been relentless. I guess if we were going to break the rules, there was no reason to do it half-assed. I was pretty experimental, not much I hadn't tried, but it wasn't even about that. It was how absolute we gave ourselves over to each other, wholly letting the passion take us. Neither of us held back, and it was the most amazing night of sex I ever had.

And it may be the last. *It has to be*, I told myself.

I watched a slight smile trace her mouth, her fingers touching her lips, a deep blush coloring her olive complexion. *Oh Jesus, is her smile because of me?* Air retracted in my lungs, and my skin prickled, rushing with the need to make sure that smile stayed on her mouth forever, always for me.

"Hey."

"Dammit." Rez jumped, spilling a little liquid from her cup. "You scared me." She hurriedly wiped her leg dry.

"Sorry." I planted my feet on the ground, the blanket barely covering me.

"It's fine. You simply caught me daydreaming."

"About me, I hope?" I grabbed for my boxer briefs off the floor, my gaze never leaving her.

"Maybe." She blushed deeper.

"I'm gonna take that as a yes." I winked. "Hope I'm as good in the memories as in person."

She looked away from me, her whole body flushing. Heat radiated from her like a kiln, hardening me like a freakin' piece of pottery. The beast picked up his head, sensing the change. I inhaled and forced my legs into the fabric of my boxers. Normally I would walk around naked and not even blink an eye, but I needed to draw the line between us again, much as I hated it.

I stood, thinking I was headed for the bathroom, but my beast took me straight to her. She gazed at me when I reached the chair, her eyes so dark, rich, and deep they matched the coffee in her cup. I bent over, my fingers grazed her jaw, pulling her head toward me. My mouth took hers and my body responded. The beast wanted her. My willpower might have been stronger if she didn't kiss me back with such emotion. The ceramic hit the floor with a crash, hot liquid splashing our legs, but we ignored it. I enfolded my arms around her waist, pulling her to me. Our breaths grew labored as our kisses became more eager and intense.

"As much as I like you in my clothes, I need this open now." I unzipped the hoodie. My hands moved over her body. She had only put her underwear back on, which I wiggled off quickly, leaving my sweatshirt on her. Her fingers yanked down my shorts. Lust filled the space, blurring my mind and vision. Our mouths never left each other, I picked her up, and she wrapped her legs around me. This time I took her back to the window and pressed her against it. She broke the kiss, her eyes on me, pulling herself up higher on me before sliding slowly down again.

When my brain short-circuited and I suddenly forgot how to speak English, Gaelic would flow out instead. This usually happened only when I was livid, drunk, or sleeping. I knew Rez had twisted my mind when all I could speak were swear words in my old language.

"Gaelic with a southern accent. Gods, that is hot," Rez gasped as I picked up the pace. The sunshine flickered off her skin as I pounded her into the window. With a loud crack, we splintered the glass.

"Shit, West. The window is breaking. I can feel it." She struggled to speak, gasping for air, her body demanding more from mine.

Without a pause, I gripped her ass with one arm, the other swept everything off the table. Maps, cups, and dishes all hit the floor with a clatter. Her thighs clung harder to me as I moved her to the edge of the table. She hit the top and arched back for me, and I knocked the table into the wall.

The beast took over. I lost all my senses except pleasure, which was heightened. Neither of us was quiet or gentle. All the power of earth and water collided in an explosion. And more Gaelic erupted from my mouth as we plunged over the edge. At least the beast was polite enough to make sure she went first, then followed, wholly letting go.

She fell back on the table, gulping for air. I leaned over her, her legs still tight around my waist. I placed my forearms on the table next to her head, catching my breath.

"I hadn't planned on doing that," I panted. Where was that line I talked about earlier? *What the hell happened to backing away?*

"Me neither." She smiled, her body still not ready to let me go. "But I wanted you. Badly."

"Me too, darlin'." I bent to kiss her when a ringing noise erupted from the floor. Lying near my foot was the walkie-talkie mobile device.

I froze.

Rez looked down and then both our gazes locked on the caller ID.

Lighting up the screen in bright, bold yellow was the Unseelie King's code name and number.

Reality came streaming into the room so fast it spun my head. It seemed surreal. I was still deep inside Rez, and her muscles clasped in orgasm around me at the same time as her man called for his update. He probably never imagined someone would consider screwing his woman. His ego was too vast, his power too unequivocal.

Rez jerked, going up on her elbows, staring at the phone like it was a deadly snake. Not far from the truth.

I slid out of her. A wave of shame, anger, and sadness pummeled me. With one call our little bubble blew up. There was no need to say we could never do this again. It was clear. She swiftly dropped her legs, covering herself with my gray hoodie she was still wearing, her gaze on the floor.

Neither of us moved to pick up the call. I was excellent at lying, pretending all was good when it wasn't. But right here, standing naked, Rez all over me… I wasn't that good. Lars was too perceptive to not sense something even over airwaves. He wasn't the high demon king for nothing. Eventually the buzzing stopped. The silence filled the room with awkward tension.

I ran my hand through my hair; the feel of it flopping back in my eyes annoyed me. Everything pissed me off all of a sudden. "I'm gonna jump in the shower. We need to plan for tonight to find the spear and get the hell out of here." And most importantly, far, far away from each other. Not saying it made the inevitable moment hang heavier in the room.

Rez nodded, her eyes still on the ground by the window. I glanced over my shoulder as I moved to the bathroom. The rays streaming through the splintered window reflected rainbows all over the room and covered her body. My muscles trembled with the agony of turning away from her. The beast demanded I return, but for once I had to override him. Logic had to win out over primal reactions.

I didn't do grief or sadness well. Dark Dwellers weren't built that way. We always turned to anger. I slammed the bathroom door so hard it shook the cottage. Huffing, I leaned over the sink. I had let my hair grow long, to my shoulders, but now I picked up my razor and turned it on. Eli shaved his head when he lost Ember. For three years he thought his mate was dead. I was understanding my brother more every second. Rez was not dead, but she was lost to me just the same.

I knew my life was on a timer now. Even if a miracle happened and Lars didn't find out what had passed between us, it would kill me to know she was sleeping with him every night. To come to the house and pretend she was nothing more than Lars's secretary would be impossible. I could only keep the beast behaving so long.

The last of my dark blond locks fell into the sink. My head and face held a shadow of scruff, drawing more attention to my eyes, which looked cold and ferocious. All I wanted was to shift into the beast and forget everything. Run, fight, have sex with other women till I forgot.

Blistering rage shot through me, my arm slammed into the mirror. Similar to the cracked window in the main room, the mirror fractured into a thousand small pieces, crumbling into the sink as I hit it again. Blood covered my knuckles and smeared across the glass. Morweena was right. If I couldn't become a beast, I was lost. I was merely a weak, pathetic man who fell for someone I couldn't have.

Everything in my past, all the relationships that had gone to hell—my mother, father, Cammie, Aneira—caught up to the present. They all came crashing over me at once. A roar tore through my throat. Anything that was not built into the foundation I tore free and smashed into chunks against the walls. I ripped the bathroom apart, as if it were my prey. Time seemed irrelevant. Blood trickled down my hands and arms as I demolished the space. The beast bashed and banged against its cage, and pain ripped through my veins as I tried to shift.

A scream bellowed from me as I pushed against the invisible barrier with everything I had. My eyes watered, veins and muscles straining. For one brief moment a large paw, daggered with claws, protruded from my hand. I squeezed my lids together, trying to hold the shape, but my body gave out, and I fell to the floor with a pained cry.

"West!" I heard Rez scream over and over again until she finally broke through the door. I lifted my lids but didn't turn to look at her. "Dammit...West." She collapsed next to me on the stone floor. She was still wearing my hoodie, smelling of me. Of sex. My lips pursed in a grim line.

"You need to stop doing that," I growled.

"What?"

"Wearing my clothes." My nostrils flared.

"Sorry. I didn't have time to pick out an outfit before you decided to destroy our bathroom," she snapped, then grabbed my bloody hand with hers. "Gods, West, you pulverized your hands."

"I'll heal." I shrugged.

"Don't move." She stood and stepped out of the room.

I hadn't planned on moving. Pain, both emotional and physical, drained me. My lids drifted closed until I sensed her back in the room, sitting next to me. The smell of rubbing alcohol tickled my nose. My eyes went wide with the first stinging dose of antiseptic.

"I swear, I leave you alone for five minutes and you demolish the room, shave your head, and turn yourself into minced meat." She kneeled over me, my hand in hers as she cleaned it. "I once had a Siberian husky that did the same thing when I left her alone too long."

"You had a dog?" I tilted my head to look at her.

"That's what you picked up from what I said?" She guffawed. "Yes, I used to have a dog. I love animals. Lars isn't fond of them, so I couldn't get one. I miss having a dog. She was so sweet. No matter how bad I felt, she always made me feel better."

"Never had a pet." I let my head roll forward again. "Didn't really need one. I am one."

Rez snickered. "Yeah, you guys make the best family pets. So cuddly and sweet. Great with kids."

"Hey. We are good with kids," I grumbled, a flash of Jared as a baby, him only a few months old, curled around my front paw, stroking my fur and babbling like I understood. I would have destroyed anything to keep him safe. "We're extremely protective."

"I don't doubt that." She met my eyes. "I'll bet you'd be an even better father."

My body went rigid. Her gaze went to my hand, her head shaking. "Sorry, I didn't mean that."

"What? I wouldn't be a fantastic dad?" I quipped back.

"No. Just..." Red colored her cheeks. She paused and grabbed my other hand, inspecting it. She was doing a good job pretending I wasn't still naked.

"We can't do this anymore," I said softly.

"I know." She nodded. Her expression struggled to stay impassive.

"Hey." I grabbed her chin with my free hand, lifting her face to look at me. "If it was anybody else, darlin', I would fight. I would kill anything and anyone in our way."

I held her chin, but she dropped her gaze. "Why does it make me feel worse?"

"Tell me about it."

"West." Her gaze lifted back up. "I never imagined this… you… I wasn't looking. I wanted for nothing. I have a great life. Happy. A family and they need me."

"That's why—"

"Let me finish," she demanded.

"Yes, ma'am." I grinned, dropping my arm.

She smiled back, but a sadness reflected in her eyes. "You messed everything up. I feel torn in two now, between what I should do and what I want. I never wanted more than my life there. Now you've changed everything. How can I go back and pretend? Be happy in my old existence? I will be a shell, knowing I have had a taste of something exceptional. I won't be able to see you walk into the house pretending we are barely friends, and I won't be able to fight the need to see you. It will be torture either way."

"Well, sweetheart, either Lars will kill me or the creature will tonight. Problem solved."

She dug her nail into my cut knuckles.

"Ow, evil woman."

"Not funny."

"Come on, it's a little funny." I nudged her.

"Why, because it might be true?" She glowered at me.

"There is no 'might.'" I tipped my head against hers. "There's no way Lars won't find out."

She tipped back, staring. "Why?"

I wasn't about to tell her my beast set up camp when it roamed between her thighs, positioning a huge neon arrow that proclaimed: *West claimed this one...move along. Nothing to see here.* It would do no good.

"He's a smart man, darlin'. He will sense it. Also, when he touches you, I'm not sure I could sit back and be the obedient pet."

"That's the last thing I would ever want you to be," she whispered, dropping my hands. She unfolded her legs and sat against the wall, her shoulder brushing mine. "We really are in a mess."

Oh, we were beyond that. I don't think she completely understood the severity of it. She must still hope we could tuck it away without Lars ever noticing. I didn't want her to know the truth. She couldn't do anything about it anyway.

"Speaking of mess, you really obliterated this bathroom, didn't you?" She waggled her head, taking in the bare walls, splintered mirror, broken cupboards, and knickknacks on the ground.

"I think we might lose our deposit."

She sniggered, tapping her shoulder against mine, her gaze scouring my head. "I like it." She nodded at my absent hair. "Very tough, Mr. Moseley."

"Thank you, Ms. Mareza."

She jabbed her finger into my side.

"Damn." I jerked with a laugh. "You really hate that name."

"Yes." She turned to me and drooped her head on my shoulder. "But it's not so bad when you say it."

"Really?"

"That doesn't mean you can keep using it. But I will forgive you…and not shave your eyebrows as you sleep."

"No, not my eyebrows." I wiggled them. "They're the only thing that brings in the ladies."

She tipped her head back so she could see me. "It's definitely not the only thing."

"You shave *that* and we are having words, darlin'."

She grinned, and her eyes lit up. She looked…happy. It was the most beautiful I'd ever seen her. And it killed me.

I was on a slippery slope. But my future was pretty much over and not for one moment, staring down at her, did I regret a second of it.

*Hell, West, you're going to die anyway. You might as well jump.*

---

The rain and wind lashed brutally down on us, punishing any exposed skin. The windows of the lone cottage glowed with buttery light, and smoke curled out of the chimney. I hopped over the thigh-high stone fence, taking Rez's hand to help her. She trembled with cold under my grasp, her jacket and pants saturated. Keeping my fingers twisted with hers, I hustled up the hill to the door.

The sun had only lasted till lunch before another gale swept over the land, the temperature dipping low, and rain saturated the already sodden dirt. It was growing dark when we reached Olwyn's cottage. The only thing that kept us moving through the mucky hills was hope Olwyn would know of some old Druid roaming around these parts. Our options were thin; we needed help.

I rapped against the door and tucked Rez close to me to keep her warm. No sound of movement came from inside, but I could smell life in there.

"Fionna?" I hit the door again. "Olwyn?"

Nothing. Rez and I exchanged glances.

"I know you're there. Please, open up." I beat my fists against the wood, rattling the door.

Not a thing stirred. A warning nipped at my neck. I took a deep breath. The smell of oils, herbs, spices, dense magic, and old animal blood filled my nose. It covered the scent of whomever was inside, my ears picking up only one heartbeat.

"Olwyn?" I rammed my shoulder against the entry. I couldn't stop the rise of apprehension. It tapped the base of my neck. I took a step back and kicked my foot at the door. It took two more tries before the old latch broke free, the door bursting open and crashing against the wall.

Rez and I stepped in. Only the fireplace gave off dim light, laying heavy shadows over the room from the table pilled with pots, books, and potions.

"Fionna?" I called out again, my eyes moving slowly over the space. A creak of wood shot my gaze to the hearth. Low flames consumed the tiny chunks of wood left.

Olwyn sat in the rocker. Her eyes focused on the fire as she rocked back and forth in a slow rhythm. She didn't notice our intrusion, her eyes void, her face slack. Something was very wrong. She even smelled different.

"Olwyn?" I walked up cautiously. She continued to stare at the embers like I wasn't there. "Hey." I touched her shoulder.

With a snap, her head turned to me, her eyes glazed. "Who are you?"

"West. I came here a couple of days ago?"

Rez moved around to her other side; Olwyn's gaze slowly tracked her.

"I don't know you." She stared blankly.

"My name is Rez. I am a friend of West's."

"I don't know either of you. Why are you in my house?"

"Olwyn, where is Fionna?" I bent over and placed my hand on her arm.

Her mouth opened to speak then shut, her lips smacking together a few times as she frowned at us. "I-I-I don't know a Fionna…should I?"

"Fionna, the girl who was living here with you. I sat at the table two nights ago, drinking tea. I asked for a locator spell." I motioned back to the table.

"Tea...spell…" Olwyn blinked and stared off past me, lost in her thoughts again.

"Olwyn?" I could feel irritation crawling up my throat.

Rez stepped in front of me, placing her hands on top of the woman's. "What happened to Fionna, Olwyn?"

"Fionna." Olwyn said her name with familiarity, a soft smile. Then it dropped, her head tilted. "I don't know any Fionna."

"Damnit." I turned away, rubbing my hand over my shaved head. What if those men followed my car and kidnapped Fionna, thinking she was with us?

"I think she's been spelled to forget." Rez leaned into Olwyn, staring deep in her eyes.

"What?" I moved around her to see Olwyn. She looked stoned. I took in a deep breath, letting her smell drift over my tongue. My lids popped open. "Holy shit." I could taste the intense magic covering her, but it wasn't her magic. The strong energy pounding off her a few nights ago was gone. Olwyn was barely a witch by magical standards. Not even close to the force I experienced here before.

"What?" Rez tensed, standing to her full height.

"She hardly has any magic, almost none... Either it had all been a front or someone took it. Someone powerful enough..." Fear coursed up my spine. "Look at me, Olwyn." I got in the old lady's face. "Where is Fionna? Did someone take her?"

Olwyn stared at me, emptiness behind her expression.

"Goddammit!" I stomped my foot onto the wood floor, leaning over her chair, my hands gripping the rocking chair, shaking it slightly. "Wake up, Olwyn! Tell me where they took Fionna."

"West, stop. It's no use." Rez pulled me back, my muscles stiff to move.

"Those men took her, I just know it." I gritted through my teeth.

Rez bit down on her lip and looked back at the old woman. I followed her gaze. Olwyn stared at the flames, rocking, empty again. She couldn't help us. Not only did I have to deal with a brought-back-to-life demon, but a missing Fionna as well. If anything happened to her it would be all my fault. Another woman to get hurt because of me.

Unfortunately, Fionna's absence would have to wait, time was ticking down on our chance to obtain the spear, and we needed to go now.

"What do we do?" Rez grabbed a blanket off the bed in the corner and covered the old woman.

"The only thing we can. We go for Balor."

"How do we do that?" Rez moved to me, her face twisted with worry.

"We kill him."

Rez's eyes went wide. "Don't you recall last night?"

"Tonight we purposely go for his third eye. It's the source of his power and his weakness."

"Oh yeah. Easy as that."

I stared deep into her eyes. "Nothing worth getting is ever easy, sweetheart."

# TWENTY-THREE

The beast was the first to rub along my ribs, pricking at my instincts as Rez and I neared the beginning of the trail atop the cliffs. Below lay the small section of beach where we left the diving gear. The trail down to the coast was steep, dangerous, and off limits. I glanced at the woman next to me. *None of those have ever stopped me before.*

The moonless night made it hard to see anything far out. Even though my senses weren't top notch anymore, they still were better than most fae. I took in deep breaths, trying to taste what my gut was warning me about.

Magic. A shit-load of it.

I grabbed Rez's wrist, stopping her in place.

"What?" Her voice spiked with anxiety.

"There's something ahead. Very powerful," I whispered, my head swiveling around, trying to see through the darkness. Tasting the dense air on my tongue, I found it heavier and braided differently than fae's.

Druid magic.

My back stiffened as I noticed a hooded outline a few yards away.

Rez gripped my elbow, and her eyes also locked on the figure.

The petite shape moved forward, hands clutching the hood and pulling the cloak back.

I inhaled sharply. *Holy. Shit.*

"Fionna." My head swam, trying to clear the confusion, but my gut understood immediately.

She grinned smugly. The shy girl I met in the cabin was absent. The power and confidence thumping off her doused the air.

I couldn't believe I had been so blind.

"You aren't a witch at all, are you?" It was less a question and more a statement.

"No." Her voice was strong and fluid. "I am *far* more than that."

"You're a fuckin' Druid." I curled my hands into fists. "How could I not see that? Sense it?"

"Because I didn't want you to," she stated, taking a step closer.

"Why?"

"Because you can get away with a lot more when people don't suspect you or know how powerful you are. No one assumes it's you," she replied. Power controlled every word. "Being the sweet, young ingénue comes in handy."

"So you hid behind an old lady, using her as your front?" I exclaimed. "Did you have to hurt her? Fry her brain?"

"People never saw me as a threat. They always thought it was Olwyn. She looked the part. I didn't. So yeah, I used that. But I'd never hurt her. Olwyn took me in; she is the only family I have."

"You spelled her."

"I enchanted her to keep her safe. She is old and dying. I have kept her alive. What you saw was Olwyn's normal state."

A flame erupted out of the darkness, landing on a stack of wood on the ground. Fire exploded high, displaying the woman behind it clearly. Fionna's arms were outstretched; her lips moved in recitation.

Her actual physique was tiny, but the way she held herself was solid and commanding. Her homogeneous brown pants and tunic top had been replaced with brown leather pants and boots. A brown cloak draped her shoulders. Her long brown hair was pulled back in a high ponytail, showing off her beautiful face.

I had totally underestimated her. "Something's different about you." I cocked my head to the side. "Is it your hair? Get it cut?"

A smile curved her lips.

The fire crackled and spurted. The same feeling went up my spine.

"You're amusing, Mr. Moseley." Her glance darted back and forth between Rez and me, an eyebrow lifting. "I might have liked you. Very much."

I never told her my family name, but I wasn't about to ask now how she knew it. Another ting of warning bells brushed at my skin, stirring my feet.

We fae never underestimated what women were capable of as humans did. Fae women could kick ass. And even though Fionna was barely five foot three and petite, the power emanating off her held the power of a tsunami. You didn't mess with that.

"What's happening here, Fionna?"

"Something that should have centuries ago." Her jaw flexed. "For so long, Druids were persecuted, killed...slaughtered by the thousands. My friends...my family. My mother and father hid me right before they were killed along with my baby sister. I've had to conceal my true nature so I would not be found. But no more..."

"Things are changing. We even have a Druid Queen now."

"That toddler?" Fionna snorted derisively. "I see how well the fae are listening to her. The world is in chaos. She is *not* one of them. They will never fear or respect someone who barely knows how to conjure a basic spell," she growled. "It may not be out in the open anymore, but we are still being hunted and killed. The same fear and ignorance rules you fae."

"Not all of us feel that way. The new Queen is my friend. She is trying hard to change things."

"Please. You can't believe that." Fionna's lids tapered. "I know what you are, *Dark Dweller*...who you work for." She came around the fire; her glare pinned on me. "How stupid do you think I am? The Dark doesn't work with the Light. And *neither* work with Druids. Especially the Unseelie King. And if you believe he will, then you are more of a fool than I thought." Her shoulders lifted with anger. "Do you think he would ever allow someone to rule with magic he can't control? Someone who could possibly destroy him?" Energy pumped through the air, colliding into my bones. My beast growled, sensing a threat. "Why do you think he wants *it*, Dark Dweller? Think about it. To merely display on his shelf?"

The same thought had come to me on *many* occasions, but I pushed it away, not wanting to think about the why as long as I got what I wanted in the end.

"I've been aware of what he was after for a while." She shrugged. "The moment his private jet landed here...I've been watching you."

The dots connected as understanding washed over me. *Shit.* "It's been you," I whispered. "It's been you the whole time."

Rez's head snapped to me, then back to Fionna, sucking in air.

"Those men weren't searching for the spear," I said. "They were trying to keep us from it."

"They didn't do an especially good job," she replied, then moved her hands around. The air thickened, swirling the wind with magic, winding around me like a funnel. I sucked through my nose, trying to move oxygen in. "Maybe this time…" Energy dissipated, clearing the way for what was hiding behind it. The cloak of magic dropped.

*Fuck. Fuck. Fuck.* Five men circled around us, seeming to come out of nowhere.

Rez jumped, her back knocking into me as she looked around. "Oh gods," she muttered, her hand clapping her mouth. There was no doubt she recognized them as I did. Her abductors—Yogi, Boo-Boo, and Hiss, along with the two other fae from the warehouse—circled us. The human men were absent. *Probably still pancaked under a hopper tank.* They had been chasing us since the beginning. Every attack led by Fionna.

They had acted like zombies because they were under the influence of her magic. They could only do what she forced them to do.

I went to the cottage for a locator spell and walked into the wolf's den, buying Fionna's entire act, never believing she had anything to do with it.

"You kidnapped me?" Rez whipped to Fionna.

"It was nothing personal, but I will do everything in my power to keep the item out of the King's hands. You are merely the messengers."

"But why kidnap just me?" Anger rose in Rez's voice.

"It should have been both of you." Fionna's hands curled into fists.

"Then why help me…?" Halfway through my question, I understood. She hadn't been helping me. She'd been escorting me right where she wanted. All they had to do was capture me again. But they failed. That's why I felt they had been ready for me. Every moment I had spent with Fionna had been carefully orchestrated to keep us from finding the spear.

"You are the one who brought Balor back." My body was alert, taking in every nuance around me.

"Very good," she replied. "No one would ever have suspected *me* of being capable of that level of magic. It comes from years of hiding with nothing else to do but build up my magic." She spread her arms wide. "It was my duty to guard it from you fae, and no better way than to raise a vengeful demon king from the sea."

Most Druids could revive beings who were close to death, but not the actual dead, unless they were extremely powerful. Certain Druid lines were more formidable in particular powers. This was a top-tier Druid. But even then, it took "special" magic to bring something back from the dead.

"Walkin' on the dark side, are we, sweetheart?" I arched one brow.

"Fae don't play fair. Why should I?" Fionna replied, then uttered something under her breath. The men shuffled closer to Rez and me. Each one moved like a robot under Fionna's control.

"Forcing fae to do your dirty work, to take away their will? It only proves your adversaries' point." I turned to

Fionna. "You are doing the exact thing they fear. This is why they hate Druids and want you dead."

"Your kind gave me no choice. I will protect the treasure." She moved several feet closer to me. "None of them should have ever been made. They hold too much power, power which seduces and bends the carrier to their will. You fae aren't strong enough to fight it. How many times must a world undergo devastation and annihilation because a fae lost control? How many times before you understand?"

What was twisted…I agreed with her. I saw what the previous Queen did to the Druid line, the centuries the few survivors had to go into hiding, everyday living the question of whether they'd be caught or not. I saw pain etched in Fionna's face because of the family she lost concealed behind her anger. It was the same pain in mine, hidden by wrath and resentment, building thick walls.

But she still wanted to get rid of Rez and me, which I was not cool with.

"You think killing us will stop the King?" I took a step to her. "Our deaths will only evoke a wrath so intense you can't possibly imagine. He will not stop, sweetheart."

She grinned smugly. "I say *bring it on. Sweetheart.*" Her hands waved in the air, and with a rush of magic the men charged.

Straight for Rez and me.

Hiss was the first to strike, his forked tongue darting out to taste my fear. His lean body flew in the air and collided with mine. The beast within snarled, saliva filling my mouth with the urge to tear into flesh. I could feel his desire to come forward, to protect Rez. I pressed my lips together, pushing back the pain. *If you continue to push to get out and cripple me, she gets hurt,* I shouted at my beast. It surprised me and instantly backed off. She came first, no matter how bad it wanted to surface.

My fists slammed into Hiss's ribs, laying him out flat. Yogi and Boo-Boo charged for me as the other fae went for Rez. She pulled out her knife. Twisting, she swung out her arm, slicing the chest of the black-haired fae like some warrior goddess. *Damn, that's hot.* I didn't have time to worry, knowing she could hold her own.

Claws swiped at my belly and chest. I jumped, twisted back, and came at Boo-Boo from the side, hitting his kidney.

A force smacked into me from the opposite direction, and I sailed to the ground with a slam. It stole my breath, and I grunted, trying to get up. A booted foot slammed into my gut, crumpling me back over, and a fist creamed my temple. Blood trickled into my eye as I took another kick to my stomach.

The beast was getting pissed, paralyzing me in place, pawing at the surface. Claws and boots struck my body over and over. Blood pooled from my mouth. With each hit, my beast tried to rise to the surface to fight back but merely pinned me in place. Dots impeded my vision, throwing my heart into a panic. I couldn't black out. I couldn't leave Rez.

*Fuck.* Was this it? How we ended? So close to getting the treasure?

"Stop," Fionna ordered and immediately the bears backed off, standing like robot soldiers. If they were ever freed, they'd probably spend their lives hunting her down. No fae wanted to be a Druid's bitch, which was why so many believed they should be eliminated.

"I'm truly sorry about this, West." She leaned over me, my vision slowly taking in details. "But unfortunately you two are the messengers Lars used while he stays safe in his tower. I can't let you have the Spear of Lugh. And I'm not stupid enough to think you will back off. He would never let you."

She stood and looked beyond me. I lifted my head and saw Rez standing there with blood and cuts on her face. The black-haired fae was lying on the ground. The other now stood like a zombie.

"But I only need one of you to relay to Lars he is not in charge here, nor does he have the most powerful magic. If he wants a fight, he will have one." Fionna raised her hands, muttering.

A scream tore from Rez as magic crashed into her. Her body lifted and power dragged her forward, her shoes digging trails in the dirt.

It took a moment for me to realize what Fionna meant. Rez was the sacrifice. She meant to kill the King's mistress and send back his lackey broken and defeated to deliver her message. With every inch Rez neared the edge of the cliff. The ocean far below was hostile with rocks sharp as knives.

My brain shut off. The beast only saw its mate about to be impaled below. I roared. Twisting, I rolled up and dived for Fionna, my body crashing into hers like a linebacker. I hit her with a sickening crunch, her tiny body flew under the force of my anger toward the ledge.

Rez cried and dropped to the ground on her knees, broken free of Fionna's magic.

Fionna smashed onto the ground, her form tumbling toward the edge. She let out a cry, her hands scraping for a surface to grip on to. She drilled her fingers into the rocks and tried to pull herself up. A rock gave way under her hold, and she started to slip down the cliff, her nails digging into the dirt to stop her descent.

"Fionna!" I leaped for her, my fingers skimming over hers, losing touch as she dropped farther down. I could be soulless, but deep inside I knew Fionna wasn't bad. She was actually the smartest of us here. Letting the current demon king have the spear, a weapon so powerful, was stupid. She was only protecting it, no matter the costs. Just like Lars would find it, no matter the costs. I couldn't let her die.

Her mouth opened, a start of a chant slipping from her lips, but it was clogged by her scream, her fingers slipping through the earth.

It was only a second.

Horror covered her features in utter sadness. Then she slipped from the edge and plunged into the void.

"Nooooo!" I wailed.

Her scream crashed into the night as she disappeared over the cliff. The howling wind and waves below drowned her cries as the sea claimed its next victim.

A flurry of magic shot over the mountain and erupted. Any fae under her control still standing dropped to the ground, unmoving.

A Druid's weakness was they had to verbalize to formulate their magic. It couldn't be conjured through thoughts like fae can do.

I stared into the darkness, lost in a rush of guilt. I should have saved her. She was only a hurt girl, not some evil monster.

"Hey?" A hand touched my back as Rez knelt next to me.

"Ahhhh!" I bellowed, rubbing my face. Another girl's death was on my conscience.

"It wasn't your fault." Rez ran her fingers along my chin, turning my face to hers. Her brown irises penetrated mine. "And neither was Cammie," she whispered.

I grunted and shoved myself back onto my feet. Rez rose with me.

The men were still out cold. They probably would be for the rest of the night. This kind of magic, the bending of your will, depleted you. They'd be fine. Angry as hell, but with no one to take their revenge out on, they would leave this place.

"Let's go," I mumbled. "Fionna is dead, which means the spell on Balor is broken. He will start to grow weak."

I was more than disgusted with myself for continuing, for so callously using her death as our gain, but I had sold my soul to the devil, and there was no getting it back till he got what he wanted.

# TWENTY-FOUR

"I'll distract Balor while you go all the way down and find it." I heaved the air tank on my back, already dressed in my wetsuit we left in the crevice the night before, otherwise hypothermia would set in for me in minutes. I was kind of envious of Rez's power to feel at home in the waves.

Rez's gaze lowered down my body.

"You're checking out my package, aren't you?" I waved down, trying to lighten the bleak mood set over us. My only way of dealing with things. "Go ahead. It's impressive, I grant you, and just think, it's freezing out."

"Shut up." She smiled, rolling her eyes. "Wait till you step in…little chicken nuggets."

"Oh come on, darlin'. Don't scare them."

Rez stripped to her underwear. The wetsuit ground against my erection. *Maybe I should step in the cold water now…* I went to the edge, sliding my bare feet in. "Holy shit!" I hadn't bothered getting water gloves or booties and now regretted it. When led by a siren's call, freezing to death didn't seem to matter. Tonight the water was like blades scraping at my skin and lungs.

"Okay." Rez came next to me. "I will lead him to you. You distract Balor while I go back and get the spear. Easy."

I snorted. Fionna's hold on him was gone, but it would still take a while for him to lose power. We needed to deplete his energy as much as we could.

We both stood another moment. This was it. No need to go over our pathetic plan again. It was time to act.

"You ready?" I glanced over at her.

"Yeah." She sounded more sure than I felt.

We already decided once Rez got the spear, we had to kill him. I was sure the spear acted as his power center for his third eye.

"Okay, darlin'. Let's go piss off a demon king."

"We're extremely good at that."

"Well, at least two of them."

Rez smiled and then dived in. I followed behind, stuffing the tank's air piece in my mouth.

The water was murky from the angry waves twisting and rocking, and it only grew darker the deeper we went. I followed Rez, the slight glow she gave off leading the way.

We had to be careful about communicating. With only a few words from Rez, I'd be consumed by her, trailing her to the trenches. Her speed quickly left me in the dust. And utter oblivion. I stayed in place, trying not to panic. The darkness engulfed me, and I struggled to keep my breath steady and know which way was up. This was not my happy place. At all.

The hum of sea life buzzed around me, keeping me focused. Soon a dim light seeped into my sight. It grew closer and closer till I could make out Rez's shape.

And what was behind her. Nipping at her heels.

*Shiiitttt.* I had tried to forget how massive and frightening he was.

Balor moved with speed and agility, only a few steps was like a city block to us. Thank the gods, Rez could move faster. I didn't have the same hope for me.

Rez had almost reached me when she darted away, disappearing in the darkness. The large creature stared around the water, whipping his head back and forth, searching for her. Rez swam far enough away her glow no longer could break through the depths of the darkness.

I waved my arms and legs and yelled over my mouthpiece, causing bubbles. Balor didn't seem to take notice, already heading back to guard.

I couldn't let that happen. I swam to him, propelling myself as fast as I could. I reached his eyeline, and his head snapped to me. Naturally, I flipped him off. Old school—with two fingers in a V.

Fury filled Balor's face. I guess he recognized the insult. He came for me, and it quickly hit me this wasn't a well-thought-out plan. How the hell was I going to outswim him? I had no time to contemplate it. My legs and arms kicked as fast as they could, taking me to the surface.

I felt Balor's arm cut through the water, trying to grab me. *Swim faster!*

My ears filled with a rumble, Balor's yell bubbling the water around me. He moved quickly. I tried to zigzag clear of his hands, but it only tired me out.

Foam and ripples above my head suggested I was close to the surface. *Come on, West. Almost there!* I really didn't know what I'd do with him when I got above, but at least there I had a chance.

As I was about to breach the surface, I felt Balor push

out of the water. The force of his body shot everything in his vicinity into the air like a cannon. Fish. Seaweed. Me. We all went flying into the sky, flailing like socks in the dryer. The air tank tore from my back and mouth, letting a scream escape me.

Like the old saying, *everything that goes up must come down*. And I did. My face and torso hit the water with a harsh slap, punching the air from my lungs. The waves forced me forward, and my skin brushed against the rocks and grainy sand.

The ground shook as Balor took a step. *Get up! Get the fuck up!* I screamed at myself. I pushed up and scrambled forward. Water gushed right where I had been; Balor's toe now occupied the space.

I hauled myself up on the rocks, clamoring toward the strip of beach. I heard his roar behind me, then heat and magic exploded next to my head. The boulders broke off, sending smaller parts of themselves out like shrapnel from a bomb exploding. I tried to get up the beach to hide from the attack.

Another burst of heat exploded rubble on me. I dived behind a rock, folding over, trying to screen myself from the brunt of the fallout.

Balor's large hand scraped by my head, his fingers trying to fit between the boulders. A sharp point came close to my hip, and I jumped, shoving myself to the other side. His harpoon stabbed at the earth barely inches from me and pierced the ground.

He grunted, pulling it out. I looked up and saw the spike tilted, heading straight for me. This was it. I was going to be shish-kabobed. West on a stick. I tucked myself in and closed my eyes, preparing for the pain.

"Heeeeyyyy!" a voice screamed into the night. "You're an awful security guard, you ugly ogre."

*Rez!*

The lance passed over me, then disappeared as Balor turned to his new taunter. Relief rushed into my lungs, and I swiftly crawled out of my hole to the sight of Rez running onto the beach, a wrapped item in her arms.

*Holy. Shit. She did it!*

Balor snarled; his eyes locked on the object. His hand reached out for it, but instead of grabbing it, his fingers curled around Rez, knocking it out of her grip onto the sand.

"Rez!" I screamed her name as he picked up her body, glaring down at the thief in his hand, then back at the item left on the shore. Why didn't he take it? It lay right there. He would be able to get it before I got there. Why take her instead?

He stared at it with hatred, fear, and longing but didn't grab for it.

Then it hit me. Balor couldn't touch it. He could guard it. Defend it. But he actually couldn't touch it. It held the magic that ended him the first time. The spear was the one thing that would kill him. Take him out for good.

My feet sprinted for the object. I tore the cloth tied around it and grabbed the spear.

Magic surged along my back, bending me, my back curling over. I dropped to the ground on all fours. A grunt surged from deep inside, my muscles stretched, expanding my body, tearing the wetsuit and my boxers into shreds. Claws grew from my hands and ripped at the rocky beach. Fur, black as night, covered my body. A crest of daggers trailed down my spine.

It felt so familiar, so much a part of me, but one I thought I'd lost forever. It brought me back to life. My body returned to the shape I was the most comfortable in.

The most real and true me. A roar came out of me, shaking the ground underfoot. I was a killer. Feared. A horror story you told to scare people.

A scream wailed in the distance.

*Rez.*

*Mine.*

Protective rage filled the beast, consuming it with the need to kill anything touching its mate. A thunderous sound came from my lungs when I spotted Balor, his hand around Rez, holding her like he was freakin' King Kong.

*Hell. No.*

My claws sliced through the sand, heading for her. I only got a few feet when pain exploded through me, my legs faltering, and my face hit the ground. My form turned back into a human.

*No. No. No,* I screamed. Panic flooded me that the beast was leaving. My gaze went back to the spear, laying where I left it. *Shit. That was it. I had to be touching it.* I inched back. The moment I touched it, the beast rushed back to the surface, exhilarating every nerve in my body with euphoria.

The only thing about being a beast was it was hard to carry stuff, but I had more chance against Balor in that form. I bent over and slipped the spear into my mouth, nestling it between my razor-sharp teeth. Magic crashed into my tongue, giving my system a shock, as if I touched an electrical fence. My muscles constricted, and I froze, struggling for breath.

A cry came from Rez as the demon shook her.

*Fuck. Fuck. Shit. West, you don't have time. Rez is in trouble. Go!*

Pushing against the paralyzing power, I sped down the beach to the demon, rage growing in my shoulders with every step. If he hurt her, nothing would stop me from tearing him into tiny little pieces.

I had to get up to his eye. At any point he could open it and destroy anything near him, but it would be harder to do if I were on him.

Leaping for his ankle, my sickle claws sank into his skin, and I climbed his leg like it was a tree. Balor bellowed and swiped at me with his free hand. I curled around to inch up the back of his leg, making it difficult for him to grab for me. Anger and fear propelled me up his body in fierce determination.

Rez's name constantly drummed in my heart and pounded out a savage beat. My ascent claimed all his attention, giving Rez relief against his hold. She didn't waste it. I saw her wiggle, pulling herself out of his hand. Balor's head snapped to her, and he grappled with re-catching her as she ran up his arm.

I dug my nails in deeper, willing his attention to me, my goal to get her out of his reach. His hand swung around and slapped hard on my back. With a cry, his palm impaled on the poisonous razor-sharp blades along my spine. His hand crunched me harder into his hip. Bones in my body cracked and popped. Pain snapped along with each bone, his massive hand flattening me like a bug. I grunted as my lungs compressed under the weight, tearing oxygen from me. Spots darted around my vision, my grip slackening. Air rushed around me as my body slipped and fell.

"West!" I heard Rez's voice scream for me. Like my own personal siren, she beckoned me through the pain to follow her. My beast would do nothing less than comply or die trying.

Reaching out, my claws caught into his skin, digging trenches down the back of his leg as I caught myself. His hand swung for me again. I craned my head. I slipped the pointy end between my teeth and rammed my head forward. The spear sank deep into the back of his knee.

An ear-shattering roar pelted from his throat, and his entire body shuddered with violent convulsions. I didn't give myself a chance to think past the result, just reared back and sliced the blade into the thin skin behind his knee joint. His leg dipped to the ground, water gushing straight up around me in walls. I dug in deeper, holding on as he tried to rise and steady himself on his feet.

Balor's wails broke like waves crashing against the rocks. He died once by this spear; I would make sure he died by it again. Even without Fionna's hold, it was the only thing with enough power to kill the rejuvenated demon king, his own magic working against him.

I leaped back up his hip, climbed steadily, and dragged the spear along, scraping a line into his skin. His shrill cries chilled the air.

"West!" Rez yelled from his shoulder, her voice full of relief. I couldn't talk to her, but my eyes connected with hers, and unspoken words passed between us.

*I need you to take the spear. Stab his eye with it.* My gaze drilled into her. She blinked and then nodded. Holy crap. She understood me.

Before Ember became part Dark Dweller, she could communicate this way with Eli, but it became even stronger after. We all always thought it a "them" thing. But maybe it was more. Maybe it was a "mate" thing. Eli was the only one who ever found his. Even Owen never said he'd claimed Jared's mother. *Shit, this made it even more real.*

I'd almost reached Rez, who stood on his shoulder, when Balor started to sway like a tightrope. "West, give it to me." Rez leaned over, reaching for the spear in my mouth. She strained to reach me, her arm shaking with effort. Balor swung forcefully to the side, flinging my body.

I gripped his skin with all my might and inched closer and closer to Rez. I knew the moment she took it I would lose my hold and return to my human body.

"Almost." She labored to reach farther, sweat and salt water beading her hairline. With a snarl I pushed my chin up, her fingers brushing the spear.

She let out a groan, her fingertips curling. Rez closed her eyes, pushed out farther, and grabbed the spear, my teeth still holding it.

"Ahhhh." A cry broke from her lips, and her face scrunched with the overbearing power. She locked her jaw and blew out through her nose. "I got it."

My teeth loosened their hold and let go. Heat and agony shredded my veins as my body reshaped into my human form.

With a bellow, I dropped and crashed into the sea far below.

# TWENTY-FIVE

Water tumbled around, tossing and spinning me. I swam for the surface and broke through with a gasp. I dug my fingers through the water, trying to keep afloat.

Balor roared, snapping my attention to the tiny figure who crawled up his ear. He swatted and waggled his head, trying to dislodge the pest. My stomach knotted in a ball. I could do nothing. It was all up to Rez now.

Balor raised his arm, his hand on a direct path with her head. "Rez!" My voice was lost in the crashing waves. My heart locked in my chest as his palm smacked into his ear. "No!"

My beast tore at my flesh, desperate and frantic to reach her. Locked back inside, it screamed with rage. To be released for only a moment and then returned to my human form, caged and useless, was worse than if it had never come out.

Balor lifted his hand away, looking at his palm for the squashed bug. Rez crawled out of his ear, relief flooding me but only temporarily. She hitched herself up, gripped his dreads, and scuttled to the crown of his head.

There was no ceremony or final words. She wasn't one to waste time or make final taunts. Rez's arm reared back, the spear glinting in the night. With a cry, her arm swung down. The sound of flesh being sliced in two, like chopping into a watery head of lettuce, resounded off the cliffs.

Balor went still. It was only a second before the most horrific bellow pierced the night. His hands moved to his third eye, and he wobbled on his feet. Deep wails ripped rocks from the surface, plummeting them to the ground.

Rez held on as he teetered wildly, twisting the spear in deeper. The howls were bone chilling. Balor stumbled forward, his knees crashing into the shallow water.

"Rez!" I screamed, dread weighing me down. Her head turned to me, and her eyes met mine, fear opening them wide. Then it happened.

Balor tipped forward. Rez slipped, grabbing on to the embedded spear to keep herself from plunging to the ground. Then like a tree being cut down, he fell, taking Rez with him.

A guttural cry emanated from me as I watched Balor's face smash into the rocky beach, water and rocks spewing up like a giant water fountain around him. The debris crashed back and rained down on the back of Balor's body.

*Rez!*

My feet hit the seabed and pawed through the waves, fear so deep in my gut my brain shut down. All I could think of was Rez. Reaching her.

*Please...don't take her from me...*

My toes hit the rocks, which then scraped my hands to shreds as I climbed over them. Balor's head took up the strip of beach, his lifeless body half in the water, half out. He was dead. Once again. Without Fionna, his eye was the only source of energy, and Rez destroyed it.

My heart thumped her name. I didn't want to think about the sharp rocks where Balor was implanted. The chances of her being alive underneath…

I moved toward his eye, where the end of the spear protruded.

"Rez?" I called, desperate now. I shoved at his head, but it didn't budge an inch. Panic danced my human form around like a hummingbird.

I grabbed the end of the spear and tugged it out with a slurping sound. Pieces of his eye dripped off the end. As my hand curled around the spear, my body shifted, the Dark Dweller stretching out again. I tucked the spear in my beast's mouth but felt no enjoyment in being back, only fear for my mate.

My beast rushed at the creature's head, pushing it back. It took four times ramming the demon king before it tipped to the side.

Blood.

I spit out the spear, pain rolling back, converting me back to a man. Black splotches dotted my eyes, but I pushed forward, crawling farther under Balor. His head slipped a little more, revealing what was below.

"*REZ!*" I howled. Her lifeless body was shoved between boulders and covered in blood and wounds.

Adrenaline thudded in my ears. Her mostly naked body was so wedged in my knuckles bled over the rocks trying to get her out. "Please…Rez. Don't leave me," I begged, lifting her broken body. She was mostly whole, but gashes cut deep holes into her back, head, and sides from crashing into the rocks. Her chest was motionless.

"Shit! Shit!" I picked her up, cuddled her body into me, moving out from under Balor, and laid her down. I put my ear on her ribs. Nothing.

I had never taken CPR or practiced it. I didn't even know if it necessarily worked on fae, but I was willing to do anything. I pumped her chest, then stopped to breathe into her mouth. I knew it was pointless, but doing nothing was not an option. Violent shivers wracked my body, and I struggled to keep up the motion, despite a mounting black panic that filled my head with a wretched buzzing.

"Rez. Please. I finally found you. Don't make me live without you." I shook her, demanding she wake up. "I'm not strong enough." The darkness already beckoned me, ready to push me off the cliff. If Rez died, I would gratefully go over.

My beast knew the truth. The connection to her was gone. Empty. Like someone cut the wires between us. But I ignored the gut-tugging sickness, my palms pressing into her chest with desperation.

Minutes passed. Maybe hours. Rez flopped under my hasty movements, life vacant from her body. In the middle of pumping her chest, I felt myself snap. Curling over her body, my forehead tapped her stomach. A wail gutted my insides, and I howled like a lone wolf into the night. I had lost her. And soon I knew I would lose myself. I couldn't take the pain. Not this.

It's strange when you are hit with grief so overwhelming you think it will freeze you. I expected that would come later. Now all I could think was Rez would want to be in the water. It was where she belonged, where she would want her final resting spot to be.

Now full of magic since the worlds had crashed together, the earth made the fae less invincible to death by human ways. We still lived millenniums or longer, and we didn't die as easily as humans, but we were a lot more susceptible than before.

My arms curled around her back and legs and picked

her up. Her head fell over my arm, her long, wet hair tickling my thigh. Her bra and underwear were soaked with blood, water, and dirt. Her skin was covered in gashes. She still was the most beautiful woman I had ever known.

My knees buckled with anguish, tripping me forward into the waves. A part of me wanted to go under with her. Just let go… My heart split. The sobs in my chest clogged my throat, my eyes blurry. This wasn't simply losing the woman I had fallen completely in love with, but my mate. A doomed love…

I placed her in the water. It circled around, embracing her. I swore I could hear the sea crying for her, mourning the loss of one of their own.

"I am so sorry, Rez." I leaned over, brushing my lips with hers. "You deserved better than this. A life full of love, laughter, checklists, a dozen pets, or… kids." A hiccupped cry strangled my esophagus. I clung to her body but knew I had to let go. I kissed her again and then released her.

Rez floated for a while before the waves took her and pulled her under, taking her home.

My breathing grew strangled as I stood there, not understanding the freezing water swirling around my waist. An anguish gutted a hollow abyss through my body, baying in the night with tormented cries. I could barely feel my hands and feet, and I shivered so violently now my teeth clanged together. Most likely hypothermia, but I didn't give a shit. The only thing tugging my feet toward the shore was the thought of Rez getting mad at me. To not let her death be in vain. Not yet.

I trudged through the water, my feet skimming the rocks, moving like a robot, empty of a brain, or heart. I glanced over my shoulder. The waves lapped at the shore as if nothing had changed. Grief turned to emptiness. My muscles no longer able to hold me up, I crumpled into the wet sand; the spear was just out of reaching distance. I didn't even have energy to take a few more steps, grab the spear and let it envelop me in the beast. Turn off.

I sensed that would be the next stage. Right now I sat facing the water, drawing my arms around my legs and stared out, vacant and lost.

The constellations moved in the sky, telling me time was moving on and morning would be coming. The world continued on. The shivers jerked and twisted my body, but each one only reminded me why I was here. Why I didn't care.

Cammie. Rez. The only two women I ever loved and I was the reason they were dead. Cammie had hurt deeply, but Rez was obliterating.

Nothing was left of me.

The sea crashed up on shore, hitting my toes. It felt as if she had reached out and touched me. That's when the pain flowed from my eyes.

She was really gone.

---

The night lightened at the edges, proclaiming dawn had arrived. I knew I had to move soon, but by walking away, I felt it would mean she was actually no longer here.

With a heavy sigh, I got to my feet. She *was* no longer here. I needed to accept it and leave.

"Goodbye." My voice cracked, and I turned away. The farewell was final. For good. I would never return to Ireland. Grabbing my jacket, I picked up the spear, the energy still bleeding through the fabric, wanting to turn me, but for some reason I didn't want to. Like I deserved to be tortured even more.

I absently tugged on my jeans, shirt, and boots, heading for the steep incline.

I would finish this job, then disappear. My family couldn't save me anymore. The hollowness inside was too dark.

I was too far gone.

# TWENTY-SIX

Each step up the face of the dune was like dragging my feet through glue. I reached the first resting spot almost halfway up, when my head automatically glanced back, needing to see her grave one last time before I walked away forever. My chest froze, causing me to stumble.

A spot in the ocean glowed, illuminating the surface. I whipped around, my ears catching a beautiful chant, flourishing from the spot. Voices so beautiful I wanted to fall to my knees. My gaze caught eight dots circling around the light. It took me a moment to realize they were heads. Of people.

Sirens.

The women sang, their music requiring I go out to them, my boots smacking the earth, taking me back to the beach at a run, dropping the spear at the base of the cliff. Was this a funeral? A way sirens said goodbye to one of their own? I couldn't do anything but watch, lost in the beauty of their voices, of their movements around the glow. It felt like a dream.

Then I saw Morweena. She moved to me, rising higher in the water the closer she got. She got waist deep and stopped, my boots splashing back into the sea.

"My daughter may think I never loved her, but it couldn't be further from the truth. I was not a good mother. I know that, but there isn't anything I wouldn't do for her." She started to descend. "Tell her that. Tell her I love her very much. I wish her the best." Morweena sank below the surface.

The area where the water glowed shot into the sky, magic crashing against me so hard I went flying back on my ass. It went silent. The light, the sirens, everything gone. I sat, gazing around in confusion, trying to understand what happened. My heart thumped in my chest counting off the seconds like a clock. A minute passed when I felt another barrage of magic slap my skin.

Then, like Aphrodite, a woman rose up, walking from the water, wearing only a bra and panties. My whole world stopped. "Rez?" My knees lurched deeper into the water, my breath clipped, not believing yet what I saw.

She smiled, her skin flawless. No cuts or gashes. "Yes, Mr. Moseley?"

A guttural cry broke from my heart. There were no words. I ran to her, picked her up in my arms, and crushed her into my chest. Her arms curled around my neck, holding me just as tight. We stayed this way for a long time, my need to feel she was really in my arms kept her pressed to me firmly.

She was the first to tip her head back to look at me, her hands going to my face, running her fingers over it like she was trying to memorize me.

"How…?" I looked into her face.

"The sea brought me back. Returned life into me." Her eyes were bright, energy rolling off her. "It can only be done if someone is still holding on to life. Guess I wasn't quite ready to go." Her gaze met mine.

"Your mother was here." Words came from my mouth,

but my brain was still grasping she was in my arms. Alive.

"My mother? Did she say something to you?"

"Yeah." I nodded. "She said there wasn't anything she wouldn't do for you. That she loves you. Wishes you the best."

I lowered her to her feet, but my arms wouldn't let her a breath away from me, my hands roaming every inch of her skin.

"She's never told me she loved me before." Rez glanced over her shoulder. "Even when she almost lost me, she still had to tell someone else. Not me."

"I'm sorry." My lips grazed her forehead.

"Don't be." Rez turned back to me, her gaze going to my mouth. "At least I know she is capable of saying it, even if she can't say it to me directly."

Was I any better? The words wanted to come out, but instead of saying them I brought her mouth to mine. "You scared the shit out of me," I mumbled against her lips. "Don't *ever* do that again."

"I don't have it scheduled any time soon." Her mouth grew more demanding, excess energy quivered her muscles and pulsed into me, blurring my brain.

There remained no more thoughts about staying away from her. Losing her had made me understand I would never again. Whatever was in front of us, I didn't care. Tonight it was only us, and I was going to take advantage of every moment. I needed to see her smile, to hear her voice cry out my name, laugh…everything. Be so deep inside her I no longer could find my way out.

---

Our mouths were frantic, my need for her bursting out of me. Every part of me never wanted to stop touching, kissing, or fucking her. But Rez's body shivered against the harsh breeze, the sky lightening even more along the horizon.

"Let's get back to the cottage." I kissed her softly, wrapping my arm around her, carrying her to where her clothes laid. "I need to be inside you, like, now."

Rez sucked in a breath, her gaze meeting mine with the same intensity. Rez got dressed, the tank and wetsuit victims of the battle. After collecting the spear, we headed back to the cottage, running most of the way home.

Every step it became harder to ignore the intensity of my need to get her home and fuck the ever-loving daylights out of her. It was feral and raw. My beast needed to claim again, understand she was really here.

"I saw you change." Rez hustled next to me, the cottage in the distance. "The spear gave you the power."

"Yes." I peered down at it, still in shock I was actually carrying one of the treasures of Tuatha Dé Danann.

"I'm not surprised. It's an exceptionally powerful weapon." She looked at it in my hands. I kept it wrapped in my jacket since touching it brought out the beast in me. Literally. I longed to change again, but right now I needed to stay in human form more.

"What if you kept it?"

"Don't." I shook my head. "Don't even think it. It's not an option. Lars said if I fulfilled my deal, he would help me out. Maybe he can figure something out. But it's being handed over to him." I wouldn't screw that up too. I already was screwing his woman.

We reached the door, and I practically shoved her in.

"Hmmm…starting to think someone is in a hurry." Her eyebrow quirked up. I grabbed a towel hanging off the bed frame and wrapped the spear, putting it in the heavy safe in the closet.

"To touch you. Yes. But once I'm in you…there's no hurry to ever leave."

She sucked in a breath as I seized her, pulling her into me. My lips were quick to part hers, exploring her mouth with my tongue. I picked her up, and she wrapped her legs around me.

I tugged off her jacket as I carried her to the bathroom. Shower and sex. Two birds…one very large cock.

Neither of us cared about all the reasons not to be together, and we let ourselves be in the moment. Stumbling into the demolished bathroom, we tore our clothes off. Under the spray of water, my fingers opened her legs, but she didn't need any encouragement. I let out a groan, feeling how wet she was.

"Now, West. Foreplay later."

I didn't stop exploring her, my finger moving deep in her.

"West." She panted, her head rolling back.

I picked her up, her back hitting the tiles, and plunged into her, making her gasp. As we moved together, with desperate need for each other, I realized an undeniable truth. I was in love with her.

The fact I could still feel love surprised me. But it came barreling into me like a cannon as we went over together. My sight went black for a moment, her cries matching mine.

I never exited her when we moved together again. This time we were still wild, but we took our time, really tasting, feeling, learning each other. We moved to the bedroom and spent the rest of what was left of the night breaking more furniture and cracking glass with our bellows. When we needed a breather, we talked. We laughed. We raided the last of the cookies I bought.

Eating them naked on the floor, we teased and joked with each other until we couldn't stay away any longer and started again.

Finally when the sun was high over the hills, we collapsed in each other's arms. My lids drifted closed from exhaustion, contentment, and dare I say…happiness?

***

*"Oh my pet. Did you think I would leave you so easy?"* *Aneira swished her elaborate robe, pacing in front of me while she played with the loose, braided belt on her hips. We were back in her chamber. I stood before her naked and vulnerable, as she preferred me. "I hoped pretending to be your little human the other night would have finally brought you to me. But she saved you. From yourself."*

*I glanced away, trying to ignore her.* She's not real, West. This is all you. She's dead.

*"She won't be able to save you forever. She will go back to where she belongs, with whom she belongs… and you, my pet, will come to me." Her long red hair hung freely to her hips. "I mean, really, you are doing her a favor. Haven't you already gotten her killed once? You know it will happen again, only a matter of time."*

*I stiffened against the sting of her words.*

*"Think about it, you didn't even need to shift into the beast to murder the delicate human girl." Aneira sneered. "You can't help yourself. It is who you are, what you were born to be. Why ignore the beast inside? Merely because he can't come out doesn't mean you've stopped being a killer. You love the taste of blood. Fighting it will only repeat history."*

*"No." I flinched against her words. "Cammie's death was an accident."*

*Aneira let out a peal of laughter. "Oh pet, we both know that is a lie."*

*She moved to me, her nails raking down my torso. "You loved rolling with me…giving over to your darkest desires." Her fingers trailed all the way down. "You couldn't stop abusing me as much as I tortured you. We can have it again. Just come with me. Give yourself over to me."*

*"No." My nostrils flared as she worked her hand over me, my teeth gritting. "I will never give myself over to you again."*

*"You already did. You simply need to accept it." She palmed me tighter. "I am the darkness inside you, the vile secret you have not told anyone, festering deep in your memory. Because even you know no matter what your brothers and sisters have done, what despicable, evil deeds they undertook, they could never forgive this. They could never accept what you did." Aneira let me go, reaching for my cheek. "You will always be alone, lost and searching. I am the only one who accepts you completely."*

*The truth of her words slammed into my chest like a wrecking ball. Aneira laughed as a tortured grunt twisted from me. Breath moved in and out of my lungs in hasty gulps.*

*"Do you think the siren would love you knowing what you did? How we got off when I tortured my own personal knight?"*

*The ground gave way. There was the recollection I never let enter my mind. The act I pushed so deep I pretended it was a nightmare.*

*But it wasn't. It became the lowest of my depravity. My mind was lost by then, reveling in the evil. All my abhorrence for the Light, for fairies, was twisted by one. I watched her torture and become aroused by the same one who had protected my friend. My family. The one who later reached out and pulled me from my twisted obscurity. He was there because of Ember…but I only saw everything I despised. I saw myself.*

*Torin was never aware of me. And he never would be. Disgust, rage, and regret filled my veins.*

*"Don't tell me you didn't enjoy that?" Aneira's mouth turned up in a wicked grin. "We could have that all the time. Just you and me."*

*"You are not real." My knuckles popped, my fingers digging into my palms. "You. Are. Dead. Only a figment of my imagination."*

*"I'm more than that." She leaned back into me. "I am part of you. The deep part of your soul you hide from the world where it's only us. Or if you want, I can change back into your beloved human girl?"*

*"No." I shoved her back. "You can no longer use Cammie against me. I will not be crippled by her death. The Cammie I knew, the girl I loved, would never want me to. I will not let you take her from me, twist her into something awful. She was beauty and light. You are merely regret."*

*"Ouch." Aneira's lower lip stuck out in false hurt. "I don't think it would be the little human I should be portraying anyway. I think this is more what you want."*

*Aneira's façade dissolved, reshaping into Rez's features. I could hardly swallow.*

*"Yes. This is exactly what you want. What your beast wants. The precise thing you can't truly have."*

*Aneira pulled on her loosely tied belt around her queenly robe, letting it fall away. Rez stood before me. Naked. Her expression wanton. Long hair covered her breasts but nothing else as she walked to me. Her fingers trailed down my arm.*

*"Not real. You're not Rez," I chanted to myself, but my body couldn't help but respond to the doppelgänger.*

*"Yes, this is what you want." Aneira nipped at my lip. "You want her so badly you're willing to die for her." She kissed me again.*

Pull away, West, this is not Rez.

*But my body wouldn't move.*

*"How noble of you. Not you at all. You are a beast. You do not sacrifice for others. You sacrifice them. And you will end up butchering her in your selfishness to have her. You did it before and you are doing it again."*

*"Shut up!" I bellowed. I reached for her throat and began to squeeze. Rez's image faded back into Aneira's, her beautiful, cruel face grinning at me like she had won. "You are dead! Leave me in peace."*

*"The only peace you will have is when you surrender to me. Do it! Strangle the life from me. Don't fight it. It will only bring you closer to me."*

*I couldn't stop, fury and hate controlling my actions. My hands squeezed, throttling Aneira's neck. I just wanted it to end. The pain to be over. Her eyes widened, but the smug smile still curled over her red lips.*

*"I fucking hate you. Die!" I did loathe her, but really the words were meant for me. I compressed down, the softness of her neck bending under my fingers.*

*A strangled gasp came from her, her eyes widening. This only gave me a sick pleasure. Rage shook my body and drove adrenaline in my muscles.*

*"We—st." My name came out in a choked cry, a tear leaking down her face.*

*"Yes," I seethed. "Die! Give in to me."*

*The beast hit at the cage, throwing itself against my ribs. Clawing. Roaring. It took me a moment to realize it wasn't because it was excited, wanting this kill...*

*It was panic. Fear.*

I blinked. Aneira's creamy white skin and flaming red hair grew darker. Her violet eyes became a rich shade of coffee.

Every muscle locked up, dread paralyzing me. *Oh gods, no.* I dropped my hands and backed away so fast I crashed into the wall and knocked down a framed painting, which shattered into pieces.

My eyes widened with complete horror, staring at the woman through the shadows, the curtains only letting in a slice of late-afternoon sun. Rez bent over, rubbing at her neck, coughing, trying to recover from what I did to her. Oxygen couldn't get into my lungs fast enough, disgust at myself blocked it from reaching. Acid burned up my throat, and I felt the vomit dancing in my stomach.

I would have killed her. If it wasn't for the beast, Rez would be dead. By my hands.

*"You are a killer. Fighting it will only repeat history. And you will end up butchering her in your selfishness to have her. You did it before and you are doing it again."*

Rez straightened, her fingers still at her throat, her gaze meeting mine. She looked so beautiful and vulnerable. Her hair draped over her front like it had in my dream.

There were no words I could say that could take it away. No apology good enough. Staring at Rez made me wish I had let Aneira take me. Give myself over. End it. Save everyone from me.

"West." The sound of her rough voice broke me from my torment for a moment.

Liquid tickled the back of my lids, and I looked away. I needed to run. To get far away from the cottage. From Rez.

"Look at me," she demanded, taking a step toward me.

I stirred against the wall, ready to bolt.

"Look. At. Me."

A pathetic whimper caught in my throat. I could not refuse her, but gazing upon her might destroy me. I turned my chin to face her. She stood far enough away but instinctively blocked my exit to the door.

No fear showed in her irises, only concern, which forced more repulsion through me.

"I know you would never hurt me."

A crazed laugh ascended from my throat. "I just did."

"You were not here. Not with me." She shook her head. "You were with her."

My head jerked, my torso puffing in defense.

"She's taking you away from me." Rez approached me slowly. "I will not allow that."

I scoffed, but it was heavy with agony.

"She can't have you." Rez stopped in front of me, her naked body eclipsed by mine. "Aneira's ghost can't have you anymore."

I sucked in like someone punched me in the gut.

"And I certainly won't lose you to yourself. Whatever you're fighting, whatever horrors you went through, tell me. Let me help." She reached for my face.

"No." I grunted, pulling away. "No one can help."

"You're letting them win." The tenderness dropped from her voice. "I thought you were stronger than that."

Anger bristled up my spine.

"You think you're being so strong by protecting us

from the truth? From sharing your pain?" She snapped at me, her hands going to her waist. "You are being a coward. Hiding behind your ghosts. You're letting your fears rule you instead of letting them out."

"You have no idea what monsters I hide inside." I leaned into her face, baring my teeth. I was trying to scare her. I needed her to back off. "If you knew half the things I've done, you'd be *running* back to your demon lover."

She inhaled sharply through her nose. "You think attacking me is going to get me to run?" She let out a derisive laugh. "Give it your best shot, *sweetheart*. I will go toe to toe with you. You think I don't have ghosts that haunt me? You only know the basics of the things I've done in my past."

"That's the family channel compared to mine."

"You think you know it all?" She puffed up, getting right back into my face. "Because I told you a tiny portion of my life at the club? You have no idea what I let be done to me. The number of lives I took when I needed a new high. But I don't let it destroy me anymore. I faced them."

"You think we're alike?" I snorted, cruelty in each word. "Being a fucking *whore* to get high doesn't even come close."

At that she slapped me. Blood thrummed in my cheek and temple. "Fuck you. At least I had the strength to talk about it. To not be afraid of my past anymore." Her lids fluttered; tears pressed behind them. "Not you or anyone else will shame me. I own it. It's made me who I am."

Sorrow and guilt tumbled over me like an avalanche. What did I do? Did I cause her pain only to ease mine? To stop her from poking at the wound? I covered my face with my palms, my legs gave out, and I slid down the wall. *Jesus, I was a piece of work.*

The suffering I kept sealed away for so long rose to the surface. I wanted to smash things, to get my pain out through my fists, but instead it ransacked my chest, roaring out of my throat in a guttural wail.

Rez dropped to her knees and put her arms around me. I hated feeling weak, vulnerable, like I needed someone. But I didn't have the energy to push her away. Nor did I really want to. I liked feeling her arms around me, the way she brought my head to her chest, holding me.

The dam broke and the words flowed out, uncensored. Most fae knew of Aneira's cruelty, but only her guards and the ones she took to her "special" chamber realized how sick and twisted she was. I didn't know if she was always like that or losing her sister pushed her over, but with no one to tell her no, nothing checked her hunger for power from turning perverse and cruel.

"She brutalized me for weeks." I let the memories flood over me. "Name it…she did it. She moved between her sick games of horrendous punishment, then granted me pleasure, warping me into something I didn't recognize. I tried to hold on, fight her. But one day I snapped."

Rez's hand stroked over my temple, staying silent. I pulled away, needing distance to get through the rest. "I gave in to it." I swallowed back the lump in my throat, my voice a whisper. "I enjoyed it...wanted it." My vision blurred with the admittance. Saying it out loud held a power I wasn't ready for. Emotion choked me. "I despise her to the core of my being. What she did to my family… And I didn't only let her break me. If I had become a shell, let her do what she needed to, and just shut down…" I pulled my knees to my chest. "I could have forgiven myself. *That* I could live with."

Something wet slid down my cheek. Shit. A tear? I rubbed my face on my arm and wiped it away.

"You didn't simply enjoy it?" Rez asked, her voice even.

"No." I shook my head. "I relished in it. I went to her bed eagerly...I fucked her...over and over. And she loved it. We took turns punishing each other."

Out of the corner of my eye I saw Rez gulp, her lungs sad with my truth. My lids squeezed together, another tear escaping.

"And?" Rez's voice wavered, seeming to know there was more.

"She brought me to her when Torin was caught helping Ember. At the time I didn't know that, nor did I really think about the man she had chained in her chamber. He was fay. A fairy. And the delight of him being tortured..." I broke off, liquid fell, and I stopped trying to wipe it away.

"You liked it."

I let my lids drift closed again, taking in fact, not letting myself run from it.

"After he went unconscious, I screwed her against the wall next to him, his blood over both of us. Another piece of me died there..." I licked my lips, opening my eyes. "Ember came to my cell that night. Telling me not to give up. That she would be back for me." I rubbed harshly at my face. "Seeing her brought the tiniest part of myself back. That little piece wrapped around her words and held on for dear life. After that, I refused Aneira. I was punished more for it, but I took the beatings with a different kind of pleasure. I became a shell. I no longer enjoyed feeling only hate and disgust. I crawled out of the pit that night and never looked back. Ember rescued my soul, but part of me wished she hadn't saved my life."

"West…"

"When I returned, all I could do was lock it away. Believe it never happened. No one could ever know. Not the real truth. So I became the carefree guy they knew me as. It was the only way to survive. But then when the beast started struggling to come out, the nightmares of Aneira and Cammie began. Dark Dwellers are used to the dark, being reprehensible, but this went far beyond that. I hadn't only slept with the enemy, I gave myself to her."

"Not all of you." Rez touched my arm lightly.

"Don't." I flinched away. I couldn't have her touch me, not anymore.

"Do you think what you told me makes me feel different about you?"

"It should." I rubbed at the dried salt trailing my face, feeling the anger rise. "You should get far from me."

"You say we aren't alike, but we are." Rez only moved closer and tilted my face to look at her. "I gave myself over, gladly. You have no idea who I let between my legs to keep from ever having to climb out of the darkness."

A growl rumbled in my chest at the thought of any other person inside her.

"I understand your self-loathing, your disgust, more than you know. I lived it. I also let the vileness take me, twist my brain. Break me." She cupped my cheeks firmer. "Ember gave you the power to pull out, but *you* did it. You had the strength. And that is why, no matter what you confess to me, I am in awe of you. I didn't have the strength at first. Lars forced me out. And I fought him every step. I didn't want to come out. I never wanted to look at myself in the mirror again."

"But you did."

"And you will, too." She leaned forward, and her gaze filled with something I couldn't quite decipher. "You have finally let her out. Aneira can no longer flourish in the darkness. She will not hold you captive again. I *refuse* to let your guilt, demons, and self-hatred take you down. You need to forgive yourself."

I tried to turn my face, but she gripped tighter, and her gaze drilled into me.

"Gods, West. What you've been through. No one could have gone through that without succumbing. It doesn't make you weak because she got in your head and twisted you. But she *didn't* break you. A broken man wouldn't have held on to hope and pulled himself out. He would have stayed there. But you didn't. You fought back after all she did." She rubbed a thumb gently over my cheeks. "You don't even see how unbelievably amazing you are."

I huffed. Amazing…right.

"They will not have you anymore because I want you *here* with *me*. So whatever you have to do, you *fuckin'* fight. You forgive yourself. You got it? Fight…fight for yourself, your family. For Cammie." She glanced down. "For me."

Emotion twisted in my chest and obstructed my throat. I traced her jaw and ran my fingers through her hair, cupping her head. I needed to taste her lips, to feel her mouth, breathe her words to life. I brought her to me. The kiss was hungry, demanding, consuming. I knew a struggle was before me, but she gave me strength to face it without hiding.

She broke away, stood up, and tugged me with her. Walking backward she led me back to the bed. She brought me down on top, her body open for me. I felt lighter, like confessing did release the burden I'd been holding in me. I would probably never tell my family, but that was okay. My tormentors had been freed: Cammie, Aneira, myself...

It would always haunt me, what I did, what I was capable of. But this was the first time I ever felt there might be a chance to absolve some of my horrors and be able to breathe again.

Rez gasped as I slid into her and rocked our bodies together, slow and deep.

Every thrust breathed life back into my lungs.

# TWENTY-SEVEN

The howling gusts drummed at the broken window and poked at the fissures, prodding me awake. I blinked, staring out into the evening sky. Hints of the impending night sank over the land. My stomach was telling me it should have been fed hours ago, but after the night and afternoon we had, our bodies needed the rest, taking the full day to recover.

What a wild night full of highs and lows. It had been a roller coaster of death, terror, bliss, secrets, and confessions.

I told her the vilest part of myself, and she wrapped it in her arms and took it. Bore it with me and shared hers. I don't think I could express how she soothed my soul, quieted the horrors which had haunted me. It was the first time I slept without being terrorized. As if her saying they could no longer have me came true.

I don't think Aneira or Cammie would ever disappear completely, but I needed to learn to accept them. They were parts of me I would have to live with. Rez gave me strength to let in happiness again.

The sex after my confession had been different from anything I had ever experienced. Intimate. The shared secrets fused us further together. Not even with Cammie had I ever given so much of myself. The passion was consuming, and I let myself go. Rez and I surrendered, not thinking of what it meant or that it could crush us in the end.

We finally got some sleep, my body still humming from the contact with her. I was also aware we now had the spear close but was too relaxed to think much of it.

I still couldn't believe we killed Balor and took the spear, which let my beast free again. Now I had to hand it over to the King...along with Rez. I didn't know how I was going to let her go. But neither of us had a choice.

*Right?* A voice inside told me different, knew what it had to do. *Don't think about it. Just enjoy right now.*

I glanced over at the woman lying next to me on her side. Her back rising and lowering slowly, her hot skin brushing me. *Mine.*

The beast pawed, and I could feel him wanting to come out, to be released again, but not in the way it had at the beach. No, he wanted release in another way.

I had taken her every way possible. Hard and wild, slow and tortuously good. And she took it, gave it back, and wanted more. The woman almost depleted me. *Almost.* I rolled over, pinning her tightly against me. My hand curved over her hip, her ass taunting my dick.

Air hitched in her throat as my hands moved down, exploring her. She panted harder the more my fingers greeted her. She reached back, palming me. Both of us flourished under the other's control. Breathing grew tense, and she began to mutter. I opened her more, dragging her leg back over my hip. I leaned over, kissing her neck and behind her ear.

"Tell me," I whispered. "What do you want?"

"I want you." She squeezed her lids together.

"No. Tell me. How do you want me to fuck you?"

She wiggled back, tilting her ass into me, her words low but commanding me to take her.

The beast came alive, wanting to take her the way he preferred.

I grabbed her by the waist, pulling her up on her knees as I kneeled behind her. She curved her back, wiggling her gorgeous ass at me.

"Oh, you are so going to pay for that, darlin'."

"Then teach me a lesson." She grinned over her shoulder.

*Hell.* I was already neck deep. With her smile, I went all the way under.

Every time I took her, I knew it was wrong. The beast marked her more and more. But this looming threat didn't stop me. I took her harder than ever, matching the headboard to the broken footboard. I was going to have to fork out a lot of money to help Cara rebuild the place. *But it was worth it.*

Sweat dripped off both of us and she let go, screaming and begging for more. I willingly gave it, bending her farther over, allowing me to go deeper. She cried my name, her body clenching as she climaxed. I continued to pound into her, roaring as I released into her. We both collapsed face-first into the pillows, my chest landing on her back.

"Okay. Wow." She sighed, then rolled her cheek over the pillow to look at me with a grin. "Exceptional work, Mr. Moseley."

"Thank you." I kissed her shoulder blade, her skin tasting of a mix of sex, my sweat, and salt. "I'm a stickler for making sure I do things well."

"You call that well? I'd like to experience your idea of outstanding. Think you underestimate your talents."

"I don't like to brag." I winked, twisting to lay on my side, one leg still over her. She snorted cutely, knowing how little modesty I had. "I am starving." I continued to kiss her body. "I say we get into the shower, then go for a huge Irish breakfast."

"It's dinner time."

"So? You can have breakfast for dinner." I brushed back her hair, letting my hand run along her neck to her back. "Another rule I'm going to make you break."

"I'm not sure I can move."

"I have little doubt I could get you moving again and shrieking like a banshee and screaming out the most *dirty* words."

"Don't you sound so sure of yourself?" she challenged, but we both knew I was right.

"You know how fast I could put your words to shame?" I raised an eyebrow, leaning my head against my palm.

"Gods, you are full of yourself." She rolled over onto her back, staring up at me.

Our eyes locked and we watched each other. In the quiet I felt a strange aura in the air, secure, but with none of my usual walls. An emotion stirred inside, far beyond lust. Far beyond anything I had let myself feel in a long, long time. And if I was being completely honest with myself, if ever.

Her hand met my cheek, and I leaned over, capturing her mouth with mine. This time she kissed me like she was marking *her* territory. And I welcomed each stamp, wanting her to possess me.

Only a few weeks ago, I barely slept with a woman more than once. The idea of being with only one terrified me after Cammie. The beast was restless and demanded to run. Now the idea of not being with Rez—forever— rendered him frantic and irate.

*Shit. Shit. Shit.*

When did this happen? When did I fall *in love* with her? How did I let it? But with each kiss, I realized I didn't care. I was more than okay with it.

"Breakfast can wait a little longer," I mumbled against her lips, making her laugh. My hand caressed her body.

"Oh no, Mr. Moseley," she said formally. "If you want me screaming like a banshee, you need to feed me."

"I can fill you up." I winked.

"With actual food."

Food sounded like heaven, but we had nothing left here. We'd have to leave the bed and get dressed to eat, which wasn't something I wanted to do.

"Fine." I rolled off her onto my back. "But we get it to go…bring it back here and eat…both food and each other."

Rez groaned with amusement. She was getting used to my constant dirty mouth. She said it turned her on, which she'd never have admitted a few weeks ago. Hell, a couple times the night before and even just a moment ago, her mouth rivaled mine, at least in bed, which I loved even more, where it was only for me. I loved she showed me the private side no one else knew. I felt this was the true Rez, the unguarded woman who no longer let her past dictate and control her.

She leaned over and kissed me, her smile turning serious.

"What?"

She shook her head, and I felt my stomach clench. I could sense her thoughts brush against my mind, conveying her words through her eyes.

*Lars.* We were gonna have to deal with him soon. We found the spear and should have already contacted him. We should've been on a plane back to the States by now. Our little world was coming to an end, reality dragging us out.

"Yeah. I know." I cupped her face, bringing her back to my mouth. The thought of this ending, of her no longer being mine to kiss, spread desperation through me. My lips became frantic and incinerating, wanting to taste her. Consume her.

*Bang.* The door to the cottage whipped open and crashed against the wall. Cool, wet air swept into the room with a blistering gush.

I leaped from the bed with a growl, the Dark Dweller startled and on defense. My body instinctively curled forward, shoulders rigid. I had to fight not to shift since fear incited our protective mode.

Rez moved swiftly, jumping to her feet on the other side of the bed.

Two large intruders entered the cottage. Their familiar faces iced my lungs like the Arctic.

I froze, swallowing the panic edging along my body. I was beyond screwed. If I hoped by a slight chance we could have stayed a secret, fate came up and slapped me across the face. Hard.

Goran stepped into the room, his gaze roving from my naked body to Rez's. Goran was Lars's lead henchman. If Lars asked him to bend over, he would do it without a thought. I didn't know why, but Goran was so loyal to him he'd clean his boots with his tongue.

The new guard, Travil, moved in, sliding away from the door. He could not hide his shock or his disgust.

But they were not my focus or my worry. They never went anywhere without their leader.

Thumping energy crackled at the already broken window, sending more fractures trailing out. My heart slammed against my ribs, and I heard Rez gasp, grabbing for a bedsheet to cover herself.

Then *he* entered the room. His yellow-green eyes rolled over us, taking in what was before him. His face was stone, but with one inhale, blackness filled his eyes, and his shoulders strained his dark gray suit.

Dead. I was going to die right here, I knew it. It had been inevitable since the moment Rez stepped in the plane with me…possibly before that. No part of me regretted her. I was only afraid she would.

Lars inhaled sharply, his pupils vacant with emotion, his body motionless. But I could feel the fury rolling underneath, pumping magic in the room with dense waves, bending my legs.

"Lars," Rez spoke.

"Don't." He growled the syllable so low and twisted, it almost didn't sound like a word. "If you open your mouth, I. Will. Kill. You." His hands became fists, his shoulders vibrating.

I had seen Lars pissed before. At me. At Eli. At Ember… Actually, there wasn't anybody he hadn't been furious with at one time or another. This was not like those times. The ground trembled with his rage, as did every nerve in my body. Sweat trickled down my face, my teeth gritting as the pressure grew.

Lars's skin changed to the palest white, thinning to a translucent texture. Bones protruded from the shallow skin, resembling a Day of the Dead skeletal mask. Black pupils dug into me, scouring my body. Then pressure like a sonic boom slammed me to my knees with a groan.

"You. Dare. Take. What. Is. Mine?" Lars took a step forward, his voice low, but it boomed in the room, slashing at my eardrums. "You go against your King? Disrespect and insult me?"

"Lars, it wasn't—" Rez stepped forward.

"Silence!" Lars yelled, and Rez sailed back into the wall and smacked into the paneling, pinned in place. "I don't want to hear anything out of your treacherous mouth. Everything I've done for you…" He shook his head, his cheekbones protruding garishly from his face. "I gave you a home, a job, a family…a place in *my bed*."

Magic poured in the room, twisting me over my knees. Even Lars's guards bent to their knees beneath the pressure of his fury.

"Lars. Please…" Rez cried out, but I couldn't turn to look at her. Lars's will kept me locked in place.

"What?" He opened his arms, stepping closer to her. "Do you not think I have the right?"

"You have every right." She struggled to talk. "But I hope you will hear us out first."

"Why?" Anger lashed down on the room again. I groaned, my bones close to cracking under the force. "Why should I give you that right? What have you done except betray me? You deserve nothing. I should kill you right here."

"Then do what you must, Lars," Rez ordered. "But know I did love you…even when I knew you would *never* love me back. I loved what you did for me, how you took care of me, treated me with respect and decency. Something I hadn't had in a very long time. You are an amazing man, and an even better King. I will always cherish the time we had together. You saved my life. Showed me love and kindness. I am so sorry. I never planned on this."

"Do you think flattery will help you?" He gritted his teeth. "You think I will forgive this treason?"

"No," she replied, still locked against the wall. "It's the truth. Go ahead. Kill me if it would appease you."

A rattling noise started in the back of Lars's throat. My mouth opened, air ripping out from my lungs, the pressure bearing on me like a vise, cranking in, squeezing my mind. It grew and sprouted until I felt my body start to bend and twist. Screams and wails tore through the room when the magic swirled into a tornado.

*Crack!* The window splintered, and daggers of glass exploded through the room, slicing at my naked body like thousands of tiny warriors. The wind swept into the room and blew the papers and curtains around in lashing circles.

Lars bellowed, shaking the cottage with its violence. The magic popped like a balloon, the force evaporating, and oxygen zoomed back into my lungs.

A couple of minutes that felt like years passed before Lars spoke. "My desire to kill you both overrules any logic." He turned for the door. "There is still a mission to complete and then you will account for your crimes.

"Goran, have them outside in ten minutes. I need a moment," he barked at his rising guard.

"Yes, my liege." Goran got to his feet and nodded.

Lars stalked out the door and slammed it, the frame cracking behind him. Cara would never rent her place out to fae again.

Goran and the other man quickly righted themselves, glaring at us. "Get up," Goran snarled. "You heard the

King. Ten minutes!" I pushed myself back up on my heels, glaring at him. "I never thought Dark Dwellers were this stupid and suicidal." Goran's revulsion toward me combined with rage.

"Ah. That's because you never got to know me well enough." I stood and folded my arms.

"Did you want to get caught?" Travil sneered at me. "You ignored his calls for four days. What did you think would happen?"

*Damn.*

I should have known that would bite me in the ass.

Goran glowered at me. "Normally he'd send someone over to check on you guys, but for *some* reason he didn't trust you completely." Goran stepped up to me. He was an inch shorter but well built. He was meant to be intimidating. Scary.

I could be scarier.

"Tell me, dweller, when he assigned you to obtain the spear, when did you figure putting your spear in his woman was what he meant instead?"

My chin stayed level, my nose flaring, I staying silent.

"I'm not anyone's." Rez walked around the bed, the thin sheet barely covering her. "No one owns me."

"Really, Rez?" Goran snorted as he turned to look at her. "You are not a fool. You knew what you were signing up for when you moved into his bedroom. You made the choice, and now you are going to have to deal with the consequences." Goran face me. "Outside in ten." Goran and Travil trampled out the door and slammed it, splintering another hole in the door.

Rez and I both stood for a moment before I heard her exhale shakily. I rubbed my face, moving to find my jeans.

"West?"

"Are you all right?" I asked evenly.

"Yes." She twisted the sheet around her fingers. "What are we going to do?"

"Go out and face him." I jostled on my pants, not looking at her. "It's all we can do." Out of the corner of my eye I saw her nod, then go hunting for her scattered clothes.

Our only choice was going forward. Even if death was in my near future, I had no doubt I would do it all over again. I would do anything for her.

*Mine.*

I actually had to push back the urge to grab her, claim her so vigorously and loudly everyone would know she was mine without a doubt. I'd battle all who came to separate us. Permanently.

It was a fight I would lose. Badly.

"You didn't tell him we have it." Rez slipped on her sweater, her eyes going to the safe.

"Neither did you." We both understood the moment we handed it over, we'd lose any power we might hold. It was a tiny bargaining chip, though it wasn't enough. He could easily take it and kill us anyway.

I knew what I had to do. What flittered through my mind earlier was the only thing I could do to protect Rez. The exact thing I didn't want her to know was the one thing the King needed to know.

I couldn't do it alone. I snatched an object off the floor, hiding it under my clothes as I headed to the bathroom. Rez stared after me, clearly sensing the abruptness in my movements. I shut the door, needing a moment when she was not next to me.

This was a long shot but all I could think of to do. I hoped she would forgive me.

And I hoped they could get here in time.

347

# TWENTY-EIGHT

Goran and Travil led us like criminals out toward the bluff. The evening sky was clear, which made the air even colder. It gnawed on your bones and slapped your face with painful stings. Darkness slipped quickly over the countryside, no streetlamps or city buildings to dilute the night. The moon was low, the stars only starting to wake up.

Lars paced back and forth, one hand in his pocket, the other pinching his nose. His eyes were back to normal, but his skin was still stretched and thin. The demon was still very close to the surface.

I had to give it to him for not killing me already. I can't say I would have done the same if I found Rez in bed with someone else. The beast snarled at the mere idea, ready to dissect and maim anyone who even thought about it. *Shit. He's going to have to kill me. I won't be able to handle her going back to him...fucking him...*

Goran halted me in front of the King; Travil stopped Rez next to me.

"Leave us," Lars ordered his men, sending them away with a flick of his head. They nodded, let us go, and moved back toward the house where Lars's car waited.

Now I wanted that burly, blond bastard to stay. Without him and Travil, the ground felt a lot more unstable. I didn't know why since they would happily throw me over the cliff or bury my ass six feet under, but anything was better than being alone with Lars.

Lars turned to me, clasping his hands, his voice tight. "Where is the spear, Mr. Moseley?"

Uhhh... "I don't have it." Technically true. It remained in the closet where we left it.

"But you know where it is?" Lars's lids narrowed.

"Yes."

"You have it." Lars's eyes flashed, puncturing my soul, picking out the truth among the weeds of lies. "And you *keep* it from me as a bargaining tool?" He seethed, his eyes turning black again.

I had the distinct impression he wasn't too happy about that. Wonder where I got that idea?

"Where is it, Mr. Moseley?" The demon king came back to the surface. "You do not insult me, bed my mistress, and squirm out of our deal."

"We're not!" Rez held her hand out. "It's yours, Lars. We were only keeping it safe."

"That is not what he was doing." Lars leaned into my face, his black eyes sparking with rage. "I was going to kill you quickly, but you do not deserve that kindness."

Agony squeezed my throat. Lars's invisible hold on me was like a python, constricting my esophagus in a death grip. I couldn't gasp for air, even though my mouth opened to try. Pain sliced down my throat and tore at my lungs. I heaved but no sound emerged. Panic gripped my muscles, and I clawed at the nonexistent hand.

"Noooo... Please stop!" Rez begged. Her pleas were lost on him. His entire focus was on me, drilling pain throughout my body. Dots popped up in my vision, the pain of his power mincing my insides.

*Shit, I really am going to die tonight.*

My ears buzzed, but in the distance I heard someone call through the night. Or was I imagining it?

"Lars! Stop!" A woman's voice grew closer, the familiarity ringing in my chest, but my mind did not yet want to believe. It might be a hallucination. I wanted it to be true so badly I was making it so.

But then the hold around my neck loosened, letting a trickle of air slip into my throat. I gulped it, coughing and gasping with the tiny bit of air that slipped in.

"Lars. Please. Don't do this." Her voice caught the wind and sailed right for us.

I jerked my head to the side and saw two figures jogging to the edge of the cliffs. Their dark clothes blended with the night. They were so well known to me that my beast leaped up my throat. I wanted to run to them, tackle and hug, like wolf pups. *Oh thank the gods. They made it.*

"Don't hurt them." The woman ran in front of me, her arms outstretched protectively against both me and Rez.

Lars halted, his eyes widening. "Ember?" He gaped, his eyes returning to their normal chartreuse. "What are you doing here?"

"Stopping you." Ember reached back, gripping my hand. She glanced at me with those two different colored eyes. Her black-and-red hair was pulled back in a ponytail. She wore dark jeans, knee-high black boots, and a puffy black jacket. It was good to see her.

Lars's glower narrowed, anger sharpening his teeth. "Get out of the way, Ember."

I knew both Eli and Ember would sense me when they got close enough. They could also feel the magic pounding off Lars, both of us a beacon to lead directly to our location.

"No." Ember's shoulders stiffened as she leaned forward with determination.

Eli came to her side, blocking me from Lars. "You'll have to go through us first," Eli growled.

His bright green eyes glimpsed over at me. He had let his light brown hair grow long again. He wore a similar black winter coat, dark jeans, and the same worn motorcycle boots he had for years.

*Thank you, man, I know this was a lot to ask,* I sent him through our link.

*Not too much for you, brother.* Eli shot me a quick glance over his shoulder. *I'm not letting anything happen to you either. I am not losing any more of my family.*

"I said move. That's an order!" Lars bellowed, his eyes so black all I saw were pits.

"You *do not* order me." Ember took a tiny step closer to Lars. "I am not your employee. You can force me, we all know that, but I hope you won't. You're my uncle. I love you."

Or her father. The verdict was still out. My gut had little doubt Lars was actually her father. I was sure Ember and Lars felt the same, but without proof, they kept to the Aisling story that Devlin, Lars's twin brother, was Ember's father.

"West is part of my family too. I am Dark Dweller as much as I am a demon. I protect my family. Rez is also part of that. I will not let you hurt either of them." Ember's long ponytail whipped across her back as the wind tore over the cliff.

"They have dishonored and insulted me. They must pay for their crimes." Dark, indignant energy pumped off Lars.

Rez shifted next to me, her chin tilting higher, not shying away from his threat.

"I understand that." Ember took another step toward the demon. "And they will, but not with their lives. That I can't let you do. I will fight you, Lars, to the death."

Eli snarled in front of me, his shoulders curling forward, his fingers twitching. I knew he was fighting the urge to change. His mate merely mentioning the word *death* aroused his beast.

"No." I stepped out of his shadow. This was my battle to fight. "This is not why I asked you to come. This is my problem to face."

"You asked them to come?" Rez swung to me.

"Yes." I kept my eyes on Lars. "And not to stand behind them. I will take my punishment."

Ember's unnerving eyes, one yellow-green, like her uncle's, one blue, shot me a warning.

"This was completely me. Punish me. Kill me." I stabbed a finger at my chest.

"What?" Rez floundered with confusion. "Completely you?" She faced forward, walking around Ember to Lars. The demon tracked her, his magic sparked, and his lips hitched in warning.

Ember reached over, her fingers gripping the King's hand, speaking his name so softly the wind blew it over the land like dust. Ember's touch flatlined his mouth, but his muscles were still locked with fury.

I think she was the only one in the entire universe who could calm him. His love for her transcended his rage and impulses. At least for now.

"Lars," Rez stood proudly, "there are not enough apologies in the world to tell you how sorry I am. It doesn't matter we never really loved each other or I lost you a long time ago to a ghost. But right here and now, I am so sorry for what happened. It was not planned. I did not consider I would ever fall in love with a Dark Dweller, especially West."

My body jerked. *Love? She loved me?*

"Wait." I stepped closer to her, Ember still in the middle, holding on to Lars, keeping him grounded. "What do you mean *especially* me?"

She tipped her head to the side. "Really? Is this about your ego?"

"Well…"

"You idiot. I just said I loved you, and you are preening over your self-importance?" She waggled her head, her hair blowing loosely in the wind. "Seriously, West, it's no secret you are the biggest player out there. Girls drop at your feet by the dozens. I've seen it. So falling for you, admitting it out loud, was never something I thought would happen, nor really wanted. But it did. *I did.*"

All I wanted to do was kiss her. To pull her into my arms and let her know she had ruined all other women for me. All I could see, feel, and want was her. But a livid demon stopped me from acting. The more she talked, the more magic spilled from him and was so thick it warped the air around us and halted my words in my throat. At my stunned silence, she bristled and turned back to Lars.

"Your liege, whatever you feel you must do, I am at your will." She bowed her head before the King.

Lars pulled from Ember's grasp and moved to Rez. He placed one finger under her chin and lifted her head. "You are right. I never loved you like you deserved, nor did you love me. But you are still mine. There is no greater weakness than a King losing what is rightfully his. I cannot let this go. I am remorseful for that. You have been a great addition to the house, and your loss will be greatly felt."

My beast reacted. "No!" I lunged for Lars. Eli was swift to grab me, wrapping his arms around me, and walked me back. "Don't touch her!"

"West, stop," Eli growled.

"Fuck you," I lashed out. If it were Ember, there'd be no question. "She's *mine*. It's why I called you."

Eli exhaled, running a hand through his hair with frustration. He knew what that meant. What extent he would go to for Ember. Hell, the man already offed himself once for her. Left the pack to follow her across the world.

*What?* Ember's voice came into my head. Her eyes wide, head snapping back and forth between Rez and me, realization dawning. Over time she was getting better at linking with us. *Are you telling me the beast claimed Rez? Seriously? Eli, did you know this?*

Eli glanced at the sky, a half-guilty, half-smug smile on his mouth.

*Oh crap on ash bark...* Ember let her head fall back.

When the beast found its equal, its mate, there was nothing it wouldn't do. At our core we were animals. It was hard to explain the feeling. When I called Rez mine, it didn't mean I "owned" her, but I would fight to the death for her. The term "mate" almost surpassed "family." They became family as well and would be protected as fiercely by the clan.

It had been the only card I could play against Lars. I would have preferred the whole clan here, surrounding

Rez, protecting her, but in the time frame I had Eli and Ember were my best bet. Ember knew the doorways better than anyone and could get them here fast.

Eli swung around, still holding me back. "Lars, if you touch her, you will have to contend with me as well." Ember moved next to Eli as a solitary front. Lars dropped his hand, watching me through his black holes, cold and empty.

"What?" Rez's forehead lined with worry.

Everyone looked to me.

"What? What is going on?" Panic curled around Rez's vocals.

"Oh Jesus, West. She doesn't know?" Ember threw out her arms.

"Did Eli tell you?" I shot back.

She angled her head, her gaze on Eli. "Actually, no, *he* didn't. Gabby told me."

"Thanks, man," Eli grumbled over his shoulder at me.

"If I'm going down, so are you," I mumbled back.

"Someone tell me what's going on," Rez exclaimed.

I opened my mouth to tell her.

"It means I cannot kill you." Lars spoke, his voice void of any emotion. He pushed back his shoulders, tugging at his sleeves. The demon shifted slowly back into the man. "Not unless I want to start a war with the Dark Dwellers." When he spoke, all attention was pinned on him. "I am a smart enough man to understand what Cole and I have built to keep this new world moving forward is far more significant."

Confusion still etched over Rez's face. I strode to her. "What he is saying is my beast claimed you, darlin'."

"Excuse me?" Rez faulted a step back, keeping a slight distance between us, her shoulders rising defensively.

"*Claimed* me? I will not go from one keeper to another. I am not a dog."

"See?" Eli said to Ember, motioning to Rez. "Exact reason we never had this conversation."

"I think it's because you are a weenie." Ember folded her arms, teasing.

"Can't go five minutes without bringing up my weenie, can you?" He lifted one eyebrow.

Ember blushed and she shook her head. Then she turned to Rez. "I know it's scary to hear. *Believe me.*" She went to Rez, taking her hands. "Especially to one of these Neanderthals. But it's not like that..." She cleared her throat. "You love him, right?"

Rez glanced over at me, then nodded.

"Then that's all that matters. Just because he claimed you doesn't mean you aren't free to decide what you want. You can walk away whenever you want." Her eyes filled with compassion, then turned harder. "I threaten to walk daily. Keeps him on his toes."

Eli snorted behind me. I almost burst out laughing as well. Those two couldn't go a few hours without tearing each other's clothes off. The love they had for each other was nothing I had ever seen. They were in it for life. And Dark Dwellers lived a hell of a long time.

"This does not interest me." Lars pulled focus again, snapping our heads forward. "I may not choose to kill either of you for reasons I feel are far more important. However, this offense cannot go unpunished. You've made me look weak. The influx of people vying for my spot will hinder our ability to move this world forward." He rolled his head and slowly moved to me, magic punching my chest. "Now for the one thing you did promise me. The spear."

My beast growled inside, angry at the thought of giving it up. The moment I handed it over, the beast would be confined again, locked behind agonizing bars of torture. It was like handing my soul over to the devil. But I made that deal long ago.

"You will not hurt her?" I asked.

"No, I will abide by this favor. Nonetheless, she will still pay."

"But she is free to go. Do whatever she wants?" All I wanted was to know she was alive and free to choose whatever she desired.

Lars pinched his lips together. "She will be free of my bed and banished from the house, yes."

It wasn't exactly what I wanted, but I knew he would not do better. I nodded. "The spear is in the safe so no one could sense it."

Rez came to me, and in her gaze I knew she understood what it meant to lose the artifact. I was giving up an entire part of me, my identity, my being.

I glanced into her chocolate brown eyes, full of love and concern for me. I may have lost part of me, but I didn't lose my soul. That was with her.

I reached up, running my hand over her cheek. "I'm in love with you too, darlin'." I didn't care if the Unseelie King was watching. I leaned over, bringing her mouth to mine, kissing her deeply. It was quick but filled with everything I didn't say. Then I turned to Lars. "Okay, I'm ready."

He stared at me, then gave me a firm nod.

"What are you doing?" Ember moved toward Lars and me, but Eli was quick to grab her. "No! Let go. Lars, you said you wouldn't hurt him."

"Ember. Stop." Eli drew his arms tighter around her body, pulling her into him. "This has to be done. West has to pay for his crime."

Ember was still new to the Otherworld rules. She didn't understand how honor and appearance ruled our world. I defied the laws and stole from the Unseelie King. There was no way around it. Rez's silence showed how well she understood this. And for Rez, I would take whatever punishment he felt I deserved, tenfold.

"I will not kill him, Ember." Lars clasped his hands. "But just." When he faced me, his yellow-green eyes glowed. "West Moseley, from here on out you will be bound to me, to use as I see fit. There is not one thing you will refuse to do for me. I own you. Do you understand? By taking something of mine, I take from you."

"Yes." The weight of his words yanked me to my knees, the beast growling to fight back, but it could not rise above the damage. Between the pain of not shifting and Lars's magic, sweat oozed along my hairline, locking my jaw.

"Do you agree to the terms? Night or day, you are at my whim? My slave, my killer, my messenger."

"Lars, don't! Please," Rez pleaded, falling on deaf ears. Taking a Dark Dweller's freedom was like putting a leash on a wild panther. It was an act of great power and cruelty. Some things were worse than death. This was the only way he would not lose respect for keeping me alive.

"West understands if he doesn't agree, he gives you up," Lars coolly replied. He was right. This was how it worked. If I kept the girl, I lost something equally important. "I think we all know he won't do that."

Even if she chose not to be with me, I still would have agreed to his terms. The beast allowed for no less when it came to its mate.

"Do you consent?" His voice growled, and his eyes returned to black. The demon fired under the surface.

"Yes."

The connection came down on me like a noose. I heard Ember whimper. She knew the sensation of one of Lars's binds. In fact, everyone standing here had been bound to Lars one time or another.

"Elighan." Lars's skin faded from olive to white again, sharpening the features of the demon always simmering underneath. "Please take Ember and Rez away."

"No!" Rez's knees skated over the dirt, falling next to me. "I'm not leaving him."

"Rez…" the demon king warned.

"No." She shook her head.

"Go." I angled my head to her, fighting against the pressure curling around my muscles as sweat poured down my temples.

She cupped my face, her eyes wild. "I can't leave you."

"Yes, you can." I leaned my head into hers. "I don't want you to see this, darlin'."

She gave a choked whimper.

"Please?" I whispered. "Let me have some dignity." The legend of Lars's torture was gut twisting. I had no doubt it would not be pretty, and I didn't want her to see me weak and whimpering.

"Damn you." She gripped my face tighter. "Using your southern charm to make me weak in the knees and agreeing to whatever you say."

"That's the plan." I winked.

She inhaled a choppy breath and pressed her lips to mine. She stood, keeping her back rigid as she walked over to Ember. Eli stood in place when the girls reached for each other. They took each other's hands and disappeared into the night.

*I am here for you*, Eli sent me through our link.

*Thanks. Let them get far enough away.*

*Don't want them to hear you blubbering like a baby?*

I was gonna say something smart-ass, but all I could say was, *No.*

Eli nodded in understanding.

*I can't turn anymore, Eli.*

*I know. Cole told me.*

*Damn, Cole knew?*

*I don't care, brother. You are a Dark Dweller, whether you shift or not. That doesn't change who you are.*

I blinked, looking at the ground, then back at him.

Eli's mouth pinched together, fighting back the wave of grief and indignation he felt on my behalf that came rushing through our link. It's funny when you realize how much you love someone. Because I was older, Eli and I hadn't been terribly close growing up. But that had changed. Now I sensed a million threads binding us, making us closer than any blood brothers. When I'd been closest to death and useless, Eli had carried me out of the Otherworld, ignoring my pleas to be left behind. We never spoke of it, but from there on out, there was no one I trusted more. I had always been restless, searching for home, when I had it all along.

I nodded but said no more; I didn't need to. He felt it. He gave me a nod back, bowed away, and followed the girls into the darkness. He would stay close. I knew it without a doubt, and he would be the first to retrieve me.

I sucked in breath and pointed my gaze at the King. This was going to be bad. And not being able to shift after to heal more quickly would only make Lars's sentence sweeter for him. Lars would be able to kick the ever-loving shit out of me without moving from his spot or getting his knuckles bruised.

Lars didn't utter a word but transformed completely to demon as the first surge of pain burst into my head. I crunched my teeth together, trying to keep the wails beating against my ribs from leaving my throat as more abuse hammered my mind. He growled and my body flew, slamming my back into the earth. An invisible hand clenched my throat while I felt my mind was shoved through a grinder. Every muscle strained and burned, feeling like I was stretched on a rack while being burned alive. Sounds came from my throat, tearing across the sky like lightning.

The worst of this was being frozen in place, not able to curl in a ball under the onslaught of pain. Lars's black eyes held nothing but cruelty. He clenched his fist and agony slashed up my spine like nails being driven into my skin.

Lars stepped over me, reached down, and grabbed me by the throat. "I. Am. King."

Then his face pinched, and it felt like my head split in half, shredding my entire body head to toe. I bellowed, quickly losing logic or reasoning, my beast pulling my mind in protectively. I was sure vomiting and screaming were involved, and the world spun in the most agonizing anguish I had ever known.

Time and objects around me lost meaning, I was simply one long nerve being twisted in ways it never should. Eventually I succumbed and pushed out the torment while my mind sheltered itself in a sea of blackness.

# TWENTY-NINE

Pain thrust me into the dark and it brought me out. Sharp and agonizing. My head was the first thing I sensed. It throbbed like it had its own pulse, leaving my thoughts stuck in thick mush. Every nerve in my body burned and zapped through the hurt in my body.

I was awake, but I couldn't seem to drag myself past the paralyzing pain. All I could hear was a beeping noise along with low murmurings. They slowly grew clearer till my brain could make out words and comprehend them. Then I fell back into nothing. Several times I reached consciousness only to be pulled under again.

My mind started to fill the darkness with images. A beautiful woman, her smile, brown eyes…her musical laughter. Food smeared over her face; her singing at the top of her lungs to the radio; eating cookies naked on the floor.

*Rez.* I called her name in my mind, pulling me through the murk. My lids jolted open, blinking to clear my vision until an off-white ceiling came into focus. Because of the smells, the feel of the bed underneath me, I knew instantly I was home, tucked in my own bed. How and when I got here, I didn't know. Right then, nothing felt better. Home.

For centuries I struggled to find mine. To find my place. And in my journey it only led me back to the family I walked away from, never thinking I fit in. It was now the only place I knew I did, with people who loved me, who would die and kill for me. I had been too selfish before to see what I had, too stuck in what I didn't have to see what I did.

"West?" Eli's face loomed over me, lined with worry. His brown hair messy, his scruff appeared a little thicker than normal.

"Hey," my parched voice cracked.

"Jesus, man." He raked his hand roughly over his face then into his hair. "Fuck, you gave us a scare."

"Rez?"

"She's fine."

"Where is she?" I felt she wasn't near; my body had its own GPS for her. Once your beast claimed, it was part of the package deal. Eli had talked about this when Ember left him the first time. No place on earth existed where he couldn't find her.

I could still "feel" Rez, but some internal instinct said she wasn't close.

"Drink this." Eli held out a cup of water.

I tried to sit up but balked against the shooting pain. Eli stuffed a few pillows behind me, pulling me up. I took a long drink while my gaze scoured the room. Chairs, blankets, and a couple of mattresses stuffed every free corner.

"Did Cole rent out my room to a bunch of vagabonds?" My voice sounded raspy and could barely be heard.

"Most of us have been sleeping in here, or at least taking turns." Eli pulled up a chair and sat down. "Like I told you, you gave us a scare."

"So you have a slumber party without me? Nice, brother. If you tell me the girls had pillow fights, I'm going to kill you."

"Nah." A cheeky grin hinted at his mouth. "But Cooper and I did."

"Ugh."

"Naked."

"What's sad is it wouldn't surprise me," I rasped.

"There might have been a couple games of pin the tail on the jackass."

"Let me guess…"

"We didn't want to leave you out. It was your party." Eli smirked.

"Nice."

Eli's gaze dropped, his expression turning serious. His voice sounded low and gruff. "We didn't think you were going to make it." He leaned forward, gripping his hands together. "Lars was a little angrier than we thought."

I bobbed my head, looking at the cup in my hand.

"Man, what the hell were you thinking?" Eli shook his head.

"I wasn't." I shifted higher and my jaw slammed together. I took a few breaths, letting the sharp sting disappear. "I did at first. Tried to ignore it. But…"

Eli laughed harshly. "Yeah, that damn *but*…"

"You of all people should know." I rubbed between my eyebrows. "Believe me, she was the last person I expected or wanted for the beast to claim."

"I do know." Eli grinned; his green eyes glinted. "I fought Ember as hard as I could and somehow I would still find myself near her. Now that fuckin' woman has my balls wrapped so tightly she could place me under a Christmas tree."

I guffawed, which switched into a groan. We sat a few moments in silence.

"I'm sorry, man," I said quietly.

"For what?"

"For everything. For choosing Lorcan. Blaming you for Cammie. Disappearing for so many years. Not being here."

"There's nothing to be sorry for."

"I was such a dick. Took my past out on you guys. Lost my way."

"Jesus, man. I went AWOL for over two years. I was unbearable. I misplaced my way so bad Cooper threatened to challenge my ass for my position." He held up his arms. "But we're family. We love each other no matter what. You have never been excluded from that...ever."

"I know."

"And for Cammie. Fuck. I carry that around every day. I was so young and new to being second-in-command. I handled it all wrong, and a girl died because of it. I'm the one who's sorry, man."

"It was my fault. I freaked out and thought if I told her the truth, tried to force the beast to claim her, everything would be all right. And eventually she would accept what I was. I was a fool." I shook my head. "You can't force the beast, and now I understand the difference of loving someone and finding your partner in life. I'm forgiving myself for Cammie. I hope you can, too."

Eli nodded and cleared his throat.

"Yeah, enough sappy shit."

I set my cup next to me, realizing something.

"Wow, it took me nearly croaking to get you to come home."

Eli sniggered, rubbing his face again. "Yeah, everyone thanks you for almost dying."

I knew why they didn't want to come back. The ghost of Jared, Owen, even Samantha, haunted this house. They would always be here, but every day it eased a little.

"How did we get back here?"

"Em," Eli replied. "Only she seems to understand how the doors work."

Cole barreled through my door, followed by Cooper and Gabby.

"West? Shit. You're finally awake. I was about to come in here and kick your ass till you woke up." Gabby came stomping up to my bedside.

I couldn't help smiling. "Missed you too, Gabs."

"Screw you! You totally freaked us out." She leaned over me. "Never do that again. Do you hear me?"

"Yes, ma'am."

Cooper pushed his twin sister away, moving next to the bed. His bleach-blond hair a contrast to his sister's hair, which today was black with pink tips. "So glad you are awake, man." He gripped my hand in our special handshake. I tried not to look like a pussy and flinch at the jerky movement.

"Aw. The love." I grinned playfully.

"Nah, man, I just need you to get back to work. I've had to take on more than double without you. I'm tired. And needing a night off to get laid."

"Not something I need to know." Gabby shuddered.

"Like I need to know about you and Alki," he bickered back. "Need to bleach my brain."

"Oh please, living in this testosterone-filled house is bad enough. I hear you guys have sex all the time. Eli and Ember in the shower this morning? I still can't eat."

"You were eating *my* peanut butter right outside the door when we came out." Eli turned in the chair, shouting back.

"That was only to piss you off." She smiled evilly. "And when did it become your peanut butter again? You haven't been home in six months."

"It's always my peanut butter. You never, ever touch a man's peanut butter. Have I taught you nothing?"

"All of you. Shut up." Cole rubbed his forehead with a groan.

Oh yeah. I was home.

"How are you feeling?" Cole patted my leg from the end of the bed.

"Fine. Will be dancing on pool tables and causing mayhem in no time," I lied. Lars had left his mark. The beast was locked away again, a slave to the Unseelie King. I was far from all right. But the reason I did all that was what was still foremost on my mind. "Where is Rez?"

"She's with Em. She'll be fine." Eli faced me again.

A tickle of warning tugged at my gut. "What aren't you telling me?" I ignored the pain and sat up higher in bed. "Where is she?"

Cole and Eli exchanged a look, probably communicating privately with their link.

"Tell me!" I exclaimed.

Cole sighed. "If I tell you, you can't leave this bed. You can't do anything to help her anyway. I will force you to stay in it if I have to."

"Cole..." I growled.

"She's meeting with Lars."

"What?" Fear struck at my heart.

"Rez cannot go unpunished for her actions. Lars sent for her this morning."

I moved without a thought.

"West. Stop." Cole put his hand on me, but I ignored him and continued to struggle to get out of bed, involuntary noises wheezed from my chest. "I warned you." Cole's voice went deep and powerful. "I order you to *stop*. Get. Back. In. Bed."

I grunted against his control, but it was a lost cause. He was my alpha, and I would always have to bow to his order. Cole barely used it, so I never felt resentful. Most of the time it was only to protect us from doing something at the extreme end of stupid. I eased back on the bed, already panting with exertion.

"Sorry, but you need to stay put. You can't do anything for her." Cole softened his alpha stance. "Rez is an amazing and strong woman. She'll be fine." He said it with such familiarity, like he knew her character.

"What am I missing? You don't even really know her that well."

"We've had time to get to know her." Cole shoved his hands in his jeans. "I understand what you see in her."

I gazed around my family, still confused. "Had time? How long have I been out?" A couple days, surely. A week, max.

"Four weeks," Cole replied.

"Four! Four weeks?" I sputtered, looking to Eli. It had been a month since the night on the cliff?

"Lars was true to his word. You were an inch from death." Eli clasped his hands together.

"And Rez has been here the whole time?"

"Never left your side, until this morning." Cooper folded his arms. Even in the middle of winter he wore a black tank and jeans.

My heart tugged at the thought of her being here for me, while I couldn't be there for her now.

"Jesus, West, claiming the Unseelie King's mistress?" Gabby put her hands on her hips, dressed in tight ripped jeans and a tied-up T-shirt. "Could your beast be any more of an idiot?"

She was right. It was an idiot, but it wanted Rez just the same.

"Though at least I can tolerate her." In Gabby language this was the closest to praise as you'd get. It had taken Gabby a little while to accept Ember. Gabby was raised with mostly boys and guarded us carefully. Even when Samantha was alive, they never got along.

Cole rolled back his shoulders and took a deep breath. "You know this will not stop our work relationship with the King. It can't...no matter what you feel. Or how we feel." Regret shone in Cole's hazel eyes. I could tell this was weighing heavy on him.

"I took my punishment. I was in the wrong. I don't have any hard feelings for Lars. He did what any leader would do." Except, if he hurt Rez, things would be different. "I know with work, with Ember, all our paths will cross. Plus..." My tongue locked momentarily on my confession. I would always be tied to Lars. His slave.

"I told them," Eli informed me.

I nodded, grateful I didn't have to relay it.

"Actually, Lars was the one to send his own personal healer here to check on you several times a week, till you were okay. He knew we didn't have one since we lost Owen." Cole folded his arms, his blue flannel straining against his muscles.

Lars sent a private doctor to heal me? You had to give it to him: He was a considerate asshole. In the fae law,

Lars was more than lenient. Simply the thought of being anyone's bitch was still a hard pill to swallow. To be with Rez, I would gulp down a dozen of them.

"It took him four weeks to call for Rez?"

"I think he needed to cool down," Eli said.

"Alki told me it's a mess over there. Rez was the glue, and losing her hit the house hard, especially after the loss of Koke and Maya. Only Marguerite is keeping them going." Gabby played with the side knot of her rocker shirt.

"Do you have any idea what he's going to do?"

"No." Eli shook his head. "That's why Em wouldn't let her go alone. If anyone can keep Lars somewhat grounded, it's her."

I took tiny comfort Ember went with her, but still my stomach twisted with worry.

"He won't hurt her physically. That's not Lars's style." Eli sat back in the chair.

"I know. But that actually makes me more nervous."

"Yeah." Eli frowned.

I did not believe in hitting or hurting women in any way. I killed a man once for slapping his girlfriend around in the parking lot of a bar. I showed him what it felt like to be on the receiving end. He was an evil son of a bitch. No one missed him.

But fae lives were different. Even though violence was part of it, I knew there were other things which could hurt worse.

Cole's walkie-talkie buzzed, and he reached for it on his belt loop. "We're going to let you get some rest." Cole gave my leg a last pat and motioned to Cooper.

"Get better. I can't do this without you," Cooper yelled over his shoulder, exiting the room.

"I'll fix you something to eat." Gabby ruffled my hair.

"Oh no. Please don't." I shook my head violently.

"What? I'm a great cook."

Both Eli and I lifted our eyebrows at her.

"Okay, I nuke things well."

We still stared at her.

"Oh, shut up," she grumbled, stomping toward the door. "I'm excellent at ordering delivery."

Eli and I snorted. I loved my family.

Eli rose from his chair.

"Thank you, Eli." I looked up at his towering frame. "For coming and standing next to me. For protecting Rez."

"I know you lost your chance to be able to turn again, for Rez." Eli shuffled his feet. "To me that makes you even more of a beast."

Moisture stabbed behind my eyes, but I blinked it back. "Thanks, man."

He nodded. "We won't give up. If Lars refuses to help you, I will."

Damn emotion wouldn't leave my chest.

"Weeeeeee." A tiny voice tore down the hallway toward my room, jolting Eli and me from our mushy moment. "My wee bits are freeeeee!"

Eli groaned, palming his face.

"Cal! Sir Eli said for us to stay in the kitchen." A buzzing sound like an electric fan filled the room.

A six-inch, dark-haired man dressed in only a belt with a plastic sword hanging off it came flying into my room. "Siiir-stttick-up-hizz-ass can kess miinee. MY BITS WANT TO BE FREEE!"

I couldn't help but laugh. Cal and Simmons were two

pixies who had attached themselves to Ember, and by association, Eli. The bemused annoyance Eli showed them only made me chuckle more. I had grown used to them when Em and Eli lived here. Kind of missed the buggers.

"Theerre youz are." Cal weaved in the air, heading for Eli. "My poo empty."

"Your poo?" I chuckled.

"My poooz...that thingy, you know… holding liquid love."

"You mean the kitchen sink, your pool?" Eli scoffed.

"Yes! That thingy! Need more!" Cal was sobering up by the second. Pixies couldn't stay drunk for long with their hummingbird metabolism.

Another pixie flew into my room. He was blond and wearing an old 1960s-style pilot outfit. A winged machine Lars had someone construct sat on his back. He lost his real wings in the war.

"I apologize, sir, I tried to keep him in the room like you asked," Simmons said to Eli.

"Oh, crackled crackers. Have some fun, Simmons. Let your wee lil' bits loose."

"*My* wee bits are *free*." I nodded at Cal.

"See?" Cal waved toward me. "Even Mr. Direction is joining the party." He turned to me. "There'll be booze and floozies at this party, right?"

"Floozies." I chuckled. Yeah, I taught him that one.

"Harlots…whatever! Oh speaking of, where is the girlie?"

"The girlie is at Lars's," Eli answered.

"What? And she didn't take me?" Cal huffed.

Simmons landed next to Cal on the bed frame. His foot caught the rung, and he fell face-first onto my bed, his wings still flapping so hard he began to spin around.

"Ahhh!" he yelled as his body swung in circles.

"Let go of the button!" Cal tossed up his arms.

The mechanical wings puttered to a stop, and Simmons slowly lifted his head.

"Every. Damn. Time," Cal muttered.

Simmons stood tall, straightening his clothes. "Still working out the kinks," he said to me.

"Yeah, *that's* the problem," Eli mumbled.

Simmons's chest puffed up, and he stomped to Cal. "Our lady told us we were needed here. You know..." Simmons thumbed at Eli.

"Jumpin' junipers. We're always stuck babysitting him."

Eli rolled his eyes. "Come on. I'll fill your pool again. Just try not to swim naked on the counter or use the light as a sunning bed. Your butt cheeks are still imprinted there from last time."

"One time! Jeez, he never lets it go." Cal sighed.

"How about when we found you curled around that squash?" Eli lifted an eyebrow.

"That was a simple mix-up anyone could have made."

"Or when I woke up to you snuggling my leg."

"It was cold."

"Or the time it was my di—"

"Okay, okay!" Cal cut Eli off and took flight. "Marshmallow brownies. Someone has issues." Cal zoomed out of the room.

"Spoken by the naked pixie flying around the house with only a sword." I chuckled.

"Like you haven't done that," Eli teased, heading for the door.

Pretty damn close.

As Eli exited, Simmons turned to me.

"I am glad you are safe and home, Mr. West. My lady was quite distraught. Miss Rez was as well."

"Thank you, Simmons."

He bowed. The buzz of his wings filled the room as he took off, following Eli.

It was only a minute before I heard Eli's voice bellow from the hallway. "Dammit, Cal, get out of the butter! Your wiener is not a cob of corn."

I lay back on my pillow, a grin engulfing my face. This was how this house was supposed to be—with laughter, voices, and full of family. Losing Jared killed that for a while, but I felt a spark of it coming back. Maybe happiness could be found here again.

# THIRTY

To heal itself, my body hauled me into a restless sleep, but Rez flitted through unsettled dreams. What would Lars do to her? What did he consider punishment? What if he decided he did not want to give her up? I couldn't blame Rez if she chose to stay. Her family was there, along with financial security and comfort I could never give her. Rez's world was so different from mine. I was leather. She was lace.

My mind was just drifting deeper into slumber when energy shot up my back, zapping at every nerve with vigor, causing me to sit straight up in bed. Her name rolled from my lips. The beast roared to life. She was here. I could feel her.

I leaped out of bed and didn't even bother getting dressed, my impulse stronger than pain or politeness. It felt like I was caught on a rod and she was reeling me in.

*Damn. This bond is powerful.*

"Rez!" I bellowed, running on shaky legs out of the large ranch house.

"West, what the hell are you doing?" Gabby yelled at me from the living room, but I ignored her.

The weight of Rez's presence came from everywhere outside, as though she were the air, the sun. I gazed around trying to find her, my heart slamming into my chest. The beast pawed excitedly. This was insane. I suddenly realized I could never have pretended she was nothing to me. I wouldn't have lasted five seconds.

"West?" A voice came from the opposite way I was looking. My head jerked around, air sucking in my lungs.

Shit. There she stood, beside Ember, more beautiful than I remembered. Dressed in dark gray cargo pants, boots, a black tank under a fitted black puffy jacket. Her long, dark hair hung around her face. Casual and real. The girl I had fallen for. I couldn't breathe.

"Oh gods…West." Her hand went to her mouth. "You're awake...you're okay."

No words came. My body moved toward her.

Both of us were on a collision course. My arms swooped around her, pulling her tight as we slammed into each other. My lids lowered with contentment the moment I felt her in my embrace—right where I always wanted her to be.

She let out a bubbled laugh/cry and tightened her arms around me until I let out a groan.

"Sorry!" She pulled back, her fingers running over my shoulders and the scars on my chest.

"Never be sorry, darlin'. I can handle this kind of pain." I cupped her face, bringing it to mine. I could feel people around us, but they were all a blur. Rez was my only focus.

"I was so scared," she whispered.

"I'm a Dark Dweller. Believe me, we are almost impossible to get rid of…no matter how much you might want to." I grinned.

Ember snorted and walked to the porch where Eli stood. He looped one finger in her belt loop and tugged her to him, his gaze on her full of lustful mischief.

"Brycin."

"Dragen." She grinned at him before he crushed his mouth to hers passionately. She pulled away, her grin widening, her eyebrow lifting coyly. "Why don't we give them some privacy?"

Eli smirked, already pushing her for the door. "Right behind you, woman."

Everyone else followed, leaving Rez and me alone.

"Are you all right?" My gaze wandered over her.

She took a deep breath, her eyes lowering. "Yes..." Her voice went hesitant.

"What? What did he do?" I gritted my teeth, dropping my arms.

"Less than I thought. Lars was extremely lenient, considering." She licked her lips. "He said I would be banned from ever stepping foot on his grounds."

"Which means being banned from your family?"

She nodded, tears hinting in her eyes.

"He offered me the chance to stay. Not in his bed, but in the house and run it like I always have. Live there with my family like nothing happened."

My shoulders tensed, my chest walling up for protection. "I wouldn't blame you. He can provide you with a much better life. What you're used to. I can't. Plus, your family is there—"

Her finger went to my mouth, quieting me. "I told him no. If I chose to stay, then I give you up. That is *not* something I am willing to sacrifice."

"So...you gave up your family for me?" My mouth dipped open.

She blinked her tears back. "West, you are my family."

Her words detonated my heart with happiness. Family was so important being a Dark Dweller. They were the *only* people we trusted.

My hands slid along her jaw. Vigor incited the instant our lips touched, flaming down my back. With those few words, she had bonded us further together. I couldn't get enough, my mouth devouring hers.

"Guess some of you is healing and working again." She laughed against my mouth. My body reacted to her fingers skimming over my bare ass, forgetting the pain.

"Darlin', with you around, that part will *always* be working in overdrive." I kissed her again. "And you better get used to seeing naked asses around this house…" I tipped back a bit. "If you are planning on staying, that is."

"There's nowhere else I want to be, Mr. Moseley."

"Good thing, Ms. Mareza…because I wasn't planning on lettin' you go."

Her smile widened, and she gave me a quick kiss. But I still had a feeling in my gut, like a thorn, something she wasn't telling me.

"Tell me." I brushed my hands over her hair.

"What?"

I tipped my head to the side. "This mate thing comes with a bullshit detector. I know Lars…he wouldn't leave his punishment at mere banning." As the King, he could not leave the punishment appearing so little to outsiders. Even though being cut off from Marguerite, Alki, and Nic was cruel, it seemed too easy.

She inhaled, glanced away, and licked her bottom lip. "You and I have something in common right now."

My stomach dipped. "What?"

She pulled her head up, looking me straight in the eye, and cleared her throat. "He stripped me of my powers. I am no longer a siren." She gulped.

"Oh shit." Taking away a fae's magic was like ripping out half of our souls, splitting apart our identities. Physically and emotionally painful as hell.

"Stripped? He didn't just bind them?"

"No, stripped." She pinned her lips together, as though trying not to cry. Binding them inside was more like what I suffered. They were still inside, but they couldn't come out. Stripped was having the power taken out of your body. You were still fae but no longer had your own magic.

Rez could never breathe underwater or glamour, but she also didn't have to kill to fuel her magic either.

I hadn't known Lars was capable of stripping, a certain type of magic, exceedingly powerful and old. The kind of power you'd find in the spear…or the sword. The thought of Lars already obtaining two of the treasures of Tuatha Dé Danann scared me shitless. Two I knew about, what if he had more? What would happen if he got all four? I quickly pushed the idea away. Surely he was too smart to mess with that kind of magic.

"I've struggled with being a siren, but after this trip I felt myself take control. Loved being one again. I came alive." A sob caught in her throat. "The moment he took it away from me, I felt that light die. I feel so lost."

"I am so sorry." I brought her in, kissing her forehead and temple. She was still in shock. It would hit her soon, and hard. All I could do was be there for her. Love her.

"He told me he's holding my powers in a safe place. Someday I can get them back."

Asshole. Keeping them over her head like a dog biscuit. If she was obedient and did what he said, she might get them back. He now had two slaves.

"They're gone." She looked up at me, tears trailing down her face.

I held her to my chest for a long time, letting her cry. Slowly her tears ebbed, and I kissed the top of her head when I felt her body relax. "I won't lie and say this will be easy for you."

"No. It won't." She wiped at her face. "Besides my powers, I'm going to miss my family like crazy. I'm going to be disoriented and lost for some time," she said matter-of-factly. "I could only leave there with what I walked in with. I have nothing. No money, no magic, no clothes, or a home."

I lifted her chin to stare into her eyes. "You have a home. Here with me. Clothes are easy enough to get. As far as money, we have it. Don't worry about it right now. We'll figure it out." I tucked a strand of hair behind her ear, a mischievous smile hitching my lip. "I know ways you can earn your keep, darlin'."

A single eyebrow lifted. "Benefits?"

"I would say so." I glanced down, my body eager with need. "Can you start now?"

A coyness inched up her lips. "Do I get a company uniform, Mr. Moseley?" She nestled in closer to me.

"We don't have a dress code here. At all." I smirked. "But on Fridays you're allowed to wear something fun...like a maid's outfit, nurse, leather dominatrix, naughty librarian...whatever."

She went on her toes, her mouth claiming mine. I pulled her in, our mouths growing more and more desperate. My dick twitched needing to be inside her.

"You probably need to rest," she muttered, nipping at my bottom lip.

"I rested for four weeks," I growled into her ear. "What I need is to be deep within you. That is the best medicine for my pain."

"I'm at your command, darlin'," she teased, repeating what I had said to her the first night we were together. She stepped away, grabbed my hand, and towed me toward the house.

I was a goner. And I loved it.

These people, these walls. With her. I wanted to be nowhere else in the world.

# EPILOGUE
## (Six months later)

I hit the gas on my new bike, pushing me faster down the road. The new motorcycles were much better than the last pieces of shit, but still was nothing to how a Harley felt between your legs. The breeze felt good against my skin. The warm sun dipped low in the sky, hinting at the evening.

What I really wanted was my girl on the back, driving around Black Lake, where we'd stop and fuck relentlessly on and over my bike or a picnic table before continuing on. Then we'd get dinner and finish back in my bed with a very long dessert. Unfortunately it would have to wait.

It had been six months since Rez came to live with me. Six months of unbelievable bliss. Everyone, except Eli and Ember, wanted to kill Rez and me. Probably more me. I was a smug fucker, and I couldn't keep my hands off her. Thankfully she struggled as well, or I'd feel bad for how many times a day I wanted her. My libido had no discretion on where either.

Cooper was taking it the hardest. He would never show it, but I could sense his envy of the love Eli and I had for our women. He always grumbling about having to jerk off because he had to hear it from both ends of the house now. Gabby merely spent more time off with Alki. Cole was so deep in work he didn't notice much else. With the loss of his nephew and brother, work was the one thing that got him through the day.

Rez's presence brought new life to the house with happiness and laughter, which had gone missing. Even Eli and Ember were back to using it as their base between hunts. Their job as bounty hunters, keeping the new world of fae and humans in check, was endless. But instead of staying away like before, Ember wanted to be around more for Rez. Their return to the ranch also brought back two pixies, which caused a lot of mischief and fun, and was exactly what the house needed. The ghosts of those we lost were always there but didn't haunt us like before.

Ember returning home resulted in Mark, Lily, Kennedy, Ryan, and his boyfriend Castien coming around the ranch. Even Lorcan dropped by a few times. That relationship was still strained, but it was getting better. I couldn't figure out him and Kennedy, but he had changed...and I would bet she had something to do with it.

To welcome Rez to "Camp Dwellers," Ember got permission from Lars for Marguerite, Nic, and Alki to come for dinner. Rez cried like a baby and hugged them the entire night. During moments like that I felt awful. I was the reason she couldn't see them, but she convinced me later this was exactly where she wanted to be.

There were rough times for her. For the first month I would wake up to hear her crying. All I could do was hold her. It was easing day by day. The loss of her powers and her family was not easy, but she was trying to accept it.

She was not one to sit around, especially when trying to forget her sadness. It hadn't been long before she was running everything, giving Cole more freedom to go out with us. Cole claimed daily he never wanted to be without her.

I could see how Lars's house fell apart without her. We tripled our income, inventory, and speed, which did please the King. Although I was sure he had no doubt why we were suddenly running more efficiently, he never said anything.

I tapered my speed, nearing my destination, and sucked in my breath as I rolled up to the gate. On cue, an enormous man stepped out from the shadows. "Hey, R-Man. It's been a long time."

"Not long enough," Rimmon rumbled.

"Aw. You missed me, don't deny it."

"Like I miss a knife to my gut."

"Did you…did you make a joke? I'm so proud." I lived to taunt the shit out of him. Some things would never change. Born a cheeky bastard, I would die a cheeky bastard. "My grumpy ogre is growing up." I wiped my eye.

"Someday the boss will let me kill you," he grumbled, his palms fisting.

"But today is not the day, Big R." I grinned.

"Password," Rimmon growled, folding his grotesquely huge arms.

"'West is super sexy' is still not it?"

Rimmon took a step closer and leered at me. He still wore the patchwork pants, the only ones that would fit him.

"Password, Dark Dweller; my patience is thin tonight."

"How is it different from any other night?"

Rimmon snarled.

I shook my head and uttered the password. The spell released its hold, and Rimmon unlocked the gates. This time when I rode up to the front of the house, Rez was not there waiting for me. Everything about my return to this house felt so familiar, but not in a good way. Did I ever imagine the last time I came here that in six months Rez would be waiting for me back at *my* house, in *my* bed?

I had seen Lars from afar when we dropped off inventory, but we never spoke. He dealt with Cooper now. I would be alone in a room with him for the first time since the night we made the deal. His summons didn't come in a nice note or phone call. No, he summoned you through magic that pulled on you like a giant magnet. Your muscles moved as if by themselves to follow the pull.

Ember was the only one around here who understood the sensation. She told me the longer I ignored it, the worse it became till you felt if you didn't go to him your insides would shred into pieces. Sounded like fun.

The aggravation eased the closer I got to him. This was my future. Always his bitch. I couldn't even hate him because he gave Rez and me our lives, our love.

I set my kickstand down and swung off the bike. The front door opened.

"Mr. Moseley?" A woman's voice came out into the warm evening. My head shot to the doorway. This woman towered in six-inch heels. She was lean, with long blond hair tied in a slick ponytail, and fitted into a gray skirt and bright red blouse, which matched her lipstick. Professional and beautiful. The way Lars liked his business managers. "His Royal Highness, the Unseelie King, is waiting for you in his office. I will show you the way."

*His Royal Highness? Show me the way?*

"You must be new, sweetheart." I snorted and walked up the stairs. Right then Marguerite came running to the door, her arms outstretched, and knocked Blondie out of the way.

"Mr. West! Oh, *hombre guapo*, you are here."

I wrapped the small woman in my arms, kissing her on the cheeks. "I've missed you, *mamacita*."

"*Me duele el corazon*." She placed her hand on her chest, as though to tell me how much it ached. I nodded, fresh with guilt for how badly Rez must feel. Hell, I did too. I missed this woman who treated all of us like her children.

"Hopefully we can get you over to the house again soon."

Her eyes teared up, and she nodded furiously. Then swished her hands. "You are *muy flaco*. Must eat!" She turned, motioning me into the house.

"Mrs. Gonzales, Mr. Moseley has a meeting with the King."

"Hush!" Marguerite waved her hand at the woman. "Mr. West needs to eat."

I grinned and shrugged at the blond, enjoying her outraged expression, and followed Marguerite.

Nothing appeared different. Same sofa and table, same paintings and rugs, but I could feel the loss of its soul. Rez had been so much a part of this house it felt like the house itself was mourning.

Marguerite was already in the kitchen pulling out pans by the time I caught up to her. Damn, she was fast. "Mr. Moseley, please—" the blond tried again.

"*Mamacita*, I will eat after." I leaned in and gave her temple a kiss. "Don't want to give newbie here heart failure."

Marguerite glowered at the blond and mumbled something about being a pain in her ass. Rez's name was definitely mixed in there. I bet this was the hardest on Marguerite. She and Rez loved each other more than anything and worked well together over the years. Blondie didn't look like she was faring well with Marguerite.

The woman walked me swiftly toward Lars's office, eyeing me like I was going to pocket the china on the way.

"Highness?" She tapped on the door. "Mr. Moseley is here."

"Send him in," Lars's familiar, cool voice spoke through the door. My heart couldn't help racing. We'd finally be face to face, alone, since Ireland. I had no idea what mood or plan he had for me.

She opened the door and gestured me in, her nose scrunched like she did not like my kind near her. "Anything else, my lord?" she asked.

"No, Elise. Thank you." Lars did not look up, and Elise shut the door behind me.

I strolled across the floor to the Persian rug worth tens of thousands of dollars. My eyes locked on the man behind the desk. How many times I had come here, how many times Lars and I met, but this was not the same. We were operating with different terms. I licked my lips nervously, but Lars's attention remained on his writing, which he continued to do for the next few minutes. The tactic was nothing new. He wanted me to wait, to feel uncomfortable. It worked, but I forced my feet to stay still with my gaze trained on him.

Finally he set down his pen and sat back, his eyes drifting slowly to me. "Mr. Moseley, it has been a while." Not one inflection of emotion sounded in his words. I gave a nod to his comment but stayed quiet, as did he.

My throat felt tight. I couldn't take it anymore. "I see you got a new assistant." I thumbed toward the door. "Think she might pat me down on the way out and check my pockets for stolen goods."

"She won't last." A slight frown twitched his mouth. "Marguerite does not like her." Lars rose from his seat, motioning me to sit. "But she won't like anyone. None of them are Rez." My gaze went to the floor as I sat. Lars came around the desk and sat on the edge. "I hear she is flourishing with you. By the profits, I can see she is a great addition."

"She is." I clasped my hands together, leaning my elbows on my legs, which vibrated with energy.

"I am glad to hear it." Lars glanced out the door into the violet sky. He cleared his throat. "She is greatly missed here."

I stirred in the chair.

"Professionally speaking, of course." Lars turned back to me, his green-yellow eyes meeting mine. "I will not apologize for what I had to do to the both of you. I should have done worse."

"I know." I nodded.

"But it is in the past now. I want to move on. Go forward from here."

"I would like that as well."

He stood, slipping back behind the desk. "I summoned you here tonight for a particular reason, for a mission extremely sensitive and secret. I need to know I can count on you and you will do anything to fulfill this quest for me."

I swallowed. "Do I really have a choice?"

Lars smirked, taking a seat in his chair.

"No, I guess you do not, but your willingness will

make it far easier and less painful for you."

*Shit.* This did not sound good already. "What is it you want me to do?"

"Your skills and dedication in retrieving the spear greatly impressed me, Mr. Moseley. I knew killing you would be a serious waste. But in my anger, I might have been a little shortsighted in one aspect. What is ahead of you is dangerous."

"Like getting the spear wasn't?"

"This might be even more so."

"Your sales pitch is in need of a little help."

"I don't have to sell it to you, Mr. Moseley. Like you said, you don't have a choice." He sat back, lacing his hands. The smug bastard. "Are you regretting your choices?"

"No," I growled. "Not for one moment."

His smile looked genuine. "Good. I would not want to lose Rez to anything less. Whatever you think of me, I care for her. I want her to be happy.

"But back to you, Mr. Moseley." He sat forward, his clasped hands on his desk. "I once promised you I would help to find a way to restore the beast. I might be willing to again."

I stood straight now, my attention focused on him. "Why?"

"Two reasons. You will be much more useful to me in beast form when challenged by enemies." He drew his arms off the desk. "And because what I want is the precise thing you will need to shift into Dark Dweller again." He settled back in the chair. "Rez explained to me, when she was here, the spear gave you power to change back without pain." He paused.

I ground my teeth, fighting back any emotion.

"Letting you have the spear is out of the question." His clipped tone left no room for doubt. "It is not the spear anyway. It is the type of old magic it holds. What all of the four treasures contain."

For some reason with every word he uttered, oxygen went in and out faster through my lungs, my gut ahead of my thoughts.

"Any of the treasures would always have to actually be in your hands to siphon off the power...except one."

"Which one?" My voice was a croak.

"The Cauldron of Dagda."

*Fuck. Fuck. Shit.*

"You want me to retrieve it for you." I gulped. So I had underestimated him. He would collect all the treasures, which turned my fear to full-blown terror. Then what?

Two down, two to go...unless he already had the Stone of Fál. I shook my head, pushing out the thought. That could not be true. No one should have that much power. Especially the high demon king. I saw what too much power did to prior demon kings, like Balor. Yet I had no choice but to do what he asked. Shit...

"And if you do this, I will give you my word I will find someone to produce a spell from it to reclaim the beast." He tilted his head. "Beneficial for both of us."

*Right.* "What's the catch?" My heart thudded against my ribs like a flat tire.

An eerie grin curved Lars's mouth, his eyes glinting. "I think we will work together quite well."

I knew how he worked. Nothing was upfront or as easy as it might seem. There was always a catch—a sacrifice in some way.

"As you know, these treasures have not been easy to come by and are extremely well guarded."

"Yeah, yeah, dangerous and hard to find. Get to the point."

He steepled his fingers, his elbows resting on the chair arms. "My two men who flew over to Ireland with you were able to uncover the high Druid family who created the cauldron for Dagda. An exceptionally important family. Powerful. They were the last to be seen with it before it went *missing*."

"What family?" Acid trickled up my esophagus.

Lars only smiled.

*Aw, fuck...* Ice filled my chest, my voice barely breaking a whisper.

"Kennedy's."

His gaze met mine, a smug smile hinting on his mouth. "Are you ready to seek the Light, Mr. Moseley?"

No. But as we both knew, I had no fuckin' choice. My will was his, and now it would be centered on Kennedy. My friend.

The Druid Seelie Queen.

*Oh darlin', I hope you know what's coming for you.*

*Thank you to all my readers. Your opinion really matters to me and helps others decide if they want to purchase my book. If you enjoyed this book, please consider leaving a review on the site where you purchased it. Thank you.*

*Want to find out about my next series, **The Collector Series**? Sign up for my newsletter on my website and keep updated on the latest news. www.staceymariebrown.com*

## City In Embers

There is something unique about Zoey Daniels.

She can see the fae—a species kept hidden from the human world.

Because of her talent, she is hired as a Collector by the Department of Molecular Genetics (DMG), a secret government agency that uses fae blood to save human lives, curing things like cancer and birth defects. She is trained to collect the fae, never considering them anything but soulless monsters who feed on humans like their personal buffet.

When devastation strikes Seattle, everything Zoey knows is turned upside down. An electrical storm tangles her with Ryker, a ruthless wanderer, who looks like a Viking and kills like a brute. His hate for humans is as equal as her hate for fae.

When DMG turns on Zoey, she can no longer trust the government agency she had spent years dedicating her life to and is forced into an alliance with the callous Viking.

Ryker and Zoey's connection sends them down a road of lies, deceit, corruption, and murder.

It won't be just the city left in embers…

**This is set in the same world as Darkness! And both connect to The Lightness Saga!**

# Acknowledgements

West only came to be because of you readers. Your love of these characters, your need to want more, let me expose all I saw going behind the scenes. Thank you for wanting me to bring him to light.

I am a very lucky girl. I get to work with the best of the best in this business. A HUGE thanks to:

Jordan, the woman that can make me fly or bring me to my knees, but always in the end it's a far better story. Thank you. http://jordanrosenfeld.net/

Hollie "the editor", how can I put into words what you have come to mean to me. My friend, my editor…you're like my happy place. You are always there anytime I need. No question. Thank you so much! http://www.hollietheeditor.com/.

Jay Aheer for making such stunning covers!

To Judi at http://www.formatting4u.com/: Always such a pleasure. You always got my back.

Mom, my alpha, beta, bouncing board, and helper of all the yucky business stuff. There'd be no books without you. Nor would there be a me…guess you can thank Dad for that too.

To all the readers who have supported me: My gratitude is for all you do and how much you help indie authors out of the pure love of reading.

To all the indie/hybrid authors out there who inspire, challenge, support, and push me to be better: I love you!

And to anyone who has picked up an indie book and given an unknown author a chance.

THANK YOU!

# About The Author

Stacey Marie Brown is a lover of hot fictional bad boys and sarcastic heroines who kick butt. She also enjoys books, travel, TV shows, hiking, writing, design, and archery. Stacey swears she is part gypsy, being lucky enough to live and travel all over the world.

She grew up in Northern California, where she ran around on her family's farm, raising animals, riding horses, playing flashlight tag, and turning hay bales into cool forts.

When she's not writing she's out hiking, spending time with friends, and traveling. She also volunteers helping animals and is eco-friendly. She feels all animals, people, and environment should be treated kindly.

# To learn more about Stacey or her books, visit her at:

**Author website & Newsletter:**
www.staceymariebrown.com

**Facebook Author page**:
www.facebook.com/SMBauthorpage

**Pinterest:** www.pinterest.com/s.mariebrown

**Instagram:** www.instagram.com/staceymariebrown/

**Tiktok:**
https://www.tiktok.com/@staceymariebrown

**Amazon page:** www.amazon.com/Stacey-Marie-Brown/e/B00BFWHB9U

**Goodreads:**
www.goodreads.com/author/show/6938728.Stacey_Marie_Brown

**Her Facebook group:**
www.facebook.com/groups/1648368945376239/

**Bookbub:** www.bookbub.com/authors/stacey-marie-brown

West

www.ingramcontent.com/pod-product-compliance
Lightning Source LLC
Chambersburg PA
CBHW070818190726
48292CB00006B/2045